*Writing Women
in
Modern China*

MODERN ASIAN LITERATURE SERIES

Writing Women
in
Modern China

AN ANTHOLOGY OF WOMEN'S LITERATURE
FROM THE EARLY TWENTIETH CENTURY

EDITED BY

Amy D. Dooling and Kristina M. Torgeson

COLUMBIA UNIVERSITY PRESS   NEW YORK

Columbia University Press
Publishers Since 1893
New York   Chichester, West Sussex
Copyright © 1998 Columbia University Press
All rights reserved

Photograph of Qiu Jin courtesy of the Qiu Jin Archives in Shaoxing, China.
Photograph of Chen Hengzhe courtesy of Special Collections, Vassar
    College Libraries.
Photograph of Lin Huiyin courtesy of Wilma Fairbank.
All other photos courtesy of the authors or their family members.
Chinese calligraphy copyright Xu Bing.

Library of Congress Cataloging-in-Publication Data
    Writing women in modern China : an anthology of women's literature
from the early twentieth century / edited by Amy D. Dooling and Kristina
M. Torgeson.
        p.   cm. — (Modern Asian literature series)
    Includes bibliographical references.
    ISBN 0-231-10700-5 (alk. paper). — ISBN 0-231-10701-3 (pbk.)
    1. Chinese literature—Women authors.   2. Chinese literature—20th
century—Translations into English.   3. Women and literature—China.
I. Dooling, Amy D.   II. Torgeson, Kristina M.   III. Series.
PL2515.W75   1998
895.1'0809287'09041—DC21   97-19306

Casebound editions of Columbia University Press books are printed on
permanent and durable acid-free paper.
Printed in the United States of America
c 10 9 8 7 6 5 4 3 2 1
p 10 9 8 7 6 5 4 3 2 1

To our families

CONTENTS

All selections translated by Amy D. Dooling and Kristina M. Torgeson unless otherwise noted.

Acknowledgments	ix
Introduction	1
1. Qiu Jin Excerpts from *Stones of the Jingwei Bird*	39
2. Chen Xiefen (*translated by Jennifer Carpenter*) "Crisis in the Women's World"	79
3. Chen Hengzhe "One Day"	87
4. Feng Yuanjun (*translated by Janet Ng*) "Separation"	101

5. Shi Pingmei
   "Lin Nan's Diary"
   "Lusha—A Letter to Lu Yin"
	115

6. Lu Yin 135
   "News From the Seashore—A Letter to Shi Pingmei"
   "After Victory"

7. Lu Jingqing 157
   "Random Notes: Number Nine"

8. Chen Xuezhao 165
   "The Woes of the Modern Woman"

9. Ling Shuhua 175
   "Intoxicated"
   "Once Upon a Time"

10. Su Xuelin 197
    "Harvest"

11. Yuan Changying 209
    Southeast Flies the Peacock

12. Xie Bingying (*translated by Lin Yutang*) 253
    Excerpts from *War Diary*

13. Ding Ling 263
    "Day"

14. Chen Ying 275
    "Woman"

15. Lin Huiyin 299
    Three poems

16. Bing Xin 307
    "Our Mistress's Parlor"

17. Luo Shu (*translated by Janet Ng*) 331
    "Aunty Liu"

18. Xiao Hong 343
    "Abandoned Child"
    "A Sleepless Night"

Glossary 367
Supplemental Readings 377
Contributors 387

ACKNOWLEDGMENTS

The intellectual collaboration that produced this anthology began several years ago, when as fellow graduate students in modern Chinese literature at Columbia University, we realized that our mutual interest in and commitment to the study of women's writing in China would best be served by pooling our resources. At the time, the works of few early twentieth-century Chinese women writers were available in print, let alone in translation, and thus sharing the fruits of our own painstaking explorations beyond the canon became a crucial labor-saving strategy and, soon, the basis of a rewarding extracurricular course in modern women's literature. As we went on to undertake research projects abroad—Kristina Torgeson on a Fulbright-Hays in Beijing, China and Amy Dooling on a Fulbright-IIE in Taibei, Taiwan—the specific inspiration for an anthology of translations began to take shape. Poring through stacks of old journals, newspapers, and books in the archives at Beijing University Library, Beijing Library, and Academica Sinica, we came to realize just how much women's writing had been produced in the first three decades of the twentieth century—and how little was readily available to readers in any language (even Chinese!). It also became increasingly apparent to us that if scholarly work on women's cultural production in China were to make any difference, more had to be done to redress the underrepresentation of women's writing in translation. Encouraged by the sincere interest and enthusiasm of the many scholars, writers, and friends we met along the way, we decided that some of the materials we had amassed—enough for several volumes on Chinese women's writing from the first half of this century—belonged in an anthology.

This anthology would not have been possible without the tremendous support we have received over the years from numerous institutions and individuals. Generous grants from the American Council of Learned Societies, the Graduate School of Arts and Sciences and the East Asian Languages and Cultures Department of Columbia University, the Fulbright Foundation, and the Mellon Foundation have supported our research at Columbia and in Asia. We would also like to thank the staffs of the many libraries we worked in over the past years, especially the C. V. Starr East Asian Library at Columbia University, the Kroch Library at Cornell University, Barnard College Library, the New York Public Library, Vassar College Library, Beijing University Library, Beijing Library, Capital Library in Beijing, the Qiu Jin Archives in Shaoxing, Shanghai Library, Taiwan University Library, the Kuomintang History Archives, the National Central Library in Taibei, and Academica Sinica.

In addition, we are grateful to Ba Jin, Chen Shou (writer Chen Hengzhe's sister), Feng Zongpu (Feng Yuanjun's niece), Ma Xiaomi (Luo Shu's daughter), and Su Xuelin for graciously providing biographical materials and photographs for the authors represented in this volume. We would like to thank Wilma Fairbank for entrusting us with one of her treasured photographs of Lin Huiyin; and Robin Visser, Zhou Zhunnan and Professor Yin-nan Tang, and Leif Carlsson, whose heroic efforts in Shanghai, Tainan, and the darkroom, respectively, provided us with additional photographs.

Many scholars in China, Taiwan, and the United States helped us with research, ideas, encouragement, and logistical support. We particularly thank Professors Rey Chow, Peter Hitchcock, Jing Wang, and Marcelle Thiebaux, who set aside time from their busy schedules to read and provide critical feedback on our introductory essay. In addition, Professors Paul Anderer, Tani E. Barlow, Chen Pingyuan, Miriam Cooke, Howard Goldblatt, C. T. Hsia, Ke Qingming, Jeffrey Kinkley, Sally Lieberman, Qian Hong, Paul Rouzer, Shen Naiwen, Wang Xiaoming, Xia Xiaohong,

Jean Jingyuan Zhang, and Zhu Weizhi all generously gave of their time, knowledge, and assistance. We are also grateful to our fellow contributors, Janet Ng and Jennifer Carpenter. For showing us the importance of women's writing and the value of making Chinese writers more accessible to a broader audience, thanks are due to Professors Carolyn Heilbrun, Barbara Ruch, Jennifer Wicke, and Marsha Wagner. Professor David Derwei Wang has also been a staunch supporter of our long-term research in women's cultural practices and feminism in China, and we deeply appreciate his understanding that this project was relevant to the dissertations we were each writing.

Special thanks go to Julie Rousseau, Kathryn W. Torgeson, and Rachel Wang for enthusiastically reading, editing, and checking the translations. Margaret Bishop, Charlotte Dooling, Béatrice Laroche, Giles Richter, Sarah Schneewind, Wang Yu, Professor Yunzhong Shu, and Professor Gopal Sukhu also read texts and answered questions in their particular fields of expertise. John Weinstein and the actors at the Adams House of Harvard University performed the first dramatic reading of the Yuan Changying play, art historian Francesca Dal Lago researched the cover art, artist Xu Bing provided the calligraphy, and poet Bruce Tindall helped to rework the poems by Lin Huiyin. Jennifer Crewe, Leslie Kriesel, and especially the anonymous readers at Columbia University Press, whose comradely critiques raised thoughtful questions, all helped to make this book possible and shape its present form.

Peter Hitchcock, who read countless drafts, offered endless words of advice and encouragement, and was always prepared to mix martinis to celebrate any increment of progress on the project, deserves a special award of honor. His unflinching support and inspiring sense of humor about things academic and otherwise helped more than he knows. Amy Dooling would also like to say a heartfelt word of thanks to her mother, Bob, and her sisters (Daniella, Charlotte, Jennifer, Eleanor, Maggie, and Leslie) for their loving confidence in her. Many thanks also to Xiao Qiang, who answered numerous last-minute translation questions. Kristina Torgeson is especially grateful to her parents, Dewayne and Kathryn Torgeson, who in addition to providing endless love and support, helped out with editorial advice and many trips to the Cornell library.

We have tried to make this anthology as representative of a wide range of texts by women in early twentieth-century China as possible. As with any anthology, however, ours reflects personal interests and biases for which we take full responsibility. In making our choices, we were lucky to have the work of pioneering scholars in modern Chinese women's literature to challenge and guide us, in particular that of Tani E. Barlow, Rey Chow, Yi-tsi Mei Feuerwerker, Dai Jinhua, Wendy Larson, and Meng Yue. Of course any mistakes or oversights contained in this book are entirely our own. It is our hope that this anthology will inspire future scholars of women's literature to correct them.

*Writing Women
in
Modern China*

INTRODUCTION

WRITING WOMEN IN MODERN CHINA

For the editors of *Woman Writer Magazine*, a literary periodical launched in Shanghai in 1929, the connections between modern gender debates and the works of modern female novelists, poets, and essayists seemed self-evident. "It is precisely due to the contributions of women writers," they claimed in their first issue, borrowing the words of Soviet feminist Alexandra Kollontai, "that we are able to know the New Woman who is now being created." Nearly three quarters of a century later, such connections seem far less obvious. Most of what we know about the New Woman (*xin nüxing*) and the array of new feminine identities constructed in modern Chinese literature comes from texts by leading male writers, while many women writers of the early decades of this century have fallen into relative obscurity. This anthology, a collection of women's literature from the last years of the Qing dynasty through the eve of World War II, focuses attention anew on the ways Chinese women wrote themselves into literary modernity. It foregrounds texts that self-consciously address matters of gender and, in so doing, invites readers to consider the diverse strategies and perspectives female authors brought to bear on the complex subject of modern Chinese women.

The "writing women" who penned the fiction, drama, essays, and poetry in this volume lived and wrote in an era of tremendous social, political, and cultural turbulence and transition. There had always been a minority of educated women who wrote in China, including courtesan poets, Confucian moral handbook authors, and gentrywoman lyricists, but the early twentieth century brought profound changes in both the material conditions and the cultural conceptions of women's writing. The rapid expansion of female education, the emergence of professional literary opportunities for women, and the conceptualization of women's writing (*funü wenxue*) as a gendered aesthetic category are just a few of the factors that helped transform the roles of "writing women" in modern China.

"Writing women" also describes the project in which the literature collected in this volume was primarily engaged: the broad cultural enterprise of rethinking and redefining what being a woman meant or could mean as China sought to reinvent itself in terms of evolving definitions of modernity. Beginning in the late Qing period (c. 1890–1911), when debates on women's role in national renewal precipitated a far-reaching critique of the established gender order, the Woman Question (*funü wenti*) came to occupy a prominent place on the country's cultural-political agenda. Whether taking up themes as broad in scope as the nature of feminist revolution or as specifically defined as the benefits of bobbed hair, modern poets, playwrights, filmmakers, novelists, and journalists were among those who helped produce the new narratives, images, and theories that defined modern Chinese women.

As texts written by women, the pieces collected in this volume offer readers an opportunity to consider the complex ways in which literary women expressed the experience of gender at a moment when the category of woman itself was in the process of being radically rewritten. The multiple connotations that "woman" accrued in modern Chinese cultural discourse and the feminist ramifications of her symbolic centrality have been provocatively dealt with in the recent scholarship of Tani Barlow, Rey Chow, Lu Tonglin, and others.[1] The works translated here will facilitate new avenues of research, alerting us to the (sometimes overlooked) fact that intellectual women in early twentieth-century China were not waiting passively on the cultural sidelines while men battled over what role the New Woman would play in the shaping of Chinese modernity. Instead, women were actively engaged in the debates and reformulations of what it meant to be a woman in a modern cultural context.

The selections in this anthology reveal that there was not a coherent movement by women writers to arrive at a unified notion of what the modern woman was or should be; rather, efforts to redefine "woman," "femininity," and "women's literature" were decentralized and complex, informed by a broad spectrum of ideological perspectives and aesthetic tastes. Some of these works resonate deeply with prevailing paradigms about gender and genre that have been shaped by the literary canon, while others call them into question. Yet if a thread of meaning can be found to link these diverse works together, it is their preoccupation with "woman" not merely as literary subject matter, but as a meaningful participant in the Chinese project of modernity. This collection is, then, not about women as much as about their struggles to find ways to write "woman," and thereby themselves, into the discourse of Chinese modernity.

Until quite recently, the prevalent assumption (among Western sinologists and Chinese scholars alike) has been that besides Ding Ling, Ling Shuhua, and Xiao Hong there were few other "worthy" or "significant" women writers during the formative stages of modern Chinese culture. This view has been perpetuated by mainstream literary histories and anthologies of twentieth-century Chinese literature in China and in the West. In recent years, however, a significant body of archival, historical, and interpretive scholarship has begun to emerge from inquiries into women's participation in early twentieth-century literary production. New theoretical critiques, reference works, reprints of women's literary histories from the 1920s and 1930s, and republications of May Fourth women's writing are transforming the ways in which modern Chinese literature and culture are both taught and discussed. In presenting these translations of women-authored texts from the late Qing up until the Sino-Japanese War, we envision this volume as part of the burgeoning effort among Western sinologists, Taiwanese and Mainland Chinese scholars, and feminist activists to rethink questions of women, writing, and gender in modern China. It is our hope that by introducing some of the less familiar women writers of the first three decades of this century and placing their work alongside selections by more canonical authors, *Writing Women in Modern China* will further contribute to this important critical endeavor.[2]

In order to provide the reader with a clearer view of the cultural and historical context of the writing in this anthology and the conditions that helped to shape the ways these writers "wrote women," the remainder of this essay charts some of the major developments affecting concepts of gender, literature, and women's writing. Proceeding chronologically, we begin our discussion with women's feminist-nationalist activism and writing in the late Qing, move on to examine the connections between the new social and political status of female intellectuals and the burst of literary production by women in the May Fourth era (c. 1917–1927), and conclude with sections on the burgeoning "women's culture" of the late 1920s and early 1930s, as well as the tough political choices facing women writers during the years leading up to the outbreak of the Sino-Japanese War in 1937. Not trying to fit this particular story of women's writing into any of the prevailing narratives or timetables of modern Chinese literature (although many readers will discover numerous overlaps in addition to significant divergences), this essay is a preliminary attempt to construct a new narrative of literary production in modern China—one that foregrounds women's literary expressions on the subject of women. The essay is not intended to be exhaustive or all-inclusive, but instead aims to prompt questions, offer arguments, and provide information that will provoke further discussion and research.

Radical Women's Writing in the Late Qing (c. 1890–1911)

"With all my heart I beseech and beg my twenty million female compatriots to assume their responsibility as citizens. Arise! Arise! Chinese women, arise!" Thus Qiu Jin (1875–1907) dramatically calls her fellow countrywomen to action in the opening pages of *Stones of the Jingwei Bird*. Executed for treason before she could finish the piece, Qiu Jin clearly intended it to inspire women to overcome the ignorance and traditional restrictions that she felt blocked them from the right and duty they had to play active and productive roles in Chinese society. The contributions of women poets and artists—*cainü*, or "talented women," as they were called—had challenged the popular stereotype that a virtuous woman was an uneducated one for hundreds of years.[3] But the radical way women like Qiu Jin and her friend Chen Xiefen (1883–1923) intervened in the debates on culture, nationalism, and gender in the late Qing marks this period as a critical turning point in women's literary history.

The threat of foreign imperialism in the late nineteenth century spurred this transformation by prompting intellectuals to link the need for women's liberation with national salvation. Male reform intellectuals of the late Qing such as Kang Youwei and Liang Qichao advocated female education and the abolition of foot binding by rationalizing that if China could not exploit all its productive resources, including women, the country would be unable to compete in what was seen in Darwinian terms as a struggle for national survival on a global scale. The "natural feet" societies and female academies that sprouted up at the *fin de siècle* were conceived, therefore, not as tools for radically overturning traditional gender ideologies, but as part of a patriotic enterprise to create "enlightened mothers and wise wives." Interest in these issues also stemmed from an awareness that prevailing standards of femininity clashed with visions of the woman ideally suited to mother or marry a "modern" man. Chinese reformers began to see bound-footed and illiterate women as an embarrassing symbol of China as a nation held back by outmoded traditions.

These and other historical developments set in motion a transformation of women's social, political, and cultural roles that went far beyond the expectations and aims of early nationalist reformers. New institutions, including organized political parties and study associations, opened unprecedented avenues for women to participate in political discourse, while the modern newspaper and periodical press provided a crucial public forum for broader discussions of women's issues. In 1905, the dismantling of the imperial civil service exam system, which had sustained male domination in both literary and political culture since the sixth century, removed a formidable roadblock for women pursuing careers in those arenas. New ideas about women filtering into China via the foreign colonial and missionary presence, translations of Western fiction and political-philosophical tracts, and firsthand reports from Chinese travelers abroad further broadened discussions of the place of women in China.

From the late 1890s on, a small group of women feminist writers turned to the nascent periodical press to launch their own critique of the prevailing condition of women in Chinese society.[4] Primarily members of the educated elite, these women published essays, poetry, and fiction in reform journals and newspapers of the period and founded their own magazines devoted to the promotion of feminist causes. Chen Xiefen, daughter of the editor of *Subao*, an outspoken nationalist journal, started one of the earliest "women's magazines" (*nübao*). In 1902, she began editing a small insert devoted to women's education and rights for *Subao* that she soon expanded into a monthly magazine called *Women's Studies*. Between 1898, with the founding of a journal in Beijing also called *Women's Studies*, and 1911, over thirty periodicals dedicated to bringing both women (as writers and readers) and women's issues into the arena of public debate began circulation in the treaty port cities of China and the Chinese emigré communities in Tokyo.[5] Because of their dependence on private funding and donations from readers, many of these early women's periodicals, including Chen Xiefen's *Women's Studies*, were extremely short-lived.

The feminist vanguard's appropriation of the press as a tool for propaganda and education was part of a widespread discovery of the modern mass media by the progressive literati of the moment. In the wake of repeated failures to reform late nineteenth-century politics and escalating resentment of the Manchu rulers of the Qing dynasty, progressive intellectuals turned to the circulation of news and information, as well as the so-called "new novel" (*xin xiaoshuo*), as the primary vehicles for effecting serious social change. Expanding literacy among the urban masses of China's treaty-port centers had already created a huge market for a popular periodical press, and many reformers now believed that the key to national renewal lay in tapping into and transforming this audience. As Liang Qichao optimistically declared in 1896, "The more the people read the press, the more intelligent they become; the greater the press, the stronger the nation."[6]

The founders of the feminist press adopted this logic (and indeed the inflated rhetoric) and announced their mission to be nothing less than the transformation of the Chinese "women's world" (*nüjie*). In the editorial statement of the monthly journal *Chinese Women's News* that she launched in 1907, Qiu Jin wrote, "Who is responsible for controlling the force of public opinion and taking charge of guiding the citizens of the nation if not the press? Today, this magazine will unite our two hundred million women by circulating our news and serving as a general headquarters of the *nüjie*. It will enliven them and rouse their spirits."[7] In practice, of course, these journals reached a minute female readership limited primarily to educated women of the urban elite and the newly literate students of female academies. Still, for those women whose daily lives remained largely confined to and defined by traditional domestic roles, they served as an unprecedented source of political ideas, news, and information, including such practical knowledge as how to enroll in a female school or the best methods for caring for recently unbound feet. These magazines contrasted sharply with the traditional handbooks for women, whose primary function was Confucian moral edification. Instead they employed biographies of non-Chinese women, utopian feminist fantasies, reports on extraordinary contemporary Chinese women, and numerous other genres to introduce a wide range of alternatives to the traditional Confucian ideals of womanhood. The magazines encouraged readers to critically reflect on the norms governing their own lives. For the first time, women readers were interpellated as political subjects, both as citizens of the nation (*nü guomin*) and as members of the collective population of Chinese women.

Just as male nationalists advocated female education and the abolition of foot binding in the name of the national interest, so the majority of late Qing radical women writers framed their critique of women's social status as part of the broader project of China's modernization. But when women themselves took up these issues, the late Qing debate on women and the nation changed in significant ways. Most obviously, women ceased being simply objects of nationalist discourse and asserted their own historical agency in improving women's lot. As Qiu Jin once exhorted her female readers, "You must realize that just as the rulers of an empire do not cede the conducting of state affairs to others, we must depend on ourselves in matters affecting us. . . . Men fear that if we gain knowledge we will surpass them so they prevent us from seeking education; but why should we submit to this? If we do, we women are simply surrendering our own responsibilities, accepting the dominance of men, and being too lazy to resist."[8] In her 1904 essay "Crisis in the Women's World," translated here, Chen Xiefen went a step further by specifically linking women's rights to national liberation. "Since we women have a common responsibility, can we simply stand on the sidelines and allow the nation to be destroyed?" she asked. The national crisis, she suggested, was a crucial opportunity for women to exert their political agency and take the first steps toward obtaining social rights.

Critical also of what they perceived to be a paternalistic and superficial treatment of women's issues in the reform press, women writers used their magazines to significantly expand the content of the gender debate. Going far beyond the narrow parameters of the current nationalist discussions of foot binding and female education, Qiu Jin, Chen Xiefen, Luo Yanbin, He Zhen,[9] and others took up a broad range of topics related to women, including issues of economic autonomy, free choice in marriage, political rights and responsibilities, domestic reform, and Confucian gender ideology. Many of the issues that would be addressed under the rubric of the Woman Question in the May Fourth period of the late 1910s and 1920s were prefigured in late Qing women's writing.

Remarkable in terms of its political content, the writing of this generation of women is also notable for several important formal developments that signal a break from prior modes of women's writing. Most significant was the deliberate shift to a vernacular style of written language (referred to as either *suhua* or *baihua* at this time), which, it was widely believed, would be more accessible to the generally less-educated audience of female readers. Proficiency in classical Chinese (*wenyan*), the terse written form that by the twentieth century bore little syntactic relation to spoken usage, required years of formal training. Therefore, like some of their male counterparts, women radicals recognized the political imperative of employing a more popular linguistic medium in their writing. *Beijing Women's Post*, for instance, announced: "The Chinese language is exceedingly difficult and women's education in China is extremely underdeveloped, therefore this paper will use vernacular Chinese (*baihua*) and simple grammar to facilitate the understanding of women of all classes."[10]

Writers were also compelled to develop a new terminology capable of expressing notions central to their feminist-nationalist agenda. Qiu Jin and Chen Xiefen's writing, for instance, is filled with newly coined phrases and terms (often adapted from Japanese approximations of Western concepts) to describe women's political struggles against male domination. Terms first introduced during the late Qing, such as "independence" (*duli*), "women's rights" (*nüquan*), and "gender equality" (*nannü pingdeng*) would remain central to subsequent debates on women. Although modern *baihua* did not come into full usage until the May Fourth period, the hybrid of colloquial and classical written Chinese deployed in the late Qing feminist press shows that consideration of gender played an early role in establishing a connection between literary language and sociocultural transformation.[11]

Late Qing women writers also appropriated a variety of traditional fiction and nonfiction forms as part of their endeavor to "enlighten" their female readership. In imaginative literature, for instance, one finds examples of traditional forms of poetry, drama (*zaju*), and linked-chapter novels being used for feminist ends. In *Stones of the Jingwei Bird*, Qiu Jin adopts the *tanci* (literally, "plucking rhymes"), a popular narrative form with both an oral and written tradition, to recount a utopian tale of the political awakening and rebellion of five talented beauties-turned-revolutionary heroines.[12] Aware of the popularity of the *tanci* form among women audiences as well as its potential to reach nonreaders through oral performance, Qiu Jin chose this semilyric, semiprose traditional form for her radical narrative. Although the text was left unfinished at the time of Qiu Jin's execution for her role in a plot to overthrow the Qing government in 1907, we have included excerpts from the first five chapters of this monumental work in order to demonstrate how she attempted to transform a traditional narrative form for very revolutionary purposes.[13]

The richness of the language Qiu Jin employs to do this is remarkable in itself. By switching easily between classical literary tropes and newly coined feminist vocabulary, and by alluding to eminent women in Western history in the same breath as the heroines of the Chinese tradition, Qiu Jin manages to tell a very modern feminist story while still adhering to the familiar conventions of the classical Chinese storyteller. And lest one be too drawn into the story itself and forget its purpose, Qiu Jin's narrator cautions, "I pray that my readers ponder these words and that they don't treat this book like an ordinary novel. All the tears and blood are meant to awaken my compatriots from their living hell. I only hope that every one of my sisters can find a way to become independent and stop relying on men."

Feminist poems, songs, and dramas also appeared in the late Qing, but the essay, as exemplified by Chen Xiefen's "Crisis in the Women's World," prevailed as the most popular form used by radical women writers to express their political beliefs. Essays generally occupied the most prominent positions in women's magazines of the period. They frequently were styled as speeches addressed to a female audience and were written in highly colloquial Chinese. In some cases, however, including the essay translated here, they were written in a more formal style of classical Chinese, as if to demonstrate the intellectual authority of the author and to persuade male intellectuals as much as (or perhaps more than) women readers. Literary expressions of female frustration and dissatisfaction are certainly not unprecedented in Chinese women's literary history. However, writers in the late Qing enlisted the essay form to carry out a much more explicit and far-reaching interrogation of women's roles in society.

Both essay writing and experiments in literary form were to become key elements of women's writing in the May Fourth era of the 1920s. Yet this is not to suggest that May Fourth writing was self-consciously modeled after women's writing from the late Qing. Despite the relatively brief span of time that separates the women writers of these two periods, the dramatic historical events that took place—the fall of the ancient dynastic system, the failure of the newly established republican government, the harsh suppression of the women's suffrage movement,[14] the patriotic demonstrations following World War I—created a sense of enormous historical distance. As a result, the iconoclastic leaders of the May Fourth Movement saw themselves as rebellious pioneers of the modern era who were breaking with "tradition" for the first time. Indeed, the mythologies of the May Fourth generation—myths that still dominate contemporary views of Chinese modernity—either overshadowed or simply repressed from historical memory the late Qing attempts at literary and gender reform.[15]

Although many May Fourth intellectuals would continue to champion Qiu Jin as a symbol of modern female rebellion, women writers of the 1920s and '30s did not look back to her generation as their own literary foremothers. By including two examples of women's writing of the late Qing period in this anthology, we are not suggesting that they should be considered the long-forgotten "first" generation in a self-consciously evolving tradition of modern women's writing in China. Instead, we hope to point to another moment of modernity in such writing that will encourage further inquiry into women's literary production during the transformative decades of the late Qing and provide a new literary-historical perspective on women's writing in the May Fourth era.

New Culture and New Women Writers in the May Fourth Era

In June of 1917, with little fanfare or notice, a young Chinese woman studying at Vassar College in the United States wrote a short story called "One Day" for the *Chinese Students' Quarterly*. As an unknown woman publishing in a minor journal, Chen Hengzhe (1890–1976) was never crowned the "mother" of new fiction in China (the title of "father of new literature" went to Lu Xun, the famed writer whose short story "Diary of a Madman" was not to sweep through intellectual circles for another year), but Chen's simple account of a day in the life of a group of students at an American women's college still stands as the first piece of literature in modern vernacular Chinese (*baihua*). As such, it marks the beginning of the dynamic period of literary output in China associated with the May Fourth movement.

Broadly speaking, the May Fourth movement refers to the tremendous creative and intellectual ferment beginning in the late 1910s that followed the demise of China's dynastic system in 1911. Against a backdrop of rising anti-imperialist sentiment, intellectuals and youth alarmed by what they viewed as the slow progress of China's modernization mounted a radical re-examination of the country's cultural heritage. Traditional values and beliefs, especially those associated with Confucianism, were now virulently denounced as the source of a spiritual "disease" afflicting the

Chinese people and rendering the nation incapable of withstanding the challenges of foreign imperialism. Paradoxically, what was needed, according to this iconoclastic generation, was a cultural renaissance through the appropriation of new—namely Western—ideas and methods.[16]

At the heart of the cultural modernization project was a renewed interest in the issue of linguistic and literary reform. According to Hu Shi, an acquaintance of Chen Hengzhe and one of the leading spokesmen for the New Culture Movement, classical Chinese (*wenyan*), the official language of China's literati for over two thousand years, was a "dead" language incapable of describing the reality of China's current social and political problems or verbalizing the fresh ideas needed to overcome them and establish a new culture. In an essay that would later be regarded as the opening volley in the May Fourth literary revolution (*wenxue geming*), Hu Shi challenged his compatriots to create a new national literature by adopting as their medium a vernacular Chinese cleansed of the stagnant stylistic and ideological conventions of the past.[17]

Without engaging in the polemics of the heated debate that ensued, Chen Hengzhe accomplished what male intellectuals were still only talking about in 1917, a feat that reportedly caught even Hu Shi by surprise.[18] For her part, however, Chen remained remarkably nonchalant about the textual breakthrough her story represented. As a student in one of the first girls' schools in Shanghai during the last years of the Qing dynasty, the apparent ease with which Chen abandoned the classical style may have to do with her status as a female intellectual in the early twentieth century. Unlike for most of Hu Shi's detractors—men who, having been trained in the classical literary tradition, would have been entitled to social power and privilege had the imperial exam not been dismantled in 1905—for Chen, classical Chinese arguably had rather different symbolic implications. By late imperial times it was not unheard of for women of Chen's social class to have some degree of mastery of the traditional literary canon, but this would never have led to public office or its attendant rewards. Hence, the displacement of classical Chinese by the vernacular didn't pose the same kind of threat to the identities of female intellectuals. From the standpoint of women's history, one could argue that it was the very demise of classical literary culture and the institutions supporting it that ushered in a new era of intellectual possibilities and empowerment for women like Chen.[19]

Support for female education had grown steadily since the late nineteenth century. Whether they attended schools with curricula based on traditional women's subjects such as music, painting, and sewing, as were many provincial girls' schools, or on training for careers as doctors, nurses, or teachers, urban women who could read and write were no longer as rare as they might have been during Qiu Jin and Chen Xiefen's time a decade earlier. Government statistics estimated that 6 percent of the students attending state-run primary schools in the early 1920s were girls. By the early 1930s, this percentage had risen to 15.1, and the averages were significantly higher in Christian missionary schools, where girls made up nearly 40 percent of the students. Only 887 out of the 34,880 students (or 2.5 percent) attending college or university-level courses in 1923 were women, but by 1934 the proportion had risen to 15.02 percent, with higher averages in Christian-run colleges.[20] In noting the advances in female education during the May Fourth era, however, it is important not to underestimate the often bitter personal struggles many young women of this generation underwent to secure the right to a formal education. Though May Fourth reformers enthusiastically embraced education in their effort to improve women's lives, the majority of society still saw marriage and motherhood as the proper feminine destiny. Thus, as the biographies of several writers in this collection reveal, women who took it upon themselves to defy this norm often did so at the risk of losing both the moral and the financial support of their families.

For the generation of young women who did enroll as students, the school campus represented an unprecedented social space that afforded them a vast array of new experiences, including the opportunity to interact with peers outside of the mediating control of the family. The campus was also an important breeding ground for the heightened political consciousness and activism that characterized the new female students. During the nationalist demonstrations of 1919 from which the May Fourth Movement took its name, for instance, young women were visibly present in the crowds of angry students and citizens who marched through Beijing and Tiananmen Square to protest a provision of the Versailles Peace Treaty that handed former German territorial rights in China over to the Japanese. Students from Beijing Women's Normal College, the first public postsecondary educational institution for women in China, smashed the locked gates of their school to participate in the May Fourth demonstrations and were followed by several hundred women and girls from schools around Beijing. As the protests swept through other cities across China, female students mobilized, openly defying rules of social decorum in order to meet with male students, organize rallies, deliver public speeches, and work on propagandist journals. Much of this activity was originally patriotic in focus; however, the informal and formal networks that emerged among female participants during the heady days of mass demonstrations and political protests in 1919 were soon to have a discernible impact on the women's movement. In addition to many feminist groups, dozens of new journals and magazines aimed specifically at providing forums for women to address gender-based forms of oppression were launched in the months and years immediately following the 1919 demonstrations.

Contact with progressive male teachers and students involved in the May Fourth Movement, as well as greater access to public life through new educational and professional opportunities, expanded women's abilities to voice their opinions on many issues, including what was now specifically referred to as the Woman Question. Much like the reformers at the end of the Qing dynasty, intellectuals of the early May Fourth period had again pointed to the status of Chinese women as the most glaring symptom of China's backwardness and as an impediment to national modernization. Taking their cue from the recently imported theories of John Stuart Mill, August Bebel, and Friedrich Engels, intellectuals often considered progress in resolving the Woman Question a yardstick for measuring China's advancement toward modernity. The journal *New Youth*, the main propaganda organ for May Fourth ideology, had reserved a special section for discussions of the Woman Question since 1917. Along with hundreds of other new journals appearing around the country, *New Youth* often published articles critiquing Confucian gender ideology; introductions to "emancipated" foreign women like Alexandra Kollontai, Sophia Perofskaya, Emma Goldman, and Ellen Key; and translations of contemporary writing by foreign women writers such as Katherine Mansfield, Olive Schreiner, and Yosano Akiko. In 1918, the journal devoted an entire issue to the work of Henrik Ibsen. Nora, the main character in his play *A Doll's House*, who walks away from her unfulfilling role as wife and mother, instantly became the symbolic heroine in China for both women's emancipation and the liberation of China's youth from traditional Confucian moral codes in general. Countless stories and plays featuring sinified Noras who rebel against their old-fashioned families (often to assert their right to a modern romantic union) appeared in print and on the stage in the early 1920s.

In the aftermath of the student protests of 1919, an increasing number of women began contributing essays, stories, and poems to the most prominent political and literary journals in the country and to dozens of new local and national journals devoted exclusively to women's issues. It is no coincidence that the vast majority of the *nüshi*—"woman scholar" or "Miss," as they were invariably called—whose works appeared on the pages of the major progressive literary journals in the early 1920s were students at educational institutions in Shanghai and Beijing, most notably Beijing Women's Normal College. Acting upon their political commitment to women's education, the main male architects of the New Culture Movement (including Chen Duxiu, Li Dazhao, Lu Xun, and Hu Shi) often taught classes and gave speeches at women's universities and high schools, influencing several of the writers included in this anthology.

Editors of progressive magazines also began actively recruiting young college students like Bing Xin (1900–) and Lu Yin (1898–1934) to write for their journals.[21] Having women as contributors was clearly considered a rather politically correct and "modern" thing to do. But such encouragement also stemmed from an understanding that women would provide new insights into the issues critical to the Woman Question. Discussions of female emancipation, women's suffrage and education, and even marriage and foot binding in the early May Fourth press had become largely dominated by male voices, giving rise in certain circles to concerns about the role women themselves were to play in resisting patriarchy. At the same time, emergent notions of authenticity in literary expression helped shape assumptions that only women themselves could truly give voice to their gendered experiences. As Zhou Zuoren urged in his 1922 article "Women and Literature," modern Chinese women needed to "take advantage of their own creative abilities to express their true feelings and thoughts and to eradicate age-old misunderstandings and misgivings about women."[22] As theoretically naive as these may seem from the standpoint of late twentieth-century feminist criticism, such views were crucial in both legitimating women's writing in the 1920s and informing the ways in which it was publicly received.

At a moment when literary culture in China was being shaken to the core by a flurry of iconoclastic intellectual and creative activity, most young women hardly needed an invitation to put their pens to paper to express their views on the Woman Question or other matters. The act of writing was fast becoming an integral aspect of an educated woman's modern identity and part of the current rebellion against conventional definitions of femininity. The prolific May Fourth writer Chen Xuezhao (1906–1991), for instance, once recalled that her literary debut, an essay entitled "The New Woman I Want to Be," marked her first step in liberating herself from the authority of her traditional family.[23] Chen not only wrote and submitted this essay to a major Shanghai newspaper without asking permission from her strict older brothers but in doing so she discovered that writing could provide her with the income necessary to live independently. The flourishing of women's writing in the May Fourth era is inseparable from the fact that literary publication offered educated women one of the few means of earning an income and, therefore, a potential alternative to a life of financial dependence on parents and/or husbands. While many early May Fourth women writers also held teaching positions in the newly established women's schools and colleges, the money they earned for the publication of stories, poetry, or essays supplemented their meager wages and contributed to their already growing financial independence. In Chen Xuezhao's case, the income she earned from her essay writing eventually financed a lengthy stay in France where she was able to earn a Ph.D. in literature and sidestep her family's pressure to get married.

While May Fourth women writers published in the leading journals and newspapers, they tended to remain peripheral to the frequent theoretical battles between contending literary factions that dominated early May Fourth cultural politics. Whether they were simply not as caught up in the particular issues involved or felt ill at ease dueling with their male colleagues, the women whose names appeared in the rosters of prominent literary associations (Bing Xin, Lu Yin, and Feng Yuanjun [1900–1973], for example) rarely publicly voiced their opinions on such matters as "art for life's sake" or the merits of romanticism versus realism.[24] This does not mean, however, that they were either cut off or detached from the sorts of cultural debates taking place in meeting rooms at Beijing University or teahouses in Tokyo. The halls of the Chinese literature department at Beijing Women's Normal College, for example, were similarly abuzz with discussions of what direction new literature should take and what role women should play in its creation. Lu Yin, Feng Yuanjun, Su Xuelin (1897–), and later Shi Pingmei (1902–1928) and Lu Jingqing (1907–1993), all attended Beijing Women's Normal in the early 1920s and formed their own loose literary cliques and associations, networks whose impact on May Fourth literary culture and women's writing deserves further examination.

As many scholars have noted, dominating all these debates was a new focus on the interior realities of emotional and psychological experience.[25] Though this literary introspection manifested itself in exceedingly diverse ways—some writers narrativized new notions of the individual's relationship to society and social change, while others reveled with lyrical abandon in the depths of romantic turmoil—what many of these writers shared was an intense preoccupation with the subjective self. Accordingly, the period witnessed an outpouring of autobiographical and semiautobiographical writings. Even fictional stories purporting to probe social problems objectively often betrayed a great fascination with the unique consciousness of the I-narrator who encounters a problematic "other."[26]

On one level, women's writing was clearly influenced by this overall trend, evincing highly subjective tendencies as the narrative gaze increasingly turned inward to the realm of the personal. But on another level, the question of subjectivity in May Fourth women's writing raises issues that are specific to this body of writing as writing *by* women. This is not least because the project of representing the self at this historical moment was complicated by the highly public manner in which womanhood was being discussed as a sociopolitical problem. Whereas a male writer such as Yu Dafu could confidently claim with respect to May Fourth culture that the individual self had been "discovered," many women writers during this period articulated a far more ambivalent view of the so-called modern female self.[27]

Feng Yuanjun's 1923 short story "Separation," for example, begins to reveal some of the particular characteristics of women's self-representation at this time. The story is usually categorized as a "question story" (*wenti xiaoshuo*), a popular genre during the early May Fourth period that typically employed a first-person narrator, often an intellectual not unlike the writer, to scrutinize and expose a social problem. In "Separation" the issue at hand is modern love, namely the conflict a young educated woman experiences between the love and filial obligation she feels towards her traditional mother and the promise of romantic fulfillment in a modern relationship based on love. But the female narrator is not simply an objective observer pondering an external social dilemma; she is also the subject of the experience—it is her own mental and emotional turmoil that is foregrounded through the first-person narrative. The exploration of the Woman Question through a highly subjective point of view—whereby the educated female I-narrator stands simultaneously as the critical subject and the object of critique—characterizes much women-authored fiction of this period, and can be seen as a key device employed to capture the complex emotional and psychological effects of sociopolitical transformation.

The title of Lu Xun's oft-cited 1923 speech referring to Ibsen's defiant heroine, "What Happens After Nora Leaves?," delivered at Beijing Women's Normal College, asked the question that many May Fourth women intellectuals were asking themselves. Lu Yin, for example, who had begun her literary career squarely within the Woman Question story genre, abruptly switched the focus of her work from the problems of other women to the frustrations of women like herself, who had devoted themselves to ideals of modern marriage and career only to find that being a "modern woman" was fraught with difficulties and disappointments. In contrast to the confidence with which writers of the late Qing and early May Fourth periods often wrote about women's liberation, Lu Yin's best-known work, the novella *Seaside Friends*, published in 1923, and the 1925 short story translated here, "After Victory," are imbued with a deeply pessimistic attitude toward women's roles in contemporary society.

Reflecting an emergent motif in women's writing from the mid-1920s, Lu Yin's work foregrounds the disillusionment of educated young women who had spurned social conventions and even their own families to obtain an education and marry a man out of true love, only to find that life after this supposed "victory" was less rosy than anticipated. In part, Lu Yin's bleak attitude, like that of many of her contemporaries, was influenced by the rise of a realist aesthetic that emphasized the experience of social injustice. For many women writers, however, such experience and its literary expression took on a very personal dimension. As they watched many of their women friends and even themselves revert to traditional female models of good wife and mother and their once-progressive male classmates turn into domineering husbands, many women writers realized that behind the emancipatory rhetoric of May Fourth culture loomed traditional assumptions and expectations about women's place. In the view of writers such as Lu Yin, Chen Xuezhao, and an increasing number of feminist intellectuals, only a more fundamental socioeconomic restructuring of gender roles in Chinese society would enable an egalitarian relationship between China's "new" men and women. Devoid of the iconoclastic idealism driving earlier discussions of the Woman Question, Chen's essay "The Woes of the Modern Woman," translated here, challenges the May Fourth myth of the new reformed family by exposing just how little women's domestic status had changed by the twentieth century.

While they would continue, almost as a matter of course, to produce the type of overt political writing exemplified by Chen Xuezhao's essay, women writers of the May Fourth era also began to show a preference for personal modes of literary expression in which to explore their own anxiety and ambivalence about the current state of the "modern woman" in China. These writers' diverse experimentations in subjective voice and form, discussed further below, both increased the variety of women's writing being produced in China and provoked a multiplicity of fresh configurations of the "modern woman" as well as the "writing woman."

Creating the Modern Self: Public Forms of Private Expression in May Fourth Women's Writing

In her 1925 story "After Victory," Lu Yin constructs a complex narrative of female friendship and alienation by weaving together fictional letters written by a group of former classmates from a women's college. The epistolary form allows Lu Yin to reveal the confidences these women share with each other while maintaining the semblance of a private, unself-conscious conversation. Such public-private forms, as we will call them, became increasingly prevalent in women's writing in the mid- to late 1920s. The first-person short story, particularly the diary or epistolary forms that lent themselves well to exploration of the feelings and psychological motivations of the female protagonist, became a favorite narrative mode among women writers of this period. So too did an array of personal genres such as lyrical essays, intimate poetic and letter exchanges between women writers, and longer forms of memoir and autobiography. More than the realist short story (the genre long privileged by literary historians), these personal genres provided women writers with valuable space for self-inscription as well as channels of dialogue with other women.

Unlike the Woman Question stories and analyses written during the period immediately following the May Fourth demonstrations, these subjective writings tended to focus on the problems of women close in class and educational stature to the writers themselves. Typically, the "I" who speaks is a woman who has managed to obtain some measure of independence in her marriage and career—the quintessential New Woman—yet still feels a deep, if undefined, emotional angst. As one of the characters in Lu Yin's story wonders, "Before getting married we dreamt of full and satisfying lives, but in the reality of this flawed world, we end up with nothing but regrets!" What the imperfections of that social reality might be, or what measures should be taken to fix them, however, are not the focus of such writings. Instead, they probe the subjective consciousness of the individual woman within the context of this reality.

One of the most striking aspects of public-private women's writings of the 1920s was the practice of publishing letters, essays, and poetry of such an intensely personal nature that a reader unfamiliar with the authors' individual circumstances would have trouble understanding their subtle references and allusions to people and events. These often highly autobiographical works appeared not only in women's magazines, but in mainstream journals and the literary supplements found in major urban newspapers. Lu Yin, Shi Pingmei, and Lu Jingqing, all graduates of Beijing

Women's Normal College, were the most popular authors of public-private writings during the mid-1920s. Under the auspices of a loosely knit literary group known as the Wild Rose Association, Lu Jingqing edited *Women's Weekly*, a supplement to *Beijing Post*, beginning in 1924. From 1926 to 1928, she co-edited, with Shi Pingmei, *The Wild Rose Weekly*, a literary supplement to another prominent Beijing paper, *The World Daily*.

The intimate and rather cryptic exchange of poetic letters between Lu Yin and Shi Pingmei that is included in this anthology is typical of the style of works published by the Wild Rose Association. Although publishing personal expressions of emotion and private memory in such public forums may appear unusual, it should be noted that not only was there a long tradition of letter writing by women in China, but famous romantic couples of the May Fourth period frequently collected and published their love letters in book form. Yet in departing from the heterosexual norm of romantic discourse of that era and celebrating the intense affections between women, these exchanges exemplify how women writers used personal forms of writing to establish a separate yet public space for dialogue among themselves. The familiar and exclusive nature of such writings occasionally sparked critical accusations of lesbianism and solipsism, but the fact that these literary supplements remained in print for several years—during a time when journals often folded within a few months—shows that they had a substantial audience among middle- to upper-class educated women like themselves (not to mention curious male readers).

Women writers of the 1920s also favored the personal essay and a form known as "little works," or *xiaopin*, to depict moments of self-discovery or despair in an extremely impassioned and poetic style. The brief, lyrical sketches of a scene or a memory found in Lu Jingqing's collection *Random Notes*, most of which were first published in Wild Rose Association journals, are typical *xiaopin*. Addressed to an unnamed "you," the essay from *Random Notes* translated here adopts an intimate tone that invites the reader to share in the narrator's recollection of a past friendship. Characteristic of Wild Rose Association *xiaopin*, Lu's focus in the piece is less on the male "you" and more on the narrating "I" as she re-creates the past in order to formulate a clearer picture of her present self.

The short, descriptive first-person essay was also the preferred form for recording travel adventures. For the few Chinese women who managed to study abroad during the early twentieth century, the experience of leaving behind parental pressures and societal norms and adjusting to the new ideas and values of a foreign culture proved an opportunity for self-reflection and invention. Several of the women writers in this collection, including Chen Xuezhao, Lu Jingqing, Lu Yin, and Su Xuelin, published moving accounts of their travels in Europe and Japan. Su Xuelin, who left her studies at Beijing Women's Normal College for a scholarship to study in France in 1921, exploited the loose definition of the personal essay to include descriptive language that borrowed heavily from classical Chinese without sacrificing a contemporary flavor and significance. "Harvest," the essay translated here, is ostensibly an account of two idyllic experiences Su had in southern France. Yet implicit in her lyrical description is the revelation that the woman living these experiences is being changed by them. Only in the final paragraph of the essay when she suddenly notes that "I love my country, but I have suffered endless disillusionments there," does Su hint to her reader that the events recorded in the essay are more than travel notes: they signify a personal transformation that has affected how she perceives herself in relation to her country.

Poetry—always considered a suitable genre for women in the classical tradition—was reappropriated by women writers in the 1920s. Virtually every woman writer included in this anthology wrote free verse poetry (as opposed to the fixed styles of classical Chinese poetry, which many of them composed as well) during her career. Bing Xin popularized the haiku-like "mini poem" (*xiaoshi*) that expressed an idea or emotion in a few brief lines. With the publication of her poetry collection *Spring Water* in 1923, she inspired numerous imitations among male and female writers alike. Women writers connected to the Wild Rose Association frequently wrote and published poetry addressed directly to each other or prompted by each other's poems or essays. Linked and occasional free verse poems by Lu Yin, Lu Jingqing, and Shi Pingmei represented an intimate form of female literary expression that recalls the tradition of women's poetry clubs of late imperial China.

Longer personal narrative forms such as the memoir and the autobiography would also emerge as popular genres of women's writing, especially in the 1930s.[28] Lu Yin, Xie Bingying (1906–), and Xiao Hong, for instance, all published full-length autobiographies of their experiences growing up in traditional families and in a society unaccustomed to independent and educated women like themselves. Although not a prevalent form, novels written by May Fourth-era women were often highly autobiographical or biographical in nature. *Ivory Rings*, a novel by Lu Yin written in 1931 and published in 1934, based on her friend Shi Pingmei's tragic love affair, is a prime example of this.

In addition to letters, poetry, and essays, women writers of the May Fourth period used subjective fictional forms to give expression to the modern female self. Even more popular than the epistolary short story form exemplified by Lu Yin's "After Victory" was the fictional diary. The most famous of these was "Miss Sophia's Diary" by Ding Ling (1904–1986), which caused tremendous controversy when it was first published in 1928 with its frank depiction of the complex sexual desires of a young New Woman.[29] In the example included in the present anthology, "Lin Nan's Diary," also published in 1928, Shi Pingmei uses the diary form to prompt the reader to consider the subjective experience of a fictional female character who is a *victim* of the revolutionary ideas regarding women championed by her New Woman counterparts. Like her contemporary Chen Xuezhao, who frequently took a critical stance in her essays against the insensitivity of China's "new men" to the consequences of their modern lifestyles for women, Shi Pingmei provides a fascinating perspective on the modern male intellectual through the eyes of a traditional woman who, by no fault of her own, has become an unwanted burden to her "enlightened" husband. The fact that Shi Pingmei herself was involved in a relationship with a man already married through a traditional arrangement makes this story an especially interesting example of the blurred lines between the fictional and the autobiographical in women's writing of this period.

Though extremely influential, epistolary, diary, and other subjective forms were not the only fictional modes employed in women's writing during the mid-1920s. Many women writers continued to experiment with the realist short story. Ling Shuhua (1900–1990), one of the most talented modern Chinese writers, composed tightly crafted short stories that delved into the psychological world of women from the upper class through a much more detached narratorial stance than the first-person stories of Feng Yuanjun, Lu Yin, and Shi Pingmei. The stories included here, "Intoxicated" and "Once Upon a Time," boldly deal with two types of female desire—sexual attraction to a man other than one's husband and strong affection between two young women—both of which were provocative topics of debate at the time. In "Intoxicated," for example, Ling exploits the concise space of the short story to intensify the protagonist's emotions without allowing them to dissipate in lengthy detail or description before the story's unexpected denouement. Similarly, by setting "Once Upon a Time" in the closed atmosphere of a girls' school, she allows the two female protagonists to explore their feelings for each other without the intrusion of an outside world that would condemn them.

Given the keen interest in the subjective dimensions of so-called feminine experience, it is not wholly surprising that drama was a literary form sparingly used by May Fourth women writers.[30] There were, however, a few notable exceptions, including Bai Wei's (1894–1987) monumental lyrical drama *Linli* (1926)—regrettably, too lengthy to be included here. Composed in a highly expressive style of verse, the work explores the emotional entanglement of three characters caught in a tragic love triangle. In *Southeast Flies the Peacock*, the play we have translated, Yuan Changying (1894–1973) rewrites an ancient folk ballad in order to undertake a sensitive, albeit melodramatic, psychological analysis of traditional motherhood. Similar to the short fiction described above, the play foregrounds not the social conditions of female oppression but the psychological effects of those conditions on women—in this case, on the much-maligned mother-in-law in Chinese culture.

The variety of literary forms, both new and old, that women writers adopted in order to explore questions of female subjectivity helped shape the May Fourth literary landscape. Creating a host of new characters, themes, and perspectives, they drew on and subverted many of the images and narratives of gender that had begun to take hold in this period. Yuan Changying's version of *Southeast Flies the Peacock* doesn't simply celebrate modern romance or bluntly reject tradition; it explores the psychological underside of old-style family dynamics by focusing on the complex emotions of the traditional mother, who was often caricatured and dismissed as a reactionary figure in male-authored fiction. Shi Pingmei used fiction to play down the popular figure of the modern rebellious woman and ponder those women left behind, while Ling Shuhua put a surprising twist on the free marriage-versus-old marriage dichotomy by questioning the desirability of heterosexual marriage altogether.

The prevalence of overtly subjective forms in women's writing in the 1920s and the historical and theoretical issues it raises is an area of ongoing research among scholars of modern Chinese literature. A number of preliminary explanations have been offered, but key questions remain to be answered.[31] How, for example, did women's writing intersect with the romantic ideologies of the self and literary self-expression in general during the 1920s? To what extent did the intense spotlight on the Woman Question in May Fourth academic and political circles, as well as the proliferation of modern women characters—the victimized peasant, the westernized New Woman, the patriotic girl student, or the robust woman worker—in popular culture influence or mediate (or, alternatively, were they influenced or mediated by) women's self-representations? And how did May Fourth women writers' specific experiences of class, race, and nation shape the ways in which they expressed themselves as women? This final question was to take on particular importance, given the plethora of styles and modes of writing by women that existed by the late 1920s.

Public Politics and Women's Writing in the Late 1920s

Even as their more creative efforts turned increasingly inward, women writers of the May Fourth era remained vocal in the social and political debates over feminist reform. The contributors to *The Wild Rose Weekly*, for instance, also routinely wrote forceful articles on topical issues such as coeducation or birth control, as well as poetic meditations on personal loss or romantic love. In the early years of the May Fourth movement, mainstream discussions of the issues that fell under the rubric of the Woman Question were largely confined to the situation of educated urban women. As the decade wore on, however, heightened awareness to both the plight and the political importance of working-class and peasant women began to substantially change the nature of feminist discourse. Challenges to the liberal social reform agenda of the mainstream women's movement had surfaced from time to time in the May Fourth press, but the eruption of fiery nationalist protests in 1925–1926 made the need for a truly mass women's movement more apparent than ever.[32] To this end, concerted efforts were initiated by feminist leaders in both the newly formed Communist Party and the liberal wing of the Guomindang (the KMT or Nationalist Party) to organize working-class women in public protests and labor strikes against imperialism and, at the same time, to develop a feminist platform that could address their specific class-based problems.

Turning out in much greater numbers than they had in 1919, female students and intellectuals now joined women workers on the picket lines and patriotic marches of 1925–1926. Many of them began to embrace far more radical political commitments, especially after the sobering tragedy of March 18th, 1926, when forty-seven unarmed Beijing students were brutally gunned down by government soldiers during a protest against Japanese imperialism. The victims included several students from Beijing Women's Normal College,[33] and this unprecedented episode persuaded many women that they had as much at stake in political change as men. By the end of the 1920s, a growing number of women intellectuals began heading south to join the women's movement under the joint leadership of feminist activists like Xiang Jingyu of the Communist Party, and He Xiangning and Song Qingling (Madame Sun Yat-sen) of the liberal wing of the Guomindang.

One such woman was a defiant young graduate by the name of Xie Bingying, who would emerge as an important new voice on the literary scene. Like many of her generation, Xie saw political participation as the solution not only to the nation's crisis but to her personal plight as a woman. In her case, enlisting in the nationalist army allowed her to evade the arranged marriage awaiting her at home. After graduating from the Wuhan Central Military and Political Institute, Xie Bingying became one of a small contingent of female propagandists on the Northern Expedition and worked in Hubei and Henan provinces to promote gender reform at the grassroots level.[34] *War Diary*, her firsthand account of these experiences, catapulted Xie Bingying to fame in China and, through translation, in the West. The excerpts presented here, from the 1930 translation by Lin Yutang, contain vivid anecdotes of Xie's political work among peasant women. Chinese critics praised the bold unadorned syntax, revolutionary spirit, and social content of Xie Bingying's work for what they saw as a new (and, as some even characterized it, "unfeminine") mode of women's writing. Images of intrepid revolutionary women quickly began appearing in the fictional narratives of a wide range of authors.

The revolutionary fervor of the mid-1920s proved short-lived, however. After the collapse of the tenuous coalition between the Communists and the Guomindang in 1927, the prospects for progressive social change once again seemed remote. Many intellectuals previously sympathetic to the Guomindang were now disillusioned by the "white terror" carried out by Chiang Kai-shek's forces in Shanghai in April 1927 against union organizers and suspected Communist Party members. Historians have noted that this was a particularly grim moment for women, as latent resentment toward the ever-bolder feminist movement now exploded into a frenzy of outright retaliation against women activists.[35] Hundreds of women workers, students, and citizens were killed, including leading political activists like Xiang Jingyu, many simply for having bobbed hair, a reputed sign of radical allegiances. In 1927, Xie Bingying's female propagandist brigade was disbanded and she barely escaped arrest and execution herself.

In the years immediately following the bloody crackdown of 1927, the cultural climate in Shanghai, Beijing, and other major cities grew even more tense, especially for intellectuals with any significant political conviction. Many writers went into hiding or self-imposed exile; bookstores and publishing houses with suspected leftist ties were closed, and censorship rules tightened. The intellectual center of China shifted from Beijing to Shanghai as writers and political activists sought temporary refuge in the International Settlement there. Bitter squabbling over the role of culture in saving the nation left literary circles divided and directionless.

Nearly every writer included in this anthology was affected by the political and cultural changes taking place during the late 1920s. Lu Jingqing, for example, who had actively participated in the fatal demonstrations at Beijing Women's Normal College in 1926 and had gone south to work in the women's movement, decided to remain in Canton rather than return to school in the north. Others, like Chen Xuezhao, determined that even life in Shanghai was too dangerous and went abroad to France. Chen Hengzhe, Feng Yuanjun, Yuan Changying, and Su Xuelin, all of whom had been active as creative writers in the early May Fourth period, felt that they could now contribute more to China's social and cultural growth by translating, teaching, and researching in areas such as Western history, foreign languages, and literature—all of which were still very new academic subjects in China at the time.[36] In addition, a whole new crop of writers was emerging that had been educated not only on the curricula of the progressive women's schools, but on radical political protest as well.

Ding Ling, a newcomer to Shanghai who had stunned literary circles with her candid short story "Miss Sophia's Diary" the previous year, was in hiding in the International Settlement in Shanghai when she wrote the story translated here, "Day," in 1929. Opening with a long panoramic description of Shanghai and the sordid underside of its cosmopolitan exterior, "Day" captures the city as a center of material luxury and frenetic human activity as well as a site of colonial privilege and capitalist exploitation. This dual-sided landscape serves as a metaphor for the internal tension Yisai, the story's protagonist, experiences over her own inability to act upon her surroundings. But Ding Ling is also plainly critical of her middle-class heroine, and the sights and sounds of the urban environment that intrude on Yisai's life radically relativize the angst and ennui she feels. The story ends abruptly almost before it begins, highlighting the young woman's failure but also revealing how the story is for Ding Ling a transition piece between the subjective style of "Miss Sophia's Diary" and a more socially oriented (and eventually socialist) realist mode of writing. Less than two years after writing "Day," Ding Ling fixed her political resolve after her husband, the poet Hu Yepin, was arrested and executed for his involvement with the Communist Party.[37] Ding Ling herself joined the Party in 1932 and was detained by the Guomindang before her escape and reappearance in 1936 in Yan'an, the Communist Party base in Shanxi province, where she would help develop cultural policies and practices to further the cause of socialist revolution.

As many women writers began rethinking their own literary methods in the late 1920s, the very notion of "women's literature" came under particularly intense, often hostile, critical scrutiny. Once praised for their unique insights into the realm of feminine experience, women writers were now frequently criticized for focusing narrowly on women's subjects, in particular their own emotional experiences. In 1929, for example, the influential critic Qian Xingcun (A Ying) wrote disdainfully:

> Most works by women writers seem to bear a telltale and indelible mark so that all one has to do is open a book to know whether the writer is a woman. This is primarily because women use their fervent emotions as ink and base their depictions of all human characters on their own old-fashioned natures. Their works are lyrical and autobiographical, their material never extends beyond their personal spheres, and their works contain more emotion than reason.[38]

The critical backlash against women's writing at this historical juncture is an exceedingly complex issue, at once entangled with the shift toward a revolutionary aesthetic in the late 1920s and with the masculinism that continued to hold sway in cultural discourse. New interests in the proletarian fiction, social and socialist realism, and later resistance literature that had emerged in response to China's national crisis led to a turning away from the highly subjective mode of much May Fourth writing. Among those who condemned the bourgeois limits of the romantic mode of May Fourth literature were women writers involved in leftist politics, such as Ding Ling, Bai Wei, and Feng Keng, all of whom began testing out new forms, styles, and points of view that expressed their radical political convictions.

What many critics of "women's writing" (*funü wenxue*) seemed to forget, however, was that subjective literary tendencies were not unique to women. Male "romantics," as they were to be called later, had been equally absorbed with the self and self-expression in the May Fourth era. By specifically aligning the now-problematic characteristics of May Fourth literature (extreme emotionalism, privileging of the individual self, inadequate attention to social reality, bourgeois ideological stance, and so forth) with women authors and feminine writing, however, theorists were able to posit a superior brand of literary practice. The delineation and subsequent denigration of such writing functioned in large part as a way of valorizing the new paradigm of revolutionary literature.[39] The criticism leveled at women's writing, moreover, tended to rest on the now all-too-familiar opposition between the personal and the political common to masculinist discourse, which in turn underpinned the dismissal of women's concerns as irrelevant to politically engaged literature.

The notion that women's concerns and women's self-writing were unrelated and inferior to "broader" political and national concerns unfortunately began to pervade analyses of *funü wenxue* by Chinese critics of all political persuasions by the early 1930s. How women writers of this period, particularly those consciously dedicated to "politically engaged" literature, dealt with the critical devaluation of gender and gendered writing and its implications in terms of their own textual practices remains an important but as yet little-explored topic in Chinese literary history. What is clear, however, is that such assessments served to initiate a process of critical marginalization and omission of women's writing, particularly that by May Fourth and nonleftist writers, that persists in accounts of modern women's writing in China by Chinese and Western critics, who tend to reiterate that women writers, unlike their male counterparts, "were unable to move on to a broader vision of reality."[40]

But it would be a mistake to take the views of the literary critics who demarcated and then rejected works by May Fourth writers such as Chen Hengzhe, Ling Shuhua, and the members of the Wild Rose Association as evidence that women's writing or interest in women's issues was at an ebb during the late 1920s or early 1930s. On the contrary, this period witnessed such a massive outpouring of fiction, journals, and books devoted exclusively to concerns of women that one suspects much of the criticism directed at *funü wenxue* and the woman writer at the time was actually a symptom of the popularity women's writing and women's culture were then enjoying.

Women's Culture, Leftist Politics, and Women's Writing in the 1930s

By the early 1930s, a substantial increase in female literacy and an expansion of employment opportunities for women, who could now be found in factories, schools, and department stores, had created a new social atmosphere in international Chinese cities like Shanghai. Along with these changes came an increase in the popularization and commodification of the New Woman. The image of the cosmopolitan New Woman, sporting Western clothing and bobbed hair, graced cigarette advertisements, captivated moviegoers with her liberated "modern" antics, and filled the pages of popular glamour magazines. Not surprisingly, she also came to symbolize urban decadence for progressive writers and filmmakers of the 1930s, and the "woman writer" (*nüzuojia*) herself, often portrayed as fickle and self-absorbed, was frequently cited as the quintessential New Woman. But as the selling power of the New Woman grew, so did the influence of New

Woman consumerism. The real "new women" of Shanghai and other urban centers—middle-class office workers and store clerks, teachers, and wives who had been educated in the women's schools, as well as an underclass of female factory workers, an increasing number of whom had some degree of literacy—and their purchasing power stimulated growth in what they themselves began to refer to as a "women's culture" movement.

In 1929, the first issue of an ambitious journal entitled *Woman Writer Magazine* appeared on Shanghai newsstands and contained the following statement of purpose: "By responding to current trends, this magazine is the only existing vehicle devoted to the promotion of the new women's culture movement (*xinnüxing wenhua yundong*). The content is dedicated exclusively to masterpieces of literature and art by Chinese and foreign women. The contributors are all famous contemporary women poets, writers, playwrights, painters, and musicians."[41] The editors went on to note that they had decided to publish the new magazine after a double issue of the Shanghai literary journal *Zhenmeishan* on women's writing, published earlier that year and republished in book form under the title *Women Writers Special Issue*, had "sold over 10,000 copies within two months and broken all previous publishing records." While the readership was still small in relation to China's massive population, it is nevertheless a remarkable number considering the minuscule audience for serious literature at the time. Inexplicably and unfortunately (but not unlike many journals then being produced in the unstable political and financial atmosphere of Shanghai), *Woman Writer Magazine* folded after a single issue. Yet along with *Women Writers Special Issue*, the magazine is important as an indication of a burgeoning urban women's culture that was to have a far more diversified and wide-ranging influence during the 1930s, at least within Chinese cities, than women's cultural efforts had had in the late Qing or May Fourth eras.

Located in the French Concession area of Shanghai, the Women's Bookstore dominated publishing by and about women from approximately 1933 to 1936. When a reporter visited the Women's Bookstore in 1936 to interview the editor of *The Ladies' Monthly*, a journal published by the store, for her column "Interviews with Shanghai Career Women" in the Shanghai newspaper *Dagongbao*, she was greeted by a young assistant editor for the press who also doubled as bookstore clerk:

> Are you interested in purchasing books? Please, take a seat and have a good look around. Here is the latest issue of *The Ladies' Monthly*, and this is a collection of short stories by Miss Lu Yin;

here is a book of poetry by an Indian woman, and over here we have a collection of works written and selected by Miss Lu Yi [the pen name of Su Xuelin]. They are all very good and worth reading. Please sit down and have a look![42]

Publicly eschewing allegiance to any specific political party or feminist agenda, the collective of women intellectuals associated with the Women's Bookstore defined its mission in cultural terms. The charter stated its objective as: "Utilizing women's strength to publish useful books that will raise women's knowledge and encourage women's writing."[43] Given the extreme conservatism of the New Life movement started by Chiang Kai-shek in 1934, which advocated a return to traditional "family values," this neutral stance may have been more strategic than real. Despite the political turmoil and chaotic climate of the Shanghai publishing world during the early 1930s, the Women's Bookstore managed to publish several dozen books dedicated to an eclectic range of women's issues, including *Chinese Women: Past and Future*, *A History of Women's Lives in England*, and *China's Female Labor Problem*, all by women, as well as practical guides such as *Women's Legal Knowledge* and *Women and Bee-keeping*. They also published a series dedicated to fiction, drama, and poetry by women writers such as Feng Yuanjun, Zhao Qingge, Wu Shutian, Chen Baibing, Lu Ping, and many others. The relative success of the bookstore and journal was likely due to prudent efforts at downplaying any "political" implications to these endeavors as well as efficient management by, at different times, well-known women writers and activists like Huang Xinmian, Zhao Qingge, and Fengzi. The management even incorporated the Woman's Bookstore as a business in which interested supporters could purchase subscriptions to future publications and shares at a number of banks, including the Women's Bank located on Shanghai's famed Nanjing Road.

The existence of a thriving market for women's writing and books on "women's culture" in the 1930s is also demonstrated by the anthologizing and packaging of women's writing by more mainstream, popular publishing houses such as the Shanghai Commercial Press and Guangyi Publishers. The 1930 "Women Writers Mini-Book" series, for example, featured the works of several young writers such as Li Tiwei and Wei Yuelu in an attractive boxed set marketed for the new woman reader (and indeed the new male "voyeur" as well).[44] Anthologies, not only of fiction but also of poetry, drama, letters, essays, and diaries, and collections of works, often hastily assembled, by May Fourth era and new women writers went into multiple printings.[45] Translations of literature and writings by foreign women increased, with the Commercial Press taking the lead in publishing books on controversial topics with its 1931 translation of Margaret Sanger's sexual education handbook, *What Every Girl Should Know*.

That the "woman writer" herself was something of a hot commodity in the 1930s is especially apparent in the new Chinese cinema. In the 1934 film *The New Woman*, for example, the famous Shanghai actress Ruan Lingyu plays a struggling woman writer dismayed to learn that a publisher wants to put a glamorous photograph of her on the cover of her novel to increase sales. With glamor came gossip, and just as Ruan Lingyu's character in the film becomes the subject of a scandalous rumor in the tabloid press, actual women writers and artists were increasingly becoming fodder for the rumor mills themselves: Lu Yin traveled to Japan in 1930 in order to escape public ridicule over her "little lover" (referring to her second husband, who was nine years her junior), and Bing Xin's 1929 wedding was covered with an elaborate photo spread in *Woman Writer Magazine*.[46] But the public culture also fostered new forms of solidarity among women writers and their female following. When Bai Wei revealed the shocking consequences of her disastrous romance with the poet Yang Sao (including the sexually transmitted disease that she had contracted from him) in her 1936 autobiography, *My Tragic Life*, it triggered such a flood of sympathetic letters to the journal *Women's Life* that the editors were prompted to take up a collection for the treatment of her illness.

The attention to women's culture and the accompanying commodification of women's writing in the 1930s led some scholars to address women's cultural roles as topics for serious study. Veteran women writers and activists such as Wang Liming, Guo Zhenyi, and Tan Sheying published historical analyses of the Chinese women's movement.[47] In addition to Lu Jingqing's groundbreaking *Women Poets of the Tang Dynasty*, published in 1931, there were a large number of historical studies and critical works by male scholars on both classical and modern women's writing.[48]

But what of New Women's writing itself? While a growing number of leftist women writers had, by the late 1920s and early 1930s, begun to broaden their literary scope to include, among other topics, the plight of rural and working-class women, many other women writers found a booming market for their New Woman fiction. Although such fiction typically centered on modern urban women, usually from Shanghai, and clearly catered to the interests and concerns of a sophisticated urban female readership, it frequently dealt with topics of a far more serious nature than the critics who trivialized it were willing to admit. Chen Ying

(1907–1986), for example, one of the most popular and prolific women writers in mid-1930s Shanghai, was usually characterized as a light, romance writer. Yet the women characters she portrays in stories with titles such as "A Woman Writer" and "After the Wedding Banquet" go beyond superficial notions of women's concerns. "Woman," the story we have translated here, unfolds through the eyes of a sensitive "new man" who observes how his wife agonizes over her decision to undergo an abortion rather than jeopardize her intellectual ambitions. Chen Ying's exceedingly graphic description of the actual abortion confirms that she was more than just a writer of frivolous love stories. Though her writings differed dramatically from the overtly political style practiced by leftist women writers, she portrayed New Women as complex beings whose actions and ideas were far from irrelevant to contemporary society. Chen Ying's popularity—her short story collections all went into multiple printings—also attests to the fact that women's issues, while being relegated to an inferior position in political circles, were far from being marginalized in women's writing. In fact, writers like Chen Ying continued to write ever more boldly about them.

This is not to say, however, that women writers were uncritical of the privileged class of modern New Women who were now visible in cities like Shanghai. Sharply contrasting the often-melodramatic depictions of the struggles of intellectual women in the work of Lu Yin and Feng Yuanjun, Bing Xin's tongue-in-cheek "Our Mistress' Parlor" caricatures the heroine, a cosmopolitan Shanghai lady whose intellectual pretensions are undercut by subtle details emphasized by the narrator. A hostess of a sophisticated intellectual "salon," the protagonist claims to support women's rights, yet puts down women more successful than herself and hypocritically retains the maid who had been part of her dowry.

There were other women who eschewed overtly political art in the 1930s, attempting to attain a high "modernist" aestheticism in their writing. Like her better-known male contemporaries Dai Wangshu and Shi Zhicun, who were part of the so-called neoimpressionist movement (*xin ganjuepai*) in the late 1920s and early 1930s, Lin Huiyin (1904–1955), for example, utilized stream-of-consciousness and imagist techniques to compose fiction as well as free-form poetic sketches. Her impressionistic 1934 story "Ninety-Nine Degrees" uses a dizzying array of descriptive detail to conjure up the flurry of activity surrounding a birthday banquet on a sweltering Shanghai day. In the poems translated here, such as "On the Gate Tower," Lin Huiyin plays with voice and image to skillfully transform the sometimes distracted yet always romantic thoughts of a new woman into subtle verse vignettes.

But as China's political situation grew ever more volatile with the Japanese invasion of Manchuria in 1931 and the escalation of hostilities between Guomindang and Communist forces, other women writers chose to align themselves with literary groups advocating radical social change. The most influential group of the period was the League of Left-Wing Writers, a loose-knit organization of progressive intellectuals with disparate, and occasionally antagonistic, agendas that had been established in Shanghai in 1930. Among the founding members of this organization were a number of women writers—including Ding Ling, Bai Wei, Yang Gang (1905–1957), Guan Lu (1907–1982), and Feng Keng—who eagerly collaborated with male comrades in fashioning a new brand of revolutionary culture.

When Xiao Hong (1911–1942) and her husband, Xiao Jun, both writers from northeast China, sought refuge in Shanghai in 1934, they received an enthusiastic welcome from League members, who heralded them as authentic voices of patriotism from a region already under Japanese occupation. Lu Xun, the head of the League of Leftist Writers and the single most powerful figure in the literary world, was particularly supportive of the young couple, helping them publish their work and often featuring their stories in his own journal. Yet while Xiao Hong's writing was praised by critics for its nationalist sentiment, her portraits of rural China under Japanese occupation were a far cry from the idealistic visions of China's vast peasantry held by many other leftist writers of the period. Most notably, as a careful reading of her longer works such as *The Field of Life and Death* reveals, her sense of the national situation is heavily mediated, if not subordinated, by concerns about gender-based forms of oppression. The suffering of the female characters in this grim narrative is represented not (as it so often would be in the resistance literature of this period) as a pretext for condemning Japanese or foreign incursions on Chinese soil, but as an indictment of the deeply ingrained, homegrown system of patriarchy that still thrived in rural China.[49] In "Abandoned Child," translated here, Xiao Hong acknowledges the revolutionary context of her story in only the most oblique manner at the very end, choosing to focus her narrative on the effects of poverty on a young pregnant woman. Xiao Hong's ambivalence toward national liberation is captured even more powerfully in "A Sleepless Night," the brief essay included in our collection. Published shortly after the outbreak of full-scale war with Japan in 1937, the story expresses the complex nostalgia she feels for her homeland in Manchuria, now under Japanese occupation, when she realizes that as a woman in a male-dominated culture, she would have no real home of her own to return to—even without the ravages of imperialist aggression.

Despite her problematic relation with her native Manchuria, Xiao Hong was among a number of "regional writers" who made their literary debuts in Shanghai in the 1930s. Mounting demands for a literature of national resistance prompted new interest in representations of China's rural masses, and leftist literary circles championed regionalist writers' work as a needed alternative to the Westernized fiction of urban writers. Luo Shu (1903–1938), a writer from Sichuan in southwestern China, is one such example. Although she was a sophisticated intellectual who spent several years studying in Europe, her portraits of rural women from the Sichuan hinterlands reveal an acute sensitivity to the nuances of class and gender difference. The short story translated here, "Aunty Liu," dramatizes a privileged I-narrator's encounter with a downtrodden "other" in a manner highly reminiscent of the "question story" format of the early May Fourth period. Yet here the narrative is more self-conscious in portraying the discomfort the young narrator feels with her old nanny, who has been ravaged by abusive husbands, poverty, and alcoholism. Like Xiao Hong, Luo Shu refuses to either romanticize the suffering of peasant women or gloss over the intellectual, economic, and experiential distance that separates the different women in the story.

Luo Shu and Xiao Hong both died tragically at very young ages (Luo Shu in childbirth in 1938, and Xiao Hong of an illness during the Japanese attack on Hong Kong in 1942), abruptly bringing their promising literary careers to a close. But the works of these young women writers anticipate many of the issues that would frame women's writing in the decades to come: How could educated, urban women writers represent the rural women of China without eliding the vast differences that invariably arose between them? In the context of foreign invasion and civil war, was it the "duty" of women writers to write on behalf of national resistance, or should their first allegiance be to the "women's world," that female collective that Qiu Jin had referred to three decades earlier? What should they do when the interests of the nation and those of the "women's world" diverged?

In the decades since Qiu Jin and Chen Xiefen had first begun writing women into the discourse of Chinese modernity, the circumstances and context for writing had been radically altered. After 1937, when China faced a full-scale invasion by Japan, the conditions imposed by war greatly changed, and ultimately fragmented, the literary world. Whether they remained in occupied Shanghai or Beijing, followed the exodus of refugees fleeing from the advancing Japanese army, or established themselves at the Communist Party base in Yan'an, veteran women writers and newcomers found themselves facing very different challenges, questions, and expectations from those confronted by women in the previous few decades. The project and process of "writing women" that we have been describing in this essay did not come to an end, but it did change substantially. Writers of the Shanghai occupation period, such as Yang Jiang (1911–), Su Qing (1917–1982), and Zhang Ailing (1921–1996), for example, would bring a new level of literary sophistication and intellectual cynicism to their fictional treatments of modern gender relations. Resistance writers like Chen Xuezhao, Xie Bingying, Yang Gang, and An E (1905–1976) turned to reportage to capture life during these unstable years, producing an important record of women's perspectives on war and revolution. Ding Ling, Bai Lang (1912–), Cao Ming (1913–), Yang Mo (1914–), and the many others who contributed to the development of socialist culture in Yan'an struggled to find the best ways to address women's needs in the context of revolutionary transformation.

Women's literary production during World War II and in the postwar era was so enormous and informed by such a diverse range of concerns that the period could not be adequately represented in the present volume. Readers will have to wait, therefore, for a future anthology devoted to Chinese women's writing of the late 1930s and 1940s.

NOTES

1. See our supplemental reading list for works by these and other scholars of modern Chinese women's writing.

2. For a more in-depth historical overview of Chinese women's history during the period than we can provide here, see Kazuko Ono, *Chinese Women in a Century of Revolution, 1850–1950*, Joshua A. Fogel, ed. (Stanford: Stanford University Press, 1989).

3. For more on women's writing prior to the twentieth century, see Ellen Widmer and Kang-I Sun Chang, eds., *Writing Women in Late Imperial China* (Stanford: Stanford University Press, 1997), Dorothy Ko, *Teachers of the Inner Chambers: Women and Culture in Seventeenth-Century China* (Stanford: Stanford University Press, 1994), and Susan Mann, *Precious Records: Women in China's Long Eighteenth Century* (Stanford: Stanford University Press, 1997).

4. For more on the rise of the women's press, see Charlotte Beahan, "Feminism and Nationalism in the Chinese Women's Press 1902–1911," *Modern China* 1 (4): 379–416.

5. See Fang Hanqi, *Zhongguo jindai baokanshi* (A history of the early modern Chinese periodical press) (Taiyuan: Shanxi jiaoyu chubanshe, 1981), 558–71.

6. Liang Qichao, "*Lun baoguan youyi yu guoshi*" (On the value of the periodical press in national affairs), 1896. Quoted in R. S. Britton, *The Chinese Periodical Press, 1800–1912* (Taipei, 1966), 88.

7. Qiu Jin, "*Fakanci*" (Journal statement of purpose), *Zhongguo nübao* (Chinese Women's News), 1907 (1).

8. Qiu Jin, "*Jinggao Zhongguo erwan wan nütongbao*" (Warning to two hundred million women compatriots), *Baihua bao* (Vernacular News), 1904. Reprinted in *Qiu Jin ji* (Collected works of Qiu Jin) (Shanghai guji chubanshe, 1979), 4–7.

9. Luo Yanbin (b. 1869) was the founder of one of the most successful late Qing women's papers, *The New Chinese Women's World*, which she launched in Tokyo in 1907. He Zhen (dates unknown) cofounded the feminist anarchist paper *Tianyi*. For more on these two pioneers in feminist journalism, see Li Youning, "Zhongguo xin-nüjie de chuangkan ji neihan" (The founding and contents of *The New Chinese Women's World* magazine) in Li Youning and Zhang Yufa, eds., *Zhongguo funüshi lunwenji* (Taibei: Taiwan yinshuguan, 1981), 179–241; Peter Zarrow, "He Zhen and Anarcho-Feminism in China," *The Journal of Asian Studies* 47 (4): 796–813.

10. Advertisement for *Beijing nübao* (Beijing Women's Post), 1905.

11. For more on how new words and meanings made their way into modern Chinese discourse, see Lydia H. Liu, *Translingual Practice: Literature, National Culture, and Translated Modernity—China, 1900–1937* (Stanford: Stanford University Press, 1995).

12. For more on the *tanci* form and its popularity among women and women writers, see Marina H. Sung, "T'an-Tz'u and T'an-Tz'u Narratives," *T'oung Pao* 79 (1993): 1–22.

13. Another such experiment, and possibly the first woman-authored feminist novel of the modern period, is Wang Miaoru's fantasy novel *Flowers in the Female Inferno*, published in 1904, which chronicles the successful liberation of Chinese women through the combined efforts of several intrepid heroines.

14. In the years immediately following the overthrow of the Qing dynasty in 1911, feminists called for women's suffrage and started several journals dedicated to the cause. In 1914, however, President Yuan Shikai implemented the Police Regulations on Public Order, banning women's political groups and their publications and forbidding women to give public lectures or attend meetings or rallies.

15. Ding Ling, who examines the political awakening of her mother's generation in her unfinished semiautobiographical novel *Mother* (1933), is an important exception.

16. For more on the May Fourth movement, see Chow Tse-Tsung, *The May Fourth Movement: Intellectual Revolution in Modern China* (Cambridge: Harvard University Press, 1960) and Vera Schwarcz, *The Chinese Enlightenment: Intellectuals and the Legacy of the May Fourth Movement of 1919* (Berkeley: University of California Press, 1986).

17. Hu Shi, "A Preliminary Discussion of Literary Reform" (*Wenxue gailiang chuyi*), in William Theodore de Bary, ed., *Sources of Chinese Tradition* (New York: Columbia University Press, 1964, c. 1960), 2:158–62. Original version in *New Youth* 2 (5) (January 1917): 1–11.

18. Hu Shi, "*Hu xu*" (Preface by Hu Shi), in Chen Hengzhe, *Xiao yudian* (Little Raindrop) (Shanghai: Xinyue shudian, 1928), 1–7.

19. Chen Hengzhe's willingness to flaunt tradition and experiment with the new language may also have been influenced by the success her Vassar classmate Edna St. Vincent Millay had in writing what the American literary establishment considered "unfeminine" verse.

20. Colin Mackerras, "Education in the Guomindang Period, 1928–1949," in David Pong and Edmund S. K. Fung, eds., *Ideal and Reality: Social and Political Change in Modern China, 1860–1949* (Lanham, Md. and London: University Press of America, 1985), 171. For an early but still informative study of women's education in China, see Ida Belle Lewis, *The Education of Girls in China* (New York: Teachers College, Columbia University, 1919).

21. Beginning in 1919, Bing Xin and Lu Yin became familiar names in the influential journal *Short Story Monthly* and the literary supplement of Beijing's *Morning Daily*, which regularly featured their poems and short stories. Both of them were daughters of former Qing officials attending women's colleges in Beijing (Bing Xin at Yanjing University and Lu Yin at Beijing Women's Normal College) whose activism in student politics following the May Fourth demonstrations led to writing and publication.

22. Zhou Zuoren, "Women and Literature" (*Nüzi yu wenxue*), in *Women's Review*, June 7, 1922, 1–2; and in *Ladies Journal* 8 (8) (1922): 6–8.

23. "Wo de diyi pian sanwen" in *Chen Xuezhao yanjiu zhuanji* (Hangzhou: Zhejiang wenyi chubanshe, 1983), 299–300.

24. For examples of the kinds of essays May Fourth women writers published on aesthetic issues, see Kirk A. Denton's *Modern Chinese Literary Thought: Writings on Literature, 1893–1945* (Stanford: Stanford University Press, 1996).

25. See, for instance, Leo Ou-fan Lee, *The Romantic Generation of Modern Chinese Writers* (Cambridge: Harvard University Press, 1973) and Jaroslav Průšek, *The Lyrical and the Epic: Studies of Modern Chinese Literature* (Bloomington: Indiana University Press, 1980).

26. For an insightful examination of this particular narrative pattern in May Fourth writing and its gender implications, see Yue-ming Bao's "Gendering the Origins of Modern Chinese Fiction" in Tonglin Lu, ed., *Gender and Sexuality in Twentieth Century Chinese Literature and Society* (Albany: State University of New York, 1993), 47–65.

27. Yu Dafu makes this claim in his 1936 article included in *Zhongguo xin wenxue daxi taolun xuanji* (Shanghai: Liangyou tushu gongsi, 1935–6). Quoted in Leo Ou-fan Lee, *The Cambridge History of China* (Cambridge: Cambridge University Press, 1983), 12:476.

28. For a selection of autobiographical writings, see Janet Ng and Janice Wickeri, eds., *May Fourth Women Writers: Memoirs* (Hong Kong: Renditions Press, 1997).

29. Translated in Tani E. Barlow, ed., with Gary J. Bjorge. *I Myself Am a Woman: Selected Writings of Ding Ling* (Boston: Beacon Press, 1989), 49–81.

30. Successful women playwrights like Bai Wei and Yuan Changying may have been rare, but we should note here that as an art form, drama (and increasingly, film)

was instrumental in the May Fourth period in changing the public perception of women in another way: through the presence of women actors on stage, beginning in the late 1910s. Such performances shocked theatergoers, who were accustomed to seeing men play female roles in traditional Chinese opera but had never before seen women on stage.

31. See Yi-tsi Feuerwerker, "Women as Writers in the 1920s and 1930s," in Margery Wolf and Roxane Witke, eds., *Women in Chinese Society* (Stanford: Stanford University Press, 1975), 143–68; Wendy Larson, "Female Subjectivity and Gender Relations: The Early Stories of Lu Yin and Bing Xin," in Liu Kang and Xiaobing Tang, eds., *Politics, Ideology, and Literary Discourse in Modern China* (Durham: Duke University Press, 1993), 124–43; Wang Jialun, *Zhongguo xiandai nüzuojia lunwang* (A discussion of modern Chinese women writers) (Beijing: Zhongguo funü chubanshe, 1992); Meng Yue and Dai Jinhua, *Fuchu lishi dibiao: xiandai funü wenxue yanjiu* (Emerging on the horizon of history: A study of modern Chinese women's literature) (Zhengzhou: Henan renmin chubanshe, 1989).

32. The first of these protests is usually considered the May 30th Incident of 1925, in which British police in the International Settlement in Shanghai opened fire on a group of workers and students protesting the death of a worker at a Japanese-owned textile factory. The event had immediate and major political repercussions as anti-imperialist protests and boycotts erupted throughout the country.

33. Liu Hezhen, a classmate of several of the women writers in this collection, became the symbolic martyr of the March 18th Incident after Lu Xun published an essay decrying her death. The woman writer Lu Jingqing, who was also actively involved in organizing students at Women's Normal, also wrote of Liu in her 1932 memoir *Wanderings*.

34. The Northern Expedition refers to the 1926–1927 Guomindang-led military operation to wipe out powerful local warlords and unify the country.

35. See, for example, Elisabeth Croll, *Feminism and Socialism in China* (New York: Schocken Books, 1978) and Christina Kelley Gilmartin, *Engendering the Chinese Revolution: Radical Women, Communist Politics, and Mass Movements in the 1920s* (Berkeley: University of California Press, 1995).

36. Chen Hengzhe, who was the first woman professor at Beijing University, also produced the first Chinese textbook on Western history. Feng Yuanjun devoted herself to research on the classical Chinese literary tradition; her *Outline History of Classical Chinese Literature* has been translated into English. Yuan Changying wrote on and translated French literature, as did Su Xuelin, who also went on to teach and write the history of modern literature in China.

37. Leftist woman writer Feng Keng (1907–1931) was also among the four others detained and executed with Hu.

38. Qian Xingcun, "Guanyu Chen Hengzhe chuangzuo de kaocha," in Huang Renying, ed., *Dangdai Zhongguo nüxing zuojia lun* (On contemporary Chinese women writers) (Shanghai: Guanghua shuju, 1933), 251–57. First published on December 12, 1929 in *Haifeng zhoubao*.

39. For further elaboration of this point and other matters related to the interpretation of the critical discourse on women's writing of this period, see Wendy

Larson, "The End of 'Fünu Wenxue': Women's Literature from 1925–1935," in *Modern Chinese Literature* 4 (1988).

40. Yi-tsi Feuerwerker, "Women as Writers in the 1920s and 1930s," in Margery Wolf and Roxane Witke, eds., *Women in Chinese Society* (Stanford: Stanford University Press, 1975), 145. For a critique of such views, see Rey Chow, *Woman and Chinese Modernity: The Politics of Reading Between West and East* (Minneapolis: University of Minnesota Press, 1991), 158–59.

41. *Woman Writer Magazine* (Shanghai: Jinwu shudian, 1929), 1 (1): 156.

42. Yu Xiao, "Miss Jixing Gan, editor at the Women's Bookstore," in *Dagongbao*, Shanghai, September 1936. We would like to thank Susan Glosser for bringing this article to our attention.

43. *Nüzi shudian tushu mulu* (Index to the publications of the Women's Bookstore) (Shanghai: Nüzi shudian, 1933), inside cover.

44. *Nüzuojia xiao congshu* (Women writers mini-book series), (Shanghai: Guangyi shuju, 1930), 10 v.

45. See, for example, the five collections of contemporary women's diaries, essays, and short stories edited by Wang Dingjiu for Shanghai's Zhongyang Bookstore in 1935, or the seven anthologies of modern women's writing edited by Jun Sheng for Shanghai's Fangguo Bookstore in 1936.

46. In a tragic twist of fate, shortly after the release of *The New Woman* the actress Ruan Lingyu found herself at the center of unwanted media attention and committed suicide.

47. Guo Zhenyi, *Zhongguo funü wenti* (The Chinese woman question) (Shanghai Commercial Press, 1931); Wang Liming, *Zhongguo funü yundong* (The Chinese women's movement) (Shanghai Commercial Press, 1934); Tan Sheying, *Zhongguo funü yundong tongshi* (The history of the Chinese women's movement) (Nanjing funü mingshe, 1936).

48. Lu Jingqing, *Tangdai nü shiren* (Shanghai: Shenzhou guoguangshe, 1931). See also Chen Dongyuan, *Zhongguo funü shenghuo shi* (A history of Chinese women's lives) (Shanghai: Shanghai Commercial Press, 1928); Tan Zhengbi, *Zhongguo nüxing de wenxue shenghuo* (The literary life of Chinese women) (Shanghai: Guangming shuju, 1930).

49. For an illuminating discussion of Xiao Hong's treatment of gender and nationalism, see Lydia Liu, "The Female Body and Nationalist Discourse: Manchuria in Xiao Hong's *Field of Life and Death*," in Angela Zito and Tani E. Barlow, eds., *Body, Subject, and Power in China* (Chicago: The University of Chicago Press, 1994), 157–77.

1

Qiu Jin

Qiu Jin (1875–1907)

Remembered for her pioneering role in Chinese feminism as well as her flamboyant participation in the nationalist revolutionary movement during the waning years of the Qing dynasty, Qiu Jin belongs to the extraordinary first generation of radicals who actively searched for solutions to China's political crisis at the turn of the century. In Qiu Jin's view, the problems of "woman" and "nation" were intimately connected, not least because she believed that the liberation of Chinese women from patriarchal domination would have little meaning if China as a nation were subjugated by foreign powers. Much of her political work and radical writing was devoted to this dual agenda.

Born into a scholarly family from Fujian province in 1875, Qiu Jin was brought up in a traditional manner, although her parents were at times lenient in allowing her to pursue activities normally deemed unsuitable for young ladies of her social class. Her mother reputedly gave up trying to teach her the "feminine arts" of sewing and embroidery when Qiu Jin insisted that she preferred practicing archery and reading martial arts novels. Qiu Jin also received outstanding training in classical literature, which is reflected in the traditional lyrical poetry (*shi* and *ci*) she composed as well as the wide range of poetic allusions in her more explicitly revolutionary writing.

Qiu Jin was first exposed to radical nationalism in 1903, when she moved to Beijing shortly after her marriage. The imperial capital was still reeling from the repercussions of the disastrous Boxer Rebellion of 1900, and it was amid this politically charged atmosphere that Qiu Jin started reading periodicals such as Liang Qichao's *New Fiction* and meeting other progressive intellectuals who shared her growing alarm over China's current situation. To express her deep dissatisfaction with the status quo, Qiu Jin began composing patriotic verses and, much to her husband's dismay, appearing in public in Western male attire. Thoroughly disillusioned by her marriage and determined to contribute personally to the revolutionary movement, Qiu Jin left her husband and her two children in 1904 and embarked for Japan, a venture that she financed by selling her dowry jewelry.

In Tokyo, where she enrolled in Shimoda Utako's Girls' Practical School, Qiu Jin quickly distinguished herself as an ardent advocate of nationalist revolution as well as a leading voice in the nascent feminist movement. In addition to delivering fiery speeches at meetings of Chinese students in Japan, Qiu Jin helped to reorganize the Encompassing Love Society, an early all-women's political association whose members included the future suffragette Lin Zongsu. In 1905, Qiu Jin formally joined Sun Yatsen's Revolutionary Alliance, becoming one of the first female members of that organization.

Like many late Qing activists, Qiu Jin regarded the burgeoning print media as an indispensable tool for galvanizing her compatriots to reform society. In Japan, she began writing for the *Vernacular News*, a revolutionary journal that advocated the use of a more colloquial form of written Chinese. After returning to China, Qiu Jin launched her own journal, *Chinese Women's News*, at the end of 1906. Like many of the periodicals that comprised the so-called women's press at the turn of the century, Qiu Jin's magazine was explicitly addressed to a female readership and took up a variety of feminist issues, including women's education and economic autonomy. The goal of the magazine, as stated in her editorial introduction, was to "unite all Chinese women." Due to financial difficulties, however, only two issues of this ambitious journal ever appeared in print. In 1907, Qiu Jin was arrested and beheaded in Shaoxing for her role in a conspiracy to overthrow the Qing government.

A versatile writer, Qiu Jin was admired for her lyrical poetry as well as her political writings. The latter category included feminist-nationalist songs, patriotic ballads, and impassioned essays on the relationship between women's emancipation and nationalist transformation. Qiu Jin's most ambitious revolutionary opus, however, was the *tanci* she began composing in 1905 in Japan, *Stones of the Jingwei Bird*. A traditional oral narrative form that alternates in performance between recited prose and sung verse, the *tanci* was seen as an ideal medium for reaching the illiterate and semi-illiterate masses. (The alternating verse/prose style has not been maintained in this translation in the interest of preserving the flow of the narrative in English.) The *tanci* held particular appeal among female audiences, which might also explain why Qiu Jin choose this particular narrative mode. Originally conceived as a twenty-chapter work, *Stones* was left unfinished at the time of Qiu Jin's execution, but it remains an important example of this formative moment in modern women's writing in China. The full text appeared in print for the first time in 1962 in Qian Xingcun (A Ying)'s anthology of late Qing literature.

Excerpts from
STONES OF THE JINGWEI BIRD[1]
(1905–1907)

Preface

I live in an era of transition. Taking advantage of the light of the dawning civilization and the paltry knowledge I possess, I have thrown off the yokes of the past. Yet I am often pained that my sister compatriots remain in a World of Darkness, as though drunk or dreaming, oblivious to the changes around them. Even though there are now schools for women, few enroll in them. Let me ask you, of our twenty million women, how many still grovel at the feet of tyrannical men? Alas, today they continue to powder and paint themselves, chatter about their hairdos and bind their feet, adorn their heads with gold and pearls, and drape their bodies in brocade. Toadying for favor, they ingratiate themselves to men—obey-

---

1. The *jingwei*, a mythical bird, attempted to fill up the ocean with pebbles. Although traditional proverbs about this bird connote an endeavor carried out in vain, here Qiu Jin reappropriates the image to convey in a more positive sense the idea of a monumental yet achievable task.

ing their commands like horses or cows. They are no more than the servile and shameless playthings of men. But though they are subjected to immeasurable oppression, they are unaware of their pain; though suffer abuse and humiliation, they have no shame. They are completely blind and ignorant, saying with idiotic serenity: this is our fate. They feel no disgrace in begging like slaves and groveling on their knees. Instead of supporting their compatriots, they stand on the sidelines obeying their husbands and sons and opposing those who build schools and factories for women. Then there are those delicate ladies of noble families, with their fancy houses and fine appearances, their piles of pearls and gold, who willingly worship stupid temple idols and fatten the Buddhist monks and nuns to pray for their happiness, yet when they see other women who are engulfed in suffering, they don't even offer a helping hand. Alas! Do they feel no compassion?

I continued to be baffled by this situation until, after long reflection, I suddenly awoke. Now I declare: wherever there are women, are there not also heroines, philanthropists, and exceptional individuals to be found? I am not referring to those women in scholarly circles, for they have already been nurtured by civilization. But are there not also heroines even within the World of Darkness? Unfortunately, women suffer from ignorance and limited experience, and thus no matter how many books they may have in their possession, they have a hard time understanding what they mean. For this reason, I have composed this *tanci* in plain language, hoping that all women will comprehend its content and that it will enable them to leave the darkness behind and ascend to the civilized realm. I have tried my best to write systematically about the demeaning realities of women's existence, about their suffering and shame, in hopes of startling my readers, making them aware of their own shortcomings, and rousing them to further enlighten our women's world.

Every day I burn incense, praying that women will emancipate themselves from their slavish confines and arise as heroines and female gallants on the stage of liberty, following in the footsteps of Madame Roland, Anita,[2] Sophia Perofskaya, Harriet Beecher Stowe, and Joan of Arc. With all my heart, I beseech and beg my twenty million female compatriots to assume their responsibility as citizens. Arise! Arise! Chinese women, arise!

---

2. Anita Garibaldi (1821–1849), the Brazilian-born wife of Italian revolutionary Giuseppe Garibaldi. She appeared as the heroine of a short work of fiction by the late Qing reformer Liang Qichao in 1902.

I lament that the Chinese motherland has descended into darkness. How can we bear to have our magnificent rivers and mountains swallowed up by foreign races? We forty million heirs of the Chinese motherland are but slaves, useless to the bone. We willingly cower before others and seek glory by ingratiating ourselves to them. Fortunately, among us loyal subjects have been reincarnated who will rebuild this entire nation from scratch.

But the pathetic world of women remains without glory, complacently awaiting death amid these seas of sorrow, these cities of sadness. Forgotten are the unwavering courage of Mulan[3] and the heroic spirit of Hongyu.[4] However, the winds of Europe and the rains of America are suddenly surging forth and are beginning to revive such spirits. Chinese women will throw off their shackles and stand up with passion; they will all become heroines. They will ascend the stage of the new world, where the heavens have mandated that they reconsolidate the nation.

[Editors' note: Chapter 1, "In Slumberland, muddled women suffer in their Dark Prisons; In the Enlightened Heavens, lucid heroines descend to the City of White Clouds," begins with an allegory of "Slumberland," a nation plagued by incompetent officials and corrupt traditions. The Queen Mother in Heaven is so outraged by the oppression of women in Slumberland that she dispatches a troop of immortals to intervene. Interestingly, the divine intervention plot remains undeveloped in the remainder of the narrative and the possibility that the main characters are incarnations of these immortals is only hinted at. As the narrator herself carefully reminds the reader, deities and immortal beings are fictitious creatures worshipped by the ignorant and superstitious. Our excerpt picks up at the end of chapter 1.]

So let us return without further delay to the main story about one particular family. In the Huang clan of Zhejiang province, there was a prefect by the name of Huang Sihua. He had realized his ambition of attaining high status while a young man, and thus did not bring shame upon his illustrious ancestors, officials who had served in the customs bureau in Fujian Province for generations. As they had been frugal officials, their sleeves were empty[5] and all they bequeathed to their sons were the teach-

---

3. The legendary woman warrior who disguised herself as a man and took her ailing father's place in battle.

4. A female general who distinguished herself in battle.

5. In reference to an official, having empty sleeves means to be honest and upright.

ings of the Classics. Though the traditions preserved in this family were all very proper, it was an inflexible, old-fashioned family that did not easily accept new ways. For example, girls had never been sent to school and learning was strictly for boys. But enough said about Prefect Huang. His wife, Lady Sang, was extremely virtuous and capable. They were cousins, and after they were wed, she aided her husband in his studies of the Five Classics.[6] Her mother-in-law died young, leaving behind three sons: Prefect Huang, who was the eldest son, and two others, both young boys. Lady Sang had married into the family when she was eighteen years old and had served her mother-in-law with such obedience that she gained a reputation for being virtuous. After her mother-in-law's death, she devoted herself to raising the two younger boys, as though they were her own sons. When they came of age, she married them off and assumed full responsibility for domestic matters in the household. She had suffered a great deal in the past, and now the prosperity she had long deserved arrived. But who could foresee that Heaven does not always obey people's wishes? Although her family now enjoyed prosperity and rank, Lady Sang was not happy. If you want to hear why, allow me to take a rest, and in the next chapter I will continue our story.

Chapter 2: Huang Jurui is born amid the Sea of Remorse; Little Jade laments in the Fragrant Boudoir.

A brisk wind accompanies the winter season, and the Japanese landscape evokes a thousand emotions.[7] I contemplate the crisis now facing China and how hopeless the situation is without any heroes to come to the rescue. My emotions overwhelm me, making it impossible to study, so I sit here before the lamp and continue to write our story. I had written that Lady Sang was a virtuous woman, but even though the family now enjoyed prosperity and rank, she found family life unbearable. It turns out that her husband Prefect Huang was fond of women, and had all manner of liaisons outside his marriage. Naturally, his infidelities sparked frequent conflicts and quarrels between husband and wife at home. It was not that Lady Sang enjoyed getting angry, but Prefect Huang was simply

---

6. The core texts of a traditional Confucian education, the Five Classics are *The Book of Songs, The Book of History, The Book of Changes, The Book of Rites,* and *The Spring and Autumn Annals.*

7. Qiu Jin started composing this work in 1905 while living in Japan.

out of control. Men as a rule are accustomed to rejecting the old and coveting the new, and officials are even worse in this regard. Thus, troubles arose between a husband and wife who had once suffered through so much together. As a result, Lady Sang had grown very unhappy. She had given birth to four sons, but only the fourth, a boy named Zuyin, had survived. She cherished her only son and treated him like a precious jewel.

Prefect Huang had been sent to Shandong to await a vacant position. Now the career of an official is one of competing to get to the top and either maneuvering or begging to secure positions. If you don't beg or maneuver but rely solely on your abilities, then you will never get anywhere. Prefect Huang came from a poor family and he was upright by nature, so he didn't scheme to acquire a position. Thus, even though he had attained a high degree, he was still unemployed and passed his days drinking, writing poetry, and frolicking in the brothels. By this time, Zuyin was already six years old, and due to many childhood illnesses, he was a very frail boy. Lady Sang was pregnant again, and her due date was drawing near. Time passed quickly; the season was already autumn.

It was the auspicious Double Ninth Festival,[8] and the chrysanthemums by the bamboo fence in the courtyard had sprouted branches that withstood the frost. Refusing to yield to cold or snow, yellow flowers piled upon purple ones. Thousands of resplendent branches produced a wondrous sight and the flower blossoms themselves were of a rare beauty. It was as though they were proud to be so spectacular in such a late season—the sole lords of autumn. Prefect Huang said to his wife, "This year the flowers have lasted a particularly long time. They have bloomed in an unusual manner as well, with strange colors and blossoms that illuminate the courtyard. Moreover, this is just the time to celebrate the Double Ninth Festival. Hurry and order a jug of wine and some cups so we can enjoy the flowers." The servant girl relayed this order to the kitchen, which immediately prepared a small feast in the courtyard. Husband and wife came and sat down, with Zuyin and his nanny to one side. They had drunk many cups and were enjoying themselves when suddenly the Mistress wrinkled her brow in pain, pushed back her chair, stood up, and returned to her living quarters. The servant women were all very alarmed. When they inquired after her, they learned that she was about to give birth, so they hurried about in preparation for the delivery. During the delivery, the midwife made her drink some ginseng broth; after a few

---

8. A traditional autumn holiday observed on the ninth day of the ninth lunar month.

minutes, the room was filled with a scarlet light that dazzled the eye, and a crying baby girl was born. In past years, Lady Sang had suffered through many difficulties in childbirth, but this time it had been as simple as a crow alighting momentarily on a branch. But when the maid reported the good news to the Master, he immediately exploded in anger: "What is there to report about having a daughter? What is there to be happy about? She is nothing more than money-losing goods. How can she ever bring honor to our ancestors?" He raised the goblet in his hand, but his expression revealed his displeasure. Meanwhile, inside, Lady Sang overheard her husband's words and could not help feeling angry. The weakened bonds of affection between husband and wife were such that he casually made these comments and did not even bother to go view his newborn child. Reader, let me ask you: a boy and a girl are both one's children, so why did he treat them so differently? Well, it turns out that in Slumberland people were accustomed to looking down on girls, so that while giving birth to a boy was considered a joyful event, having a girl was a tragedy. That is why Prefect Huang was so unhappy. As for Lady Sang, though she did not attach special importance to having a daughter, the difference was that she possessed a mother's affection. Thus although the father was severe, she, the mother, was kind. She may not have loved her daughter, but since the baby was her own flesh and blood, she did at least treasure her. She named her Jurui,[9] since she had been born at the very moment the yellow chrysanthemums reached their fullest splendor.

Alas! Poor girls born in Slumberland, we know full well the difficulties you face from the minute you are born until old age. Moreover, the custom of privileging the male and despising the female and the precept of honoring men and disdaining women have been passed down for thousands of years from father to son, from older brother to younger brother, so that now there is no escape from them. Women of the literati class have even less freedom. How will Huang Jurui, who was born into this sleeping country as well as into a rigid, old-fashioned family, ever be able to free herself and mount the stage of liberty? One mistake and she could pay for it with her life. But, so much for this digression, let me return now to the main story.

Like a shooting arrow or the shuttle of a loom, time flew by quickly. After a few years, Lady Sang gave birth to another girl, who was named Shuren, and who had a gentle disposition. The passage of time ages peo-

---

9. The first Chinese character of her name, Ju, is a homophone of the character for chrysanthemum.

ple quickly, and Jurui had already turned seven years old. Her brother, Zuyin, had long since begun his studies under the instruction of a tutor named Yu Zhubo. Yu, a cousin of Prefect Huang, was a gentleman of more than forty years old; since he often helped those in distress, he was known as "Old Buddha." As his wife had passed away without leaving him any children and he had no valuable possessions, he drifted from job to job. So Prefect Huang hired him as his secretary, and even though he also had to teach, his duties were very light. He spent every morning reciting new poetry and he often searched high and low for new and amazing books. He had always adored little children and doted on the Huang sisters and their brother. He loved Jurui the best of all and would often amuse her and read poetry to her.

Unexpectedly, the superiors sent down an order: Prefect Huang was to proceed without delay to a post in Jinan. After he obtained his appointment, Prefect Huang was extremely busy entertaining his colleagues and friends, who all came to congratulate him. He thanked those who had appointed him, accepted the official seal, and then entertained his guests. Naturally, he was quite busy with these social calls; however, he also found time to marry two concubines. One, named Hou, was the daughter of a common family. The other, named Tao, was a prostitute in a private brothel. They accompanied Prefect Huang and his family to his new post. At this time, Jurui was seven years old.

It is said that Jurui had been heroic since her birth, and despite her youth, she was resolute by nature. Her face had a chivalric aura about it and because she was independent, she disliked dressing up according to the decadent fashions of the boudoir. Whenever she heard tales of women who had been mistreated or abused, she would suffer alone in silence. She watched the cunning and perverse behavior of her father's concubines and how they would often underhandedly stir up mischief to make her father insult her mother for no reason at all. Her mother was very frail by nature and was unable to resist the ever-increasing insolence of her rivals. For her part, Jurui felt more and more indignant but could do nothing about these tyrants. All she could do was secretly plot her revenge as she hid behind sweet words. She yearned to dispel her mother's anger, fearing that she would fall sick and further aggravate the situation. Jurui often stole off to the classroom with her brother and learned to recite a few chapters from his books. When Tutor Yu saw how intelligent she was, he began instructing her as well. Who would have thought that she could memorize texts at a glance and read ten lines in one go? Tutor Yu was extremely pleased and reported to Prefect Huang,

"My niece is remarkably intelligent, and I think your family may produce the second Huang Chonggu."[10] When Master Huang heard this, he replied in shock, "How is it that Jurui is also studying? Only women without talent are virtuous, so what is the point of her studying?[11] This must be her mother's cursed idea. After I have a word with her, she'll tell Jurui to go back and practice her needlework! Why would a girl ever need to study?" Having said this, he was about to leave.

Tutor Yu hurriedly stopped his cousin. "Please wait a moment and listen to me. It was not her mother but I who encouraged her to study. Because she is naturally so intelligent and refined, would it not be a shame to leave such a precious stone unpolished? You say that only untalented women are virtuous, but then why has that legend of Cao Dagu[12] been handed down to the present day? There have been numerous talented women ever since ancient times, and all have admired them. If women are to be virtuous wives, how befitting can it be for them to be completely illiterate? I am but a lowly relative of an official's family, but unlike others I don't think men and women are different. Thus, I have chosen to teach both my nephew and niece. In any case, it does not take any more of my time." At this, Prefect Huang responded, "But cousin, it is not necessary. What's the use of study to a girl, since it's impossible for her to bring glory to the family like a man? Even if she were endowed with eight bushels of talent, when did the government ever establish official exams for women?"

Tutor Yu replied, "Even though there are no official exams for women, I have heard that they are planning to establish women's schools. Cousin, have you ever met a man from Canton who calls himself a great loyal official?[13] Didn't he present a clear proposal for implementing a new government? He has many followers, who are called something like the Bao Kuang Party![14] They advocate all sorts of reform, including one that

---

10. A woman poet of the Tang dynasty (618–906).

11. "To be virtuous is to be untalented" is a saying applied to women that became popularized in the late Ming (16th–17th centuries), a period when, perhaps not coincidentally, significant strides were being made in gentrywomen's education. The term *talent* refers in a general sense to knowledge beyond the traditional feminine arts of needlework and embroidery.

12. A respectful form of reference for Ban Zhao [Pan Chao] (c. 49–c. 120), the famous woman historian of the Han dynasty (206 B.C.–A.D. 220) and author of the Confucian classic *Precepts for Women*. A translation can be found in Nancy Lee Swann, *Pan Chao: Foremost Woman Scholar of China* (New York: The Century Co., 1932).

13. Most likely a reference to the late Qing reformer Kang Youwei (1858–1927), a native of Canton province.

14. Literally the "Full of Madness" Party. Qiu Jin, who was vehemently opposed to the Manchu court, here seems to be punning on "Bao Huang Hui," Kang Youwei's Protect the Emperor Society, which he founded in 1899.

is argued something like this: 'In order for the nation to nurture talent, we must have education, therefore we must build schools everywhere. Since women are the mothers of civilization, and family education in the home depends on women, we must build schools for both women and men.' So you see, the establishment of schools for girls is not far off, yet you still object to my niece studying a bit? If you allow her to get an education now, in the future not only will she not fall behind others, but all her talents and intelligence won't have gone to waste. At the very least she could become a teacher!"

Prefect Huang laughed at his cousin. "You believe the strangest things! Are the ancient customs of the ancestors so easily changed, so easily replaced by barbarian fads? Is not abolishing our traditional schools an insult to Master Confucius? If men and women possess no differences, won't such anarchy make the rest of the world mock us? If women change the way they dress and cut their hair short, won't this insult the ways of the Han Chinese?"

Prefect Huang was about to continue when Tutor Yu stopped him by bursting out in laughter and pointing at his clothes and queue.[15] He asked his cousin, "Is this the attire of the Han dynasty? The only people who still don Han-style clothes are those actors who dress up in ancient costumes that cross in the front and who sport yarn hats on their heads. Nowadays, with a new dynasty, we have queues and shaved heads and narrow sleeves. These peacock plumes, the decorations on our hats, and the official insignias on our robes are all foreign dress. My virtuous cousin, you wear these yet you do not think it strange. When the Empress Dowager came to power and implemented the rule of might, she was respected like the Virgin Mary and her righteousness and charity were praised; only later were her evil ways revealed for all the world to see. Yet when had she ever entered a school that offered equal education for boys and girls? The schools of today won't be like those in the past, because male and female education will be based on the same principles. When people are well-educated, they naturally become noble; equal education will certainly not lead to licentiousness and corrupt ways. Let me ask you, do prostitutes and women of that sort know anything about literature and the classics? Yet there have always been 'talented girls' who do know of such things and I have never heard complaints about them. So, based

---

15. These are all Manchu fashions, which were introduced during the Qing dynasty (1644–1911). Although by this time few real distinctions still existed between the Manchus and the Han, the dominant ethnic group in China, the nationalist sentiment of this period renewed perception of the Manchus as foreign.

on this comparison, it would in fact seem imprudent for women not to be educated."

When Prefect Huang heard this, he heaved a long sigh. "Cousin, when you put it this way how can I refuse? But once she gets educated and becomes talented like Xie Daoyun,[16] all she'll be able to do is write poems lamenting the bitter fate of being a talented beauty."

Tutor Yu laughed and replied, "Cousin, how can you believe such nonsense? Surely you have read the poems that Yuan Mei[17] wrote for his wife Wanqing, which illustrate that talent and happiness are not incompatible! But later on, it will be you who wields the power to choose a good husband for Jurui, so be careful. Don't make the mistake of marrying her to a rich merchant. I have heard that you don't care much for your daughter, and I'm afraid you might throw this precious pearl away by marrying her off to the wrong kind of man."

Prefect Huang was silent, then said, "What parent on earth does not love his own sons and daughters? But even though I will permit you to teach them both, don't go preaching to them about the damned revolution or some nonsense about freedom and equality. The Huang family has been honest and virtuous for generations and I don't want to bring injury to our ancestors by earning a reputation for being rebels. As for topics like foreign clothes, don't go talking about them either!"

Tutor Yu responded, "Cousin, don't worry, how could I ever bring harm to your family? But wouldn't it be marvelous if your family were able to produce a female heroine, a female knight-errant to be admired and worshiped by everyone? I fear more that your family will miss out on such fortune!" Having said this, he walked off with a smile.

After that, Tutor Yu went back to the classroom and Jurui was ecstatic when she heard the news. From then on, she was exceedingly diligent in her studies, and the years raced by. Before you knew it, she had already turned fourteen, and her knowledge was like a vast array of jewels and her writing like a rich brocade. Tutor Yu could not have been more pleased, for to have a disciple such as her was rare indeed. By this time, Jurui's brother Zuyin was already twenty years old and had been married for two years. He had a son who had turned one and was just learning how to talk. At this time, Jurui was busy with her studies, and she didn't have to worry about assisting her mother.

---

16. A woman poet and calligrapher of the Eastern Jin dynasty (c. 221–207 B.C.).

17. Yuan Mei (1716–1797) was a poet from the early Qing famous for his patronage of female poets.

One morning, she was sitting at her desk writing when the maid from her mother's quarters, Fragrance, came to announce that guests had arrived and wanted to see her. Jurui reported to her tutor, then took her leave. When she arrived in the hall, she looked up and saw on her left a guest dressed in silk, wearing a formal imperial necklace and insignia. At her side was a girl with delicate features. She was dressed in brocade, and wore a long necklace. She looked about fifteen or sixteen and conveyed an air of intelligence and competence. As soon as Jurui gazed upon her, she felt an immediate affection for her, as though she had known her in a previous life. As she was turning these thoughts over in her mind, her mother ordered her to quickly pay her respects to Lady Liang, so she made a deep bow and stood in the middle of the hall. Lady Liang took hold of Jurui's jadelike hand, and scrutinized her from head to toe. She saw that Jurui was not inferior in appearance: her complexion was like beautiful jade and her mouth the color of rouge. Her lightly painted eyebrows contained a chivalric air and her clear eyes displayed dignity. When she raised her eyes, she appeared at ease yet not at all vulgar, and her deportment was modest and unaffected. But her independent and heroic nature was apparent, and her behavior seemed easy and carefree. When Lady Liang learned that Jurui studied and attended school, she felt that such an intelligent and refined look suited her well. She called Little Jade to her side to meet Jurui and when they had made their greetings, they clasped hands and gazed at one another, both thinking that they had known each other before. When Jurui asked her name, she learned that her childhood name was Little Jade. Then Jurui said to her attentively, "Sister! Were we not destined to meet today? I hope that you will never abandon me, but that we will always cherish and comfort one another."

When Little Jade heard these words, she felt very sad, and her jadelike countenance looked mournful as tears welled up in her eyes. She lowered her head and clasped Jurui's hands and said, "Your words will remain etched on my heart. I have heard that you are a fine poet[18] and that your talents are immense. Would you be willing to accept me as your disciple? I fear only that I have not been fated to receive such happiness!"

Jurui promptly responded, "Why be so modest? Between sisters, let us not use such formulaic and polite speech."

---

18. Qiu Jin is alluding here to the talented woman poet Xie Daoyun mentioned earlier, who, according to legend, impressed people with a poem she composed on the subject of the snow.

Lady Sang smiled and said to Lady Liang, "Listening to them talk and looking at the way they hold each other's hands so affectionately, they must have been fated to meet!" Then she said, "Jurui, why don't you take Jade to your room and show her your books. I'll order some snacks for you to relax with." Jurui was extremely pleased, and Jade just looked at her mother without saying a word; the two then went hand in hand through the inner chambers. They arrived at the Perching Phoenix Pavilion.

These were the living quarters for the Huang sisters. Shuren was slightly unwell and was in her room to avoid the cold, so she did not come out. Jurui's room was to the left. When they entered, all Jade could see was a paper screen, a bamboo bed, and a desk in front of the window upon which books and various writing utensils were laid. Next to the desk were several cases of books and a few chairs. The room was simple but elegant. Jurui, with her unadorned dress and dignified manner, was the perfect occupant of such a room. All of Jade's feelings of envy and jealousy about such wealth were instantly dispelled.

They sat together and talked about their families' difficulties and honors. Only then did Jurui learn that Jade was actually the daughter of a concubine. Even though Lady Liang, her father's first wife, had three sons of her own, she was exceedingly jealous and mean by nature. She was completely unforgiving toward her husband's concubines and merciless in her curses and beatings. Even Jade's father, who was now old and sickly, feared his first wife. Jade's mother was a concubine who had been purchased by the wife, and so whenever they were in the presence of other people Lady Liang always acted very kind and generous, but at home she treated Jade's mother like a prisoner. When they went out Lady Liang would tell people that they got along like sisters, and she was so good at pretending that people would have been hard pressed to believe otherwise. When they were in public, she would act polite and courteous to Jade's mother, but at home she would pick fights with her. Little Jade's life had been hard; being at home was worse than being a bird in a cage. Lady Liang treated her harshly and Second Brother was even more cruel. If she and her real mother ever wanted to speak to others, the servants were to follow and watch over them like prisoners or criminals. Lady Liang also seldom let them accompany her on her outings. "But today, because she was coming over here, she called me to her room to help her dress. She then instructed me carefully that I should often accompany her to your house. My real mother could not object, and today my visit makes me feel happier than passing the civil service exam. Jurui! Today, I am pouring all this out to you, but please don't pass it on to anyone. If Lady Liang ever found out, she would definitely be infuriated. I wouldn't complain if I were blamed, but I'm afraid my mother would suffer."

Jurui nodded her head to indicate she needn't worry. "Sister, I won't say anything. My father has two concubines who run the whole house and get whatever their hearts desire. When they are dissatisfied, they curse and yell at the maids until they're blue in the face, so everyone rushes about to please them. They're ten times more powerful than my mother. They are only satisfied when they provoke quarrels between my mother and father, and my mother has no choice but to give in. But even still, the two of them often quarrel with her. Who would have thought that in your family, it's the concubine who is good while the wife is lacking in virtue. The ways of Heaven are certainly not flawless. I would like to call upon Heaven to explain this inequality, but at the moment I can only think of how oppressed you have been. The fragrant boudoir is worse than prison, so why have you been banished there? How can you bear it? What a waste of intelligence and courage.

"If you don't study, you'll never be independent and you will have to rely on people who don't care about you. When will we ever find a way out of this sea of bitterness? This oppressive system is infuriating, and our lack of independence maddening. How often I wish we women could escape these slavish confines. I deeply regret that I have no way to help you and that we can't spend time together talking every day because I believe that you and I are no less intelligent or talented than any man. In fact, those faint-hearted, shameless men don't even measure up to us. In the past, there were countless extraordinary and brave women, such as Hongyu, Xun Guan, and Mulan, or Yunying and Qin Liangyu of the late Ming,[19] who led armies with such discipline that when the bandits heard about them they lost their nerve. In strength and courage they stood alone. The ones who have surrendered and turned over their territories have always been men. I am ashamed that such men were traitors to China.

"So if you compare men and women, the most disgraceful and shameless are the men. Women ought to occupy the superior position, so why do they act in such a servile manner? Rather than striving to be independent and to make their own living, they keep their heads low and live

---

19. Xun Guan (Jin dynasty) became famous when she was just thirteen years old for rescuing the besieged city where her father served as prefect. Shen Yunying (1623–1660) was noted for her horsemanship and archery skills; when her father was killed in battle, she personally retrieved his body. Qin Liangyu (1574–1648) was a well-educated woman who took over her husband's military command after his death and defeated rebels in Sichuan province. On Hongyu and Mulan, see notes 2 and 3.

in someone else's house.[20] If I, Jurui, ever have the good fortune to become independent, I will certainly help you climb out of the pit you are now trapped in. How can you tolerate such oppression and humiliation? Even though they say suffering produces heroes, each day you pass in that dungeon must feel like a year. It saddens me to see a person of talent suffer so." Having said this, she sighed and was filled with such sorrow that tears spilled over onto her blouse.

When Little Jade heard these words, she was moved and frowned, her own troubles and worries weighing heavily upon her. She knew her ambitions were not ordinary, but why had she ended up like this? It was improper for a guest to cry, so she held back the tears welling up in her eyes. She thought to herself how brave the Huang girl was, and how uncommon her heroic manner. If they were to become sworn sisters, then in the future they could rely on each other in times of trouble. She lowered her head, but didn't say anything.

Jurui guessed what she was thinking and urged her, "Sister, if you want to say something, why don't you? We already have so much in common, what is there to stop you from speaking up?" So Little Jade revealed her wish and Jurui promised without hesitation. Instead of setting up an incense table as others would do, they knelt in front of the window and made the following pledge: "We will never forget each other if we obtain wealth and rank, and in poverty we will share our lot; we will support each other in times of extreme difficulty. Let she who forgets these words be struck down, as Heaven is our witness." After they completed this vow, they stood up and clasped hands, and their mutual love and affection grew even stronger than before. They addressed each other as Little and Big Sister, and they felt closer than biological siblings. Even if the seas ran dry and the earth crumbled, their affections for one another would not falter.

Just as they were preparing to sit down and continue talking, the maid came to report, "Lady Liang is preparing to leave. A relative from afar has arrived, so the young lady is to make haste and not delay departure." The two had no choice but to hurry, as they could see Lady Liang straightening her clothes in preparation to leave. When Little Jade came with Lady Liang to say goodbye, the latter turned her head and said, "Miss Huang, come to visit our home sometime. As your illustrious parents are so kind, I hope you will not stand on ceremony and will visit us often. The friend-

---

20. From the saying that a person who lives in a house with low eaves has to keep his/her head low; referring here to a woman who has to submit to an inferior position in her husband's home.

ship between our two families is special." Jurui promised she would do so. The two girls looked at each other and were sad, but what else could they do? Who was to know that they would soon meet many other unusual girls and that many strange events were to follow. Wait until I relate them slowly, one at a time. The chapter ends here so I can rest a moment. If you want to know what happens, please read on to the next chapter.

Chapter 3: Parents force a marriage; Deprived of rights, brother and sister fight.

The storms from abroad grow more threatening by the day and I am increasingly disheartened as I look toward my homeland. A great calamity is at our doorstep, and yet my compatriots remain deep in their slumber; I have called out to them ten thousand times, yet they still fail to respond. In the previous chapter, I ended with matters regarding the Liang family; Lady Liang and Jade had returned home and entered the hall. The maids and servant girls all came out to greet them, along with the concubines and Master Liang. They were informed that Lady Liang's sister had arrived, accompanied by her son and daughter. Thereupon, Lady Liang immediately hurried in to welcome her sister, Madame Bao. They entered the main hall to make formal greetings and the sister then presented her son and daughter.

Madame Bao was generous by nature and always kind to others. From birth, the two sisters had very different personalities, and she was not at all irritable like her older sister. Just then, everyone came in and sat down and they spoke of all their heartfelt emotions since they had last seen each other. Madame Liang prevailed upon her sister to stay so they could continue catching up on all the years they had been apart. Madame Bao agreed and ordered a messenger to go back to inform her brother-in-law, Prefect Zuo, of her whereabouts. Shortly, her personal belongings were sent over, along with Hibiscus, an exceedingly competent serving girl. The maids and serving girls were all sent to wait on Madame Bao and soon a welcome feast was prepared. By the time the banquet was over, it was already evening. Guest quarters had been prepared for her in a small lane to the west.

There were three rooms in a row, flanked by two side rooms, with an arched entrance. The door to the left led to the main quarters of the house; the door to the right led to the outside. It was very convenient, and Madame Bao was especially pleased by the peace and quiet, so she decided to stay in the room to the left. Her daughter took the right-hand room at the back. The maids stayed in one of the wing rooms, while the remaining room was used as a small kitchen, where they could prepare food to their own liking. Since the son was already grown up, he stayed in the study in the outer quarters.

The two sisters had a marvelous time talking every day, while Madame Bao's daughter Unity and Little Jade got along splendidly as well. In the mornings, they would stroll hand in hand in the garden, and in the evenings they would lean against the outer railings of the window and take pleasure gazing at the moon. Sometimes, they would discuss literature. Little Jade was extraordinarily intelligent, while Unity was exceedingly well-educated. Every day Unity would teach her younger cousin several passages from a variety of books. Naturally clever, Little Jade learned quickly and easily with little instruction. The two of them stuck together like glue, and had endless things to talk about.

One morning, as they were sitting together at the dressing table, Unity sighed that half a month had already passed. Then she mentioned, "I have a cousin in the Zuo family named Awaken, who is both kind and virtuous. She is also a very loyal friend. She is the same age as you and she is quite strong physically. Although she's not terribly beautiful, her poetry is unusually good. When we were living and studying together we would stroll about hand in hand together. We have been separated now for half a month and I miss her terribly. She once promised that she would come over to spend a few days with me here. If you like her once you meet her, you mustn't keep any secrets from her. I wonder, as you have lived here for a long time, if you have made any friends?"

Little Jade replied, "Speak of this no more. I am like a caged monkey. It's hard enough for me to move about freely at home, let alone go out to make friends. The day you arrived was the first time in my life that I had ever ventured past the front door. I paid a visit to the Huang residence in our prefecture and when I met her daughter it was as though we were old friends. We became sworn sisters at once. Her name is Jurui. She is bold and straightforward, and her face exudes character. Even though she may not be a top-notch beauty like Yang Guifei,[21] her eyes are pretty, her brows long and her mouth cherry red. Her face is egg-shaped and her complexion beautiful. Overall, she has a remarkably dignified beauty. As for her comportment, she is a champion of justice and sympathizes with

---

21. The most famous beauty in Chinese history. According to popular legend, the Tang Emperor Xuanzong's infatuation with the lovely Yang Guifei (716–756) caused him to neglect his political duties, allowing a rebellion to occur during his reign.

all who suffer. In dress, she strives for simplicity. She has been studying for many years, which isn't at all common for young ladies. Since we became sworn sisters from our first meeting, I really wonder why I haven't heard any news from her for a fortnight. I miss her dearly, and not a day goes by when I don't think of her. But Jurui hasn't come herself and I have nobody I can send to ask after her. It's terribly distressing not to have any news!"

When she finished speaking, she heaved a sigh and knit her brow. Taking her hand, Unity said, "Dear sister, why get so upset? I can send somebody over to inquire after her, though I don't know whether Jurui's mother is kind or whether she's as strict with her as your stepmother is with you."

Little Jade replied that this wasn't the case at all. "Lady Sang is modest and amiable, and very polite. Although she isn't as generous as your mother, she isn't as strict as my stepmother either. If you send somebody, I am sure she wouldn't mind." Unity nodded and promised to tell her mother to send a maid the next day to ask after Jurui. Later that evening, Unity asked her mother, who agreed to send Hibiscus, since she was both clever and reliable.

The following morning, when the dawn sun was still red, Hibiscus called for a small sedan chair and left without delay. Before very long, she reached the front of the residence of Prefect Huang, where all was a-bustle. When Hibiscus explained her purpose in coming, she was invited in and led into the inner hall. Lady Sang was busy doing something and there were two people at her side helping, with envious looks on their faces. There were holiday fruits of all varieties placed on the table and upon closer inspection Hibiscus thought it looked as though someone were getting married. But knowing that their daughter was still so young, she wondered how they could have chosen a groom so soon. Hibiscus sighed and hurried over to the center of the hall and kowtowed respectfully, then said to them, "The young lady of the Liang residence sent me to ask after Madame and the young lady of the house."

When Lady Sang heard this, she seemed to hesitate, then ordered the maid Spring to take her to see her daughter. The maid nodded in reply and led Hibiscus downstairs to the courtyard. She heard the maid muttering to herself, "I wonder if she's in her room or in the study? These past few days she has been so irritable, and it will be bad luck for me if I get a scolding." When Hibiscus heard this, she said to her, "May I ask how old you are?" The maid replied, "I'm eleven." Then Hibiscus asked her what the cause of the young miss's anger was, to which the maid swiftly replied,

"I will tell you the whole story. There is a rich man, Millions Gou, who has recently made a fortune. This year his son turned sixteen. It is said that he's very unattractive. When the Gous heard about the talent and beauty of our young lady, they hired a matchmaker to act as the go-between for them. Prefect Huang and his wife were more than willing, but that troublemaker Tutor Yu has been insisting the two are not well-suited. The young lady is exceedingly displeased herself and has hinted as much to her mother. It's not that her mother doesn't love her, but because the Gou family is rich, she just told her, "Stop interfering. This decision is up to your father and me, how can you be so shameless? Haven't you heard of the traditional rules of the Three Obediences?"[22] The young lady has been livid ever since and sulks from morning until night. Even though she has kept herself busy these days studying, she constantly knits her brows in worry. That loathsome Tutor Yu often bemoans that such a talented girl has been promised to a bandit. Even though the Gou family is rich and reputable, that tactless Tutor Yu loves wagging his tongue and the young lady is more and more persuaded by him, and secretly weeps every day, sighs, pouts, or just sits there still as a statue. She is a complete fool for not liking a family such as the Gous. But the Gou family is in a hurry, so the engagement is to take place in about ten days. Because of this, the young lady won't eat and hides herself away during the day. The Madame says that it's because she's shy and has instructed us not to bring up the subject with her. I usually wait only on the Madame, so I don't know where the young miss is right now."

When Hibiscus heard this she understood immediately. "No wonder she hasn't been over to the Liang residence. I suspect that the young master Gou is hardly a good match and is terribly unsuited to marry such a fine young lady. Too bad her parents are taking such oppressive measures and bringing so much suffering upon their own daughter. In our household, the Madame is benevolent, and the young Master Bao and his sister both support the reform movement. So I suspect that they won't encounter the injustice Miss Jurui is now suffering."

She was just pondering this when suddenly Spring called out loudly to another maid, "Maid, is the older miss in that room?" Thereupon, they heard a young maid reply, "She is in her own room." So Spring escorted

---

22. As detailed in such classical texts as the *Nü'er jing*, "The Three Obediences" (*sancong*) exhorted women to submit to the authority of their fathers and older brothers, their husbands, and their sons. "The Four Virtues" (*side*) stated that women should comply with Confucian ethics, be reticent in speech, be conscientious but modest about physical appearance, and fulfill their domestic duties.

Hibiscus to Jurui's room, where they found a girl sleeping on a small chair and saw that the bed curtain had been lowered. It turned out that Jurui was napping. Hibiscus immediately whispered, "Don't say anything, the young lady is sleeping." But Jurui had already heard them and asked, "Who is it?" Spring replied, "Young Miss, the Liangs have sent over a girl to see you."

As soon as Jurui heard this, she got out of bed and Hibiscus went over to kowtow to her. Jurui rushed to help her up and woke up the maid to move the chair over to the side of the bed. "Please sit down." Hibiscus, who didn't dare, said, "I'm just a maid so it is proper that I remain standing." Thereupon, Jurui said, "Don't be that way, there's no difference between high and low, so please stop making excuses." Hibiscus had no choice but to sit down modestly, while the maid went back to report to her mistress. Jurui sat in the middle of the bed and when she looked up she saw a pretty girl who had a face like an hibiscus flower, a willowlike waist, slender shoulders, a cherry mouth, and kingfisher brows. Her eyes were pretty and full of courage—she was not at all a common person. A character so upright and stern, yet she had the misfortune of being born a maid. Could it be that beauties really are condemned to bad fates? As a multitude of feelings surged in her heart, Jurui sat thinking to herself.

Hibiscus also took a look at Jurui and thought that she looked exceedingly noble. Her eyes were beautiful but dignified, her brows were slender but full of heroic spirit. Her manner was forthright and direct, her figure sturdy. How could she be in such distress? Thereupon, she conveyed Little Jade's wishes. Jurui asked about how Little Jade had been recently, and Hibiscus told her everything.

When Jurui heard this, she sighed and said, "I am deeply grateful to your young mistress, since now that my sworn sister Jade has a companion, I suspect that she won't have to endure so much abuse. When you return, tell her for me that I am in good health and she needn't worry. However, because of some other pointless matter, I have been terribly unhappy and depressed. In a few days, I will pay her a visit and tell her all about it in person, and then I can pay my respects to your honorable lady and the young mistress as well. May I ask how old you are and when you first came to the Bao family? How do your employers treat you? Have you ever learned to read? With such great talent and beauty as yours, it truly is an insult and great injustice to have fallen into the sordid waters of servitude. If you and I were educated, we would easily be outstanding people. Someday, if I'm ever free, I swear that I will rescue you from this dungeon. We can become sworn sisters and consult with each other on everything; we will become heroes among women."

After she finished speaking, she sighed deeply and Hibiscus knew that she was being treated like an intimate friend and felt deeply grateful for this. She thought silently about her unfortunate life and marveled at the compassion Jurui had shown her. Her passion really moves me, yet I worry for her, she thought. Thereupon, she replied, "My mistress, as well as her son and daughter, are benevolent people and don't treat their servants as others do. I have been particularly well-treated, and since the young mistress once taught me some literature, I even know a few poems. I am already fifteen years old this year. I was sold into the Bao family when I was seven, and my masters have treated me well ever since. I have never thought about freeing myself since I was sold to them, and besides there's nothing I could do about it. Thank you so much for your high regard; I will never forget your friendship."

Jurui smiled and said, "This is even more marvelous than I thought. Having such a fine poet as Unity teach you as her disciple, you must be very smart. If you become educated, one day you will surely be independent. But I am afraid you are silently laughing at me as a fool or dreamer because of what I have said about saving you, since these days I'm worse off than you." Hibiscus immediately protested, then comforted her by saying that Jurui should try to make do and that things would get better; then she encouraged her to visit the Liang residence to relieve her depression. Jurui laughed coldly, "It's not that I don't know about calmly accepting my fate, but that I'm afraid my life won't be calm. I have long since wanted to go visit the young ladies. If I don't go tomorrow, I'll certainly be there the following day."

Thereupon, Hibiscus took her leave. Then she bid farewell to the Madame, who gave her a tip and some nuts and fruit and told her to send her regards to her mistress and the young lady. As she got into the sedan chair in front of the yamen[23] to return home, she could see that the evening crows were already spreading their wings to fly. When she reached home and went inside, she did not see her mistress and the place was quiet, so she went over to the Liang residence, where she heard the sound of voices inside Jade's room. She hurried in and saw her mistress and Unity sitting together next to the canopy bed. Little Jade was lying in bed sobbing.

---

23. A government office in imperial China.

[*In the section that follows, Hibiscus learns that during her absence Little Jade has been severely beaten by Second Brother for ordering some medicine for her mother without permission from Lady Liang. That night, Jade restlessly contemplates the news of Huang Jurui's impending marriage to the good-for-nothing son of Millions Gou; she laments the lot of women and begins to wonder whether the old adage that talented women are fated to suffer might be true. The narrative picks up the following morning, in the middle of chapter 4, "The Resentful Daughter passes a sleepless night; The Four Beauties lament social customs."*]

When breakfast was over and the tea had been served, the girls had only been chatting for a short time when the maid rushed in and reported that Awaken had arrived. Unity ordered the maid to receive her and was quite delighted. Soon, a very pretty girl walked in. After joyful greetings, Awaken said that she had recently made a new friend who had come over together with her. Madame Bao immediately asked the whereabouts of this friend and Awaken replied that her sedan chair had been delayed. Thereupon, the mother and daughter hastily sent a maid to greet her when she arrived. The maid left at once, and it was not long before a graceful girl with a jadelike countenance appeared. Her eyes were radiant and her teeth white. She was indescribably beautiful and her figure was very striking. Everyone exchanged greetings and upon inquiry they learned that her surname was Jiang and she was from Jiangnan; her name was Vitality, and she was fifteen years old. Her father had come to the city to wait to fill an official post.

As soon as everyone was introduced, they were all like old friends, sitting together, laughing and talking. Vitality asked Little Jade, "Is something the matter? Your face looks so drawn. Could it be that you have been ill?" Upon hearing this, Unity sighed several times. "When did she get sick?" Then Unity described to them how Jade had been beaten. When the two heard this, they were both incensed, and Vitality started speaking. "Among those of us born on this earth as women, are there any who aren't considered inferior? In matters trivial or important, we're not even allowed to put in a single word."

At that point Awaken also sighed. "Poor women, we're considered less than human. If a daughter is born, people say she is bad luck and that she will belong to another family once she is married. Enlightened parents will still love her, but those who aren't will hate her the instant they see her. They always say that girls are useless and do nothing more than cost them a lot of dowry money. But when a son is born, everybody loves and treasures him. They let him go to school to study the Five Classics, while girls aren't even permitted to get near books. On the contrary, they claim that talented girls will suffer a bad fate. But if you think about it carefully, when have women ever been weaker than men? We are equal to men in talent and intelligence, and if we were able to get an education, we too could earn money to support our parents.

"The root cause of suffering, however, is that girls have no way to make their own living. We are kept locked away deep in the inner chambers our whole lives. I am fortunate to come from a good family, and I have studied the classics with my older brother. Although I am not what you might call a talented girl, I am better off than those ignorant illiterate men. In my heart, I often curse the world for looking down on women. My ambitions soar higher each day, yet I can't do the things I'd like to do because girls have no way to make a living; it's even impossible to go anywhere in public. It makes me loathe being a woman. Everyone knows that Unity is extremely talented. Vitality is also far from common. Little Jade, as well, seems so intelligent and pretty that I am certain that her knowledge is superior to most people's, and ten times better than all those boys who never study. Why are we all willing to submit to this? Just thinking about it makes me angry at the injustice of it all."

Vitality sighed and said, "Women suffer in so many ways! But as for the most painful—it is being mismatched to some oaf, for it's a tragedy when true beauties have such bad fates. Men have made up lies about how the husband guides his wife. They have such high opinions of themselves, yet they go out and frolic with prostitutes in the brothels and despise their wives who have lost their good looks from being locked behind closed doors. Beating and abuse is common and so is favoring concubines over the wife. There are also those merchants who go off to other provinces and marry another woman or get a concubine and simply abandon their wife at home. They couldn't care less if she starves or freezes because they have severed all feelings of duty toward her; they'll let her weep to her heart's content about her hunger and suffering or whine that she has nobody to rely on.

"Then there are those women who suffer along while their husbands study for the civil service exam, putting up with his poverty and low status. But the day he becomes a successful official, he marries a pretty concubine and abandons his wife to the wind to fare for herself, completely forgetting all that she has done for him. That's the type of man who is completely ungrateful and merciless, who forsakes the old and covets the new. Then there are women who endure in-laws no less tyrannical than

Yama.[24] They loathe their daughters-in-law but spoil their grandsons. They give free rein to their sons to play around with other women and even encourage them to do so, and if the husband and wife happen to get along, then they complain that ever since the daughter-in-law came, their son has changed; when they curse him for being disobedient, they'll blame it on the wife, saying she's the coquette behind it all. They're only happy when they have turned their son against his wife.

"There are also those husbands who are frivolous by nature and spend their time gambling and visiting prostitutes. They complain that their wives don't interest them anymore. Even in this situation, the mother-in-law will still try to sow discord between her son and his wife as well as abuse the wife herself. But what is most tragic of all is when a talented girl is married off to a fat merchant, just like a phoenix forced to follow a crow. Her great wisdom is all in vain, and all she can do is pour her grief into her poetry. There is nobody who understands her, and all she can do is sit alone in her chamber and weep despondently. How can a violent and uncouth husband appreciate the elegance of a spray of plum flowers? Having no confidantes and being stuck with a vulgar man, these women spend their entire lives deep in the inner chambers weeping in indignation. Alas, how many talented girls have been buried like this since antiquity! But the cuckoo lamented to the Eastern Wind in vain.[25] Just thinking about this situation makes me miserable. How I regret that Heaven is so muddled and unfeeling that it treats us women like this; it's as though it deliberately wants to harm us out of spite." She frowned as she said this, and when she lifted her eyes she saw that Little Jade had started crying again. She asked at once, "Sister Jade, your sadness shows that you must have strong feelings on this subject. Why don't you speak out, and we'll listen."

Jade replied, "I have a sworn sister, the daughter of the illustrious Prefect Huang. Her name is Jurui and from the age of seven until today, at fourteen, she has studied diligently and is very knowledgeable. Her personality is gallant and heroic. Who would have thought that her parents would arrange a match for her with that son of fat merchant Gou, who is the precisely the kind of irresponsible playboy you spoke of? Is this not regrettable beyond measure?" Without realizing it, she sighed

---

24. Mythical ruler of the Chinese underworld.

25. This is a reference to the story about a cuckoo who was so grief-stricken when its mate died that it cried until it spat blood and died.

several times before continuing, "Heaven is so unjust. Why create a person with such qualities as Jurui only to destroy the lovely girl with such savage storms? I don't know how she has been these days, but I fear that she has grown thin and pale. I deplore the fact that just when such a tender bud was beginning to blossom the spiteful winds and rain have ravaged her. When the talented Han Dan[26] was married off to a lackey, was not Heaven once again preventing a talented woman from marrying a talented man? How can such suffering be alleviated? But it is no use beseeching Heaven. If her own parents are behind this, how can others possibly assist her in getting out of this bad engagement?"

Jade's regret and resentment were profound, and her tears overflowed, dampening her clothes. When the others heard this they too were miserable. Unity heaved a long sigh and poured out the following eloquent words, "What woman doesn't suffer? We are confined to the inner chambers our whole lives; we have our own opinions but can do nothing on our own initiative; we are completely restricted and haven't an ounce of power, as if we were orphans who must obey our master's every word. At home, our parents won't teach us and forbid us to leave our chambers. All day long they watch over us and demand that we learn to sew, to the point where our hunched-over backs ache. When we've embroidered a pillow, we start on some trousers; after that's done, there are covers for the mirrors and the teapots, the canopy-tops and sides; then skirts and hems and painted screens. As soon as purses are embroidered, it's on to fan cases; when that's finished, there are still sleeves and collars and endless other trivial things. Every day we strive to perfect our skills in sewing and coordinating the colors of the thread, without a moment's rest to even walk around. And in the end, either our minds are completely numbed or we fall ill with consumption. Even if we don't fall ill, our shoulders and backs will have become disfigured. And the truth is, embroidery is completely useless. It's a total waste of money that buys nothing but suffering; the purpose of all that embroidery is merely to make the bridal trousseau pretty. Let me ask you, if you get stuck with an ungrateful husband, are not all those fashionable items for naught? If he's useless, all this splendor will not rescue you from poverty. If he's a playboy and later abandons you by the wayside, there's nothing you can do but suffer, since it's impossible to live off one's clothing. And if your husband is a profligate, he'll gamble it all away. All that crouching over

---

26. Another unhappily married beauty from ancient times.

your embroidery day after day will have been completely in vain, since in a single instant it isn't worth a dime."

Jade then continued, "My dear sisters, the world is so unjust. What is most deplorable is that the ancients came up with this malicious system that treats girls as lowly beings but respects boys. Even if a family has a huge estate, girls aren't entitled to a single share, while the boys inherit it all. Even though it is obvious that they belong to the same parents and are made of the same flesh and blood, when it comes to the inheritance, girls are considered to be completely different. The minute you're married off, they simply let you suffer abuse as if they know nothing about it. If you have frequent quarrels with your spouse because you've been mismatched, they simply say that you have a bad destiny. The Three Obediences are even more absurd, since they exalt the husband as if he were a god. Even though we speak of 'husband and wife,' in fact, how can the wife ever decide what goes on in the house since she is supposed to obey her husband in every minor matter? If she does one thing by herself, everyone will talk about it. And if her husband reprimands her, all she can do is meekly agree. Once she has become completely submissive and humble in all matters and gains a reputation as a model wife, she still must let her husband frolic about as he pleases; otherwise, if she quarrels with him, others will ridicule her for being a jealous wife. And, after she's suffered enough and he's become an official, she'll have to put up with his numerous concubines and mistresses.

"There are other men who ignore their families and play around, and buy new houses in which to install their new wives. Even if the first wife were permitted to be jealous, in this case she would be unaware of what is going on.[27] Then there are those who often bicker at home and abuse their wives as though they weren't human, and even when the wife is dying of anger or grief in her chambers they continue dallying in the brothels. If you are of the lower classes, you can always go out to work as a servant to make a living and avoid this horrid treatment, but if you are of the upper classes, a single move out the door requires a sedan chair and maids to accompany you. These women know little of the outside world and have no skills with which to make a living. And, of course, it's impossible for an upper-class woman to find employment as a maid.

---

27. A woman's jealousy was traditionally one of the seven grounds on which a man could divorce his wife. The others included failure to produce a son; adultery; lack of filial obedience to her husband's parents; illness; theft; and being too talkative.

"This is all so infuriating. Sometimes it's a case of you crying in the north courtyard while he's off being entertained in the south courtyard, since he loves a new woman and despises the old. You waste your youth being sick and worried every day from dawn to dusk. But if you make even the slightest protest, your husband will be rude and outsiders will all deem you an unvirtuous wife. You have no freedom in domestic affairs, and when it comes to property, it belongs entirely to the husband. We lead the lives of animals or slaves who have to obey their master's every command. In the event of the husband's death, the wife is left with nothing; everything goes to other members of the family. She won't even have control over a hundred pieces of gold. If something happens, she's not allowed to appear in public, and if she doesn't know a man who can act on her behalf, no one will believe what she says. Raising a daughter won't help her get by since even if her daughter's husband is rich, she will still be poor. For if a daughter tries to help her mother or father, she will be considered a criminal by her husband's family. On the other hand, when a woman's husband's family is poor, even if her mother's residence is wealthy, how can she depend on them? A woman has no power either way.

"How did we wind up so inferior? In this world, nothing is so unequal as men and women. It makes me furious that life is so unfair. Just because we're girls, we're not able to make our own living but have to rely on others like useless creatures. I was born a woman and I have suffered at home; I have no way to make a living, so in the years to come it's unlikely that I will have a good future. But being angry is pointless: The question is, how can I save my sisters from this hell? Since my mother herself is a concubine, how can I have a free life? I don't blame the first wife for treating us cruelly, but if she's so jealous why did she allow her husband to take a concubine in the first place? How can I hope that in this life I won't become a slave myself? Heaven is truly cruel. Why are there women in the world anyway?" As Jade said this, her heart was overcome with grief and endless tears streamed from her eyes, wetting her clothing.

The three other girls thought about this and were all depressed too, dreading what awaited them in the future. The women's world is so cruel, but who can avoid it? Unable to bear the thought, they wept silently together. Suddenly, Hibiscus came in carrying a tray of pastries for the guests. As soon as she saw this scene, she was shocked, but as she was in no position to inquire, she just murmured softly to herself: "Everything was fine just now but suddenly everyone looks sad, something must have happened. I should ask, but what can I say? Then again, I can't simply let it go by either." Extremely perplexed, she finally had no choice but to arrange the plates and invite the young ladies to sit down. "Since Madame Bao is busy discussing matters with a guest," she explained, "she is unable to join you. Please don't stand on ceremony and come have something to eat."

They all dried their tears, stood up, and forced themselves to serve each other politely, though they could hardly swallow a bite. As they sipped their green tea quietly, nobody said a word, but just sat there with their heads lowered, fiddling with their sleeves. Finally Unity broke the silence and said, "Vitality, I have long since heard that you are as fine a poet as Xie Daoyun whose verses are so beautiful. In the past I read your poems and deeply admired them. I hope that you will accept me as your pupil."

Vitality immediately replied with modesty, "Sister, why be so polite? Although I have studied a bit of poetry, how could I ever measure up to your reputation? I bow in admiration to your poetry. Yours is far superior to mine."

Then Awaken chimed in, "You two, stop being so modest! Both of you are famous for your poetry. I'm the one everyone should laugh at, with my scrawl-like writing of a beginning student and my embarrassing attempts at poetry. You would all laugh hard if I read any of it, unlike the fine verse of Vitality and Unity that one never tires of hearing."

Vitality hastily said, "Enough of this formality. I have long since heard that your poetry and essays are superb and that your reputation as a writer surpasses that of Zuofen.[28] Others hardly come close to your talent and erudition. Why are you making fun of us?" Awaken was about to reply when suddenly they heard a maid announce, "Jurui has arrived and is in Lady Liang's quarters at present. Lady Liang sent me to ask you to come." Jade stood up hastily and was about to go when the other three detained her for a moment. As for what they talked of next, the following chapter will tell the astonishing tale. At this point, let me take a rest and a sip of tea before I relate the story in detail.

Chapter 5: American and European influences suddenly cure old diseases; Rousing the deaf and enlightening the blind, heroes are born.

China has been engulfed in darkness for thousands of years; women have never had an ounce of power. But today the divisions between men and

---

28. An imperial consort during the Eastern Jin dynasty who was renowned for her literary abilities.

women are being broken down and women have risen to the stage where they rouse the world. I imagine that readers who learned of what the girls discussed in the previous section were pained. But I am ashamed that I lack the ability to write more vividly; I am unable to fully describe the sufferings of women, and who knows how many things I have left out? But in a word, women's lives are no better than those of domesticated animals—they are oppressed, imprisoned, and insulted throughout their lives. Their glory or shame is entirely dependent upon men. Westerners say that the women of China let men manipulate them as if they were five hundred times more inferior than men. Alas, the women of China are no different from cows and horses; they study neither technical skills nor academic subjects. They lack any kind of knowledge. They merely flatter men, unashamed to grovel on their knees and beg. Hearing such things makes one infinitely sad! How many times have I cried to the wind and lamented to my compatriots, "Why are women willing to be so lowly, even stooping to be slaves or animals?" It is said that women are incompetent by nature. But how can people not realize that just as women too have four limbs and five senses, their talent and knowledge are not inferior to those of men? It is simply because they don't aspire to autonomy but seek only comfort and ease. As far as Chinese society is concerned, men and women have never had equal rights. Speaking of all the ways in which women suffer, how can I, the author, prevent my tears from flowing? But I pray that my readers ponder these words and that they don't treat this book like any ordinary novel. All the tears and blood are meant to awaken my compatriots from their living hell. I only hope that every one of my sisters can find a way to become independent and stop relying on men.

But enough of this idle talk; let me return now to the main story. In the previous chapter, I had gotten to where Jurui had arrived, and Jade was just about to turn around to go greet her when the three others stopped her and said, "Why don't you send a maid to invite Jurui in here to your room? Our conversation has been so open, why must we go out there with everyone else and feel constrained?" Jade then explained that she wished to avoid being scolded by her father's first wife. Unity suggested "Why don't we say that my mother said it was fine? I'm certain that auntie won't say anything, but if she does reproach us, my mother will take the blame." Thereupon she petitioned her mother, who sent Hibiscus to fetch Jurui without delay.

Not long after Hibiscus had left, the noble Jurui came into the main hall where she first greeted Madame Bao. When she walked over, the four girls all stood up together and when everyone had completed their greetings, all retired to the bedroom. As Madame Bao had a guest, she didn't have time to stay with them, so she instructed her daughter to entertain her guests by herself. The girls all sat down politely and looked at one another. Jurui took Jade's hand and was shocked wondering what could have happened to make Jade's face so thin and pale. "Sister, why are you so thin? When I asked Hibiscus yesterday, she told me you were not ill!"

Jade heard this and explained, "My destiny is unlucky, there's nothing more to say. But you, my sister, you yourself look thin. I must urge you to stop taking things so hard. This is all your parents' doing, and it's impossible to break an engagement."

Jurui could not contain her anger and color rose to her cheeks, as she laughed wryly, saying, "Sister, what is truly intolerable is accepting this engagement and being treated like a slave. My parents gave birth to me so I ought to be filial and try my best to please them. My honor is intact and I would never do anything improper to shame them. This is all well and good, but my parents ought to let me live without regret and enjoy a full life. In selecting my mate for life, however, why do they consider only the money and not the man? They lie to me and say it's fate, but that's absurd. Accepting that women live their entire lives like beasts of burden, they don't even consider whether the man studies or whether his behavior is good or bad. They haven't looked closely at anything about him, but just listen to the unreliable words of the matchmaker. It's ridiculous and infuriating all at once.

"But I'll have you know, I will not submit. Recently, I've had the chance to read many books from Europe and America that discuss the right to liberty, and how women and men are created equal. Heaven was impartial in endowing us with rights and privileges. The strength of a nation and a race hinges entirely on women, as it is the mother who is charged with overseeing family education. And since women are capable of being independent, everyone is promoting women's rights. There are so many women heroes whom men don't measure up to. Women's schools are all equal to those of men, and at school, women are equal to men and have entered all fields. Unlike China, where we still only study the classics and history, in other countries each field is divided into many specialities. In elementary school, students first study a variety of subjects before they go on to higher education. At the university, all sorts of specializations are open, including philosophy, physics, chemistry, arts and crafts, pedagogy, and agriculture. Every field is dynamic, and men and women compete, striving for excellence in their research, so that every person can live independently. The spirit of independence burns like fire. Men respect women like their superiors, and whenever they encounter a woman, they stand and bow in humble respect.

"In teahouses and pubs, if a man is already seated and he sees a lady, he has to stand up to show respect. If the seats in a carriage are all taken and he sees a woman board, he has to give his seat to her. Women, however, don't have to do the same for men. The reason that women in other countries command so much respect is that, first of all, they are independent and don't rely on men.[29] Second of all, women always try as hard as they can in whatever they do, with the result that there are numerous heroic women who elicit the reverence and respect of others. And finally, the mother is essential in family education and in giving birth to the new citizens of the nation; therefore, in civilized nations, men value the relation between men and women and recognize that women's rights are equal.

"If they get married, women are free to choose their spouses themselves, and they don't have to blindly obey their parents. Men and women can become friends, and they respect each other, for as a rule, such friendships remain pure and proper. Often, women marry someone they have known well in school. This is because, first of all, they understand each other's individual character and educational level, and second of all, they know each other's personality and ambitions. But only if their love is profound do they get married. This has nothing in common with China, where marriage often lacks mutual love and is comparable to two strangers living together. Ordinarily, in other countries, husbands and wives love each other and respect each other profoundly, and this spares the family from contentious and quarrelsome relations. In some places, rights are even further developed and everyone is filled with the spirit of independence. Some women are employed in business, and there are even more working in education. They can both support themselves financially and have professional careers. When women and men's rights are equal, their patriotic spirits burn, and the nation grows strong and the family prosperous.

"If you compare them to Chinese women, it's as though they are living in Heaven while we are stuck in Hell—the difference seems like more than a million miles. Is it that we weren't born human, or simply that we are willing to be servile, like slaves or animals? We quietly endure

---

29. Here Qiu Jin mistakes certain customs of etiquette in Western culture for evidence of women's high social status.

our oppression. As long as we can dress up and fuss over the latest fashions, we don't complain that we are prisoners in hell with no freedom. We never try to obtain education or careers, or think about independence or self-reliance. We never consider escaping this slave trap, or becoming women heroes, or achieving a reputation that is known abroad, or making great contributions to the world or attaining the kind of success that will be recorded in history books, or doing something outstanding that will make millions of people remember our name. Nor do we think about the thousands of ways in which we suffer, or about escaping this living hell. But today, I have awoken from this former dream, and therefore I am confident that I can achieve my goals. When a phoenix is inside a cage, who can appreciate its brilliant colors? But one day it will fly to heaven, breaking out of its stupor to seek independence. I have decided, therefore, to pursue my studies in Japan, and I have come today to ask whether you would be willing to come along with me."

When Jurui finished what she had to say, all those who heard were exalted and happy. In a great clamor, they all asked at once, "Does such a wonderful possibility really exist? It's as though we have just awoken from a dream. But has any woman ever tried to seek an education before?" Jurui replied, "I read of one girl who has already gone."

The others said excitedly, "We were just lamenting the fact that girls can't be independent and that they don't live up to their talents and ambitions. But this is wonderful! Where did you learn such news?" Jurui replied, "My tutor admires reform and recently bought some books and newspapers to show to me that explained the situation of women abroad. Otherwise, how could I ever get such books to read at home?"

Jade said, "Of course I want to go with you, but where will I ever get the money?" "Don't worry," Jurui replied, "I have already thought of a way to obtain an adequate sum of money. Since the Gou family is so anxious for me to marry into their family as soon as I turn seventeen, my mother has already set aside 1000 pieces of gold to use for my wardrobe and jewelry. I can secretly steal this money. Wouldn't it be better to use this to fund our studies than to feed it to that dog? It's enough for both of us to study for two years. After that, Tutor Yu has said that he will figure something out for me, so we needn't worry."

At that point, Unity spoke up. "Sister Jurui, your words anger me because it seems you only want Jade to go. Do you mean to suggest that the three of us aren't human? Even though we might lack talent and knowledge, we too can follow remarkable people and compete for excellence. Why should we be willing to stay behind? But we would need a man to travel with us, otherwise it will be inconvenient since we are unfamiliar with the place and the people. I'm afraid we might get lost!"

Jurui hastily replied, "Sister, why would I be unwilling to have you come along? But I am afraid that, first of all, it will be difficult for you to overcome barriers at home and, second of all, you haven't enough money. But as for getting lost, stop worrying. The entire journey is by ship, so the route is simple; why must we rely on men? Do you mean we couldn't accomplish it on our own? I am willing to take responsibility for everything myself and I can assure you, sisters, we will have no problem. I have already devised a plan that will enable us to escape, but we must arrange for some more money, otherwise it'll be difficult to do anything."

Awaken and Vitality said in unison, "We both have some jewelry that we could try to sell. The problem is that we have no one to buy it." Jurui responded, "That's easy. I will provide the funds for the trip; then I will secretly give my tutor your jewelry and have him sell it for you." The two then replied happily, "Splendid!"

Jade then asked Unity, "What about you?" Unity said, "My mother has a great deal of money that I could steal, as well as gold and pearl jewelry. If there are four or five of us, I think that if we can come up with several thousand pieces of gold, that should be plenty for three years of study. But we must proceed with a single heart and mind, and shouldn't divide things up into yours and mine!" Everyone responded in unison, "You are right, if any one of us is not of one heart and mind, and doesn't share the difficulties that may befall us but is half-hearted, that person will not die a peaceful death!"

Then Vitality asked, "But how should we convene and by what means should we escape?" Awaken said, "The eighth day of the fifth month is my aunt's birthday. Let's use this as a pretext to gather, and that way we can also bring along lots of jewelry. As for escaping, we'll have to ask Jurui." Jurui thus replied that she had already made certain arrangements, which she explained to them. Everyone murmured "Splendid" in subdued voices. Jurui then said, "On that day, no matter what, we must all meet together. If someone doesn't show up, we cannot wait for her." They all nodded their heads in agreement.

Jurui then started talking about unbinding their feet, and everyone agreed, except for Vitality, who looked a little uncomfortable and said that she feared that it would look inelegant. Jurui proceeded to reveal the disadvantages of bound feet to her, saying, "Bound feet have always been a disgrace. You torture your own body to make lotus-petal feet. With such painful broken bones and withered muscles, how can you walk anywhere freely? Because of these feet, we become frail and weak and even catch tuberculosis. How can we blame this on anything but our ignorance? We're unable to fend for ourselves since we can't even walk. We have to lean on our maids for support, and if we walk more than a few *li* our feet hurt like festering sores. From morning until night, we sit still like statues, and if some calamity strikes, we're like prisoners who want to escape but can't move. The pains we suffer are self-inflicted.

"Then, there are those who are truly shameless. Since their husbands fancy little feet, they tie their bindings even tighter, into three inches which they boast are like lotus petals. When they walk, it's like a willow branch swaying in the wind, which they think is so attractive. Leaning against the door hoping that their fates will be good, they make no effort to exert themselves but actually enjoy their lives; they willingly act as their husbands' slaves. Little do they imagine that men are in the habit of abandoning the old for the new, and why should having small feet make any difference? They will still go off and find another enchanting girl, forgetting all about the love you once shared. They spoil their concubines, buy young maids with whom they spend the day teasing and flirting. What's ridiculous is that she who knows how to flatter him the best has no chance to flatter him, but is instead abandoned, like a prisoner, behind closed doors that visitors seldom pass through. How sad it is to be subjected to such humiliation, but how can your little feet alleviate your worries?

"As for those men who are so infatuated with frequenting brothels that they forget all about home, it is unlikely you can keep them with your little feet. You might as well unbind them and be comfortable. Then when you walk, even if the road is difficult, you won't have to frown. You can also develop your physical strength through sport. Whereas now you are thin and frail and everything is difficult to do, you would be able to go out without having to ask men for help; you could pursue an education so you could support yourself; you could seek a living through handicraft work. You could teach in a school to make a living and getting into business and commerce would not be difficult either. Only when you succeed in living on your own can you become independent. Through independence, women's abilities and qualities will naturally improve. What's the use of a pair of pointy feet? One day, civilization will spread throughout our land, and people will absolutely spurn little feet and regard them as a thing for animals."

When Jurui finished saying all this, everyone agreed at once. Vitality laughed like an oriole. "If I hadn't said that one thing to inspire such a response, how could we have ever had the pleasure of hearing your fluent, brilliant discussion, which has awakened me from my stupor, and made me truly admire you. I yearn to publicize your speech everywhere to enable all sisters in their inner chambers to wake up and cast aside those shameful customs of the past and engage in all manner of great deeds and cleanse their slavish hearts. Only when we've escaped this prison and have become accomplished in learning and careers will we know that women are not useless and that our independent spirits are equal to men. From now on, we will destroy the fortified walls of our suffering; why must we have daggers and spears to carry out reforms? Once we have attained education and skills we can all be independent and we won't have to worry about having anyone to rely on. How can today's swallows and sparrows compare with the phoenixes of the future? When the flowers of freedom blossom, civilization will flourish and we will rise up quickly in the world. Today I have awakened from a foolish dream, and I am determined to become independent. No matter how heavily I am weighed down by oppression, if I don't pursue my education, I would rather die." Everyone praised Vitality for being so heroic. From that moment, all the chronic ailments of the girls of the inner chambers were cured. Having made their decision, everyone was very happy.

But who would have thought that a maid was eavesdropping behind the wall?

[*The maid Hibiscus is so moved by what she has overheard that she decides to help the girls. First, she attempts to persuade Madame Bao to allow her daughter to go study abroad; when that fails, she resorts to her second plan: to steal some money and aid their escape in secret.*]

Chapter 6: Throwing off shackles, they travel courageously to Japan; Despising all abuses, they staunchly champion a grand scheme.

As I sit idle by the window, hundreds of emotions surge in me. Who has the determination to save the nation? Drinking my wine and slapping my thigh, I sigh in vain, for I have yet to master the art of the steel dagger. Saddened, my heroic spirit flags, and my grief for the nation is difficult to control. I have wept ten thousand catties of tears; amid the wind, my regrets cannot be subdued.

The previous section told how the girls made their plan to escape while at the Bao residence. Now the eighth day of the fifth month had arrived. It was the birthday of the elderly Madame Bao, though as she was only visiting, she had no relatives or friends there to celebrate. Several guests stopped by, however, including Lady Zuo and her daughter, the Jiang girl, as well as Jurui of the Huang family. Needless to say, everyone made kowtows to show their respect, in addition to all those other elaborate formalities that are so tiring. Unity reported to her mother, "This morning I will go pray to Guanyin[30] to bless and protect you from illness." Madame Bao had always been a devout Buddhist, and seeing her daughter's good intentions, she nodded her head immediately in consent and ordered Hibiscus to escort her. Huang Jurui, Vitality, and Awaken all stood up and said they would go with her to visit the temple and that after they had a look around they would come right back. Then Unity took Little Jade's hand, saying, "Sister, come with us!" Little Jade accepted this command to go. Though Lady Liang looked angry, she didn't say a word. Lady Zuo did not want to make the girls unhappy, so she too was forced to agree. So, without waiting for any permission from their mothers, they all went out into the courtyard. Madame Bao instructed them, "Hurry back so we don't have to wait for you to begin the banquet." The young ladies all promised to return soon. Then they got in their sedan chairs and hurried away like the clouds.

When they reached the temple, they all got out of the sedan chairs and Hibiscus ordered the bearers to wait in front. When they went inside, they pretended to pray to the Bodhisattva, then went to have a look around the temple, since they didn't want the monks to follow. When they reached the back gates, they found Tutor Yu there with sedan chairs. Everyone instructed Hibiscus with a few words, and she wept as she bid them to take care of themselves. She watched them get into their sedan chairs, then waited there patiently until the sun went down before turning back. At home, naturally there was a massive uproar. After Madame Bao quizzed Hibiscus, she learned the details. Some angrily cursed the maid; others wept. But there was nothing that any of the parents could do.

It is said that the girls boarded the ship, which set sail after the whistle was sounded three times. They stood at the railing holding hands and

---

30. A popular bodhisattva usually portrayed in female form.

turned to look back at their distant homeland far away, engulfed in the evening clouds. Knowing each other so well, they chatted harmoniously. Facing the wind, they clapped their hands and chatted about their lives. The author can't help but be filled with joy at this image, though I have written of it poorly in plain language.

How great these girls' ambitions must have been to break through such barriers! They had gone 1000 *li* from home, and now they were traveling 10,000 *li* as fast as the wind. Everyone on board looked at them and thought, "The new learning will surely thrive. One day these girls will act as the bells of freedom and save the motherland."

2

Chen Xiefen

Chen Xiefen (1883–1923)

Like her more famous contemporary Qiu Jin, Chen Xiefen was one of the earliest women writers to use the newly emergent radical press as a platform from which to denounce the social oppression of women. Born in Hunan in 1883, Chen Xiefen was the eldest daughter of Chen Fan, a progressive intellectual who owned and edited the anti-Manchu paper *Subao* in Shanghai. With her father's encouragement, Chen Xiefen launched *The Women's Paper* in 1902, when she was just nineteen years old. The paper advocated the abolition of foot binding, women's rights, and the improvement of female education, and was initially distributed free of charge as a supplement to *Subao*. Chen soon expanded its scope and turned it into an independent monthly magazine featuring essays, literary works, translations, photographs, and news columns. In addition to serving as the primary editor of this magazine, Chen was one of its leading contributors, and quickly established a name for herself in progressive circles for her lucid essays on women's emancipation. In June of 1902, Chen joined a group of reform-minded intellectuals in establishing the Shanghai Patriotic Girls' School, which in its early years not only offered an unusually radical curriculum to female students (including courses on the history of anarchism and bomb-making) but also supported the underground revolutionary movement.

In 1903, the Qing government banned *Subao* and charged Chen Xiefen's father and his colleagues with treason. Because of her affiliation with that group, Chen was also forced to suspend the publication of her magazine, now called *Women's Studies*. Chen Xiefen and her father managed to flee to safety in Japan (unlike several others with ties to *Subao*, who were tried and executed), where they joined the growing community of dissident Chinese intellectuals in Tokyo. Despite his progressive stance toward national politics, Chen Xiefen's father proved to have rather traditional plans for his daughter. Shortly after arriving in Tokyo, he gave his consent to a Cantonese merchant who wanted Chen Xiefen as his concubine. Although Chen Xiefen was appalled at the prospect, she was on the verge of yielding to her father's demand when her friend Qiu Jin, who had also recently arrived in Tokyo, led a public campaign denouncing Chen Fan's hypocrisy, and the arrangement was called off.

In Tokyo, Chen Xiefen resumed publication of her magazine, which would stay in print for another two years, and, beginning in 1905, worked with Qiu Jin and Lin Zongsu to resuscitate the fledgling Encompassing Love Association. This organization was initially founded by a group of female students in 1903 to protest the Russian occupation of China. Later, it adopted a more explicitly feminist-nationalist stance. The 1905 charter stated its mission as follows: "To improve the status of China's two hundred million women and to recuperate their natural rights, so that all women, imbued with concern for the nation, will be able to fulfill their responsibilities as citizens." Although Chen Xiefen was well known in radical circles at the turn of the century for her pioneering role in the women's press and for her astute political essays, little is known of her life after she married except that she went abroad to study in the United States and returned to China around 1911.

The following essay, written in a semiclassical style, appeared in the *China Daily* in 1904. It exemplifies the dual focus of Chen Xiefen's feminist agenda: to galvanize women to action against both imperialist and patriarchal forms of domination. As she suggests, not only do women have a responsibility to participate in resisting foreign colonialism, but exercising this political agency is an essential step in achieving gender equality.

CRISIS IN THE WOMEN'S WORLD
(1904)

A cold wind presses from every direction; I trim the lamp and sit alone. My mind is troubled—all at once, I hear something like a warning bell or a great drum. It cries out sonorously; it shakes thunderously. It comes suddenly, making my eyes dizzy and my brain reel; my hands shake and my feet grow numb. And my spirit trembles and falls unconscious.

What can it be? What can it be? It signals nothing less than a turning point of crucial import for us Chinese women. Alas! What kind of age is the present? Our nation is no more, and our race is about to perish. Our duty is to restore the more than one hundred million *li* of Han territory and to save the four hundred million of our fellow compatriots. Afterward, it lies in our compatriots' power to create a pure paradise and to enjoy mutual happiness. Yet it also lies in their power to allow a sacred race to be enslaved in one blow, and an ancient nation to be carved up by every land in one stroke. Compatriots! Compatriots! In this day—in this hour—we must purify our minds and set our thoughts on our goal. We must awaken ourselves; we must exert ourselves!

The inhabitants of China number about four hundred million all together. Men and women each constitute half of this. Our nation is held in common, our territory is held in common, our assets are held in common, our rights are held in common—and our misfortunes too are held in common. Therefore, since we women have a common responsibility, can we simply stand on the sidelines and willingly destroy this nation, lose these assets, cast aside these responsibilities, and throw away these rights? Can we allow ourselves to become slaves of a fallen nation—can we willingly become an India or a Poland? This is something that causes me great sorrow, great pain. Unashamed of my mere bit of strength, I would fill in the vast ocean or weep blood to warn my fellow compatriots—and, especially, to inform my fellow countrywomen.

In the academic world there are a hundred men who study in America, a thousand men who study in Japan. Similarly, in the journalistic world, there are no fewer than several dozen kinds of newspapers and magazines. "Alliances" and "organizations" with every sort of name increase daily. I would not presume to say that all this has reached a state of perfection; nonetheless, I also know that what these men have established in educating, in teaching the value of the military, in civilizing, and in awakening our people is still in its infancy. And when we examine efforts at reform in every nation east and west, we see that all must advance from a similar state of infancy to reach perfection.

Furthermore, when we look at the recent history of Chinese women, we might ask: what is the extent of our progress over the last few years? Five or six years ago, we didn't know what "restoration" was; the word "revolution" had never even reached our ears or dwelt in our thoughts. Indeed, we didn't know what an "association" or an "organization" was. But at the time of the Sino-Russian secret treaty of some years ago, noble-minded people in Shanghai held a protest meeting at Zhang's Garden and sent telegrams to protest the measure.[1] It was then that our fellow countrywoman Xue Jinqin initiated something never before seen in the several-thousand-year history of Chinese women. Laden with emotion, she stepped forward and spoke with flowing tears, and many were moved.[2] Every province heard of the events in Shanghai and emulated

---

1. Between 1901 and 1905, numerous political rallies and meetings in protest of foreign imperialism were held at the residence of the Shanghai merchant and newspaper entrepreneur Zhang Suhe. This location was so famous at the time that it was known simply as "Zhang's Garden." The meeting Chen refers to here was one of several gatherings in March of 1901 to oppose Russian incursions in northern China.

2. Xue Jinqin's speech was later printed in several newspapers in Shanghai.

them, sending telegrams of protest one after another—and the Russian treaty was stopped midcourse. After this, protest meetings grew more numerous by the day, and in recent years there has been constant talk of revolution. Indeed, those who had never awakened—women, who have been oppressed by their husbands for thousands of years, and who suffer along with their husbands under foreign rule—were also quickly enlightened! Was this not a result of establishing these protest meetings? But I ask myself: among Chinese women, aside from Xue Jinqin, who protested the Russian treaty, have there ever been those who have participated in the political realm?

Since our nation is held in common, how can we let men fulfill their duties to the utmost, while we women remain silent? Indeed, I ask, how can we not be ashamed—for not only have men despised us all along and not let us be equal, but even if men bestowed equality upon us, could we thus have had freedom? Men have always called themselves "honorable," yet everything beneficial has been held exclusively by them—they have not given even the least of these good things to Chinese women. Today, when our nation is already subjugated and our whole race is in peril of becoming slaves held in common by every land, these men who have called themselves "honorable" can indeed be ashamed! We women have been their slaves for several thousand years. How can we still remain blindly unaware and follow them, thereby becoming the slaves of those enslaved by foreign races? Or should we perhaps contend with them over past wrongs?

Indeed, if we are willing to follow men, as the slaves of those enslaved by foreign races, then in the future, when our whole race is enslaved, I fear that we still will not be treated even as ordinary slaves. I once looked over a certain French newspaper, which said: "China's land is of the highest quality; regrettably, the Chinese are but a base race. In the future, when we occupy this territory, we should wipe out this race and install a better one there." Alas! Have my fellow countrymen heard of this? In the future, they may be willing to become slaves like the masses of Poland or India, but I fear that even this will be impossible. Chinese men becoming slaves in this way—we women becoming slaves of those enslaved by foreign races—how can I bear to talk any further about such things? I imagine my fellow Chinese are also unwilling to hear about them—and, since they are unwilling to hear of these things, how much less willing will they be to solve them?

Now, some would protest men's former wrongs to them, saying: Since men have always called themselves "worthy," but enjoyed their rights alone, then they should bear misfortune alone. Why should we women participate? I, however, say that this viewpoint is greatly mistaken. When men alone enjoyed rights, we could not participate, and we ceded this participation to them. And what was the reason for this? In the past, women had entirely lost their rights; they had also lost their sense of duty. Since they didn't fulfill their duties, if they had rights, those rights were bestowed on them by others—they were not rights we women ourselves had fought to obtain. And, also, if we obtained incomplete rights, then ceding them back to the givers was permissible. But today is a day when women *can* fulfill our duty! A day when we *can* obtain our complete rights! If we don't forge ahead courageously, then it really is as men say disparagingly: "Women are slavish by nature." Therefore, if we women want to struggle alongside men, then we must first struggle to fully fulfill our duty. Then women's rights will naturally become equal! But if we persist in our blindness, merely acknowledging that inequality between the sexes is something that ought not to be, and do not think of how we can equalize things, then how can we expect our constant resentful wailing to benefit us?!

Day and night, I fear our current situation; I mourn our plight. Among Chinese women there are those more educated than I, brighter than I, and more able. I hope that the educated will teach the uneducated; the enlightened will awaken the unenlightened; the capable will help the incapable. We can save ourselves from the sorrows of an exterminated race, and restore a nation that has already been lost—of any other future, I do not dare to speak; I cannot bear to speak; I am unwilling to speak! If, by chance, I even once think of it, I am heartbroken, and if I think of it again for the sake of my fellow countrywomen, then I am overwhelmed. I weep tears as I speak of what I know and dare not calculate the numbers of those who will understand and those who will not.

Translated by Jennifer Carpenter

3

Chen Hengzhe

Chen Hengzhe (1890–1976)

Chen Hengzhe, or Sophia Hung-che Zen as she was known to her friends in the United States, achieved many "firsts" in her life. She came from a scholarly Hunanese family with a long tradition of talented female painters and poets, but was the first woman in the family to receive a formal education. In 1903, at the age of thirteen, she left home to study with a progressive-minded uncle before enrolling in one of the new schools for girls in Shanghai. When she graduated from high school several years later, however, institutions for higher education in China were still not accepting women, and Chen was forced to take a teaching job in order to stave off her father's attempts to arrange a marriage for her. In 1914, she learned that examinations for the Boxer Indemnity Fund Grants for study in the United States were to be open to women. Chen secretly applied, sat for the exam, and became one of the first women to be awarded this prestigious scholarship.

Chen sailed to the United States in the fall of 1914 and spent a year at a preparatory school in Poughkeepsie, New York, before entering Vassar College in 1915. Chen majored in history and participated actively in student life at Vassar, publishing poems in the school magazine and giving lectures on Chinese culture and politics, before graduating Phi Beta Kappa in 1919. She received a Vassar Fellowship for graduate study in history at the University of Chicago, but barely had time to complete a master's degree there before receiving a telegram from friend and progressive leader Hu Shi urging her to return to teach Western history at the newly revamped Beijing University. She accepted the offer and in 1920 became the first woman professor at China's top university.

Chen Hengzhe was a natural choice for a university bent on transforming itself into a modern educational institution and a center for innovation. She had established her reputation as a pioneer in what was by then being called the New Culture Movement long before her return to China. Answering the earliest call for a Chinese "literary revolution," Chen published "One Day," the story translated here, in June 1917 in the *Chinese Students Quarterly*, arguably making it the first piece of modern fiction written in *baihua*, vernacular Chinese. This vignette of student life at a women's college in the United States was significant not only for its conscious attention to the use of spoken Chinese language (employed in this case to approximate English conversation), but for its portrayal of a young Chinese woman in foreign surroundings. The story is constructed more like a short play than a piece of fiction, yet its attention to character and linguistic experimentation is typical of all of Chen's short stories. Other works in her 1928 collection, *Little Raindrop*, range from sparse poetic allegories of Chinese nationalism to realistic explorations of a modern woman's quest for fulfillment in both career and family.

Although Chen Hengzhe gave up writing fiction not long after the publication of *Little Raindrop*, she continued publishing outspoken essays in both Chinese and English on women's issues and political affairs, and helped found the influential 1930s journal *Independent Critic*. Her *History of the West* was the first book on European and American history written by a Chinese historian and was quickly adopted as a standard high school and college textbook; it was reprinted numerous times after its initial publication in 1926.

Married in 1920 to H. C. Zen, a graduate of Cornell University and a renowned chemist, Chen Hengzhe maintained her academic career while raising a family and moving constantly to evade the Japanese invaders and civil strife throughout the 1930s and 1940s. After the founding of the People's Republic of China in 1949, Chen and her husband remained in Shanghai, where H. C. Zen died in 1961. During the Cultural Revolution (1966–1976), many colleagues and friends in Taiwan and abroad lost touch with Chen Hengzhe and feared she had suffered persecution. Only later did they discover that Chen had passed away in 1976 after going nearly blind and living alone for years in a tiny Shanghai apartment. Unfortunately, during the Cultural Revolution she had burned many of her papers, including numerous stories and poems as well as, it is said, the manuscript of an unpublished autobiography.

ONE DAY
(1917)

Author's preface

This story describes several trivial incidents in a day in the life of new students in a dormitory at a women's university in the United States. As it has no real structure or purpose, it should be taken merely as a straightforward sketch and not as a story. The description, however, is very faithful and since it is my first portrait written from life, I feel I should preserve it.

Morning

Dong! Dong! Dong! Dong! Seven o'clock.
   In bed Anna stretches and asks, "Bertha, what time is it?"
   Bertha replies sleepily, "Huh, do you hear the bell ringing?"
   Anna falls back asleep without answering.
   Bertha falls asleep again too.
   Dong! Half past seven.

Bertha and Anna are still not awake.

The clock reads seven-fifty.

Anna suddenly wakes up. (Looking at the clock) "Oh, I've only got ten minutes." She jumps out of bed and gives Bertha a push. "Hurry and get up. The breakfast bell has been ringing forever."

Bertha doesn't answer. She turns toward the wall and continues sleeping.

Anna hurries to wash up and comb her hair and then flies down the stairs. The cafeteria servant is just closing the door as Anna bursts in. Anna goes to a table where seven or eight people are already seated. She sits down saying, "Is there any extra breakfast left here?"

Margie: "I knew somebody was sure to come late, so I asked for another breakfast in advance. You're welcome to have it." To another student: "And so what happened then?"

Anna: "Oh, Eunice has news again! Please start over from the beginning, won't you?"

Eunice: "All right. Last night a new student from outside the dormitories came to visit her friend. By ten o'clock she had still not returned home and her landlady got nervous and called the head dormitory warden. She said she thought the girl's friend lived in Raymond House, but she didn't know what her name was. Hearing this, the warden set out immediately to Raymond House and then, together with the house manager there, went into every student's room asking, 'Do you have a guest staying here this evening?'"

Emily laughs. "How amusing! And then what happened?"

Eunice: "They searched for an hour, woke up over one hundred students, and still couldn't find this student. The warden then sent a number of guards into the countryside to search for her and still she was nowhere to be found. That poor warden was so nervous she stayed up all night long without going to bed ... and can you guess where this student was in the end? This morning she calmly walked out of Josselyn House to go home and have breakfast!"

The students all laugh.

Margie: "The warden certainly was too alarmed. What girl of eighteen or nineteen doesn't know how to take care of herself?"

Eunice: "You can't blame the warden for this. Last month two upperclasswomen went for a walk in the countryside and were nearly caught by ruffians."

Anna: "Did the new student know about this?"

Eunice: "She knew. She should take care or she'll receive quite a punishment."

Anna: "What time is it now?"

Margie (looking at her watch): "Eight-ten."

Anna: "Will you please excuse me. I still have an essay to write during these ten minutes."

In Class

The clock reads twenty minutes past eight and the students are arriving one after another.

At eight-thirty the teacher enters.

Mary walks up to the teacher. "Dr. Miller, last night I had a headache and did not finish preparing today's homework."

Miller: "Fine, fine." To all the students: "Now all of you please write for fifteen minutes. The topic: 'A critique of the second French constitution written in the style of Rousseau, Montesquieu, or Voltaire.'"

The room falls silent.

Fifteen minutes pass.

Miller: "Please stop writing." To Mary: "Miss Bard, please finish writing out your answer and hand it in to me tomorrow." To the class: "You need not turn your papers in. It would be fine if now Miss Carl would please read her answer aloud so that everyone can discuss it."

At this the whole class smiles at each other as if to say, "Scared for nothing."

But the dejected expression on Mary's face seems to say, "Just my luck."

Noon

Bertha walks to the school store, buys a bag of candies, and eats it on her way to the library. Just then, Mary comes out of the library and walks toward Bertha.

Mary: "Bertha, are you coming here to study without having lunch again?"

Bertha: "Lunch? I haven't even had breakfast. I haven't done any preparation for my afternoon classes, so how can I have time to eat?"

Mary: "I'm afraid you're going to get sick."

Bertha: "I wouldn't mind getting sick, then I could go to the infirmary and have a good sleep."

The clock in the library strikes half past twelve. All the students disperse. Only Bertha remains.

The Afternoon (1)

The clock points to four-fifty. Margie walks into the room and throws her books on the bed, saying, "Thank heavens, another day is over."

There is a knock at the door.

Margie: "Come in."

Bertha walks in. "Margie, do you have any snacks? I'm starving."

Margie laughs. "Begging food again? Is an apple okay? Or would you prefer an orange?"

Bertha: "I'll take both."

Bertha eats and talks. "Margie, I think college life is really too difficult. This morning I received a letter from my mother; she said that tomorrow evening they are having another dance. Margie, do you think it's fair that they have such a good time at home while I'm here freezing and starving to death?"

Margie: "I know what you mean. Last evening I asked an upperclasswoman, 'What is the point of studying?,' and she said, 'You just arrived at college and the workload is heavy, so naturally you feel things are difficult. But you will enjoy it little by little.' Then she pulled a long face and said, 'Margie, we have this opportunity and it is a pity not to know how to take advantage of it. Haven't you seen the Chinese students here? Why do you think they leave their families and country behind to come all the way here?' I said..."

Bertha: "Margie, pardon me for interrupting you, but what's really curious to me is how anyone could leave their home and study abroad! I would never, ever be able to do it."

Margie: "Not only that, but they can't even return home during the summer."

Bertha (flopping down on the bed): "My heavens!"

Afternoon (2)

Bertha has gone. Margie is hanging a sign on the door that says: "Busy. Please do not disturb." When she finishes, she takes up her book with haste and begins reciting.

There is a knock on the door.

Margie (frowning): "Come in."

A maid enters. "Miss Adams, the Dean of Studies telephoned asking for you to see her immediately."

Margie (face turning white): "I understand, thank you."

As Margie is going out she bumps into Eunice.
Eunice: "Margie, here you are, I was just coming to ask if you would like to go ice skating."
Margie: "Ice skating..."
Eunice: "What's wrong?"
Margie: "The Dean just called for me."
Eunice (sticking her tongue out): "Sounds serious, I hope there is no problem."
Margie: "Thank you." She hurries out.

Afternoon (3)

On her way back from the Dean's office, Margie walks with an upperclassman and says to her, "It nearly scared me to death."
The upperclassman: "What exactly did she want to see you for?"
Margie: "She said that Bertha's grades were terrible and that she would have given her a second chance had Bertha always been hardworking, but now that she's not only unintelligent but also not working hard, she is going to be expelled."
Upperclassman: "What did she call you for, why didn't she call Bertha herself?"
Margie (shrugging her shoulders): "I don't know."
Upperclassman: "How are your own studies?"
Margie is silent.
Upperclassman: "What are you worried about?"
Margie: "She said... she said that as my studies are a bit better than Bertha's, she will give me a chance for four more weeks and only if I show some progress will I be allowed to stay here."
Upperclassman: "Well, now I understand."
Margie: "What?"
Upperclassman: "Nothing. I mean it is actually your studies the Dean is concerned about!"

Evening (1)

The clock reads six-thirty. The students leave the cafeteria one after another.
Emily walks over to a Chinese student, Miss Zhang, and says, "Would you like to dance with me sometime?"
Zhang: "I would like to very much, but I'm not a very good dancer."
Emily: "Do people in China dance too?"

Zhang: "No."

Emily: "How strange! Then what do you do when you have free time? Do you like America? Are you homesick?"

Before Miss Zhang can answer, a group of students begins gathering around her in a semicircle.

Bertha: "What do you eat at home? Do you have eggs?"

Zhang: "Yes, we do."

Margie: "Well then you certainly must have chickens. How strange!"

Mary: "I have a friend whose aunt is a teacher in China; do you know her?"

Lois: "Last night I was reading a book about Chinese customs and it said that Chinese people like to eat dead rats. Is that true?"

Eunice: "What are Chinese houses like? Do you have tables like us? I heard somebody say that in China people eat, sleep, study, and write on the floor. Is that right?"

Anna: "Do you have a brother in America? My brother knows a Chinese student named Zhang, so it goes without saying that he must be your brother."

Miss Zhang answers their questions one after the other.

Emily: "Do you mind us asking you to say something in Chinese?"

Zhang: "Not at all."

Emily: "Then could you please teach me a few words of Chinese?"

Zhang: "All right. For example, when you greet someone you say, '*Nong hao la fou*?'"

Emily: "That's easy, *Nong hao la fou*. What else?"

Zhang: "Then the other person says, '*Man hao, xiexie nong.*'"

Emily: "'*Mei hao, chacha nong*,' is that right?"

Zhang, laughing: "It's close."

Emily jumps up, saying loudly, "I can speak Chinese, listen: '*Nong hao la mei hao chacha nong.*'"

Dong! Dong! Dong! Six-fifty.

Mary: "I was hoping it would rain so that we wouldn't have to go to chapel!"

The students stream into the chapel.

Evening (2)

Bertha is alone studying in her room, her head in her hands. There is a knock at the door.

Lillian comes in. "Bertha, you haven't paid your Youth Association dues. Today is the last day to pay, so would you please give them to me?"

A knock on the door.

Bertha: "Please come in."

Eunice walks in: "Bertha . . . (seeing Lillian) oh, excuse me. I didn't know you had a guest. I'll come back in a little while."

Bertha: "I'll be there in a minute . . . don't eat everything!"

Eunice leaves.

Bertha: "Lillian, I don't have any money this evening. My mother is wiring me money tomorrow, would you please . . ."

A knock on the door.

Bertha: "Please come in."

Lillian: "Well, then please prepare the amount and I will come back tomorrow evening."

Jane comes in.

Lillian goes out.

Jane: "Are you Miss Whalen? (Whalen is Bertha's family name. People at the school usually call people "Miss" plus their surname when they aren't familiar.) Miss Whalen, I believe you heard the lecture last month by Mr. Pierre regarding the war zone hospitals in France. I am here representing the fund-raising effort for that hospital. I know you are a compassionate person who will certainly help those poor wounded soldiers." She brings out the contribution booklet. "Give whatever you like."

Bertha looks at the contribution list; seeing that the amounts range from half a dollar to fifty dollars, she writes "Two dollars."

Jane: "Thank you. Please have the amount ready next month. I will be sending someone else to collect it."

Bertha: "Good night." (Dropping into her chair) "I have a headache. I must go to the infirmary immediately. If I am expelled, then so be it; with all these interruptions how can I possibly study enough even when I want to?"

Evening (3)

Helen, Susan, and Judy—all upperclassman—are talking together in a dormitory room.

Helen: "Did you know that Amy already has reservations to go abroad next Saturday?"

Susan: "What? Is she really going to France?"

Helen: "Of course. Tomorrow night her close friends are even throwing her a farewell party at the Vienna Hotel—I think she really has all the luck."

Judy: "What do you mean luck? You should know that going to a war zone to be a nurse is not fun."

Susan: "How are her studies?"

Helen: "She is not going to be gone for more than a half year anyway, and besides, she is very smart. The Dean gave her a special half-year leave. She doesn't have to do anything but just leisurely review her studies over the summer vacation."

Judy: "Speaking of grades, it reminds me of my dear little sister. There is nothing I can do for that one. Today the Dean told me that she has already written a letter to her mother asking her to come take her home. Her mother entrusted her to me and I feel a little sorry about it."

Susan: "You're talking about Bertha Whalen, aren't you? She didn't have any brains to begin with. But still, the Dean is a little excessive sometimes. I heard that over thirty of the new students have already been expelled this year."

Judy: "Not only that, but . . ."

Outside the window many people are shouting: "Mark, please come out!" "We want Mark to come out!" (Mark is Susan's nickname. It is a school custom to have a nickname that everybody calls you by.)

Helen: "Oh, Mark, I haven't congratulated you yet!"

Judy: "What for?"

Helen: "You didn't know that Mark has been elected class president?" Then to Susan: "Now you better go and accept their serenade." (The English word *serenade* means a song sung under a window in the evening to show admiration for someone. Our country does not have this custom, so I've transliterated it.)

When Susan leans her head out the window, shouts ring out. Judy and Helen put their heads out the window too, waving and clapping their hands along with Susan. When they finish singing the song, the students move off to the north to serenade the new president of their own class. (Note that according to school tradition, the first- and third-year students are "sisters," as are the second and fourth. On important occasions, the students break into two groups of "sisters." Therefore, when Susan was elected the senior class president, the sophomore students had to sing to her in congratulations, and then move on to do the same for their own class president.)

Judy: "It's getting late already, let me say good night."

Helen standing up: "I should go too."

Judy goes out the door, then turns her head back, smiling, saying: "I hope that we can sleep soundly tonight and aren't woken up by that fire alarm again."

Helen: "Isn't that the truth! Those fire drills give me a headache. I think I would rather just be burned to death than have to suffer through these drills all the time."

Susan, laughing: "It is going to be eighteen degrees below zero tonight. They should have a little compassion and not call us out to freeze in the courtyard. I'm sure you won't have any problem tonight. Sleep well!"

Dong! Dong! Dong! Ten o'clock.

The whole school is sound asleep. Only the light in Margie's room is on; and she is still bent over her desk doing her math homework.

4

Feng Yuanjun

Feng Yuanjun (1900–1974)

Born in Henan province in 1900, Feng Yuanjun (pen name: Gan Nüshi) came from an educated family of officials. Her father passed the highest rank in the Qing dynasty examination system, but died soon after the birth of his only daughter, leaving his wife to look after three small children. A relatively open-minded woman who at one point ran an elementary school for girls, Feng's mother hired a private tutor for her two sons and allowed her daughter to join them in their lessons. When the boys left for boarding school, however, Feng's mother refused to retain the tutor for her daughter alone.

In 1917, Feng Youlan, Feng Yuanjun's older brother, who was to become modern China's foremost scholar of philosophy, returned home from school in Beijing with the news that the government was planning to establish a new public high school for girls. Feng Yuanjun desperately wanted to enroll in the Chinese program being offered by the school, but her mother steadfastly rejected the idea. Only after Feng threatened to use her dowry savings for tuition did her mother finally give in to her wishes.

Feng Yuanjun made the trip to Beijing with her brother in the fall of 1917 and passed the entrance exam for Beijing Women's Normal School. She quickly made a name for herself at the school as a talented and outspoken student. During the May Fourth student demonstrations in 1919, the male principal of what was by that time called Beijing Women's Normal College forbade the students to participate and even locked the school gates to prevent them from leaving the campus. Her classmates later recalled how Feng broke the lock with a stone, enabling a large group of women students to join the protest marches.

Feng Yuanjun began publishing fiction in magazines sponsored by the Creation Society literary group shortly after graduating from college. Although she wrote for only a few years during her twenties, Feng made a significant impact on the early May Fourth literary scene. When her first group of short stories, including "Separation," translated here, appeared in *Creation Quarterly* in 1923, Feng gained instant notoriety for her explicit descriptions of romantic liaisons between an unmarried man and woman. Read today, "Separation," "The Journey," and several other stories Feng wrote on the same theme would hardly raise an eyebrow, but in the 1920s, their honest depiction of a woman torn between love for her mother and her personal desire to escape an arranged marriage in order to be with her lover was shocking, particularly coming from the pen of a young woman writer. But the stories struck a cord with many newly educated young women who felt caught between the very different expectations that liberated May Fourth intellectual society and their own families had for them.

Feng Yuanjun received a master's degree in Chinese literature from Beijing University in 1925 and after publishing two collections of short fiction embarked on a successful academic career. In 1929, she married Lu Kanru, a literary scholar himself, and the two collaborated on a massive history of Chinese poetry published in 1930. Seeking a respite from the tense intellectual and political atmosphere in China during the 1930s, the couple sailed to France in 1932, where Feng Yuanjun received a Ph.D. in literature from Paris University in 1935.

From 1949 until her death in 1974, Feng Yuanjun taught at Shandong University, where she also held several administrative positions. Her niece, the well-known writer Feng Zongpu, admired her aunt's dedication as a teacher and scholar. Since they never had children of their own, Feng Yuanjun and her husband left their entire life savings to Shandong University to help needy students.

SEPARATION
(1923)

My Love!

I never thought that despite all of our careful planning, we would still find ourselves defeated by society's backwardness. Although it's true that physically we are separated, in spirit we are still together. What a terrible fate our love has met. Perhaps at this very moment you are weeping bitter tears over this, or maybe you are plotting various rescue strategies. If you are brave, you will come to my rescue.

I have been locked away in this little room since the moment I arrived home from the railway station. There is a bed, a table, a sofa, chairs, cups, a basin, and such, but I couldn't even find a scrap of paper or a frayed writing brush. If I hadn't begged my cousin to smuggle in some paper and a pen, I would have died of loneliness, and you wouldn't even have known how or where.

Today is the second day of my imprisonment. I spent the night alone in this room. Although my brother and sister are sympathetic and have tried on numerous occasions to persuade my mother to give in, they have, alas, failed. She says that what we did was tantamount to illicit cohabitation, and that not only have I dishonored her, but even my ancestors in heaven are furious and ashamed of me. She says that if my brother and sister insist on helping me, she will kill herself. My Love! How is it that our love—so sacred, noble, and innocent—has turned into something so condemned?

Life can be sacrificed, but not one's will. If I can't have my freedom, I'd prefer to die. When people don't understand that love must be sought freely, then nothing else matters. You've heard me make this declaration many times before, and I've often spoken of how our love is concrete and yet boundless. When we can no longer resist the obstructive powers around us, we will drown ourselves in the sea together. As you can see, this moment has arrived for me, but I still yearn for life. Maybe you think that I am breaking our oath to each other, but if you really believe this, you are terribly mistaken.

This world is a huge prison, and life is but a journey filled with thorns and brambles. What do I need of this world? If for some reason you were to die, how could I go on living by myself? The only reason that I did not simply jump from the train before I was caught by my mother, and take my leave from this turbid world under the train's grinding wheels, is because I still hold out some hope of an escape. The terrible day when my "betrothed," Liu Muhan, returns home is only three short days away and I am trying to get assistance from my sister and cousin. If the gods of love have any compassion for our true love, they will help us reunite. Then we will run away to another place in this world, or perhaps we will go to another world. There at least we will be together. I am afraid that if I destroyed myself now, my mother would still send this dirty corpse of mine over to the Liu family. That would be my greatest degradation.

My sister blames me for coming back to see my mother, saying "How can the earthbound not be envious of where the wild goose soars?" I do not argue with her; I appreciate her desire to help. But I know she is mistaken about me. I love you, but I also love my mother. Love is sacred, whether it is the love between a man and woman or between a mother and a child. Try putting yourself in the place of a mother already in her sixties who has not seen her child for six or seven years. Would I still be human if I did not desire to return home and be close to her while I still can? I took the risk to come home in the hope that my love could be fulfilled on all sides. I did not realize that though love is but one facet of nature, its various expressions can be mutually contradictory and intolerant.

When I was sent to this little room, I cried over my fate till my tears dried up and my voice went hoarse. My mother used to be kind, but now she has become cruel. Not only did she not comfort me, she sat in the next room listing an inventory of my crimes to my brother. She told him that our love was a betrayal and an unfilial act. I became even angrier when I heard this. The angrier I grew, the more I cried. I am utterly exhausted from crying.

Ah, My Love! How strange it was! At one point, a vision of our days together in Beijing suddenly came to me. It was summer and lotus plants covered the entire surface of the river like a jade-green blanket. The red flowers blushed the same color as my cheeks; the white ones looked pure and beautiful. Where the water was clear and shallow, one could see fish nibbling at the duckweeds. The willow strands knotted in the wind. The fragrance that wafted by was probably from the gardenias. It seemed to be morning. Dew dripped off the lotus leaves, the flower blossoms, and the grass on the roadside. We were both wearing thin white shirts and we nestled against each other as we sat on a stone bench, in the cold morning breeze. You reached out to break off a lotus leaf and placed it on my head, pretending it was a hat. I immediately put it on your head, but you took it off and threw it away. I got angry and you apologized. You held my hand tightly and smiled at me as I leaned against your chest. We forgot all about the natural scenery, feeling only the wonder of our love. Then dark clouds gathered in the sky and big drops of rain started to fall on us. There were rumbles of thunder and flashes of lightning. And suddenly, you disappeared. I was so frightened that I cried to the heavens, asking where my lover was . . . then I suddenly awoke with a start. I realized that in my fatigue from crying so much I was hallucinating. My Love! The path of roses where we used to walk is so much better than this place. Everything in the world is both a dream and reality at once. What is the difference between dreams and reality? Why don't we just dream a few more sweet dreams?

There is no moon tonight, but the sky is covered with stars. It's after eleven o'clock and everyone is asleep. It is so quiet I could hear a pin drop. Among the multitude of stars decorating the pitch-black sky is a constellation whose name I do not know. It forms a loop in the sky as if it were a diamond necklace. I couldn't sleep. I draped a sweater over my shoulders and went to gaze out the window at the sky. The array of stars, the stillness of the night—if there were a sliver of new moon, it would have been just like that night last year when we went to Zhongyang Park.

> It was on a night like this,
> The moon was slender as a brow.
> Starlight sprinkled across the sky.
> All the cry and hue
> Were abandoned to another world.
> It was on a night like this,
> We held each other closely.
> One moment, we were standing west of a pavilion,
> One moment, we were at the river's edge,
> Beneath the old cypress trees,
> Crushing the pine cones beneath our feet,
> We startled the sleeping crows.
> We listened to the trickling of the night river.
> It was on a night like this,
> We held each other closely.
> We said sad things to each other,
> Things that we had been too timid to say.
> We quarreled,
> Then we made up.
> We knew each other ever more deeply.
> It was on a night like this
> When we reminisced about how we first met.
> Talking and thinking,
> We looked at each other and laughed.
> The mystery of love
> The mystery of the night
> Became fused into one.

My Love! Is this poem nothing more than a remnant of our past? Isn't it what you would call an optimistic and realistic work? Didn't all our friends who once read this poem envy our sweet life together? When I look up at that boundless black sky and then gaze down tearfully to reminisce, the scene from that night reappears before me. But . . . but the replay of this scene is so different from reality. The more enchanted this scene appears to me now, the more unbearable the feeling in my heart. The only thing that could comfort me now would be to have you hold me in your arms again. But this is impossible.

My Love, do you remember? When we first met each other in the clubhouse, you silently stood apart from the crowd. Then you asked someone if I were Miss Naihua Wei. Do you remember? One early autumn, a cool morning, we went to visit the Three Generations Garden. At the gate of the zoo, there were a few gusts of cold wind and we could hear the rustling of leaves from the woods. I was not dressed warmly enough and tried to huddle against you in the wind. You held my hand till we came to the grove next to the Happy View Pavilion, then you put your left arm around my shoulders and held my hand with your right. We strolled together like that. You started to kiss me, but in the end you were too timid. Frankly, it was so hard to contain myself then. Werther must have had the same sensation when his foot touched Lotte's.[1]

Do you remember how I once wrote a letter to reprimand you for hugging me and putting your face against my cheek? You asked to see me at the East Gate to apologize. When we first met, we were both silent, both filled with a thousand words in our hearts. Tears flowed from our eyes. Finally, you said hesitantly, "I know that I cannot let myself develop any romantic feelings toward you. Your problem can be resolved, but not mine. I do not understand why I am forced to be intimate with someone I do not love and am called immoral when I try to get closer to the one I do." At that time, I was a little frightened that you had fallen so deeply under the spell of love. I was afraid that our romance would come to no good end. But then I heard you say, "If you think that I have offended you in any way through my actions, I can only jump into this river. I will do whatever you say, I will study hard—as long as we can be with each other like this forever." My heart softened. A desire to sacrifice myself to satisfy you spread through my heart like green grass in spring. I immediately granted you your request as if I had received a heavenly mandate. Do you still remember?

After this incident, we went to visit the reservoir. We wandered through the autumn countryside but could find no place where we could avoid the gaze of others. Finally, you had the idea of renting a boat and we hid among the reed flowers. We hugged and kissed a few times but the sun was already setting. The red of the sun's rays against the black of the distant mountains far away cast a purple hue on the evening clouds. At the river's edge and at the tips of the trees, there were a few remaining rays from the reluctantly setting sun. The grandeur and austerity of the autumn landscape seemed to make everything we did beautiful. However, the vast greyness of dusk descended. We couldn't even see the ripples on the water. The white duck-

---

1. A reference to Goethe's *The Sorrows of Young Werther*, a novel that became extremely popular among the May Fourth generation in China, after Guo Moro translated it in 1922.

lings had long been called home. We didn't want to dock and go back yet, so we sat together in the boat. I was leaning against you. As the boat drifted along, the oar dipping in the water and the rustling of the reeds sounded like sighs. But I was happy and unaffected by this. We sat even closer to each other. When I thought about the difficulties ahead of us, I could almost weep in your arms. You asked why I felt bad when our love was so perfect and so innocent. You said we must be determined to realize what even Ibsen and Tolstoy did not dare. . . .

Do you remember that winter, upstairs in Manxing Restaurant, when you tearfully declared to me that you believed in nothing but me. I was the gods' answer to your quest, you said. I responded that from that time on, I would never love anyone but you, and that we would be together forever. We would wait until the right time to. . . . Hearing these words, you smiled gently and gazed back at me through the tears in your eyes. You held my shoulders with your hands, and whispered my name softly. You said we were. . . . Then you pulled me into your arms. I stroked your neck with my hand. You lowered your head to my chest. You told me of all the sadness in your life. Your final words were, "I have not felt any happiness since I started to understand human affairs. But with you, My Love, I never feel for want. . . ." Remembering past moments is unbearable. The seed of love is more than a source of suffering. Before the birth of human beings, the God of Creation evenly strewed both flowers of sweetness and thorns of agony along the path of life. The gods mixed bitter juices in with the honey that is used to create love. But let's not talk of this anymore. How can our happy life together be fully described? My heart is broken by the memories. I do not want yours shattered too. Oh, My Love!

My Love, you are my only love. Don't make me sad. As Hamlet said, as long as my body belongs to me, I am yours. I will also say to you that as long as my spirit has any consciousness, I will never betray your love.

Yesterday, I wrote you several pages in my delirium. From now on, no matter how confused I am, I will try to describe to you my feelings while being locked up in this room. I don't think that this will bring harm to anyone but will be greatly beneficial to myself. And, even if I were never to get out of this cage in my lifetime, and were to simply cross over to the other world from here, you will still be able to learn of my days here. My cousin has already bravely sworn that she will deliver these bits of blood and tears to you. Oh, I am crying again! Is there anything sadder in this world than to not have the freedom to choose where one dies? My situation is worse than that of prisoners awaiting execution. At least they know beforehand when and where they will be executed, so that their closest family members and friends can be with them in their last moment. As for me, the only one with me when I die will be my worst enemy.

After having written you a few lines last night, I forced myself to lie in bed to try to think calmly of a way to escape. However, thoughts of our life together in the past—the happy life—immediately flooded my mind uncontrollably, like water pulled downward by gravity. People's minds are too rigid. They judge others according to their own debased outlook. Otherwise how could anyone who knows us not respect the sanctity of our love? Just imagine, a young man and a young woman who love each other enough to sacrifice their lives for one another did nothing more than hug, kiss, and talk during the ten days they spent together. Is this not rare in both ancient and modern times, within China and abroad? My Love, I will never forget that most sacred night at the inn in Zhengzhou. That was the night when we had our first lesson of love. How wonderful and mysterious! I sat shyly at the edge of the bed, refusing to get in. You helped undress me down to the last layer, then you shielded me with the clothes that I had taken off and softly asked me to please remove the last layer myself, while you stood respectfully at a distance. When you held me in your arms, I thought about how my family would oppress us with harsh measures and destroy our love and how society would be hostile towards us. I cried in your embrace and felt I was alone in the wilderness without a soul in sight. Thorns and brambles filled my path, and the sounds of the empty valley echoed around like the roars and howls of tigers and wolves. But, I believed, as long as I had you, as long as you really loved me, I would be saved. It was at that point that I started to believe that the human soul is fundamentally pure. However, this purity is only revealed in the most extreme circumstances. The purity of our souls is what makes us all human.

As I've been thinking about this, it has suddenly started to rain. Raindrops are beating on the windowpane and the banana leaves outside. It sounds like someone moaning and sobbing, or sighing and lamenting. I pray silently that the rain will keep falling, falling on the grime humanity has left behind, washing it all away, so that we can start anew, sowing seeds of freedom, honor, and love.

My life has been destroyed in the name of love. Because of my mother's love, I could not simply break off the marriage contract she arranged for me in good conscience. And because of her love, I had to come back to see her. Because of my lover's love, I sacrificed my reputation in society and the joy of being with my family. The author of my tragedy is love. The heroine is myself. I want to protest to the gods. If they cannot create a love that has no contradictions, I swear I will pluck out every seed of love they plant on this earth. I will not allow love to appear in this world ever again. Humans would be better off becoming as cruel as wild animals, eating each other alive and tearing at each other's skin.

During these days of separation, I have come to a better understanding of the human world. I have discovered that humans are selfish; although they make material sacrifices for others, they have no spiritual regard for them because they are so trapped in their historical circumstances. The bond between a mother and a daughter is perhaps the dearest in this world, but even it is susceptible to this general condition. I also discovered that no matter what kind of relationship you are in, the one who nurtures you also controls you.

It turned out to be a fine morning. The sun was shining on my bed and a touch of life filled the room. Yet when my cousin and sister-in-law came to visit me they were surprised at how much thinner I looked than yesterday. My cousin's big, bright eyes were filled with tears. This is not surprising. It is human nature to desire life. In one's life journey, which is plagued with poisonous snakes and wild animals, it is unnatural not to fight hard for survival.

Trying to cheer me up, my cousin brought me a pot of flowers. They are red with a hint of purple and their light fragrance fills my nostrils. But they only make me feel sadder than ever. I remember the pot of cherry-apple blossoms you gave me and how beautiful the flowers were against the light. I remember you reading under the cherry-apple tree in your garden. Flowers are symbols of love. I watered the flowers you gave me with the essence of my heart. When you were reading under the flowers, my soul watched over you. And now? The giver of flowers and the receiver of flowers are both victims of nature's cruelness. Seeing the flowers that I love wilt, how can I be comforted?

This afternoon, I again heard my mother talking to my sister about our plans last winter, berating us mercilessly. My Love! It is said that everything that is planned in the name of love can be forgiven. Don't they understand this?

Thank heavens! My cousin has been able to get in touch with you. Otherwise, we wouldn't even be able to die together. But I'll tell you the horrible news: According to my cousin, the Liu family son will arrive home tonight at midnight. If I do not try to leave this place before that, then, as I have said before, this enemy of mine will be the one to witness my last moments on earth. I don't have to say anymore. You can guess what I mean.

My Love, although we still have one ray of hope to see each other again, the dark-robed spirit of death is already hovering over me. We have perhaps come to the last page of the chronicle of our love. We have been with each other for about five years. We have not yet been able to contribute anything to society despite our education, but we should value our own short history. We should respect our spirit of determination. No matter what happens, we will not give in to the powers that oppose our own beliefs. We have trodden the bloody path of death in order to pursue our freedom to love. We should forge a way for other young people and wish them better success. I will not feel bad even though others might think me mediocre. If I escape, we will run away together to the middle of the ocean. We will listen to the roaring waves. We will gaze upon the mysterious moon. But if I die, you must not lose heart. You must write out the history of our love, from the beginning to the end. You must organize and publish our six hundred love letters.

My cousin is here. She is willing to deliver this letter to you. She also told me that there is a quiet alley beyond the wall next to my window. Wait for me on the other side of the wall tonight at midnight.

Translated by Janet Ng

5

Shi Pingmei

Shi Pingmei (1902–1928)

A native of Shanxi province, Shi Pingmei attended girls' schools there before enrolling in Beijing Women's Normal College in 1920. She majored in, and subsequently taught, physical education, a subject that had steadily gained support among educators who believed that modern Chinese women should be strong in both body and mind. As an active member of political and social circles associated with the May Fourth Movement, Shi Pingmei voiced her opinions in frequent essays on women's rights, Marxism, and social reform. Her poetry also appeared in prominent literary journals of the period, and she quickly became a popular member of the first generation of vernacular, free-verse poets in China. Between 1926 and 1928, Shi Pingmei coedited *The Wild Rose*, a literary supplement to a popular Beijing daily, with her friend Lu Jingqing. Shi's abrupt death in 1928 from encephalitis prompted an outpouring of grief by admirers, friends, and former students who devoted eulogies and special magazine issues to her.

Shi Pingmei produced some of the most insightful and impassioned literary works of the early May Fourth period, but she is primarily remembered in China today for her romance with Gao Junyu, a founding member of the Chinese Communist Party. Although deeply in love with Gao, Shi broke off her relationship with him so as not to harm the woman to whom he was betrothed through an arranged marriage in his hometown. After Gao Junyu's sudden death in 1925, Shi Pingmei's close friend and fellow writer, Lu Yin, turned the story of their tragic love into the novel *Ivory Rings*. Shi Pingmei was buried by Gao's side in Taoran Pavilion Park on the outskirts of Beijing, and their engraved tombstones remain a favorite pilgrimage spot for romantic young lovers.

The short story translated here, "Lin Nan's Diary," posthumously published in *Red and Black Magazine* in 1928, describes a love triangle much like the one in which Shi Pingmei found herself involved. What makes this story especially fascinating, however, is that unlike other works of the period dealing with this subject matter, Shi Pingmei's story is told not from the point of view of the modern woman lover—the character the author was undoubtedly most familiar with—but from that of the traditional wife who is left behind to take care of the children and her husband's family. Shi Pingmei uses her writing to explore how actions that may seem revolutionary and liberating to women privileged enough to be independent and educated might have serious repercussions for other women not so lucky.

In the second selection, "Lusha—A Letter to Lu Yin," Shi Pingmei also questions the meaning of life for educated women like herself who have political convictions and lofty ambitions but few opportunities to realize them. This is one of many poetic letters that Shi Pingmei wrote to her close friends Lu Yin and Lu Jingqing. She addresses the letter to "Lusha," one of the characters in Lu Yin's famous story "Seaside Friends," and signs it "Bowei," a pen name Shi Pingmei often used. Despite their obviously intimate nature and frequent allusions to private experiences, letters of this nature were often published in major literary supplements. This one appeared in 1924 in *Women's Weekly*, a supplement to the *Beijing Daily*. Although later dismissed by critics as narrow and irrelevant, this very public form of private writing was exceedingly popular among women writers and readers in the mid-1920s. The response Lu Yin wrote to Shi Pingmei's despondent letter is included in the following section of the anthology.

LIN NAN'S DIARY
(1928)

July 30

Little Rong began coughing again today. Mother said she must have caught cold last night, but the implication was that I am too careless. Little Rong is really such a nuisance these days; she never stops crying. Father and Mother have been thinking about Lin recently and it just grieves them more to hear Rong cry. When I asked Mother for some medicine, her expression was so pained that I could feel my hand shaking as I reached to take the small yellow bottle from her. After Rong took the medicine, Granny Zhang held her until she fell asleep while I went to serve Mother and Father dinner.

Lin drifts about like duckweed on the surface of a pond, and something always seems to come between him and the family. We all yearn to see him and our anticipation of his return has mounted ever since the Nationalist Party banners began waving from the walls of the old city. Yet the days keep passing without any word from him. Could Lin have forgotten his home? Or is there something else holding him back? Only Heaven knows.

At mealtime each day, the whole family sits in sullen silence. I take up a bit of food, but my throat is too tight to swallow anything. Sometimes Mother drones on and on with her complaints while Father doesn't say a word, and I just put down my chopsticks and listen to her. She interrupts the usual void of deathly silence the way an unexpected wind whips up the sea, refusing to let it remain calm.

After dinner, I was washing little Lian's ears in the bedroom when I heard Mother call me. I went upstairs to find Father holding a letter in his hand. Mother laughed and said, "Lin will be coming home soon!"

In the letter, written on the fifteenth, Lin says that he has been delayed in Shanghai for a few days, but hopes he will arrive home within a day or two. This news comes as a wonderful surprise—as welcome as the sudden appearance of a crystal-clear blue sky after the clouds and fog of a dark overcast day have dispersed. All seems brilliant and perfect before me now. A fiery-red dawn has replaced the lacquer-black night, and Lin is nothing less than a glittering star.

At that moment, the mist and gloom vanished instantly. Everybody's spirits have been lifted, and even the servants seem to be working more diligently. In no time at all they hurried to sweep the room and prepare Lin's bedding. Granny Zhang said, "Miss Rong is seeing her daddy for the first time. Let's dress her up in some pretty clothes!" I laughed and kissed Rong's rosy cheeks, and she laughed too as she clapped her little hands together.

After languishing away in pain for three long years, my heart is pounding and feels more troubled today than ever! I am a little scared to see Lin. I pulled out my light emerald-colored silk blouse from the bureau and gazed at myself in the mirror, thinking how thin and pale I have become. I wonder if I will look the same to Lin? I couldn't keep from crying! Afterward, I thought: Be patient. These tears should fall on Lin's shoulder, where he can warmly kiss them away along with all my sorrow!

As I look up, the flower vase smiles and even the lamplight appears unusually bright. It seems to be teasing me deliberately, following me wherever I go. Away with you, lamplight! When Lin comes back, you can cast both of our shadows together.

At eleven o'clock, Mother still hadn't gone to bed, so I urged her to go to sleep. He probably won't get back tonight, I told her.

As little Lan wasn't asleep either, I teased her, "Daddy won't come home until you start dreaming!" She actually went right to sleep, though after a while she raised her tiny head again and asked me, "Is Daddy home yet?"

Beneath the grape trellis in the garden, I prepared some ice cream, drinks, and fruit. The fire in the kitchen was not yet out, so the whole garden was filled with light as if it were daytime. I waited impatiently, walking quietly through the front gate. The night was still and the alley chilly; there was not a single sound anywhere. A pair of stars at the edge of the Milky Way and a crescent moon faintly illuminated this dreamlike, quiet bit of earth. Then a car horn blared in the distance, and I listened with bated breath. Could that be him? But gradually it faded away, leaving only the cold curtain of night to envelop me as I stood in my light clothes in the heavy, frosty dew.

Two o'clock. Realizing he probably wouldn't return, I let the servants go to bed. From behind the window, Mother called out, "He definitely won't be home tonight, go to sleep!" I know that Mother is still as awake as I am. Even asleep our hearts remain vigilant.

August 2

Lin returned home last night. As I lift my pen to write these words, my heart is in knots.

My brother-in-law Jing and his girlfriend Xiu Qin came back with him. Xiu Qin comes from the same village as my sister-in-law Dai, and they also went to school together, so they are very close. Even before they got here, I had already heard all about Xiu and Jing from Dai. In our house, these lovebirds are like a pair of young swallows who just flew in. Everyone welcomes them with curiosity and pleasure. They certainly are children of fortune sheltered beneath the wings of the god of love.

Xiu is an energetic and aggressive girl who radiates with a spirit of rebellion. She spent over a year in Russia, and she still possesses a bit of the zeal of "New Russia." To a family like ours, she seems like a reformer with a tocsin in one hand and a torch in the other. I, my body in chains and my heart marked with scars, am nothing like her. Although I am just six years older than she is, the times have left me behind. Mother silently shakes her head at Xiu in disapproval, but me, I yearn to discover what it is that lights up her world in order that it might penetrate the darkness of my own.

Lin! I still call him by this familiar name but I know that his soul is no longer joined to mine.

Fate warns me that a deep, dark chasm lies before me and that I ought to hold back my tears so that I can edge around it one step at a time. The future is so uncertain; I don't know where it will lead me. Surrounded by a shadowy forest, all I hear is Lin's voice gradually fading into the distance and the mournful call of a barn owl in a far-off, secluded valley. I awake from this dream to find myself crying alone, left by the wayside.

Lin has not spoken more than ten words to me since last night. Wherever I go, he avoids me. And I hesitate to approach him, with his frosty demeanor and those eyes filled with anger and resentment. Last night after he got back, he rushed the servants to make up a bed for him in the outer room and when I brought out the lilac silk comforter, he threw it on the floor. Even Granny Zhang was taken aback by his rage.

I couldn't sleep the whole night. I stood silently at the head of his bed and listened to his thunderous snoring. When I went back into the inner room, I thought I heard him turn over and then sigh faintly. I'm sure he is troubled by some deep secret tormenting his heart, but what could it be? As hard as I try, I can't understand why he is annoyed with me or why he avoids me. The third time I went over to his bed, I called softly, "Lin." But he seemed as distant from me as the most remote corner of the earth. My trembling voice echoed in the silence, yet no one answered. I collapsed on the side of his bed in disappointment. This is how I passed Lin's first night home.

August 3

As the first rays of the morning sun filtered through the gauze drapery, my heart filled with gloom. After I washed and dressed, I walked to the head of Lin's bed. His eyes were closed, but he was already awake. I had thought to go over quietly to wake him and speak to him for a while, but I dreaded his steely cold expression. I could hear my own excited breathing, and I couldn't keep my eyes from filling with tears. I was afraid of making him mad, so I quickly walked away.

I gently pushed open Mother's door, and she called from behind the bed curtain, "Who is it?" My throat was too tight to answer. Mother went on, "Why get up so early? Let him sleep a bit longer. If you're up, you're sure to wake him." I didn't know what to say, so I stood dumbly in front of the bed curtain. Mother thought this was odd and after she got dressed and lifted the curtain, she glanced at me and said, "Lin Nan, what has gotten into you?" As I folded up her flannel blanket, Granny Zhang came in with water for her to wash with.

There were many visitors today. Elder Sister and Dai, my sister-in-law, came as well, but Lin was even cold to them. Elder Sister sat politely for a while and then left. Dai was bewildered; she just kept staring blankly at me, and then back at Lin.

Lin went straight to bed after dinner. Even Father and Mother have hardly had a chance to talk with him, and Mother seems a little upset, complaining that we shouldn't have even welcomed him back. It's becoming increasingly awkward for Jing and Xiu; they have to deal with me, while at the same time maintaining their relationship with Lin. It's a very tense situation for everyone.

By chance, Mother opened Jing's leather trunk and came across a bunch of photo albums containing pictures of them all together. Besides Jing and Xiu, there were also pictures of Lin and Miss Qian together, mostly taken at West Lake. I smiled when I saw Lin's photo! Mother simply stated, "Oh, so it's her." Jing and Xiu exchanged startled glances.

Miss Qian is from our village. She was enrolled at Beijing University, but last year, during the warlord crackdown on students in Beijing, she herself came under suspicion and fled to Nanjing. At the time, Lin happened to be the head of an army supply station there, so he helped her out. As his living quarters were roomy, Xiu, Jing, and Miss Qian all lived there together. The circumstances brought Jing and Xiu together, so naturally they did the same for Lin and Qian. Love develops easily in such a romantic setting. In a letter Lin wrote me last year while he was recovering in Hangzhou, he mentioned how kind Miss Qian had been to nurse him through his illness. I thought the warm concern Miss Qian showed for him when he was sick and away from home was exceptional and I was deeply grateful. But I always believed that Miss Qian knew all about me and of course I never imagined that Lin would transfer his love for me to someone else. At the time, it didn't even cross my mind that they were more than friends.

But now I know the truth!

Oh God! I haven't the strength to quell the anguish burning in my heart. It's up to Lin what becomes of the rest of us; he can leave me, abandon me, and ruin my life. I am clearly the most pained and pathetic of women; can they really go on loving each other without any misgivings? I have come to see myself as no more than a pitiful victim taunted by human fate!

August 5

Last night I asked Lin, "If something's bothering you, go ahead and tell me about it, and I will think of a way out for you. There must be a reason why you are depressed like this all the time! You are such a determined man, why don't you pluck up a little courage?"

I asked him several times, but he only answered coldly, "Nothing is wrong, stop worrying." When I asked him again, he had already turned toward the wall pretending to be asleep; he seemed annoyed at even having to listen to me.

This time I was really angry. How I wished I could hit or bite him, only then would I feel satisfied. In the middle of the night, he got up and poured some water into a flask for himself. I slipped on my shoes and fetched sodas from the icebox for him, and he drank both of the bottles I opened. This seemed to cool his anger, so I leaned on the table and asked him, "Lin, what have I done to offend you? Whatever it is, I'm sorry. Please just tell me frankly. Surely you know that my living here at home is all for your benefit—serving your parents, raising the children, I have never once complained. Why are you so angry with me? As hard as I try, I cannot understand why your feelings for me have changed. What problem could possibly be so hard to resolve? Tell me and I will help you find a way to work this out. I'll do anything to help you succeed just as long as it makes you happy. How can moaning and groaning all day long help matters?

"Father and Mother were looking forward to your return so much that they could barely eat or sleep, but you've been so cold and disagreeable to the family. See how upset Mother has looked these past few days? Today she was crying in Father's room. You've been gone for three years and it was such an event for you to return home. I never imagined you would treat me like this."

Lin stood up and yawned, replying, "Of course I'm sorry, but Mother and Father owe me an apology too! Let's not talk about this anymore. Go to bed!" He walked straight back to his bed, turned over, covered his head with the flannel blanket, and fell asleep.

I stood next to the table transfixed, gazing at the dreary light under the green lampshade and crying. It was clear that he could hear me, but he paid no attention. Lin, my love flows like water, but your heart is as hard as iron. Lin, you used to be so tender and loving; now you're so close to me, yet so terribly far away.

August 7

This morning I had just fallen asleep when Lin started banging about as he rummaged through the chests and drawers.

Dai arrived carrying a big parcel. She sat down and spread its contents out over the bed: a little foreign stuffed dog, a diary, a camera, leather shoes, handkerchiefs, silk stockings, material, and other things. She asked me childishly, "Sister-in-Law! What did my brother bring for you? He just gave me all of this, including some things that I really like. He certainly knows how to give a woman gifts—so unique and appropriate."

I forced a smile, and she continued on, "Sister-in-Law, I get along with you so I'm going to tell you something on the sly, but you must not bring it up with Third Brother, otherwise he'll hate me."

"Whatever could deserve such secrecy?"

"Xiu came over to my place yesterday, and when I mentioned that you were not feeling well, she heaved a sigh! I asked her 'Why is my brother quarreling with Sister-in-Law?' She laughed and said how should she know. Only after pressing her did I find out what my brother's been up to. He and Miss Qian have been close friends for over a year now, and he's very serious about her. Why on earth he loves her is a mystery; no one understands it. It grew out of a particular set of circumstances—whenever he was sick, it was always Miss Qian who came to take care of him and to prepare his medicine for him. Do you think that a lonely man in the company of an affectionate and sympathetic woman could resist falling in love?! Especially in such a romantic southern setting. After she left Nanjing, my brother stopped working and applied for a vacation in order to go to see her in Hangzhou, where he rented a little house on West Lake. He claimed he was recuperating in Hangzhou, but what exactly was his illness? Her! He rarely even brings up the matter with Jing or the others, and if he wanted to settle it once and for all, he wouldn't know where to start.

"As for formally marrying Miss Qian, I'm afraid she herself would be unwilling! Perhaps she does have some ulterior motive—as they say, 'a drunkard's thoughts are never on the cup!' My brother is an honest man. If he weren't so honest, he would never have been this stupid, returning home and treating you, his own wife, as he has. Don't feel bad, he and Miss Qian won't last long together. I've heard that she wants to go back to Guangxi, and once they have separated, their love will fade. Then he'll be yours once again, Lin Nan. This time you shouldn't stay here at home, but go with him. Foreign couples never separate since there's no way of guaranteeing what might happen when they're apart. It is only in China that men go away on business and fool around for over ten years without coming home, leaving their wives behind to suffer in tears. No wonder Chinese literature is filled with so many boudoir laments that go on and on about grieving in spring and griping in autumn, and all those never-ending sad partings and joyful reunions."

I laughed at what she said—Dai certainly has a glib tongue; no wonder yesterday Lin told Mother and Father that his sister was a little like Wang Xifeng![1]

I took some lily powder to bolster my strength. Tomorrow is Father's birthday and I'll have to attend to everything, otherwise Mother will complain. Lin can go ahead and ignore and spurn me, but I won't leave his family—one day he'll have to take responsibility. Xiu laughs at how strong my old-fashioned moral outlook is, but such is my fate. In this situation, I have little recourse since I have already become a victim of the times. If someday Xiu and Jing marry properly, her position in the family will be different from mine. Everyone will assume that it's natural for her to just sit by and watch, eat, talk, and laugh as if she were a guest; in my position, however, such behavior would be impermissible. I am a daughter-in-law married into the family, not a lover invited in.

August 9

With misunderstanding comes pain. No one is willing to speak about their true feelings openly. When you want to cry, you must swallow your tears and put on a smile, and although you can't stand a certain person, outwardly you must still act affectionately. Such empty hypocrisy arises from the basic morality of the Chinese people; it permeates the society, every family, and every individual. I detest it, and yet I am unable to behave otherwise. How can anyone ever express their true self in all its nakedness within such an environment?

In my family, old and young alike have their problems and worries, as do even our guests. The only exceptions are my three innocent little children.

---

1. Wang Xifeng is a feisty, outspoken female character in the famous classical Chinese novel, *Dream of the Red Chamber*.

Yesterday, Father celebrated his birthday, and on the surface it was quite festive after all the guests arrived. Dai was particularly happy, dashing back and forth, filling the place with her voice and physical presence. Lin says she's an actress and even offstage she shines in her role. Like everyone, I really adore her; she's so competent and pretty, and her manner is so gentle and kind. No matter what she does, she does it just right and never complains in the least. The money she earns as a schoolteacher is more than adequate for a single person, so she is unfettered and free of worries. No one ever bullies her and she never has to think about pleasing anyone. How fortunate she is! If I were more like her, I would never have let Lin take over my entire existence. I have practically become his plaything: when he loves me, I am content; when he hates me, I suffer; and when he casts me aside, all I can do is sit by and cry. I would never dare take my anger and walk out the door like Ibsen's Nora.

At lunch, Xiu and Dai got drunk. Lin was a bit tipsy as well. Xiu seemed upset about something, and drinking a few cups of wine only seemed to aggravate her. She lay on Jing's bed, tossing about, crying! She really is such a liberated girl, never giving a thought to anything. Behind her back, Mother cursed her for being such an ill-mannered girl with no sense of propriety or shame about other people's scorn for her. Crying on Father's birthday like she did is considered taboo. But actually, why would any of them care about that? They're used to being on their own, so they are free to drink themselves into a stupor and laugh up a storm or wreak havoc crying whenever they feel like it. Who would dare to interfere? I think that Jing and Xiu will do best to have their own small family, as they could never survive in an extended household like this! The new and the old clash in violent opposition in too many places. Mother always says, "You all are so fortunate. Back when we were daughters-in-law, we had to do everything ourselves. We were on our feet the whole day filling the pipes of our parents-in-law and pouring their tea, and at night we still had to make socks for our sisters and brothers-in-law. We could never act like you, having fun all day long and thinking nothing of flitting off to the park or the cinema." She never mentions how many years' difference in age there are between us, but just keeps on about how she suffered in her youth. She envies our generation, and yet we are still dissatisfied with life as it is now.

Last night I didn't get to sleep until three o'clock. I hadn't much energy to start off with, and then I still had to work hard all day. After washing up, I fainted into a chair, immobilized from exhaustion. Lin saw me but didn't even come over to ask how I was.

Leaning on the wall, I made my way into the inner room where I collapsed on the bed and wept silently! I can't help thinking about my lot in life. Who else do I have in this world other than Lin? My own mother and father died long ago, and I haven't a single brother or sister. I came to the Wei family all alone and have suffered through so much abuse here, yet I always felt that as long as somewhere in this world Lin loved me, it didn't matter what I had to endure in his family. I have spent fifteen years like this and have never once complained about my fate. Now, however, my last links to happiness have been severed and I am falling into a deep, dark abyss.

Exhausted from crying, I turned to look at little Rong sleeping so adorably. My tears had trickled onto her face, leaving it stained with the tokens of a mother's broken heart. Besides her, only Heaven knows my grief. In the middle of the night, I got up and went to look at Lin, who was asleep facing the wall. When I unconsciously stroked his head, my hand came away damp. Oh! I realized then that Lin too had been crying secretly! Feeling even worse, I leaned over him and asked, "Lin, why?" He did not answer. After I asked him three more times, he threw off the quilt, turned over and said furiously, "Tomorrow I'm moving into a hotel. Every night you disturb me so I can't sleep. Why, you ask? You tell me why."

I am not scared of him, but I left it at that to avoid making a scene.

August 11th

Dai came over today. She had just come from Jing's room, and when she saw how distraught I looked she couldn't help heaving a sigh, saying, "In this family, the joys are too joyous and the worries too worrisome. I really don't know how to deal with it. I come into the eastern wing and you're putting on a tragedy; I go into the western wing and they're acting out a comedy. You had better clear this up with Lin. What an attitude he has! This is not such a big deal anyway. Times have changed, and besides, you are a graduate of a teachers' school with a decent education, and you don't deserve to endure such painful days in this kind of family. Sister-in-Law, I totally sympathize with you and pity you. Besides, I can help you. But if you keep on crying like this, you are going to get sick, and that won't help solve the problem!"

"What can I say to him?" I replied. "He just ignores me, and I realize now that the two of us are through. There is nothing holding us together any longer. Love can't be forced. Naturally he's also suffering terribly since he can't be with the one he loves, while the one he doesn't love is constantly around him and won't be shooed away. Even when he does drive me away, I keep coming back to bother him. If he officially divorces me now, that's fine, but I'm afraid Mother and Father will not agree to it.

"The truth is, I may be his wife, but I am also their daughter-in-law. They are becoming more and more dependent on me, and if I were to leave, who would be willing to spend so many years staying at home taking care of them? Mother has never been satisfied with me and thinks that I don't work as hard as she did when she was a daughter-in-law, but in comparison to someone like Xiu, I am every bit the traditional woman. She's a rebel intent on reforming precisely this kind of family. She may be Jing's lover, but she could never be a daughter-in-law.

"If I left the Wei family, I wouldn't become a beggar; even if I only worked as a servant I could support my basic needs. But I can't bear to part with my three children, Lian, Lan, and Rong. How could I be so hardhearted as to make them suffer the pain of losing their mother? Little Lian is already a perceptive child; she's not deaf, and when she sees me cry, she cries too! Sometimes at night when she hears me sobbing, she jumps out of bed and comes over and hugs me, saying, 'Mommy, don't cry, Mommy, don't cry!' Yesterday, little Lan told Mother, 'Granny, Daddy is being mean to Mommy and making her cry! Why don't you scold Daddy?' In their little hearts they already know how pitiful their mother is. It's too awful to even think about what their fates would be like if I were really to leave. I am willing to endure this miserable life for them."

As I was talking with Dai, Lin sent the maid to call her over. After a while, I heard a car horn honk as Dai and Lin left to go to the movies.

Even though it was awkward for her to broach this subject, Dai handled it in a flawless manner that revealed her utmost consideration for all those involved.

I suspect that the reason Dai pressed me to resolve this problem is that Lin had deliberately asked her to come sound me out and to get me to bring up the matter of a divorce from him. If this really is the case, he is simply being too vicious. Even though he is the one leaving me, he won't admit to anything and would rather humiliate me in front of the others. Mother's already somewhat unhappy with me; she says that before he came back I was longing for his return, but now that he's back I keep losing my temper and irritating him. She won't blame him, so she blames me.

I can't even cry anymore because if I do they'll curse me for "driving him away." Lin himself keeps saying that he can't stand these family woes for a second longer. But has anyone ever put themselves in my shoes?

Last night Xiu said to me, "This family is so stifling, you'd be better off if you went ahead and got this thing out in the open, but no one's willing to take off their mask and stop being so completely superficial. I am thinking of going home to visit my mother in a few days. It's oppressive at my sister-in-law's place as well since they joke about the issue of my marriage all day long, but staying here is too awkward. Sister-in-Law, you stay so calm, but if I were you, I would have run away long ago. Jing used to brag about how good and kind his family is, and how good-tempered his parents are. But now that I have come here and had a look for myself, I can see that this isn't the case at all. To be honest, Sister-in-Law, I am really sorry about all this. Brother Lin and you were such a loving couple, but now on account of that Miss Qian he's made such a mess of things. How do I know my Jing won't turn out to be like this eventually as well?! Hmmmm. Men are all so untrustworthy."

I don't know why she was grumbling to me like this, but I didn't utter a word and simply smiled.

August 15

I've been in a terrible mood lately. I don't even feel like writing in my diary anymore.

I think about leaving. I think about dying. I think about having to keep on living like this.

LUSHA—A LETTER TO LU YIN
(1924)

Dear Lusha,

Last night, for some reason, I paced up and down the corridors. A curtain of clouds blocked off the moonlight, and even the twinkling of the tiny stars couldn't be seen. I simply sat in silence, staring off blankly into the distant darkness, allowing my thoughts to wander wildly.

The rhythmic beating of a fortune-teller's drum broke the silence of this remote alleyway. I leaned on the balcony railing and thought of the past, back to that poetic evening and the two of us so mournful and impassioned.

I remember an ancient twisted pine drooping its long branches in the evening wind as pairs of crows flew overhead and quickly disappeared into the deep forest. You walked slowly along the silent pathway. Suddenly you stopped, grasped my hand, and said, "Bowei! Only here, on this piece of earth, among these fallen leaves, at this hour, does all the world belong to us."

Without answering, I bent over to pick up a bright red maple leaf and press it between the pages of my book. As we silently passed through the deep autumn pine forest, I slowed down, falling behind a few paces and staring after your thin, hunched shoulders and your hurried steps—they seemed to tell me of the heavy burden weighing on your shoulders.

We walked to a pavilion by the lotus pond and sat on a mossy stone, raising our heads to gaze up at the clear blue sky. The red pillars of the waterside pavilion were reflected in the pool, twisting and turning like dancing water dragons. Skylarks sang in the trees and the soon-to-be-dormant autumn cicadas began chirping. The white swans curled their necks, burying their blood-red beaks and black eyes under snowy down wings; mandarin ducks stirred up ripples, swimming here and there, heads erect. The emerald-green wooden railing erected there by the intelligent race acted as a clever barrier.

I was already feeling a bit intoxicated when I looked over to see you staring at some moss on a stone with a mysterious look of mirth in your eyes that I couldn't tell was of ridicule or praise! You slowly stood up and I walked with you aimlessly. Arriving at the vast grain altar, you gathered up your skirt and in a burst of energy boldly jumped up on the marble steps. Your face beamed with the pride and demeanor of a queen as a warm fragrant breeze seductively wrapped around and caressed you like the swan-feather fan of a lady-in-waiting. Deep in the forest to the west, among slowly drifting clouds and a thicket of leaves, the corner of a quiet, locked palace appeared.

We leaned against each other; the evening glow on the horizon resembled a silk veil covering a young girl's flushed cheeks or a bouquet of roses being offered by a lover. Slowly fading, slowly fading, until only a few streaks of a blue and purple rainbow remained; the misty dusk resonated with poetry.

Far away, a military band played a mournful tune, and you, stepping lightly in Tartar boots, belted out the "Ancient Soldier" tune. Although I wanted to laugh at your wild abandonment, as I hesitated a sudden gust of cold, wintry wind scattered the warmth of my thoughts. Dully, I circled the altar, silently counting the carved stones. Suddenly you turned and called out to me: "Life's meetings and departures are uncertain—in the blink of an eye we will part ways. Today is a rare occasion, let us try to be happy!"

I was so moved at the time that I was unable to utter a word; even now I feel the same way, and I think that in the future when I leaf back through the many pages of this history, I'll probably still be unable to say anything.

We can only chase our memories, for all inevitably fades away. But as we are deep in thought late at night, the past is not always empty. If you can picture the Bowei of this evening lost in some remote corner of the world, then you can recall the romantic vestiges of the past. But I rarely dare to think of it, I don't want to; blooming flowers fill my courtyard every month, a silver glow shines through my curtains every night; these things never change. But me! I am often caught beneath the turning wheels of the gods; what I desire never waits for me, and what I fear constantly returns. Lusha! All that I once thought and hoped for only depresses me now!

Since you've gone, a lonely atmosphere has turned the "white room"[2] into a desolate tomb under the waning moon and cold winds, and I'm like a specter haunting a dark valley or deep forest. Only now do I find that our pessimistic conversations and wild adventures of the past have all become comforting and exhilarating. During my long period of depression, I wanted to write to you countless times, but lazy as I am, I have left my pen idle until now. On my last journey from Beijing to Wuhan, I read your story "The Past" and thought of the comments you urged me to write and that I had intended to make, but this time what you hoped for will really be delivered.

In your last letter I could detect some bits of unreconciled ambition still faintly lurking in your tender words. I would feel so happy if that were true! Sometimes people get tangled in the net of the world for no reason; but when a hunter is about to shoot down the little bird soaring through the clouds, who can prevent it? Who can escape? The traps of love are the same.

You and I met by chance, and came together inadvertently—all orchestrated by the gods—everything else is unnecessary. I still have great hopes that, amidst the finery of life and aside from the daily toil, you will continue to pursue your goals and diligently persist in your unfinished work; that is why I often take the trouble to wake you up from your sweet dreams. But when a person comes from lush green mountains and streams to a rugged, thorny path and then departs from those rugged thorns again for a village shaded by willows and abloom with flowers, she's already world-weary, and in this day and age, she's already come to a new understanding of life.

---

2. The teacher's office at Beijing Women's Normal College where Shi Pingmei and Lu Yin spent much of their time while they were both teaching there.

When we were in school, I noticed your bold and spontaneous manner and once commented to Wan that you were a "female hero." Then when I saw you and Zongying gulping down food in the thatched hut in the park, I told Wan that you were a "carefree talent." Thinking of the image I have of you from your days in Japan, I see you wielding your pen like a sword, spreading out white paper like a cloud, standing atop a lofty mountain peak, overlooking the rushing waters of a mighty falls. Rapt in thought, you stood alone, facing the rivers and mountains that played before you like eulogies. At some point, however, the weathered pine tree has been transformed into a rose drooping in the sun.

But the moment we are reminded of the downtrodden state of women in China, our frail shoulders must take on the spirit of vanguards, bearing the responsibility of leading the struggle. Lusha, I urge you to work hard for the future glory of thousands of our compatriots and not to toss it all aside for your own personal reasons.

Naturally, I am still just as reclusive as ever, searching for my own peace and doing my best to avoid the dusty world, but I can't always help getting caught up by humanity. Eventually, however, I plan to follow two paths, but I've vowed not to tell you about them for now, so why don't you take a guess?

I used to laugh when you said, "I've always just played with life, never thinking that life would play with me." But lately I've come to understand what these words of blood and tears mean. Now I am extricating myself from certain bindings. I still can't predict what will happen, but the hopelessness of the situation has for the most part been exposed, giving me a hint of my future fears. But Lusha! Strong convictions have already taken root in the barren space of my heart so that even if my body degenerates, my determination will never change! As long as my blood continues flowing, my emotions will forever remain in turmoil; I know that I will cause trouble for myself as well as others, but ignorant and stubborn as I am, I've already sworn to my soul that I will forge ahead.

Bowei
September 10, 1924

6

Lu Yin

Lu Yin (1898–1934)

From birth, Lu Yin (born Huang Luyin) faced a series of challenges and setbacks that plagued her short life. Her mother, an illiterate and superstitious woman, considered Lu Yin an evil presence in the family because her own mother died on the very day of Lu Yin's birth. Lu Yin's father was an educated Qing dynasty bureaucrat but was indifferent to his infant daughter, and she was sent to live with a wet nurse in the countryside. She was later essentially abandoned by her family in a Protestant missionary school outside Beijing. Ironically, it was her family's rejection that enabled Lu Yin to obtain the education she needed to become a professional writer and teacher, and to develop the fierce independence for which she would later become famous.

In 1919, after teaching and saving her money for two years, Lu Yin enrolled in the newly opened Beijing Women's Normal College along with future women writers Feng Yuanjun and Su Xuelin, and later Shi Pingmei. Lu Yin flourished at the college. She became involved in May Fourth student politics, published her first essays and short stories in the school's literary magazine, and forged deep friendships with several of her classmates, most notably with Shi Pingmei. Like so many women writers of the period, Lu Yin launched her literary career while still a student with the encouragement of a male mentor. The well-known literary critic Zheng Zhenduo, also a native of Fujian, recommended one of Lu Yin's early stories for publication in the influential literary journal *Short Story Monthly* in 1921. Lu Yin never stopped writing after this, publishing a steady stream of fiction, essays (both personal and political), and poetry until her tragic death after childbirth, at the age of 36, in 1934.

In an autobiography written shortly before her death, Lu Yin divided her literary career into three periods. Her first stories followed patterns typical of early May Fourth realist Woman Question fiction by depicting young women and men whose lives and dreams are derailed by the dictates of traditional Confucian rules of decorum, particularly the custom of arranged marriages. After a series of ill-fated teaching jobs and love affairs, the style and attitude of Lu Yin's writing changed dramatically. No longer did she write with an optimism and idealism for the future; instead the first-person narrators in her pieces agonized over the futility of life.

The two selections translated here, "After Victory" and "News From the Seashore," a response to her close friend Shi Pingmei's letter "Lusha" (see the previous section of this anthology), are both from this middle period of Lu Yin's literary career. Before her untimely death, Lu Yin changed her style yet again as she experimented with fictional biography, travel writing, and novels in an attempt to produce the more socially engaged writing that came into vogue in the 1930s.

Published in 1925 in *Short Story Monthly*, "After Victory" is similar to Lu Yin's best-known work, the novella "Seaside Friends." Both are long, emotionally brooding pieces written in the first person and embedded with letters and conversations telling the stories of several college girlfriends. After graduating with high hopes for their futures and marrying their "true loves" (thereby, refusing to allow their parents to arrange marriages for them), the friends discover that life after the "victory" of breaking with traditional social conventions and obtaining an education does not offer them the satisfaction they had expected. The characters are lonely, despondent, and mourning the loss of the support and intimacy of close female friendships and the hopes and dreams of their college days. Lu Yin's style is not subtle, but it was hugely popular among the first graduates of women's high schools and colleges, who were by the mid-1920s beginning to feel that their aspirations were not being achieved.

Shortly after Lu Yin completed "Seaside Friends," her first husband, Guo Mengliang, died suddenly, leaving her with an infant daughter. Wandering from her in-laws' home back to Shanghai and then finally to Beijing, Lu Yin fell into a deep state of depression that no doubt influenced the dark, melancholic tone of her stories and letters from the mid-1920s. The letter translated here, "News From the Seashore," was written for her closest friend Shi Pingmei (whom she called Bowei) and published in *Women's Weekly* in

1925. The death of Shi Pingmei in 1928 plunged Lu Yin further into despair. In 1930, she married her second husband, the poet Li Weijian. Their marriage caused a great stir—particularly after the couple serialized their love letters in a newspaper in 1931—as Li Weijian was nine years Lu Yin's junior. Unfortunately, Lu Yin's tragic death came only a year after she had written optimistically, "I would like to devote my entire life to literature, and I hope that when I write my autobiography at sixty I will have written two or three successful works."

NEWS FROM THE SEASHORE—
A LETTER TO SHI PINGMEI
(1925)

Bowei!

Ever since the arrival of spring, the mornings have been overcast and grey. As I, bored, "lean on my pillow listening to the new rain, lethargically pondering the past," the copy of *Women's Weekly* you sent unexpectedly arrived. I read the column "Oceans of the Heart" and knew that hundreds of miles away an old friend still thought of Lusha, forlorn by the sea! Thank you for your compassion and good intentions! You've pulled me from the freezing depths, rekindling the ashes of my spirit that had grown cold!

How could I ever forget that beautiful autumn day in the park among sturdy pines and cypress trees. In the tranquil autumn sunlight, a light breeze gently tousled our hair and blew up the flaps of our thin gowns, as we vigorously lifted our voices to the wind, singing boldly and carefree. Before we knew it, we had come upon a bed of chrysanthemums. Those proud, wiry autumn mums stood before us smiling and nodding their heads. Staring quietly at the sky, deep in thought, you suddenly whispered, "A lone symbol of defiance, where are you going to hide? You blossom as other flowers, but why do you bloom so late?" At the time, I joked with you, "They've been left as undisturbed as water at the bottom of an ancient well, why do you make waves now? Unknowing before, will the chrysanthemums now gain boundless magical powers?" These few words were spoken in jest at the time, but thinking back upon them now, I am filled with emotions.

Since our parting, you've traveled north, getting your fill of cold indifference. And me? I've disappeared down south, my heart withering more with each passing day. How can I say I am playing with the world, when it's more truthful to say that I am merely deceiving others and myself!

I try to listen for the faint sounds of my heartstrings; but has that anguished murmur ever come to a halt even momentarily? The universe has never been benevolent—earthly matters amount to little more than sacrificial straw dogs[1]—so when we shut tight the doors of our hearts and sing the praises of an ideal life, we aren't trying deliberately to deceive ourselves, but simply doing the best we can to escape misery! Isn't the tremendous compassion with which one "watches the country's ills with great concern"[2] or "has pity for all living things" enough to pull apart one's brittle soul? Even the bonds that directly impinge upon our lives and the scars that mar our spirits are enough to keep us locked behind dungeon doors, never to free ourselves. How can we ever transcend it all? How can we ever talk about "total indifference to worldly temptations" or "complete severance from all relationships"?

Poor Lusha is a disenchanted soul lost in utopia. The few faint traces of the former "female hero" or "carefree talent" that move you to nostalgic tears intensify many of my own sad memories as well. I thank you for reminding me of the past, but I also blame you for this unnecessary act. Since coming south, I have often longed for the days of old, even shedding tears for them! I had been falling into a state of paralysis of late, when suddenly your talk of the past penetrated the fog enshrouding my heart like a bright light on a sunny day. I can't help but feel shaken by it. Oh, but this peace and contentment has never been enough to make me completely forget the past; being enlightened doesn't allow me to cast aside doubts about my future. Like a traveler treading through a wasteland, I feel noth-

---

1. Dogs made of straw used in ancient Chinese sacrificial rites; referrred to in the Daoist classics of Laozi and Zhuangzi as metaphors for things of a transient nature and value.

2. A quote from the Daoist philosopher Zhuangzi.

ing now but despair and disappointment. Oh, my dear friend, what can I say to you? The greater your hopes, the less I have to say to you!

You want me to take some responsibility for the burdens of ordinary poor women; of course I cannot object, but thinking it over carefully, what more do I know than they? How am I any more enlightened? They are living their lives contentedly, so how can I bear to tear open the thin veil shielding them, only to make them recognize their own misfortune? People find the blind pitiful because they are unable to see, but in fact, those who see are as pitiful as a mute who eats bitter medicine yet is unable to complain! Does not discord and filth of every kind constantly prick at weak hearts like a thousand thorns? Oh, Bowei! If we ever stopped fooling ourselves by fabricating beautiful, self-consoling fantasies, this world would truly have nothing to hold our interest for even a single day!

You asked me to guess your future path, but as I certainly cannot, I won't try. Actually, there's no point in guessing because the future is impossible to predict and I'm afraid even you might find yourself at a loss. Yet you will not be alone, for who alive can escape this great misfortune? Even if one manages to persevere to the end, can the scars on one's heart ever heal? Bowei, as time quietly flows on like a river, our beautiful dreams and fantasies will gradually grow faint, and finally the future will be a void where we will find absolutely nothing but an annoying sense of apathy!

Bowei! I might be too young to say such disheartening things, but my heartstrings play only this tune and I am truly unable to force myself to be happy! Just consider my words as you would a bad dream, and do not let my intolerable ranting tarnish your lively heart!

Wishing you unsurpassed joy,

Lusha, by the sea
March 1925

AFTER VICTORY
(1925)

The room here is way too cramped; a rectangular desk in front of the window occupies an entire third of the room, and with the addition of two sofas and a small tea table, there's barely enough space to turn around in. The courtyard is square and neat, like a piece of dried tofu; there are markings on the ground, but no one has ever planted any grass or flowers there. No matter how apparent the signs of spring are elsewhere, the notes of the swallow songs, the moans of the cuckoo, and the yawns of the blooming flowers never reach this little courtyard. This does, however, spare the room's occupants some sadness, for they live like old monks at the base of a deserted mountain cliff; neither the light of spring nor the hues of autumn ever disturb them, leaving their minds free and untroubled. Yet the passing breeze and the birds seem to take pity on their solitude and ennui, and occasionally drop hints that spring has arrived or autumn is drawing near. But in fact, like the sound of footsteps in a deserted valley, even these signs can be somewhat intrusive.

A lengthy spell of spring showers has filled the past few days and the grey sky and endless pattering of falling rain have naturally left the room's occupants feeling rather lethargic. When Pingzhi sat up in bed, the dark clouds were still thick in the sky. He looked about the room and, feeling cold and gloomy, yawned lazily, pulled the covers up around him, and dozed off again just as his wife, Qiongfang, came in from the rear room. Seeing that Pingzhi had fallen back asleep, she didn't disturb him but just sat down at the desk, staring off blankly. As she straightened up some old newspapers, she happened to notice an unopened letter that was, as it turned out, from her friend Qinzhi. She quickly cut it open and read:

My dear friend Qiongfang,

Life is truly unpredictable! Since our parting three years ago, your life has changed completely. I hear that you've already become a mother and your baby is even talking. Oh, Qiongfang! How strange this is! The last time I saw you, you were little more than a naive, innocent child yourself. And now, everything is completely different. It's not just you, I too can only look back on the past with a deep sense of nostalgia! I want to tell you everything that has happened to me since we parted: When I left Beijing and wrote you my last letter, I felt that I would roam about to the ends of the earth forever. Had this happened, you probably would have lamented that I was a lost soul who had never managed to find her true calling. On every clear moonlit evening, a storm would have blown up in your subconscious and you would have shed a few painful tears for the drifter! Yet truth be told, I too can be counted among those who have achieved "victory." After bidding farewell to my friends, I was planning to go abroad to study at the end of the summer, but unfortunately, once the news leaked out that Shaoqing and I were about to leave, his father learned of it and forbade us to depart without getting married. We would have to wait until after we were married to finally carry out our plan to venture overseas.

And how was I feeling at the time? Certainly I was not unhappy about bringing my life as a drifter to an end, but whenever I contemplated all the sacrifices I would have to make once I got married, I couldn't help but feel hesitant! But, Qiongfang, eventually I let my emotions win out and last spring, amid plum blossoms and narcissus blooms, we made our bows to the ancestors and prostrated ourselves before the gods of love! On our honeymoon, we went to the place where long ago you and I once spent those days by the seashore—that little thatched hut carpeted with the fallen petals of pear tree flowers and lined with bright red bricks and windows facing the white froth of the crashing waves. We sat on the rocky cliffs by the shore, quietly staring out to sea; one moment filled with joy, the next with sadness. Qiongfang, such a mood of joyful melancholy defies description. All in all, when I think back to when I first married Shaoqing after having endured so many hardships, I should be pleased to have achieved such a victory; yet whenever I recall the past, I can't help feeling overwhelmed with grief. However much a dream life may be, we were living in an even deeper dream state, for in that brief moment of infatuation we felt that the world was smiling on us and even the mountains and streams seemed happy for us!

During our honeymoon we were drunk with love; nothing could have altered our feelings for each other. We felt only the deepest devotion and everything seemed bright; we never gave a single thought to the future. Luckily, spring was just at its most enchanting; warm breezes were blowing and the blooming flowers all smiled upon us, while bees and butterflies fluttered and danced about. Whenever we got tired of staying inside our little hut, we would stroll together along a remote dirt pathway. There was a cemetery for foreigners nearby that was usually very peaceful. Often, some sentimental individual would have left bunches of fresh flowers on the graves for the departed souls. Sometimes there would be roses, their blossoms bent toward the sun, sometimes snow-white flowers mixed together with pale yellow camellias and sea roses. And all the while the holiest of tombstone angels stared up at the sky as if blessing the dead. And as we sat at the angel's shining feet, it blessed us too. This beautiful remote place brought a sense of balance to us after the frenzied lifestyle we were used to. We sat leaning against each other and, whether we were exchanging our innermost feelings or singing love songs, other than a few occasional eavesdropping spring birds or some spirits peeking at us from behind marble gravestones, nothing ever disturbed us!

But before we knew it, this pretty picture faded and our profound passionate love gradually came to feel very commonplace. Of course, reality also prevented us from going on so leisurely and carefree. Soon Shaoqing went back to work. He would leave every morning at eight and not return again until four or five in the afternoon and I would be left alone in this quiet, remote courtyard. Before long, the wheels in my mind had begun turning again as I contemplated all manner of things, both past and present. Marriage—what they call the biggest event of one's life—was resolved, yet life was not that simple and there were numerous other events aside from this major one! Housework was one. Customarily, of course, it's supposed to be a woman's sole responsibility after marriage. But I could never reconcile myself to leaving it at that, and the moment I began questioning whether women were born simply to take care of the house, I couldn't help wondering what the future held for me. It's true! I was still teaching at the time, which helped console me, and I also had a lot of free time to read, so my unsettled mind was comforted, at least temporarily.

Before long the rainy season began; the sky was dark and gloomy during the day and it rained off and on. The air was so heavy and close that I began to feel dull and bothered again. One afternoon, Xiaoyu braved a storm and came over for a chat. She talked about married life and how depressed she felt. "As for the joys of marriage," she said, "there's nothing to it." When I thought about it later, I found myself agreeing with her, but seeing how despondent she was at the time, I did my best to comfort her. I reasoned, "Our marriages may not be perfect, but marriage is nothing more than a social arrangement, and having already reached this point, we must force ourselves to cheer up. Staying single for the success of one's career is quite the rage now, but leading a spiritually empty life might only be worse. Besides, where there is a will there is always a way, and there's no reason why we shouldn't be able to make a contribution to society after getting married. One must simply not get too used to personal comfort and pleasure, so as to avoid turning as dull as a coat rack; that in itself should be satisfying enough. Why make yourself suffer for some elusive and empty notion of fame and glory?" Xiaoyu listened to my lengthy explanation but still looked quite sad. Afterward she said again, "You are much stronger willed than I am. I'm already too listless and weak, the best I can do is just accept things as they are. And then there will be children . . ."

they'll hold me down even more... how can I even begin to think about making a contribution to society?"

Oh, Qiongfang, what are your thoughts after reading about this conversation?

The truth is, Xiaoyu is not alone in feeling nostalgic about the past, troubled by the present, and fearful of the future. I was always the one who was supposed to be able to figure things out, but have I? Whatever happened to the aspirations I had when I left school, let alone the dreams I had as a child? My lofty wish to sacrifice myself for the human race still remains nothing more than a wish! It used to be that whenever I learned of some great historical figure, I would devoutly prostrate myself before him or her and cry. I remember when the famous Indian poet came to China last spring, I admired his demeanor, his shining, peaceful eyes that seemed to embrace the entire universe, and the clarity of his ideas and purpose, which revealed the most fundamental and purest human nature.[2] As I quietly listened to his magnificent theories, I was moved to tears! I cried out of admiration for him, but mostly over my own inferiority!

Last week I got a letter from Zong. She knows what an anxious mood I've been in lately and urged me not to be so bothered by the praise or condemnation of the world. Ever since I received her letter, I have really felt that she has a much stronger will than we do. Don't you agree?

The strangest thing is that I have recently grown nostalgic about the idyllic maiden days of my past. Qiongfang, you must still remember that beautiful early autumn morning when the fields were green with just a hint of deep yellow. It was very early in the morning, only about six o'clock, and although the first rays of sunlight had begun to penetrate the sky, the cold wind on our faces already made it feel like late autumn as we walked together so excitedly on that path to the park. When we entered the park, we heard the rustling of the wind blowing through dry leaves. The birds, already startled from their dreams, turned to the rising sun and combed their wind-ruffled feathers with little beaks, and the magpies flew off with their friends in search of food. We were the only people in the park other than a lone

---

2. A reference to Nobel laureate Rabindranath Tagore, who visited China in 1924.

worker sweeping the pathways and a vendor arranging his tables, chairs, and dishes. Arriving at the rock garden, you found a clean, white stone to sit on while I reclined on the green grass beside you. You once joked that I was crazy, but since that day, such picture-perfect moments seem to exist only in dreams, and my craziness exists only in your memory!

The evening before last, Shaoqing went out to see a friend and I stayed behind in this cold, desolate room all by myself. It was a beautiful, moonlit night—so bright that I turned out the light, sat on the sofa facing the window, and observed a long flower-shaped shadow cast across the snowy white curtains. I couldn't restrain myself from going out to take a closer look and discovered some wiry yellow flowers blooming by a little rock in the garden. A silvery light flooded the white-pebbled ground as I gazed up at the stars glowing in silence here and there. The tips of the willow branches in the next courtyard cast shadows on the ground, rising and falling in the wind like silver waves. As I was enjoying this scene, I suddenly remembered that spring, years ago, when you, Zong, and I were traveling together in Japan. There was one night—the evening we went by boat to Hiroshima—when not long after boarding the ship at dusk, we noticed a full moon slowly rising from the horizon where the sea and sky met. It reached the middle of the sky and its dazzling brightness as it reflected off the cold green ocean waters was overwhelming. Twinkling stars vied with the lights on shore to illuminate the ocean surface, and each time the waves surged, thousands of tiny flames sparkled on the water. Everyone else on the boat had gone to sleep by ten o'clock, and only the rhythmic sound of the sea slapping against the sides of the boat could be heard. A bleak, chilly scene—it was as if we had been plucked off of this mixed-up world and placed down all alone onto a cold, mysterious deserted island. We leaned on the railing without speaking and stared at the moon, ready to entrust everything to the care of the cloudy sky and the green ocean. Only when the boat was about to weigh anchor did we finally go back inside. Having reached such a level of exhilaration, rid of the troubles of the world, how could we imagine that as soon as we got back, daily affairs would entangle us once again? Oh, Qiongfang! The moon remains the same year after year, but people are always changing. Tonight I mourn for the past. Why do I feel so sad?

Qiongfang! All these thoughts of the past make the life before me seem dull and insipid. How can I describe my situation after "victory"? For months I've been forcing myself to act content. When others criticize me for being eccentric, I can only hang my head and accept their words in silence!

This past May, Wenqi came from her hometown for a visit and we just sat and stared at each other in silence, as if there were no words adequate to express our feelings, though a single glance into one another's eyes was enough to immediately understand the dark secrets we each hid in our hearts. Wenqi, of course, can be proud: up until now she has managed to maintain her virgin life and regard us as the odd ones. But Qiongfang, no mortal can hide from the shackles of humanity, can they? I am sure you must be curious to know how she is faring now.

Do you remember how after we all went our separate ways, Wenqi accompanied her father back to their hometown? At first she just took it easy; her family lives in the countryside in an area surrounded by water, and the beautiful scenery was enough to wash away her troubles. She'd purchased a lot of Buddhist tracts that she read with her mother every day and taught her little brothers and sisters, so life remained free from worldly cares. But who would have guessed that within six months, the people of her village would discover that she had an education and insist that she come to the city and be the principal of the first girl's elementary school there? Finally, at the urging of many people, she abandoned her life of spiritual self-cultivation for a frantic and busy job. Last month she sent me this letter:

Qinzhi,

I was so happy to receive your unexpected letter! I read the poem you enclosed over and over; it stirred up old feelings and emotions and made me feel quite distracted. I haven't been doing much writing recently other than an occasional song for my little students when I am feeling motivated. My spare time is very limited—there are so many trivial matters to attend to and my colleagues are not even worth mentioning. Only busy people can truly understand this situation. Alas, such an unnatural burden of work wears me out. How can I plan a course of self-study comparable to that of my friends who can simply sit at home and read? I'm in such agony!

Qiongfang! Just reading this single paragraph of Wenqi's letter brought back memories of our frenzied early days in Beijing, so I know how keeping busy can also alleviate boredom at times.

With all of this talk I have not yet gotten to tell you about Wenqi's recent situation. Do you know Shaoqing's friend Changjun? He's a very intelligent and warm person, about thirty or so this year, with a baby face that gives him a kind, yet very poised and unaffected manner. When I tell you he's not yet married, however, you might think it rather strange as China, after all, is a country where people marry young, so what sort of a person is it who has reached the age of thirty without getting married? Actually there's an explanation: Changjun was married at twenty, but sadly his wife passed away three or four years ago and he has never remarried. He is good friends with Shaoqing and comes to our home often; one day when I received a picture Wenqi had sent me, Changjun happened to see it and we soon got to talking about her life and studies. Changjun was very impressed and asked us to introduce them. When I thought about it at the time, I decided it would be a good idea, and immediately wrote a letter to Wenqi. However, you know Wenqi is not really very assertive and always obeys her family, so without knowing whether it would work out or not, we just thought we would give it a try. Later we had someone mention it to her father and were surprised to learn how much he approved of Changjun, so after this it was naturally easy to persuade Wenqi. Later, when Wenqi brought her students on a visit to our school, she had a chance to meet Changjun. Changjun is very learned and articulate, and Wenqi herself is a woman of high mind and spirit, so during the two weeks she was here they gradually got to know one another. But Wenqi still hesitated to make a move, mainly, I am sorry to say, because of us! A few days ago I received another letter from her:

Qinzhi!

I haven't heard from you in quite some time. Aren't you feeling out of touch? I put your last letter among those I intended to answer a long time ago, but in the end I didn't because I really am very busy and my mind is terribly dull. But why have you been so quiet? I know that you have all kinds of things to worry about now that you've started a family. I received a letter from Xiaoyu in which she wrote: "When I think back to our school days, I want to abandon my present life." Her letter brought back many memories and I began to feel that life now was dull indeed. I learned a new saying recently: "The hand that rocks the cradle rules the world." Allow me to be the one to share this with you!

During an education conference this summer in Nanjing, several of my friends started saying: "Women's education in China today is a great failure. Once women who have received higher educations get married, not only do they have little skill in managing the household, but they also lack the energy to take up work in society. They simply turn into a class of upper-crust drifters." What do you think of such talk? What's the point of higher education for women if they abandon their work in society the minute they get married?

I've let my thoughts wander and now I've written a great deal without realizing it. Perhaps you don't want to read such depressing thoughts, but now I've already written them, so I'll send the letter to you anyway! Why not give it some thought? I really want to hear what family life is like for you!

There is something else that I want to tell you, Xiaoyu, and everyone else: Even though our classmates predicted that our futures would be mediocre at best, how can we accept this? I think we should remain undaunted and work toward the future. But what can we do to forge ahead? How should we plan our futures? I sincerely hope that you can give me some guidance!

Qiongfang, it sounds as though Wenqi really has begun to have her doubts about us, doesn't it? Yet the truth is, it's hard to blame her, since even we can't say we don't have doubts about our own fates. But I feel that even though a married woman does face many obstacles that keep her from working for social change, that doesn't mean that it's absolutely impossible for her to care about social causes. We feel discouraged now, not just because we can't free ourselves from housework, but also because society doesn't have anything for us to do. In China today, it's hardly worth mentioning how the people's labor is exploited by the bureaucracy, but now even our sacred educational system has begun to decline just as quickly! Under the current system, I doubt that students can really be taught well. I doubt the sincerity of any academic undertaking, let alone any other sordid occupation. Teachers who mechanically repeat things just like recording machines, for example, simply can't live up to the expectations of their students or themselves.

I remember when I was a teacher in Beijing, one day after class as I sat in the teachers' lounge, I suddenly felt very self-conscious. My heart began to burn and I felt extraordinarily ashamed as it dawned on me that I was one of the biggest frauds on earth. I shouldn't be fooling those innocent children or myself, I thought, for when I put on that "serious face" to teach the children, did I really know anything more than they did? Perhaps I was just better at deceit and trickery! Whenever they felt upset and started to cry, adults would always say to them: "It's shameful to cry" or "One must always put on a smiling face in front of others." Oh, what can be said about such an unnatural way of life? What can an education that destroys human nature accomplish? And how many people who are working as educators really feel that education is a sacred undertaking? They just grab a book of teaching materials, muddle through an hour, collect an hour's pay, and that's the end of the story! Well, I don't think that the women who compete with men for this dirty teaching rice bowl are necessarily any better off than those who stay quietly at home taking care of the housework. They shouldn't feel ashamed of accepting any meager reward men will give them for it!

As for there not being much else for a woman to do besides teaching, simply put, in China today everything is in a state of disarray. Everyone knows that women can't find occupations, but what of all those men without work? They once received higher educations as well. Just think how many of them there are. Of course a large number of such men are just plain lazy, but don't the majority of them actually want to do something, but can't?

Qiongfang, when our school was looking for a new principal, you can't imagine how many people maneuvered to get the job.

Well, if I were to begin to tell you even some of the details about how people jockeyed for the position, education circles would really lose face. Alas, with society in such a condition, we'll never have a bright future without radical change!

But regardless of everything else, Wenqi's letter is really quite inspiring. The truth is, the Chinese family system is more than enough to wear down any woman's willpower. I feel that ever since I got married, my old friends have grown fewer and fewer, while the friends I have now are either simply social friends or else relatives with whom I have no real rapport. We either just go through the motions with fixed pleasantries to cope with each other halfheartedly or play cards or see a show. Any intellectual discussions are out of the question. I can hardly find a friend with whom I can have an intimate conversation and besides, there are so many household matters to take care of. The minute I open my eyes in the morning, I find myself hopelessly caught up in the web of daily affairs. It's not easy to sit down calmly and read, let alone take up some other activity. Oh, Qiongfang, it's pitiful how stupid people really are—before getting married, we dream of living full and satisfying lives after marriage, but in the reality of this flawed world, we wind up with nothing but regrets!

All this reminds me of Lengxiu. You probably still remember her lively and carefree personality, but have you heard about her recent situation? She's even more pitiful than the rest of us—she's really the one who's lost out the most! When we were all going to school together, no one would ever have guessed that with her proud outlook on everything, she would fall the lowest. She always said that life was a big experiment and never followed anyone too readily. She was even less anxious about the ways of love, but in the end it was with the hope of a final "victory" that she bravely stepped into this particular experiment. Although there were many sharp brambles along the way that might have pricked at her feet, she did not let them slow her down. When she was first introduced to Wenzhong, no one could foresee that the two would fall in love, as Wenzhong was already married and Lengxiu had always held herself in such high regard. In the end, however, Cupid's bow brought them together, but after the marriage they returned to Wenzhong's hometown, where his first wife still lived. Wenzhong and Lengxiu had sought the first wife's approval before marrying, so on the surface at least, everyone put on friendly smiles when they met. But according to Lengxiu's letter, her feelings changed completely soon after she arrived there; she always sensed some deep regret lodged in her heart that she could not quite express. As she lay in bed every night before falling asleep, she would ponder how true love could not tolerate a third party—even if the person were nothing more than a formality, love would be marred. Because of this, her lively spirit gradually faded. I remember some especially moving words of hers:

> I was once able to use my sharp eyes to evaluate life, just like those pessimistic, world-weary philosophers who realize that the world is a sea of suffering, that everything has a limit, and everything is a void, yet can never free themselves from the bonds of the human world. I have discovered nothing extraordinary in the course of my own life. I have been fooled by love and I have shed tears; and I have wielded the sharp sword of knowledge to stab at a fragile heart. I once resembled a weak little lamb who, full of hope, joined an enormous flock of sheep to seek the most fitting partner. In my imagination, a perfect love was as simple and clear as the cloudless autumn sky; nothing could stop me from a harmonious union. It was also like a frost-covered chrysanthemum in midautumn with a mysterious, pervasive fragrance reserved for only a few exceptional people while the bees and butterflies barely got a chance.

It isn't hard to achieve these hopes, but poor Lengxiu found that even after she had cleared a spot for a garden in a remote and barren spot and planted rose seeds, the brambles still had their roots intact and found a way to flourish. Her clear sky was eventually obscured by passing clouds and the lively fire in her soul was nearly extinguished by a gust of cold wind. What does she feel as she sits silently engulfed in her sadness before a flickering lamplight? Who can blame her each time she lets out a deep mournful sigh? Last March, she sent me the words to a new poem she had written and I was upset for days after reading it. Unfortunately I have lost her original text, but I can still vaguely remember it. It went something like this:

> The rain pours, the wind drones on,
> The stars shed tears, the clouds weep.

> I sit in silence by the lamplight,
> How deep my sorrow!
> I bemoan what is lacking on earth,
> The oceans of hate can never be filled!
> Longing for you, I grow all the more sorrowful.
> Ending my infatuation, I end up confused!
> How sad! How sad!
> Why can't I attain enlightenment?
> Why do I falter on the wrong path?
> Ashamed by the words of Western thinkers
> That say: perfection or nothing!

Qiongfang, how does reading such a mournful poem make you feel? Still, I think we should not shed tears of compassion for Lengxiu alone, but also for the countless other Lengxius living in a transitional era such as this one. If Lengxiu, having been unable to secure a flawless love, has already come to such an end, then what of all those others—such as Wenzhong's first wife—who bear empty titles but can't find even a morsel of love? How can we even begin to fathom their misery and sorrow?

Oh, Qiongfang, I used to say that Lengxiu was a free bird who became entangled in the grim net of human affairs only after obtaining the victory she fought so hard for! She gained nothing from it but a heart of misery that consumed her strong will and courage. When I think about it now, I can't help but bemoan the fact that women in China today are altogether too pitiful!

The day before yesterday, Xiaoyu's daughter turned one month old, so I went to their home and found Xiaoyu sitting with her baby sleeping in her lap. Seeing me, the corners of Xiaoyu's eyes suddenly turned red and she said, "It's still better to stay single, we've all taken the wrong path!" Oh, how painful her words were! We really were all so stupid. How heroic it seemed when we fought with our families and willingly sacrificed everything for love! We've all managed to achieve this victory, but now after victory our joys are few and our troubles great. And we have little to aspire to. What happiness is left in life, when all the thoughts that were once so comforting are suddenly wiped away? We used to think that if we found a true partner in love, then we could give up our other ideals. Now, the outcome of our experiment shows that nothing is beyond the control of circumstances.

Otherworldly joys appear to me now only late on clear, starry nights when I suddenly meet with the flower spirits and feel that I've drifted to the corners of the universe and am suspended between heaven and earth. As for the celestial island of endless skies and seas, and scenery of fine grasses and delicate flowers, I must wait a long time—till death—before I can hope to see them. Qiongfang, my days pass so slowly, and I can hardly console myself any longer. Lost in thought in this isolated room, I feel as if I'm drifting away. I had originally planned to go on vacation with Shaoqing to Italy next spring, hoping the scenery would help alleviate my malady, but that was just wishful thinking as there is always the question of money. Instead, we can only, as the saying goes, "sketch pictures of food to satisfy our hunger."

Thank you, Qiongfang, the knowledge that you are still writing helps lift my spirits. I've always wanted to do the same, but as the years have passed I've gotten caught up in life, and at some point my lofty aspirations faded away. The few times I have written, I've just been putting words on paper; where can I find any inspiration to water the barren fields of my mind and make the flowers bloom again? Qiongfang, can you predict what the future holds for me?

Qinzhi

After finishing Qinzhi's letter, Qiongfang felt as if something were lodged in her chest. She looked around at her own surroundings; natural beauty, an ideal life, these are no more than castles in the sky. Without thinking, she sighed. "This is all there is to life after 'victory.'"

Pingzhi had already awakened and could not help overhearing her. He asked, "What did you say?" Qiongfang did not want to reveal the secret in her heart, so she simply laughed and said, "It's late, aren't you getting up yet?" Pingzhi answered lazily, "What is there to do? There is no point in getting up!" Qiongfang could not hold back a sigh. "There's no point in living!" Pingzhi replied, "That's right, there is no point at all in living."

This strange conversation ended there, leaving nothing but a slight trembling in both of their hearts.

7

Lu Jingqing

陸晶清

Lu Jingqing (1907–1993)

The daughter of an antique and curio dealer, Lu Jingqing was born in the southwestern province of Yunnan in 1907. Her father was not a well-educated man himself, but he was fascinated by ancient history and literature and encouraged the young Lu Jingqing to memorize classical Chinese poetry. As a student, first at a teachers' school in Yunnan and later at college in Beijing, Lu Jingqing's own interest in poetry, particularly the new style of poetry that came in vogue in the May Fourth era, would grow.

In 1922, the same year Lu left Yunnan to start college in Beijing, her mother committed suicide. This was the first in a series of devastating personal losses Lu would suffer in her life. At Beijing Women's Normal College, Lu studied literature and became known for her frequent performances in amateur drama productions at the school. She also developed a close friendship with the woman writer Shi Pingmei, then a student several years her senior. The extraordinary relationship between these two women and the deep despair Lu felt upon Shi Pingmei's premature death in 1928 are captured in the poignant memoir Lu published in 1932, entitled *Wanderings*.

During college, Lu Jingqing became involved in the Beijing literary scene, contributing her poetry and essays to literary journals and supplements and, as early as 1924, assuming the editorship of *Women's Weekly*, an influential weekly insert to the *Beijing Post* featuring writing by and about women. In 1926, she and Shi Pingmei founded *The Wild Rose Weekly*, a literary supplement to the *World Daily*. In addition to serving as the editors of this popular supplement, Lu Jingqing and Shi Pingmei used *The Wild Rose* as a means of showcasing their own writing, including frequent poetic exchanges between themselves and their close friends. The highly lyrical quality and intimate focus of Lu Jingqing's writing is also reflected in the "little work" (*xiaopin*) translated here: "Random Notes: Number Nine" was first published in *Women's Weekly* and subsequently included in a collection of Lu Jingqing's *xiaopin* entitled *Random Notes* in 1930.

An active participant in the demonstrations that shook the Beijing Women's Normal campus in the aftermath of the May 30, 1925 student movement, Lu Jingqing eventually left the school in 1927 in protest over the administration's handling of the unrest. Like many other women intellectuals, she moved to Wuhan, the hub of revolutionary activity at this time, and joined the women's association of the Guomindang, where she became acquainted with veteran feminist activist He Xiangning. After the "failed" revolution of 1927, Lu remained in the south until the autumn of 1928, when the tragic news of Shi Pingmei's unexpected death brought her back to Beijing. Lu resumed her studies in the graduate program of Beijing Women's Normal while working on a book on women poets of the Tang dynasty. In 1931, she married Wang Lixi, a scholar who shared her love of poetry and with whom she would collaborate on several academic projects.

Because of Wang's vocal opposition to Chiang Kai-shek as well as Lu's own history of political activism, the couple were forced to go into exile in Europe between 1933 and 1938. Earning a living writing and translating, the two were also active in garnering support in England for China's war effort against Japan. In 1938, Lu Jingqing returned to war-torn China with her husband and worked for several years in the All-China Writers' Resistance Association. After her husband's death, she returned to London in 1945 as a correspondent for the newspaper *Peace Daily* and covered, among other things, the first assembly of the United Nations in London and the Paris Peace Talks in 1946. During this period, Lu also wrote a number of short stories set in Europe, one of which appeared in *Untitled*, an important collection of women's writing edited by Zhao Qingge in 1947. After the founding of the People's Republic, Lu Jingqing taught in Shanghai until her retirement in 1965. The majority of Lu Jingqing's poetry, short stories, and essays, which originally appeared in a wide variety of May Fourth and post-May Fourth periodicals and newspapers, has yet to be systematically collected.

RANDOM NOTES: NUMBER NINE
(1930)

For years I have kept a dried maple leaf that I can't bear to part with. Perhaps you'll laugh at me for being so silly. Yet you must know that I always cherish things given to me by friends, no matter how humble, or whether I like them or not. As long as a friend has given me something in good faith, I will keep it forever and never discard it. As a result, my trunk is dangerously overflowing with dozens of scraps and small knick-knacks. Whenever I clean the trunk out, I always pile them into a huge mound. As I keep even the odds and ends given me by young friends over a decade ago and carry them with me on all my wanderings, I've gradually accumulated quite a large collection. I remember how Shi Pingmei would tease me when she saw me cleaning out the trunk: "Some day you'll be buried alive under your mountain of treasures."

I've always loved preserving mementos of my friendships because whenever I take up an object a friend has given me on some occasion, even if it happened many years ago or the two of us are now at opposite ends of the earth or my friend has even departed from this life, it always brings back many memories and thoughts for me. In other words, every friend's gift that I preserve can help me relive an old dream or recapture a moment of youth or childhood as if it were frozen in time.

Take this maple leaf, for example. You picked it from a tree with your own hands and gave it to me. I have no way of knowing whether you had any special intention when you presented it to me that day, but I have kept it and I can always look at this maple leaf and at the very least remember you and that snowy day long ago.

It should not be beyond your recollection, for it was the day we took a group of small children out to play in the snow. It was a wonderful day: thrown suddenly together with those innocent youngsters, our own childish spirits came back to us and we laughed and frolicked about, forgetting all our worldly troubles.

I no longer recall whose idea it was to go out in the snow, but we were surrounded by a group of children who pushed us through the front gate and out toward a great field of whiteness. At first I wasn't too pleased by it and trudged through the snow, lagging behind. The children ran up a hill, their cheeks getting cold and looking as rosy as crabapples, and one by one they began loudly singing a winter tune. I saw you shake your head and sigh, as if deeply moved. Then I carelessly tripped on a rock buried in the snow and fell. All the children laughed and clapped their hands in delight, but only when you helped me up and saw that I was half covered with snow did you laugh and tease me: "You'll never forget this."

But the most fun was when we stood on the hill commanding the children in a snowball fight. The opposing sides even built fortresses and each of us plotted our strategies carefully, ordering the children to throw snowballs from in front one moment and then behind the next so as to be sure to hit the enemy. The children too did their utmost to show off their bravery, shouting and throwing snowballs continuously. They didn't even retreat when a snowball hit its mark. In the end, my side came out victorious and the children were as happy as if they had wiped out an army of thousands, although those that you had led cursed in disappointment.

After the snowball fight, we climbed to the top of the hill to look out and soon began telling snow stories. It was then that we completely forgot ourselves, laughing loudly and singing at the top of our lungs as we took over the silvery world that the vast snowy fields had become. In the distance, we saw a maple tree at the foot of the hill with a few leaves left hanging from its branches; set off by the snow-covered ground, it looked especially beautiful. Suddenly, without a thought to the fact that we had just met, you grabbed my hand and said, "Come on! Let's go get those leaves" as you dragged me down the hill.

When you picked three rouge-colored leaves from the tree, I was very happy because I've always loved to keep flower petals and red leaves pressed between the pages of my books as markers. After brushing the snow from the leaves, however, you didn't hand me even one, but tucked them all away in your wallet. I was very disappointed by this, but, of course, I didn't feel right asking you for them, even though I was a bit upset.

Not until evening did we finally return to Yanyan's home. After dinner everyone gathered around the fire telling stories of the day's adventures in the snow. Several of the little ones excitedly reported to their parents every detail of the snowball fight, and I proudly boasted about my battle tactics. Suddenly, you disappeared. Yanyan's mother told me that you were rather eccentric and had been depressed. She explained that you had been living at their home for over a month, but she had never once seen you enjoy a day. When everyone else was happy and lively, your brow was knit especially tight as if you were deeply troubled. She also said that you rarely went out and if by chance you did, it was always alone, never with friends. So your having gone out with us today in the snow and having such a good time was really a rare occurrence.

Then Yanyan's father went on to tell me that you were a young person of high ambitions and good intentions; that you understood several foreign languages, but were taking refuge in his home temporarily because of the failure of the revolution. He said that you had known of me for some time and enjoyed reading my essays, criticizing me only for failing to be bold enough, for you felt that my actions and writings were always too timid.

That evening we talked late into the night, but you didn't join us. Only when I went to bed did I notice you standing below the window gazing up at the cold moon in the mist. Without thinking, I called out: "Aren't you cold out there standing in the snow enjoying the moon?

"It's just right, I love this atmosphere."

Your answer really was a bit strange, so I laughed to myself all the way past the west courtyard and to the room I was staying in. When I entered the room, Nanny Wang pointed to a letter on the desk, saying "The gentleman brought this over for you." I noticed that my name was not on the envelope, but the five words: "Gift on a Snowy Evening" were written upon it. I opened it to find a white sheet of paper folded around one of the leaves that you had picked from the tree that day. On the leaf you had written two lines of poetry:

> Before others, speechless at parting,
> Of late my heart is so unclear!
>
> —haiku jotted down on a snowy evening

    The manner in which you gave me this leaf surprised me a bit because I wasn't quite sure of your intention, especially since the two lines of poetry written on the leaf suggested a deep, impenetrable meaning. But I quickly convinced myself that there was nothing profound about what you had written or the way you had presented the leaf to me as I was unwilling to think that the gift of that tiny leaf could have any great significance.

    Over the years, I haven't ventured to guess your intention in giving me this maple leaf that night, but I've continued to treasure it nevertheless.

8

Chen Xuezhao

陳學昭

Chen Xuezhao (1906–1991)

With a literary career that spanned from the early May Fourth to the post-Mao era, Chen Xuezhao was one of the most prolific women writers of the twentieth century, although she is largely unknown to most students of Chinese literature today. She was born in Zhejiang province in 1906 into a scholarly family of modest means, the youngest of nine children and the only daughter. Her father, a schoolteacher influenced by the late Qing reform movement, openly opposed foot binding and supported women's education; unfortunately, he passed away when Chen was just six, leaving her upbringing to the discretion of her often-less-than-encouraging older brothers. Still, Chen was permitted to enroll in school and in 1923, at the age of 17, she graduated from the Patriotic Girls' School in Shanghai. That year, Chen published her first article, an essay entitled "The New Woman I Want to Be," which she surreptitiously submitted under a pseudonym to a contest sponsored by the Shanghai newspaper *The Times*. Although she did not win the first prize, entering the contest was, as she later recalled, an important step in asserting her autonomy as a young woman.

Chen returned home for a brief period after graduating, but she was unhappy with the restrictions on her life there and soon accepted a teaching job at a remote school in Anhui province. This job ended abruptly when the threat of bandits sent the local students into hiding and scattered most of the faculty. The experiences Chen Xuezhao and several female colleagues had as they traveled through the countryside on their way back to Shanghai are recorded in essays she published in *The Ladies' Journal*. After returning to the city, Chen Xuezhao was soon publishing her essays in the leading literary periodicals of the day and, through the introductions of former classmates, socializing with members of the Shanghai cultural elite. The essay translated here, "The Woes of the Modern Woman," was first published in 1927 in the cutting-edge magazine *New Woman*, a frequent showcase for her work in the late 1920s. An incisive feminist analysis of the problems facing educated urban women, this text is part of a series of essays in which Chen Xuezhao takes China's supposedly "new" men to task for their traditional gender politics.

Using money earned from her writing, Chen Xuezhao set off for France in 1927 in order to escape the political chaos in Shanghai and family pressure to get married. Despite a disastrous marriage (to a man of her own choice) and other personal difficulties, Chen's years in France were a productive period in her literary career. As a special European correspondent for the Tianjin newspaper *Dagongbao* and later as a featured essayist for Shanghai's popular *Life Weekly*, Chen wrote prolifically on her experiences abroad and about the similarities and differences between Chinese and French women. Many of these essays were republished in separate volumes. During a brief return to China in 1929 to resolve a dispute with her family over the money she was earning through her writing, Chen also published a collection of autobiographical vignettes entitled *Remembering Paris* (1929), as well as her first full-length novel, *Dream of the Southern Wind* (1929), a semi-autobiographical account of the romantic entanglements and financial difficulties of a young Chinese woman studying in France.

After earning a Ph.D. in literature from the University of Clermont in 1934, Chen returned to China, where her reputation as a leftist made it difficult for her to write and publish as openly as she would have liked. As the war with Japan progressed, she become increasingly interested in the Communist movement; in August of 1938 she traveled to the Communist guerilla base at Yan'an as a reporter for *The National Dispatch*. She spent nearly a year there, interviewing participants of the Long March (1934) and gathering information for articles. Although her manuscripts were confiscated by the Guomindang, she published *Yan'an Interviews* in Hong Kong in 1940. At the end of 1940, Chen returned to Yan'an, where she became personally involved in various forms of cultural work, including serving as the editor of the Communist newspaper *Liberation Daily*. Chen formally joined the Communist Party in 1945 and after the founding of the People's Republic in 1949, she participated in the first national congresses of the All-China Women's Federation and the All-

China Writers Association. In the late 1940s and early '50s, Chen served as the Party branch secretary of Zhejiang University while publishing several volumes of short stories and essays as well as a second full-length novel, a woman-centered *bildungsroman* entitled *Working Is Beautiful*. Like many veteran writers, Chen was persecuted during the anti-Rightist campaign in 1957 and did not resume publishing her work again until 1978. Among the works she published upon her "rehabilitation" are a two-volume memoir and a sequel to her second novel.

Chen Xuezhao was a versatile writer who experimented with a variety of literary forms and styles over the course of her creative life, although of her May Fourth writings, the most well known are her essays. Two distinct styles predominate in her essay writing of this early period: highly personal, melancholic meditations on such subjects as her mother, her travels, and nature; and passionate political critiques of contemporary issues, including the controversial Woman Question.

THE WOES OF THE MODERN WOMAN
(1927)

My article "For Men" provoked so much sympathy for the woes of the modern woman that *New Woman Magazine* decided to solicit opinions for solutions. This pleased me, for it proves that some people still consider this a serious problem for which we must find a remedy.

The letter soliciting opinions went as follows: "Contemporary women have great aspirations to engage in academic scholarship and to improve society, but at the same time they cannot neglect their inherent responsibility as wives and mothers. However, in light of the actual conditions of present-day society, these pursuits often come in conflict, and consequently women are prone to feel great despair. But does this mean women should cast aside their natural responsibilities as wives and mothers and devote themselves entirely to their academic studies or to the improvement of society? Or do they have no alternative but to temporarily postpone their degrees and social work in order to concentrate on their obligations as virtuous wives and mothers? Or is there another means of resolving this conflict?"

The questions: *"But does this mean women should cast aside their natural responsibilities as wives and mothers and devote themselves entirely to their academic studies or to the improvement of society? Or do they have no alternative but to temporarily postpone their degrees and social work in order to concentrate on their obligations as virtuous wives and mothers?"* are simply wrong. Women, like men, are people, and being a wife or a mother is a human right, just like being a husband or a father is. The titles *wife* and *mother* or *husband* and *father* are merely linguistic distinctions; the duties each entails are equally important.

It is an indisputable fact that being a wife and mother is a human right, yet why is it that so many women nowadays advocate "singlehood" and are willing to devote their whole lives to either their studies or their work? Why do they believe that it is beneath their dignity to become wives or mothers?

It is precisely because women believe the burdens of marriage and motherhood are so great that they prefer to avoid or resist these roles. Some feel they are not naturally inclined to becoming wives or mothers; they consider the parameters of these roles too narrow and therefore seek to become active in society. For women in China, who have continually been shackled by Confucianism and patriarchal oppression, the desire to dedicate themselves to society or learning constitutes an awakening and an act of resistance. Most tyrannical "slave-men," who believe that women ought to become wives and mothers—*loyal* wives and mothers—feel that the women who now advocate staying single and devoting their lives to scholarship or society are guilty of the most heinous crime.[1] Concerned that this spells the end of humanity, such men voice their adamant opposition. But it is *they* who ought to be opposed. You men can say "women should not" all you like, but there is no way you can compel women to be wives and mothers. At most, all you can do is exhort them by emphasizing how much they *should* be wives and mothers! But, in the end, women who are unwilling to take on such roles will remain unwilling. Moreover, the reality is that as soon as women become aware of all the disadvantages and drawbacks of being married, no matter how you try to trick them into it, they will still refuse.

For example, when both partners in the so-called "one husband-one wife new family" have careers, the problem of dependency doesn't arise;

---

1. Chen Xuezhao is playing with the notion first popularized during the late Qing era that Confucianism inculcates a servile mentality into all its followers, male or female. Thus, in a patriarchal society, women are not only slaves themselves, but the slaves of slaves, as pointed out in Chen Xiefen's earlier essay.

however, as soon as the woman has a baby, she is no longer able to keep her job and the family's economic burden falls entirely on the man's shoulders.[2] Since there is no public child care and the average family can't afford a nanny, once a baby is born, the woman has no choice but to look after it herself. What else can she do? Naturally the man becomes the sole breadwinner, while the woman wears herself out all day long taking care of trivial domestic chores like cooking rice and making porridge. Under those circumstances, no matter how educated and talented a woman you might be, you'll be so worn out you won't even be able to move! This is not a figment of my imagination—I have plenty of female friends who have met with this unthinkable misfortune. As for men, they aren't understanding at all. Instead, they quickly forget how intelligent and accomplished their wives once were and how active they could be in society had they not chosen to take their roles as wives and mothers so seriously. They look upon their wives like they were still the illiterate women of the past, who, being incapable of economic independence, relied on men, and were the property of men, just like slaves. As a result, these educated, accomplished women are sacrificed to the hegemony of the self-proclaimed "new men" of China who still haven't eliminated their own slavish natures.

I can't help recalling all those grand theories that the new men were espousing four or five years ago. Back then, the new men believed that in order to reform the backward family and to construct a superior one, all that was needed was free love: that is, the freedom to marry an educated, talented woman with whom they could relate on an intellectual, emotional, and personal level. Such women would deserve respect from males, not to mention equality with them. These families, what we nowadays refer to as the "new family," ought to be blissful, but in fact this is not the case at all! When two people have just fallen in love, the man naturally respects the woman and the woman holds the man in high esteem; however, as soon as they become husband and wife and have children, gradually and imperceptibly the man becomes the master of the relationship; everything falls under his control and he is no longer able to respect his wife in the way he used to. Since the woman has to take care of the children and the household, she no longer has time to work in society or make a living. Under an economic situation like this, they are divided into master and slave.

---

2. Prior to the marriage reforms in the twentieth century, it was legal for men in China to marry more than one wife.

Perhaps for many "new men" this is not a deliberate choice but an unconscious manifestation of the slave mentality they have inherited from Confucianism. Such a situation indicates, however, that even when intelligent, capable men and women get married, they don't necessarily form a truly happy union. Why? Because as long as male intellectuals in contemporary China have economic control but have yet to eradicate the slavish nature that permeates all their thinking, they continue to treat educated women in the same manner in which they once treated old-fashioned illiterate women from the countryside. Therefore, I have this to say to men who insist that women must become wives and mothers: Advocate this to your hearts' content, but don't forget reality. In light of the condition of gender relations in China today, is there any way that women will willingly become "virtuous wives and good mothers?" Is there any way that they will willingly strive to fulfill their responsibilities as wives and mothers? Indeed, under these circumstances, is there any way that they—even those women who are content to be mothers and wives—will do their utmost to develop their maternal natures?

Moreover, the truth of the matter is that there are few women who become mothers or wives and who aren't subjected to the bullying of men and the burdens of children. As for those who say that women must be wives and mothers, how many have actually researched the decline of the Chinese population and worry that it's not sufficiently large? To this day, all women continue to sacrifice their lives to the difficulties, hardships, and worries of the domestic sphere. How is it that men who urge women to be wives and mothers have yet to realize this?

Why should we heed their warnings? At present, there is not an educated woman who doesn't want to develop herself, to become a person—an independent person! Therefore, with regard to those women who are willing to devote themselves to academia, to a career, or to the improvement of society, we shouldn't belittle them by saying that they haven't fulfilled their natural duties as wives and mothers, for they have created their own places in these spheres. I believe that a person's life should not be reduced to their relations with the opposite sex, for this is no more than one facet of human life. At most, all we can say is that such relations bear a tremendous influence on one's life. If we look at women poets, writers, and scholars, as well as musicians and scientists, the reason that they don't get involved in heterosexual relationships but engage in studies or careers is that their personalities, their aspirations, desires, and interests, are different. But clearly, were they willing, they too could have relationships.

With regard to any matter, we cannot rely on our own subjective views; in considering motherhood and marriage or in considering academia, to insist that every woman must be a wife and mother or that everyone must be a scholar is like trying to force an entire flock of chickens to roost. Even when it might be necessary to advise and encourage women to become wives and mothers—for example, in the event that the birthrate drops too low—it will still be up to women themselves to decide if they are willing or not. Why don't they who force women to be virtuous wives and good mothers ever think that those slave-natured men need lessons in becoming virtuous husbands and good fathers? However, I endorse neither the concept of "virtuous wives and good mothers" nor that of "virtuous husbands and good fathers"; what I endorse is the human rights of wives and husbands, mother and fathers. Women who want to devote themselves to academia or to a career have chosen the path they desire, and should not be restricted from doing so. In short, the only way for contemporary women to overcome their woes is to become fully educated and independent, and for men to thoroughly eradicate the slave mentality they have inherited from Confucianism! Otherwise, I predict that the result of women's continued depression will be that they will become even less willing to be wives and mothers—or something even worse!

Lastly, the plight of contemporary women is not limited to the two issues raised by *New Woman Magazine*; problems such as the loss of educational opportunities, unemployment, and many others are also worth discussing, though I won't go into them here.

9

Ling Shuhua

Ling Shuhua (1900–1990)

One of China's most highly regarded modern writers, Ling Shuhua was the daughter of the fourth wife of a top-ranking Qing official from the southern province of Canton who later served as the mayor of Beijing. Like many young ladies of her privileged-class background, Ling received private training in classical Chinese literature and painting. An accomplished artist, Ling continued to paint throughout her life and exhibited her work on several occasions, including a 1962 individual show in Paris where she received high praise from the French intellectual André Malraux.

These accomplishments would once have been more than sufficient for the well-bred daughter of a high official, but Ling Shuhua came of age just as the clamor for advanced educational opportunities for women reached a fevered pitch. In 1922 she enrolled, along with fellow woman writer Bing Xin, in Yanjing University to pursue a degree in foreign literature. Soon after graduating, she married Chen Yuan, the founder of the important May Fourth journal *Contemporary Review*, and in 1927 the couple moved to Hunan so that Chen could teach at Wuhan University.

During her years in Wuhan, Ling Shuhua became closely acquainted with the women writers Yuan Changying and Su Xuelin, as well as British writer Julian Bell, all of whom were affiliated with the department of literature where Ling's husband taught. Bell not only helped cotranslate many of her short stories for the English-language journal *T'ien Hsia Monthly*, but also put her in touch with his distinguished aunt, Virginia Woolf. The two women writers maintained a correspondence between 1938 and 1941. Woolf agreed to read drafts of the memoirs Ling had begun writing and encouraged her in one letter, "Please go on, write freely, do not mind how directly you translate the Chinese into English. In fact, I would advise you to come as close to the Chinese both in style and in meaning as you can." Composed in English, Ling's narrative of growing up in an old-style scholarly Beijing family within a rapidly changing society are recorded in a memoir that was eventually published in 1953 under the title *Ancient Melodies*. Ling dedicated this work to Woolf and Vita Sackville-West, whom she met in England in the late 1940s.

Ling Shuhua began writing during her college years, and the bulk of her fiction was produced during a relatively concentrated period in the late

1920s and early '30s. Because her short stories first appeared in journals such as *Crescent Monthly* and *Contemporary Review*, Ling Shuhua is often associated with the westernized literary aesthetic for which those literary journals were known, and critics dubbed her the "Katherine Mansfield of China." Ling's refined literary style and her frequent depictions of what Lu Xun once described as "the obedient ladies of the old-style family" also gained her the dubious distinction, along with her contemporaries Bing Xin and Chen Hengzhe, of being a new "*guixiu*" writer—a slightly derogatory term which at the time denoted a highly "feminine" style of writing on narrow domestic subjects. The subtle irony that runs through much of her work clearly undercuts the serene surface of her narratives, suggesting a more complex critique of the domesticity depicted in many of her stories. Ling Shuhua published most of her stories in three separate volumes, *Temple of Flowers* (1928), *Women* (1930), and *Two Little Brothers* (1935), and her work continues to be widely anthologized today.

The stories translated here, "Intoxicated," first published in *Contemporary Criticism* in 1925, and "Once Upon a Time," from the 1928 collection *Temple of Flowers*, both explore the theme of female desire, focusing in particular on transgressive acts by women who defy the conventions of sexual "propriety." In "Intoxicated," a young wife reveals to her husband that she has passionate feelings for another man. "Once Upon a Time" centers on the relationship of two schoolgirls who find (if only temporarily) love and physical intimacy outside of the institution of heterosexual marriage. The theme of schoolgirl lesbianism in this story was not uncommon in May Fourth women's writing (both Lu Yin and Chen Xuezhao, for example, also explored the subject in short stories), although the mildly erotic description Ling employs is a departure from the typically platonic terms used to describe these relationships during this period.

INTOXICATED
(1925)

It was late at night and the guests had departed. A drunken man in his thirties had collapsed and was sound asleep in a huge chair in the middle of the parlor. Next to the fire sat a tipsy young couple whispering to each other. A still, sweet aroma filled the room.

Abruptly, the woman stood up and said, "How inconsiderate of us. Ziyi is over there sleeping and we haven't even covered him up. Let me fetch a blanket for you to put over him. Turn off the lamp over there so that it doesn't shine in his eyes and disturb him."

"I'll get it," said the man, who also hastened to his feet.

But the woman had already left the room without responding and was soon back with the blanket, saying, "Take his shoes off gently. Unfold the blanket and cover up his shoulders and feet so he can sleep more comfortably." She watched her husband slip off the sleeping man's shoes and place the blanket over him, then said, "We should sit here for a while. When he wakes up he'll want a drink of tea or water. He was just telling me that he wasn't going to go home because this big chair is so much more comfortable than his own bed." As she said this she sat down again. "Oh, the poor thing, what an awful home he has."

As before, the man sat next to his wife. The room, lit now by the small electric lamp with a fringed shade, had become quite dark. The fire in the fireplace, however, projected a soft orange glow onto their beaming faces. In the warmth of the room, the bowl of plums on the side table gave off a sweet pungent odor.

The man narrowed his eyes, smiled, and turned to his wife. "Caitiao, I'm drunk too."

"Didn't you tell me that you didn't have much to drink?" said the woman, smiling.

"I'm not drunk on wine, I'm intoxicated by this ambience ... my eyes, nose, ears, mouth, my entire being feels intoxicated. But my heart is the most enraptured. Feel how fast it is beating!" As he said this, he slid closer to Caitiao.

Caitiao glanced at him with a faint smile on her face, then looking at the sleeping man, replied, "You still can't admit that you're actually drunk. Just listen to how you go on about your ears, your nose, your whole body and soul. Still, your face isn't flushed like Ziyi's. He's really drunk tonight."

Seeming oblivious to her words, the man kept holding his wife's hands and admiring her with a drunken gaze. He went on, "Darling, how could I not be utterly intoxicated, luxuriating in such company, on such a fine night, in such a lovely room. I often grow enchanted just by sitting in this beautiful warm room and contemplating all the things that my beloved has arranged. Then when I see you coming, my heart starts beating uncontrollably. With a goddess sitting here before my very eyes, my home is now a perfectly beautiful palace; the elegant music of fairies fills my ears and the soul-transporting scent of perfume assails my nostrils—sweeter than plum blossoms or roses, and even lotus petals would smell bitter by comparison. And my lips, having just savored the exquisite food prepared by my beloved, still taste of a flowery perfume, as sweet as sugar, though not quite the same, more like sweet wine yet ..."

"Enough, enough, you must be drunk, going on like a novelist to tease me like this. Talk a bit more softly so you don't wake Ziyi."

He raised his wife's hands and inhaled passionately. Then lifting his head and looking at her he said, "Aren't you just a bit tipsy too? What flower boasts a more charming color than the slightly drunken blush of your cheeks? A peach blossom? I'm afraid that's too common. A peony? No, too gaudy. A chrysanthemum? Too cold. Maybe plum blossoms? No, too dainty. None of them even come close." As he spoke, he moved still nearer to her. "Oh! Forget the rest! What could compare with these two eyebrows? Mountains in the distance? No, they're too faint. The feelers of a silkworm moth? Too curvy. Willow leaves? Too straight. A crescent moon? Too frigid. None can compare, not one of them. Eyebrows are every bit as beautiful as eyes, so why does no one ever mention them?"

Unlike her usual self, who would take in Yongzhang's words one by one, Caitiao kept glancing across the room at the sleeping man. Finally she cut Yongzhang off. "My head feels a bit dizzy tonight. I can't stand chattering after I've been drinking, but you won't stop. Aren't you thirsty?"

Still animated, Yongzhang shook his head and persisted, "Caitiao, I'm serious, the beauty of the eyebrow is really very important. However, when a man meets a woman for the first time he usually doesn't pay any attention to whether her eyebrows are ugly or attractive. It's only late at night as he sits facing her that he takes notice of them. My, your eyebrows are extraordinarily pretty!"

"Yongzhang, I'm not listening to you anymore! You're only making fun of me." She arched her brows slightly as she spoke and turned away from Yongzhang.

"Would I dare?" He promptly defended himself, gently tugging her back to face him. "Just now I was thanking Mother Nature for sending such a goddess to earth, enabling me to worship and know her intimately even though I sincerely doubt that I will ever be able to revere her sufficiently. How could I ever make fun of her? I'm convinced that if a person is truly beautiful on the outside, her inner soul is sure to be beautiful as well. Just think, has your soul ever made me unhappy or caused me not to adore you? Is there even anything in this room touched by your hand that others have not praised? If someone offered to trade me his kingdom for just the furniture in this room, not to mention you, my love, I would throw him in the madhouse for it."

At this point Caitiao, looking distracted, rested her head tipsily on Yongzhang's shoulder and stared at the slumbering man. Yongzhang continued to speak. "Well, the day after tomorrow is New Year's. What would you like me to give you? You have given me so much honor and happiness that even though I've been talking about it this whole evening, I haven't even begun to describe one iota of how I feel. My dear, tell me, what would you like? Never mind the cost. I am more than happy to spend money on whatever you want."

When Caitiao heard this she gave it a thought, then continued gazing at the man who had dozed off. Ziyi was now fast asleep and his red cheeks looked as though they had been daubed with rouge; his mysterious eyes were now shut peacefully; his jet-black eyebrows spread distinctly to his temples; his mouth, usually full of erudition and wit, was closed in a slight curve as though he were smiling. Indeed, Caitiao had seldom seen him look this way before. He always seemed so respectful and elegant, unlike his current state of mellow relaxation. After she had stared at him in wonder for a time, Caitiao's face suddenly grew flushed and she said, "I only want you to promise me one thing.... It will only take a second."

"Please hurry and tell me," Yongzhang said ecstatically. "Whatever is mine is yours. You can have a million years, not to mention one second."

"I want—I'm rather embarrassed to say."

"Don't worry."

"He..."

"He won't wake up, I assure you. You can speak without worrying about that."

"I . . . I want only to kiss his face. Would you let me?"

"Really, Caitiao?"

"Really! Yes really!"

"Really? It's not right!. . . . You're drunk tonight too, aren't you?"

"I am not drunk, no. Listen to why I am making this request and then you'll agree to it. Ever since I met Ziyi I have really admired him; his manner, the way he speaks, the way he gets along with people, these things have often attracted me to him. Since he's already married, though, I have never dared utter a word of my adoration to him. He's stuck in an unhappy situation at home and I feel sorry for him."

Yongzhang replied, "He told me that he thinks well of me and truly envies me. But since there are so many people who envy me I didn't understand what he meant. I realized that you admired him too, but I didn't know you adored him so."

"Lower your voice. Let me finish explaining what I'm feeling. As you know, I was born with a peculiar love of literature, and whenever I read a truly marvelous essay I always imagine how dignified the author looks, though writers with beautiful literary styles aren't necessarily graceful in manner or speech. But he . . . what really makes me adore him, well, everything! . . . I have never had the nerve to tell anyone about this, since the average person would misunderstand. Today after the wine the way he spoke enchanted me even more. Thinking about the aggravating situation he has at home—a wife without an ounce of affection for him, a bunch of distant relatives who only want his money—I can't help but feel profound sympathy for him. Poor fellow! . . . My dear, how regrettable it is that such a fine and noble man doesn't have anyone to love and care for him."

"Oh, so you want to go *kiss*[1] him, Caitiao?"

"Mm, because the more I look at him now the more sorry I feel for him. I've gotten to the point where I won't feel comfortable if I don't express this emotion." She gripped Yongzhang's hand tightly. "You must consent."

An uneasy look came over on Yongzhang's face and he said, still smiling, "Caitiao, can you think of another request? I can't agree to this one...."

Caitiao interrupted him before he could finish. "Since I know that you are the one who loves me most, why can't you consent to this one wish? ... It's only Ziyi, and you care for him too...."

"Dear, you really are drunk. The love between a husband and wife is different from that between friends! I'm not sure why I appreciate it when you love my friend as I do, but still I can't allow you to kiss him," Yongzhang explained hastily.

"I am not drunk, honestly," Caitiao said impatiently. "You have to let me, all I want is to *kiss* him for a second, then I'll feel better. Do you mean you still don't trust me?" She looked at Yongzhang.

Seeing the determined expression on her face, Yongzhang answered, "It's not that I don't trust you, it's just that I feel I can't agree to this request."

"If it's not a question of trust, then why can't you agree to it?" she said earnestly, standing up.

"Must you really *kiss* him, no matter what?"

"Yes, I won't feel right if I don't go and *kiss* him once."

"All right then!" Yongzhang declared decisively.

She stood up, took two steps, then suddenly turned back and pulled Yongzhang, saying "Come with me."

"What difference will it make if I sit over here and wait for you? What makes you so afraid that you need someone to go with you?"

"No, you must come with me."

"I can't go with you. Besides, if I did go with you it would be like I didn't trust you. Don't you think so?"

She moved away without replying, then suddenly halted, saying, "My heart is pounding terribly, don't go away."

"OK. I promise to stay here with you."

---

1. Original in English.

"I'm going." Having said this, she tiptoed toward the big chair where Ziyi had fallen asleep. As she drew nearer she could see Ziyi's face more distinctly, and her heart began beating faster. As she reached the front of the chair, her heart was throbbing so rapidly that the beating seemed to have become louder. Suddenly her cheeks grew unusually hot and her heart fluttered strangely. After she had fixed her gaze on Ziyi for a moment, her face cooled and the fierce pounding of her heart subsided. In two or three steps she was back in front of Yongzhang; she sat down without a word, and lowered her head. Yongzhang looked at her and asked impatiently, "What is it now, Caitiao?"

"Nothing. I don't want to *kiss* him anymore."

ONCE UPON A TIME
(1928)

One afternoon when classes had finished, the sun sat low in the sky, eagerly draping the windows of the East Building at the C— School in a curtain of golden orange. Upstairs several girl students, dressed in a variety of light blue and violet prints, were talking and laughing together. Yunluo, who was in her room tidying up, suddenly heard someone in the courtyard shout out in a loud voice, "*Juliet, Juliet, Romeo* seeks thee *Juliet!*" A burst of laughter followed.

Yunluo had recently been cast in the role of Juliet in *Romeo and Juliet*, the play they were putting on in celebration of the school's ten-year anniversary; the part of Romeo had been given to Yingman, a student in the class above her. Just over twenty years old, Yingman was a tall, outgoing northerner who loved to joke around. Yunluo had never had the nerve to talk to her before, and since Yingman had been teasing her in front of the other students during rehearsals over the past few days, she felt incredibly uncomfortable, even a bit annoyed. But then why did her heart start to pound a little each time she heard Yingman shouting "Juliet"? It surely wasn't out of anger.

"What a bother," Yunluo muttered to herself, pretending not to have heard Yingman holler, "She wants to rehearse again!"

The girl students upstairs suddenly started giggling again, and Yingman raised her voice and yelled, "Juliet, hurry up. Aren't you worried Romeo might get sick from impatience?"

Despite her slight irritation, Yunluo could no longer pretend she hadn't heard. She threw down the handkerchief she had just rinsed, stuck her head out the door of the dormitory, and replied, "Do we have to rehearse that stupid play again? I'm coming, but I'm not done reviewing the lessons we're being tested on tomorrow. . . ."

When Yunluo could stall no longer, she went downstairs pouting.

On the evening of their final rehearsal, Yingman accompanied Yunluo back to her dormitory. Sitting under the lamp, she watched Yunluo undo her hair and plait it into a loose braid, then change into her imported pastel pajamas with snowflakes embroidered along the cuffs and collar. Probably from the exhaustion of rehearsing, the tender rosiness of Yunluo's cheeks had risen to her eyelids, and she had to struggle to keep her pretty eyes open. She looked exceptionally delicate and vulnerable.

"Oh, I could die of exhaustion!" Yunluo rubbed her back with her hand, then fell onto her bed.

"Juliet, shall I massage your back for you?" Yingman said with a grin as she went over to Yunluo, gazing at the ivory skin of her exposed chest, then down past the large collar where she could make out the faint curve of her soft, slightly protruding breasts. Her small arc-shaped mouth, now slightly agape, was so adorable; two small dimples appeared at the corners of her mouth and then two more on her cheeks. She looked more enticing now than she had in the play when she was on the verge of kissing Romeo. Now and then an intoxicating aroma of Yunluo's powder, hair, or flesh—it was hard to tell which—wafted up through the bed curtains.

Suddenly, Yingman flopped down on the bed too and cradled her arm around Yunluo's neck, and said, "My entire body feels weak. What is that fragrance? Let me smell!"

"There you go teasing me again. What a nuisance!" Yunluo smiled, gently nudging her away.

"Don't be annoyed with me. I would die if you were annoyed with me!" Yingman went ahead and hugged her tightly.

When Yunluo's roommate Meiling pushed open the door and found the two of them like this, she chuckled loudly. "Romeo, don't die of heartache, I've decided to give our Juliet to you. Elder Sister Zhu, do you agree?"

Lying under her quilt reading a book, their other roommate, Zhu, smiled and said, "How could I refuse?! Meiling, you better get over to your own bed. Three's a crowd!

As the others laughed, Yingman seized the moment to bury her face in Yunluo's breast and inhale deeply.

Whether Yunluo no longer had the energy to resist or was enjoying having such a warm, soft thing hugging her chest, she didn't put up a fuss this time, but merely laughed gently and said, "You're suffocating me!"

After a while, the dormitory warden, Mrs. Zhou, came in to check the room, and Yingman reluctantly got up and returned to her own dormitory in the rear courtyard.

The next night, after the performance, it was raining so hard that Yunluo dragged Yingman into her room to escape the downpour before she went on home. When the two burst into the room clutching a single tiny umbrella and with their arms wrapped around each other's waists, Meiling greeted them with a grin. "Bravo, Romeo and Juliet have arrived as a pair. I just made some tea. Drink as husband and wife." Having said this, she gazed at Yunluo's face for a moment then fell back onto her bed in a spasm of giggles.

"You little monkey, what's so funny?" Yingman laughed.

"Backstage earlier you couldn't stop laughing—did we mess up or something?" Yunluo asked.

"It was so hysterical, tonight. . . ." Meiling was laughing so hard she couldn't finish.

"Tomorrow we should change your nickname to the laughing monkey! Can't you ever stop laughing?" said Yingman, with a silly laugh herself.

"Oh, I'm going to die of laughter!" Meiling sat up, wiping her eyes. "If I tell you, you will too. Your performance tonight was brilliant; it's just that when you got to the scene where you have to kiss each other, I was hiding in the curtains watching two boys who were sitting in the front row—the ones that looked like students—someone said they are Yang Yuqing's older cousins. Anyway, they were gawking at the two of you with their mouths hanging wide open as if they were waiting for some delicious morsel of food! As luck would have it, in the row behind them, a little kid was leaning over with his father's cane and the curved handle went right into one of the boy's mouths; the other one saw what happened and quickly pulled it out for him, but the first one sat there grinning with his mouth still wide open. It was hysterical. Didn't you see?"

They both laughed. Elder Sister Zhu threw a book down from the bed and said, "The things you say! I refuse to believe that the boy didn't even notice when there was a cane in his own mouth."

"If you don't believe me go ask someone else; I'm not the only one who saw it." Meiling laughed as she dashed out of the room.

As Yingman looked at Yunluo laughing, Yunluo's pink cheeks turned a shade darker. They sat together on the bed giggling and chatting.

After a while, Meiling bounced back in the room and yelled, "It's raining so hard I almost slipped and fell. Romeo, I have good news to report: you don't have to leave tonight. Old Lady Wu just told everyone downstairs that Mrs. Zhou isn't feeling well this evening, so she won't be coming to check the rooms."

"Let's shut the door and go to bed then!" Zhu said, shooting a meaningful look at Meiling, who got the message and went to close the door.

Shortly thereafter, the lights went out. Yingman stood up and asked, "Should I go?"

"Don't. . . ." Yunluo pulled her back down. "It's raining so hard, you . . ."

"Your bed is too small, how can I squeeze in?"

"Romeo, don't you know a good thing when you see it? If Juliet wants you to stay, how can you refuse?" Meiling said, poking her head out from the covers.

"Who's refusing? I'm just afraid we'll be so crowded that she will be uncomfortable." Yingman pulled off her jacket and skirt and lay down next to Yunluo.

The room was filled with a humid, earthy smell and the rain pattered on in the courtyard. Suddenly Meiling burst out laughing again, breaking the dark silence. "Elder Sister Zhu, do you remember the rest of the saying 'May the world's lovers . . .'?"

"Isn't it 'all become spouses'?" Zhu replied. "Now stop being so talkative and go to sleep."

Yingman nestled her face close to Yunluo's and giggled softly. "Did you hear that, you are my spouse."

"There you go making fun of me again. I'm not sleeping with you anymore." Yunluo gave her shove, but then took advantage of the moment to snuggle her head in Yingman's bosom.

Yunluo awoke in the middle of the night. Lying there under the warm covers, with a soft arm as her pillow and a hand resting on her waist, she was overcome for the first time with an indescribable sense of well-being. That feeling of emptiness, fear, and loneliness that normally came to her when she awoke late at night seemed to have been dissolved by this sensation of warmth. She covered Yingman up again with the quilt lest she catch a chill.

Yingman suddenly woke up; the rain had stopped and the faint moonlight shone in through the bed curtains. When she opened her eyes, she found Yunluo staring at her with an infatuated look. Seeing that Yingman was awake, Yunluo felt slightly embarrassed. She covered her eyes with her hand and buried her head in her arm, whispering softly, "Why did you wake up too?"

Yingman wanted to lift Yunluo's face to look at her, but she had nestled up to her shoulder laughing idiotically, which tickled her arm. Her lips touched Yunluo's forehead, and before she knew it she had started kissing her, over and over again.

Yunluo whispered, "Did you sleep well?"

"Splendidly!" Yingman's hand stroked Yunluo's velvety cheeks as she said, "What if I weren't a woman? . . ."

"There you go again. Sleep!" Yunluo pinched her gently, then put her cheek up against Yingman's face. And so they slept, snuggled up closely together.

After that, the two of them would stroll around campus nearly every evening, talking heart-to-heart as their classmates watched from afar, laughing as they walked by.

Time passed quickly and on a night half a month later, the moonlight spilled quietly over the ground like silver frost as Yunluo and Yingman walked together into the courtyard with their arms wrapped around each other's waists. First they recounted what they had each been thinking about over the past few days; after that, they sat on the railing of the pavilion and gazed at the moon, each lost in her own thoughts. Suddenly Yingman laughed and said, "How gentle the moon is! Tonight I feel that she is shining down on us with a particular brightness, and her round face looks as though she's smiling. Do you see how beautifully she smiles?"

Yunluo knit her brow and, looking at Yingman, replied, "You are always such an optimist! How is it that I can't see her smiling? If there's a smile on that frosty snow-white face, then it's a cold one! When I look at the moon, all my worries return. I shed tears of grief, for I remember my deceased father and sister as well as my living mother and brother." As she spoke, something appeared at the edge of her eye that caught the light of the moon; Yingman reached out and helped her wipe it away.

"You really are so *sentimental*;[2] you can't even bear the spring breeze or the bright moon!" As she spoke, she smiled and kissed Yunluo's cheeks repeatedly; then she smoothed down the strands of hair that the wind had blown astray. The more Yunluo's tears were wiped dry the more she cried, and finally she threw herself in Yingman's arms and started to weep. This stunned Yingman.

"What is it, my love?" asked Yingman softly, as she embraced Yunluo tightly and nuzzled her face up close.

Her sobs escalated, and when Yingman pressed her again several more times, she finally burst out, "My life is so meaningless!"

At a loss for words, Yingman looked at her blankly. Helping her wipe away her tears, she said, "Why do you always say there's no point in living? If something's worrying you, tell me. I hate it when you're sad."

Yunluo sighed; her face turned even more pale and pathetic. She stared blankly at Yingman for a while and then suddenly squeezed her hand tightly and, lowering her head, asked her regretfully, "Why aren't you a man?"

"Must I be a man in order to hear what's bothering you?" Yingman retorted, smiling faintly.

"No, did I say that? What I mean is that it's no use telling you!" She hung her head even lower.

"You mustn't hide your troubles from me; don't we share everything now? Your worries are my worries, so why can't you tell me what's bothering you?"

"I can't bear to make you sad on my behalf so I'm not telling you." She gazed silently at the moon for a while, then continued. "Yesterday my older brother wrote again and said that his section chief has begged him repeatedly to arrange a meeting with me; brother claims that this man is really all right and that he is extremely respectful toward my mother. He says he really can't refuse him." She lowered her head again. "Think about it, I have never even seen this man and, what's more, yesterday I overheard Yuying talking about him. She said that less than two months after his wife died, he was on the prowl for a new one. From Yuying's tone of voice, I think he might have even asked her. And if Yuying hasn't consented, then why would I . . ." she said, somewhat angrily. "But brother has already sent seven or eight letters saying how much he respects this

---

2. Original in English.

man, and that he's doing this for my sake, that I should save face for him and make up my mind soon and stop being so doubtful."

At first Yingman listened with her eyes fixed on Yunluo; afterward, her eyes seemed a little moist and she looked at the ground. When she realized that Yunluo had finished speaking, her tears started flowing, and she asked anxiously, "So what are you going to do?"

"I haven't written back yet. I wish that the two of us could live together for the rest of our lives. . . . It's just that I'm afraid that my mother and brother would never . . ." Yunluo glanced at Yingman, then started crying again; Yingman did not say a word but simply cried along with her. "Don't be sad. Don't be sad, my heart is going to break . . ."

Yingman took out her handkerchief and wiped her eyes. "People make their own destinies. Why can't we be together forever? Look at the primary school instructors Miss Chen and *Miss Chu*,[3] haven't they been living together for five or six years? You mean to say we can't be like them? Don't be so stubborn. My love for you is deeper and more permanent than any man's could ever be, surely you know this. Can't you just consider this the same as being married to me?"

The ashen hue of Yunluo's face seemed to have diminished somewhat, but when she heard the final question, her brow wrinkled slightly, revealing that in her heart she couldn't accept this, though she didn't dare say so openly. Seeing that she hadn't responded, Yingman touched her shoulder and, facing her, went on, "Can't you consider this being married? Write back and tell your brother to refuse that man!" Yunluo's eyelids dropped, like a coquettish young lady meeting a stranger; Yingman saw this but pretended not to notice. Her mouth was half open, as though there were something strange in the air making it difficult for her to breathe. Yunluo embraced her tightly and said, "*My God, how can I live without you! I love you. Say you love me, my love.*"[4]

When they both looked at the moon, it seemed to have changed into glittering silver dance clothes, standing in the center of the sky congratulating them with a smile. As the cool, early May night breeze blew against their faces, carrying the fragrance of the white tea roses growing beneath the western wall, it was as though the moon had opened a

---

3. Original in English.

4. Original in English.

bottle of sweet wine and poured it into their wedding goblets as she awaited them.

"You are the moon, and I am that star beside you . . ." Yingman laughed with her face turned up; hand in hand, they walked down from the pavilion.

"You'll follow me forever, and I'll always accompany you . . ." Yunluo said, walking with her head lowered.

Their affections seemed to grow like the blossoms of the tea roses, and peach and plum trees on campus, and when people at school spoke of them they no longer referred to them by their real names, as though they had always been called Romeo and Juliet. Even Old Lady Wu, who came and sold pastries at the cafeteria for an hour each day, learned of their new nicknames.

When summer vacation arrived, Yingman accompanied Yunluo to Tianjin and waited until she had boarded her train to Jinling before taking a train back to her own hometown. As they said good-bye, Yunluo grasped Yingman's hand and wept so profusely she couldn't say a thing.

The day Yingman arrived back home, she sat in her room and composed a letter, which she then hurried to have someone post. Her parents and her elder brother and sister-in-law all teased her, saying that the reason she wasn't as mischievous and playful as before was that she must be in love.

After sending off her letter, Yingman waited a week without receiving a reply, so she mailed two more express letters in a row. One day, as she was flipping through some photos of herself and Yunluo, a letter arrived. The contents moved her greatly:

> How could you suspect that I would ever forget you? I am the one who is afraid that you will forget me in the end! I myself realize that I have nothing to make someone admire me forever; for one, my intelligence can't even compare to yours and moreover I am lazy and like to play. So how could I ever rival you? I am even lazier when I am at home. Ever since I got back, Mother and I have had guests every day. It's such a bother. Whenever someone comes, my mother nags me to change my clothes and put on face powder. Yesterday I realized there was something wrong with this and refused to obey her, but that night at dinner she said, her eyes brimming with tears, "Now that you're all grown up and mature, everything your old moth-

er has to say is rubbish." I had no choice but to force a smile and hold back my tears as I listened to her chatter. Alas, since my father's death, she has suffered so much for my brother and me.

Don't blame me for taking so long to write; this is the first letter I've written since I got back. Last night, I stared at that star next to the moon for ages, as if in a trance. I suspect you are so happy to be home that you don't have time to look at the moon, do you? My star, my dazzling bright star, can you see the sparkle of my tears?

When Yingman read to this point, she lifted the letter to her lips and, teary-eyed, kissed it over and over again. That night, after everyone had gone to bed, she lit the candle again and re-read it so many times the words began to blur. She fell asleep with the letter in her hand.

At night, she would often dream of Yunluo wearing beautiful clothes, with streams of tears running down her lovely snow-white face. She would rush toward her, but then suddenly she would realize that Yunluo looked like a corpse and she would wake up sobbing. Everyone in the family laughed at her behavior.

After that letter, two weeks went by without another; Yingman was beside herself and she argued every day with her parents about returning to school early. Later, when fighting broke out in Jiangsu and Zhejiang, the Tianjin-Shanghai rail line was suspended so it took more than twenty days for mail from Shanghai to reach Tianjin. There was nothing she could do. At first, she had nightmares and would wake up in tears; later, the bad dreams stopped and she couldn't even fulfill her desire to see Yunluo in that way. She grew anxious and despondent. Sometimes, in her dreams, she seemed to hear someone say that Yunluo was seriously ill and couldn't write and that she should go see her; in the dream, she would desperately want to go to her but her parents wouldn't allow it. Her anxious cries would wake her mother in the room next door, and all Yingman could do was close her eyes and pretend to be asleep when she came in to check on her.

Week after week, she waited without hearing a single word from Yunluo. Summer vacation was drawing to a close, but the war still hadn't ended; nevertheless, a week before classes were to start, she said good-bye to her parents and returned to school in Beijing. But she was in for a disappointment, as the wardens at the dormitory still hadn't received news about the date of Yunluo's arrival.

She sent off countless express letters, though no telegrams—to send a telegram she would have to ask someone to help her, for she had never sent one herself. Besides, she had heard that telegrams from Beijing to Nanjing often didn't go through during military operations. She was so troubled that she would lie on her bed every day staring listlessly at the top of the bed canopy.

One day near dusk, as she was strolling around campus alone, she noticed that several round blossoms had appeared on the Jiangnan chrysanthemum bushes next to the pavilion; the thought of that southern region stirred up her worries and she left the garden in tears. She contemplated going back to her room to wash the handkerchiefs that had accumulated over the past few days, but this too reminded her of Yunluo, how she always used to take them away quietly and wash them for her. As she walked past the playground, she saw her other classmates strolling and chatting in couples, shoulder to shoulder, hand in hand; they seemed to her to be deliberately acting even more intimate than before. After a while, she saw one pair turn to look at her and they shouted, with a note of derision in their voices, "Romeo, why don't you come for a walk with us?" then smiled at her arrogantly. This only added to her sorrow.

The lingering pale golden sunlight streamed through the windows of the dormitory and cheerful shouts and laughs frequently emanated from inside the rooms. For some inexplicable reason she had recently come to loathe the sound of people laughing. She now thought people sounded really stupid when they laughed, and she was especially irritated when they looked at her and laughed. As she walked slowly down the corridor, she cursed the person laughing, that laughing fool, that infuriating laughter....

Suddenly, she halted in her tracks as she heard the name Yunluo. A classmate in room three was saying, "Yunluo? She's now my older sister's sister-in-law."

"She got married?"

"That's what my sister said. She wrote that her new sister-in-law's last name is Xie, that she's really pretty, and that she went to school with me for two years. Who else could it be besides Yunluo?" As soon as Yingman overheard this a loud boom filled her ears, but still she could make out the words, "Pretty ... the bridegroom is beaming ... his new bride is smiling ..." Yet she couldn't decipher what it meant. Then everything turned black; after a moment, an image of Yunluo's sad face appeared before her, then an image of her dressed up as a bride with a red veil over her head and sparkling clothes and jewelry, standing there with a slight smile....[5]

She collapsed on the floor with a thud. The people inside the room rushed out and found her there; then, their lips blue with fright, they screamed in trembling voices, "Oh my God! What's the matter with her? What happened?"

Her classmates moved her onto a bed. When she opened her eyes she could see a crowd of people and everyone seemed to be talking at once. She couldn't make out what they were saying and didn't have the patience to listen; she had no choice but to close her eyes. One moment Yunluo appeared before her crying faintly, the next she seemed to be laughing, but then she was crying again!

Yingman couldn't bear the sight of her anymore. As she let out a deep sigh, the people standing around her all said, "It's all right, it's all right, she's coming to!"

---

5. Brides in China traditionally wear red.

10

Su Xuelin

Su Xuelin (1897–)

A native of Anhui province, Su Xuelin (pen name: Lu Yi) grew up in a traditional extended family of low-level Qing officials dominated by an elderly matriarch who bound her granddaughter's feet at the age of four. Su was allowed to study classical Chinese at home and later attend an American missionary school, but only because her grandmother wanted her to read Buddhist scriptures to her. When her family refused to allow the fifteen-year-old to continue her studies, however, Su threatened to drown herself unless they permitted her to enroll in the Anhui Provincial First Normal School for Girls. She excelled at her studies and worked briefly as a teacher before enrolling in the Chinese department at Beijing Women's Normal College in 1919, where her classmates included future woman writers Lu Yin and Feng Yuanjun; she left the school in 1921 after obtaining a scholarship to study in France.

From 1921 through 1925, Su Xuelin studied literature and art in a special program for Chinese students at Institut Franco-Chinois de Lyon. Her semi-autobiographical novel *Bitter Heart*, published in 1929, relates her experiences in France and the personal struggles she overcame while abroad. In addition to describing life in rural France, *Bitter Heart* also tells the story of the author's introduction to Catholicism and her eventual conversion. "Harvest," the short essay that is translated here and first appeared in her collection *Green Skies* in 1928, is typical of the numerous short travel pieces Su Xuelin wrote after her return to China. Her poetic vignettes of the people, customs, and scenery she observed as a foreign student reveal as much about the process of her own growing self-awareness as they do about France.

Su Xuelin returned to China in 1925 to satisfy her ailing mother by marrying the man she had chosen for her. She taught at girls' schools in Suzhou and Shanghai (where she began her long friendship with fellow writer Yuan Changying), and then at Anhui University. During this period, Su Xuelin published the short stories and essays that make up *Green Skies*. Often mistaken for autobiographical writings, the lyrical sketches of blissful married life contained in *Green Skies* are what Su Xuelin once described as "beautiful lies," for she in fact was suffering through a loveless marriage at the time. While many writers of the 1920s were struggling to find their literary voices using the modern Chinese vernacular, Su Xuelin drew on her extensive knowledge of classical Chinese literature to develop a style of writing that borrowed freely from both the classical tradition and modern colloquial usage. She also produced innovative studies of classical poetry and literature, and developed one of the first courses on modern Chinese literature as a professor at Wuhan University after 1931.

An outspoken critic of the Communist Party, Su Xuelin left mainland China for Hong Kong in 1949 in a conscious protest against the new government. Her estranged husband chose to remain in China. She finally settled in Taiwan in 1952 and quickly became one of Taiwan's best-known teachers and authorities on classical Chinese literature. Although she seldom wrote fiction after the late 1920s, Su penned several pioneering studies of modern Chinese literature. Her critique of mainland China's favorite writer, Lu Xun, as a "neurotic man" unworthy of the overblown admiration he received in China made her a controversial figure. Su's vehement anti-Communist sentiments kept her early fiction from being republished in mainland China until 1994. Su Xuelin lives near the campus of Taiwan National Cheng-kung University in Tainan, where she taught for many years. In 1997, literary circles in Taiwan celebrated her 100th birthday.

HARVEST

(1928)

That summer, large empty fields near our campus were rented out for growing sweet potatoes. The soil had been left uncultivated for some time and the walls were collapsing here and there due to wind, rain, and attacks by naughty children. The school had to spend a good deal of money each year to repair the wall and it was becoming a financial burden. Finally a decision was made to rent out the land for cultivation so that the rent money could could help defray the cost of the wall repairs. Before long, farmers had plowed a portion of the land and planted a crop of sweet potatoes. I learned that once the sweet potatoes were harvested, they would plant wheat, then beans and sweet peaches. The farmers would make a decent profit once the peaches came in.

When the barren land was first cultivated and the fields were covered with sweet potato vines, the farmers came often to water them. But after a time the fields seemed to have been left abandoned and nobody paid any attention to them. Nevertheless, in the height of summer, when other types of vegetables had long since withered, the sweet potato vines continued to grow and flourish with each day and I began to suspect that they might actually be wild vines.

One day after class, I heard a steady swooshing sound coming from beyond the wall. Not knowing what it was, I went out on the terrace to see the newest development.

In the warm autumn sun, a group of men and women were digging up the earth, lifting and dropping their iron rakes in a regular rhythm reminiscent of a Tchaikovsky melody. The steady clang of the metal teeth digging into the soil mingled with the laughter of the rakers, like a harmony flowing from the keys of a piano.

"Hurry and come watch! They're harvesting the sweet potatoes!" I turned around and shouted to those lingering inside. Kang and Ahua tossed aside their books and came out to look. Before long, we decided that it would be much more fun to go out to the fields than to watch from the terrace, so the three of us opened the garden gate and made our way to the sweet potato fields.

The unearthed sweet potatoes had been collected in piles on the ground. The largest ones weighed over a pound and even the small ones were as thick as my wrist. They were red with a purple tinge, somewhat like water chestnuts just dredged up from a pond, though not as fresh or appealing. An old woman squatting on the ground was tearing the vines and roots off the newly unearthed potatoes one by one, like a midwife lifting up a newborn baby and cutting its umbilical cord. Fascinated, Ahua and I watched her and then squatted down to help.

Kang chatted with the sweet potato farmer, asking him how the harvest had been this year. The man shook his head and said, "Sweet potatoes have to be grown in sandy soil to get sweet. This is the first time this soil has been cultivated and it's too fertile here, so only the vines have grown well, not the sweet potatoes. Some of the potatoes got too large and are hollow inside so they can only be fed to the pigs; nobody will buy them." Pointing down near his feet, he continued, "Look at this one. It weighs nearly three pounds, but it's rotten inside and inedible."

The sweet potato he was talking about was the size of an average melon, but it was full of cracks and holes made by boring insects and covered with tiny roots that looked like hairs on a person's head. "Lifting the bloody head of Zizhang, I throw it back to Master Cui!" I blurted out this couplet from a poem by Du Fu as I scooped up the sweet potato and tossed it at Kang's feet.

"Why must you compare it to Zizhang? I think it's more like the head of John the Baptist that Salome carried," Kang replied, laughing, but I didn't think it was that funny. Ahua and the farmer just stared at us blankly, not knowing what we were going on about.

Since it was easy to carry the sweet potatoes from here, we asked the farmer if we could buy a *franc*'s worth, which we estimated would be about seventy pounds or so. We thought that it would be fun to roast a few while we warmed ourselves around the fire on winter nights. As the old saying goes, "I'd rather eat roast sweet potatoes than live like the Emperor." There's also the story about the lazy monk who refused to discuss even Buddhism while he was roasting sweet potatoes in fresh horse dung. Sweet potatoes might not be as tasty as the meat of the legendary falcon, but there's nothing like burying them under the hot coals of a fire while everyone is gathered around chatting or doing needlework. Just when you've forgotten that there's anything in there cooking, a fragrant odor drifts up and fills your nostrils to remind you that the potatoes are ready. Then, one by one, you pluck them from the fire, peel back the skin, and savor them while they're still hot. Oh, that sweet flavor is extraordinary!

Harvests, as I've mentioned already, are joyful occasions. While studying abroad, I took part in several large harvests, and these experiences left me with some of the happiest memories I have.

The first harvest I attended was in the spring of what I believe was my second year in Lyon. My French tutor, Mademoiselle Hémond, had introduced me to a friend who had a summer villa where we went to escape the heat. It was located near Lyon in Tain l'Ille, a village famous for its fruit.

The owner of the villa, Mademoiselle Basson, had opened a small boarding house for students of the girls' middle school near Lyon. I lived there while attending French classes at the school.

When spring break arrived the following year, most of the students in the dormitory went to their own homes or those of friends, while others went traveling. The owner of the dormitory invited several students from distant places to her villa for a change of scenery. I was one of the students she took.

On the train there, a fellow student, Marguerite, said to me, her eyes filled with glee, "This time when we go to the countryside we can eat cherries to our hearts' content." During a visit to the villa the previous summer, I had noticed several large cherry trees, but they had been covered only with green leaves and not a single cherry could be seen.

When the train approached Tain l'Ille village, the verdant green Lac Lémon Mountain stretched before the train as if it were an old man spreading his arms out wide in the spring air to greet me after half a year's absence.

Sheep dotted the flatlands in the distance like white gulls floating upon a swell of green ocean. The sharp steeple of the church towered high above the lush thicket, piercing the bright azure sky, while the slow tolling of its bell shattered the tranquil atmosphere below. The spring breeze stroked our faces with the fresh smell of new growth. As we walked along the road, we all began to feel sluggish, as if we'd imbibed some good wine or been suspended like the clouds in the sky, drunk on the fresh air.

When we arrived at the villa, the matron of our boarding house, Mademoiselle Dorothée Resson, was there waiting for us with a meal already prepared. As soon as we finished eating, we began picking cherries. Marguerite climbed up the tree, plucked the cherries one by one, and tossed them down to us. We ate as many as we could and filled our baskets with the rest. Later, I climbed up the tree too, but the matron was afraid I would fall and hurt myself and warned me repeatedly to be careful. As a child I was a natural at climbing trees, but to my surprise I found that now that I was older, my hands and feet were no longer so nimble; still, I managed to make it up.

French cherries are different from Chinese ones. They are about the same size as a longan berry, but much fleshier and with a small pit. In the heat they turn a delightful, lustrous dark purple. As for their flavor, "sweet as honey" is the only way to describe it. Lichees, mandarin oranges, and strawberries (sometimes called foreign bayberries) are the only Chinese fruits that even compare, while our pearl cherries could never be more than a handmaiden to the French cherries. I was reminded of how during the Tang dynasty, cherries were often grown in the imperial gardens and would be presented to the palace officials when the weather turned hot. This inspired many of the poets and literary men of the time to eulogize them again and again. How, I wondered, would these men have sung the praises of French cherries had they the chance to taste them? In fact, France has many rare fruits, all of which have been bred scientifically. In his play *The Blue Bird*, Maeterlinck writes that in the world of the future, there will be chrysanthemums as large as tables, and grapes the size of pears. One day, the miracles of science will make old Chinese sayings like: "In times of peace, the jujubes grow as large as melons" come true. I have a great respect for the power of science and look forward to the golden age it will bring us!

We stayed at the Tain l'Ille Villa for three days and although we stuffed ourselves with cherries each one of those days, we still had three large baskets left over. The matron wrapped them up to take back to Lyon to make jam for our desserts.

My second happy harvest experience was in the fall of 1924 when another French friend invited me to the village of Champagne near Lyon in order to escape the summer heat. We stayed at a girls' elementary school that was empty for the summer vacation. Only the school principal, Madame Julie, a woman of about sixty, and a schoolteacher, Mademoiselle Marie, remained.

As my school year always began rather late, I stayed in the countryside for the entire summer and on into early fall. I enjoyed fresh milk and eggs, huge firm pears and cherries, sweet jam, and delicious milk biscuits every day, until eventually I had put on a few pounds. When the time for the grape harvest arrived, announcements of "la Vendange"[1] were posted all over the village and everyone came to the fields to lend a hand.

I remember one day Madame Julie and I were sitting beneath the linden trees in the courtyard chatting when a man wearing wooden clogs and a calfskin apron appeared at the door and asked: "I haven't hired enough workers to pick the grapes. Would several of you be willing to come help tomorrow, Madame Julie?"

I knew he was Monsieur René, who had a good number of vineyards near the village and could be considered a small landlord. Usually he was quite elegantly dressed and dignified in manner—the very picture of a respected country gentleman—but now, in the height of the busy farming season, he was transformed into a rough workman.

Madame Julie agreed to go the next day and then asked me whether I would join her. She explained that grape picking was not very strenuous work and one could even earn six *francs* for the day plus snacks and supper. She herself went every year.

It wasn't that I wanted the compensation, but everyone else was going and it would have been dull to stay alone at home, so I decided I might as well go along with them to avoid being bored.

The next morning, as the first ray of sunlight poured through the linden trees outside the window, we prepared to go. Madame Julie and Mademoiselle Marie each wore a *tablier* (a special style of apron) and after breakfast we departed together. On the way there, we saw many other people, young and old, male and female, all heading for the fields to pick grapes. Champagne is a grape-producing area and there are vine-

---

1. Original in French.

yards for dozens of miles around, so when it's harvest time, nearly every person in the village comes out to help. It's very lively.

Monsieur René's vineyard was located behind the girls' elementary school—about a five-minute walk from the school's rear gate. Monsieur René and his four children were already there when we arrived. He was wearing the same clothing as the night before and his children were also clothed in rough workers' garb and clumsy, worn-out leather shoes. There were four or five other men and women there who I supposed were workers who had also been recruited to help.

The wheat fields were golden and deserted except for four or five dappled cows silently grazing nearby. Countless white poplar trees of equal height and distance penetrated the light morning mist like great candles. Beyond the poplars you could just make out the silver outline of a river and a high mountain range through a thick layer of fog. Copper-colored clouds threatened to cover the sun like a heavy blanket, but it was reluctant to be hidden and struggled to keep its head out. A remarkable light streamed through a crack in the clouds and, like a silver arrow shot from the sky, fell to the earth, scattering its golden rays about resplendently and painting an absolutely magnificent picture. By the time we had all reached the grape fields, the sun had made its way past the cracks in the clouds and climbed high in the sky, and the red morning glow had faded. The sky looked like an endless stretch of sparkling blue sea, and the yellow chestnuts and red maples nearby crowded together with towering dark green pines and cypress trees displaying a rich bounty of color like a gorgeous antique autumn brocade.

A cool wind tousled the tree branches as if the earth were sighing softly at the laughter rising from every row in the fields; joy filled the air. I love the European landscape because it encompasses both the cool strength of the north and the warm softness of the south. Its people are this way as well: they have both strong physiques and delicate features, resolute natures and lively spirits.

There were many varieties of grapes in Monsieur René's vineyards, white ones like crystals and purple ones like agates. Each cluster contained no fewer than a hundred grapes, every one of them perfectly round and firm. We placed them in large wicker baskets, which were taken away in a small cart to his wine-pressing room.

As we picked, we chose the largest grapes to eat, yet Monsieur René was still afraid we might be hungry and sent out bottles of pressed grape juice and slices of bread for us to snack on. Yet no one could eat any of it, for every worker had gorged on at least two or three pounds of grapes.

When evening fell, we went to the home of Monsieur René for supper. Everyone who had worked so hard that day—now made close friends by the "clogs and aprons"—sat together at a long table and drank and talked without restraint. Mademoiselle Marie told a joke, some Italian workers sang an Italian tune, and everyone urged me to sing a Chinese song. Although I had never excelled in singing class at school, I earned a great round of applause that evening.

I savored that rustic meal more than any grand banquet at a famous Parisian restaurant.

I love my country, but I have suffered endless "disillusionments" there, and have never once felt the joy of a harvest. How nostalgic I get whenever memories of my years abroad fill me again!

11

Yuan Changying

Yuan Changying (1894–1973)

Along with Bai Wei, Yuan Changying was one of the most gifted female playwrights of the May Fourth era. Although she was not prolific as a dramatist, writing for only a few short years in the late 1920s before turning primarily to scholarly research, literary criticism, and translation, her well-crafted plays reveal an unusually sophisticated sense of dramatic form and dialogue.

    Born in the southwestern province of Hunan in 1894, Yuan Changying moved to Shanghai with her father after her mother passed away, reputedly driven to her death by the fact that she had "failed" to produce any sons. Like other well-to-do young women of her generation in the 1920s and 1930s, Yuan went abroad for further academic training upon completing high school; in her case, this was a necessity since Chinese universities had yet to open their doors to women. From 1916 to 1921 she studied at Edinburgh University, receiving a master's degree in English drama. During her studies abroad, she met the economist Yang Duanliu, her future husband, and Chen Yuan, whose journal *Contemporary Review* would later feature Yuan's work. After a brief stint teaching at Beijing Women's Normal College, Yuan returned to Europe in 1926 and spent the next two years studying French literature and continuing her research in classical and modern European drama at the University of Paris.

Drawing on her immense knowledge of both the Chinese and Western literary traditions, Yuan Changying began writing drama when she returned to China again in the 1920s and accepted a teaching position at the newly established Wuhan University. *Southeast Flies the Peacock*, the title piece of a collection of works from these years that she published in 1930, represents her most ambitious and perhaps most successful experimentation with the still-nascent form of modern Chinese "spoken drama" (*huaju*). According to Su Xuelin, another prominent May Fourth woman writer and an admiring supporter of Yuan Changying's work, when this play was performed by faculty and students of Wuhan University in 1935, it received hostile reviews from leftist critics who felt the play lacked relevance to China's political struggles against Japan. True, it did not address what many progressive intellectuals then felt were the most pressing issues of the day—such as proletarian revolution or national liberation—but as an incisive exploration of the traditional family, it does engage with the deeply political topic of gender relations.

Based on the famous love tragedy depicted in an anonymous Han dynasty folk ballad (*yuefu*), Yuan's *Southeast Flies the Peacock* was not the first modern rewriting of this traditional tale: several other May Fourth writers adapted the story to explore contemporary issues. Whereas other writers focused on the theme of romance, Yuan Changying foregrounds the figure of the story's villain, Mother Jiao, in order to examine the psychologically complex, and from her perspective, tragic, realities of motherhood in traditional China.

A literary scholar by training, Yuan Changying published critical essays on literary translation, drama, and individual European writers (including Hardy, Maeterlinck, Ibsen, and Shakespeare) frequently in such journals as *Contemporary Review* and *Independent Criticism*. In addition to a collection of short plays (edited and reprinted with a new preface by Su Xuelin in 1982) and a four-act resistance play (1947), Yuan Changying's major publications include two volumes of essays, scholarly studies of French literature and Western music, and translations of English and French fiction and drama. After the founding of the People's Republic of China in 1949, Yuan Changying became a member of the All-China Writers' Union and continued publishing translations and essays while teaching at Wuhan University; however, both her academic and literary careers came to an abrupt halt after she was targeted during the antirightist campaign in 1957. Initially demoted to a job in the university library, Yuan was later charged with antirevolutionary crimes and forced out of the school altogether. During the Cultural Revolution, Yuan Changying was sent to the countryside, where she died in 1973.

SOUTHEAST FLIES THE PEACOCK
(1930)

Characters:

MOTHER JIAO	Widowed mother of ZHONG and MEI
LAN	ZHONG's fiancée, daughter of the Liu family
ZHONG	MOTHER JIAO's only son
MEI	ZHONG's younger sister
LAOLAO	An elderly widow
MATCHMAKER	Referred to by other characters as Mrs. Li
HUA	LAOLAO's granddaughter
SERVING GIRL	

Time: The Han dynasty (206 B.C.–A.D. 220)
Set: Costumes and household decorations are all of the period.

Act I

ZHONG's bedroom, prior to his wedding. The floor of the room is covered with straw mats. A small bed is placed in the right corner against the back wall. In the center of the room is a small round table with a tea set on it. Chairs are scattered about the room. One or two small clothing trunks are placed against the left wall. Next to the right-hand wall is a square desk on which lie books, brushes, ink, and a mirror. A door is located toward the front of the stage on the right-hand side. A handsome and energetic man with a round face and a square forehead, ZHONG is approximately twenty years old. When the curtain rises, however, he appears fatigued and thin. He is lying on the bed in casual clothing, flipping restlessly through a book. After a while he flings the book aside, boosts himself up, and sits on the edge of the bed. Despondently, he says:

ZHONG: Oh Heavens. Is this any way to spend my days? Is this all there is to life? This is life? Sickness! Sickness! Sick for three long months. It seems there is nothing in the world but sickness! [*Strokes his forehead with his hand. Stares idiotically at the sky as if in a trance*] But ... [*His face lights up with pleasure. He takes out a scented bag from his breast pocket, which he admires and raises to his lips, giving it a long, enraptured kiss.*] My beloved, when will I see you? ... It seems as though the days will never pass. Year after year! ... Oh, I still haven't tried on the phoenix robe your family sent on my birthday! [*He puts the scented bag back in its place, and goes over and takes a large blue silk robe embroidered with white phoenixes out of the trunk. He puts it on cheerfully and admires himself in the mirror. Feeling something in the right-hand sleeve, he hurriedly takes the garment off, turns the sleeve inside out, and sees that it has been lined carefully with bamboo paper. As he tears off the paper, a pink sash falls to the floor. He picks it up excitedly.*] No wonder everyone says you're clever! No wonder everyone says you are gentle and graceful. This pair of mandarin ducks symbolizes the two of us some day, doesn't it? I ... Oh! Why does the time drag on so? How will I endure these idle days? Ma, if only you knew how I really felt. How can I be sick? How can a mother be so oblivious? ... Heaven! Won't you come to my aid? [*He snatches up the sash again and kisses it wildly, becoming so excited that he nearly collapses. The sound of footsteps outside. He quickly stuffs the love token back into the case, dives under the covers on the bed, and fakes a soft groaning sound. The person accompanying the sound of the footsteps is his mother, a forty-three- or -four-year-old middle-aged woman. Her face is pale, her expression gloomy and worried. She carries a steaming hot bowl to the front of the bed.*]

MOTHER: Son! Are you any better today? You've already taken three doses of the doctor's medicine, but I still don't see any sign of improvement. I'll die of worry if this continues! Come now, sit up and drink this bowl of medicine.

ZHONG: [*Fighting back tears*] Ma! I don't want to take any more stupid medicine. I've had nothing but medicine for three straight months. I don't think all the medicine in the world would make me well.

MOTHER: Once you are sick, only medicine can cure you. What other solution is there?

ZHONG: I refuse to take any more. If I die, so be it!

MOTHER: [*Bursting into tears*] My son! How can you say such things? [*Wipes her tears*] Poor me, I have been a widow for over ten years, guarding you like my very life. How can you say that?

ZHONG: [*Changes tone*] Ma! Don't cry. Don't worry, I'll take the medicine. [*Struggles to sit up*]

MOTHER: [*Gently stroking his hair*] That's my good boy. [*After he drinks the medicine, his mother takes the bowl and places it on the round table.*]

ZHONG: Ma . . . [*He falls silent.*]

MOTHER: Son! [*Again she strokes his hair*] No one has hair blacker or sleeker than yours.

ZHONG: [*Smiling*] Isn't mine just the same as everyone else's?

MOTHER: Naturally no one is the same as my son! Silly! . . . It's because of the way I've pampered you. Is there anyone who has raised her son as well as I have raised you? Ever since your father passed away, there has been nothing to do except devote myself entirely to you. From morning till night, all I have done is attend to your beauty. I made this hair of yours glossy with Hundred Grasses Oil ever since you were little.

ZHONG: Thank you, Mother. You've had your hands full with me and sister. But we aren't so much trouble anymore.

MOTHER: Your sister was never a problem; after all, daughters are somewhat more docile. The naughty one was always you. But even though you are less trouble now, every now and then you are just as naughty as ever.

ZHONG: [*Smiling*] Like just now when I wouldn't take my medicine!
MOTHER: [*Also smiling*] Exactly.
ZHONG: Ma . . . [*He can't find the words.*]
MOTHER: What? You'd better lie down for a while so you don't wear yourself out. I shouldn't talk so much. [*Starts to leave*]
ZHONG: [*Tugs her to sit down*] Ma, I'm so bored. Stay and talk with me.
MOTHER: I'm just afraid you'll get tired.
ZHONG: I am not tired at all.
MOTHER: Even so, you ought to lie down. [*Forces him to lie down and tucks in the covers*]
ZHONG: [*A sort of aching yet pleasurable feeling surging in his heart*] Ma, you still treat me like a child.
MOTHER: Twenty years old is not young.
ZHONG: Twenty years old is not young. [*With a wry smile*]
MOTHER: What is this nonsense?
ZHONG: Am I not twenty-two?
MOTHER: Well, twenty-two then.
ZHONG: Ma, don't you think I've grown up?
MOTHER: How could I ever consider my own son grown up? My poor darling, you've made yourself sick thinking that now that you're all grown up, you'll have to become an official! You think you're so mature! But even if you got well tomorrow, I wouldn't let you go. We have plenty of money in the family, you don't need to go out and earn anything. All you have to do is stay here with me for the rest of your life.
ZHONG: A real man doesn't cling to his home his entire life and not go out and make something of himself!
MOTHER: A career is fine—as long as you are often by my side and let me stroke this beautiful hair of yours [*Again strokes his hair*]. Over the past twenty years, not a single day has gone by when I didn't stroke your pretty hair, this beautiful hair that is the product of my devotion. . . . Then I will be perfectly content.
ZHONG: [*Choked up*] Ma! How I wish my life could always be this way, but . . .
MOTHER: Of course it will always be this way! [*Misunderstanding him*] Who could snatch my son, my one and only son, away from me? Even Heaven wouldn't dare. I will fight for you with anyone who dares try.

ZHONG: Ma, don't misunderstand me. I am not saying I am going to die.
MOTHER: What are you saying?
ZHONG: I am saying that when your children are grown up they will inevitably...
MOTHER: [*Crying*] Inevitably leave me? How can you say this? If you leave me, who will I depend on? Then I will have to fight with you.
ZHONG: Mother, not again! How could I ever leave you? What I meant was, when your children grow up each will have their own career, their own life, and their own happiness.
MOTHER: If you stay by my side will your career be neglected? Will your life be obstructed? Will your happiness be hindered? What kind of son would say such a thing? Do you mean to say that as your mother I shouldn't treat you well? Do you mean to say... [*Angry*]
ZHONG: [*Imploring*] Ma. Ma, I beg you not to be angry. Don't worry, I won't say another word, I won't say... [*The sound of voices outside*] Someone's here. Mother, go see who it is.
MOTHER: [*Stands up*] It's probably the venerable Laolao coming to see you. I heard that she wanted to come and visit. Hurry and lie down properly. My son, I shouldn't have gotten angry and upset you.
ZHONG: I'm not upset, Ma, don't worry. [*Mei, an energetic and quick-witted young girl of thirteen or fourteen years old, enters supporting Laolao, a silvery-gray-haired old lady who is wearing undyed raw silk clothes. The old lady has an air of contentment about her.*]
MOTHER: Laolao, look what the south wind has blown in today! Please come in!
LAOLAO: I have been meaning to call on you for some time to see your son. I hear he's seriously ill. Young Master, are you feeling any better yet?
ZHONG: [*Propping himself up*] Yes, thank you, Laolao, I am.
LAOLAO: It's good that you're getting better. But your complexion still doesn't look well.
MOTHER: The poor thing has been sick for so long. Little Mei, help Laolao sit down on that couch.
MEI: Mama, I'll go tell the maid to bring some tea for Laolao, all right?

MOTHER: Good. And bring some tangerines and chestnuts for her to nibble on with her tea.
LAOLAO: Please don't go to any trouble for me. Let's just talk.
MEI: It's no trouble! [*Gives a winsome smile and exits*]
LAOLAO: I have been wanting to come inquire about your son's illness and have a chat with you. It's just that this old body of mine no longer works properly, and it's hard to get about.
MOTHER: You are really too kind to us. We don't deserve it. Since my son has taken ill, I haven't had the time to come pay my respects to you either.
LAOLAO: Don't be so polite—a sick person at home and still standing on ceremony!
MOTHER: You are the only venerable elder of the village, an example to us all. We of the younger generation ought to visit you more often.
LAOLAO: You flatter me. [*To Zhong*] Young Master, what is wrong with you anyway?
ZHONG: Thank you for your concern, but I don't know what it is myself. I'm just tired and have no appetite. I have been taking medicine every day for the past three months, and though I have seen three or four doctors already, none has been able to put his finger on the cause.
MOTHER: This child has been sickly ever since he was little. But he has never been this sick.
MEI: [*Enters with a maid who places the tea and fruit on the table*] Laolao, please help yourself.
MOTHER: It's nothing fancy, but please help yourself!
LAOLAO: Yes, I will, thank you.
MEI: Ma, the peach trees in the garden are in full bloom, so I'll go out to pick some flowers for Brother!
ZHONG: Ma, I want to go out with Mei to enjoy the garden.
LAOLAO: Since the weather is nice today, there's no harm in going outside to play.
MOTHER: All right, but bundle up, this spring chill can really sneak up on you.
ZHONG: Okay. [*Walks over to the trunk in his slippers and opens the case. The phoenix robe and sash fall to the floor. He picks them up swiftly and is about to put them away when Laolao notices them.*]
LAOLAO: Who made you such a beautiful robe?

MOTHER: The Lius sent it for his birthday. Show it to Laolao. [*Zhong gives it to her to look at.*]
MOTHER: [*Noticing the sash*] Where did this sash come from?
ZHONG: [*Blushing*] It's . . . it . . . the Lius sent it.
MOTHER: How is it that I didn't notice it the other day? Give it to me to see. [*She looks slightly irritated after inspecting it, but tries to restrain herself.*]
ZHONG: It was folded in the pocket that day, so I guess you didn't notice it.
LAOLAO: Let me take a look at it. I have heard that young Miss Lan does extraordinary embroidery. [*Examining it*] Indeed, her reputation is well-deserved. [*Notices Zhong's embarrassed but pleased expression*] I have also heard that Miss Lan is an unsurpassed beauty and a perfect match for the Young Master! Did you notice that this is embroidered with a pair of lovebirds playing in the water? [*Looks closely*] My! It looks just like the pair of mandarin ducks at Clear Water Pond! One day, the two of you will be a match made in Heaven, just like these. [*Zhong lowers his head and blushes.*]
MEI: Brother, hurry up and change your clothes, so we can take advantage of the warm weather. Once it gets cold, we won't be able to stay out for long.
ZHONG: [*Quickly dresses*] All right, let's go.
MOTHER: Little Mei, take good care of your brother. Don't let him climb on the rocks or go up on the pavilion—tiring him out is no laughing matter.
MEI: I won't. [*Looks at her brother and laughs mischievously*]
ZHONG: If you'll excuse me, Laolao. [*The two exit happily.*]
LAOLAO: Have a good time! [*To Mother*] You are fortunate to have such children!
MOTHER: You flatter me. You're the lucky one! Your grandson is now as old as my son.
LAOLAO: But he hasn't any sense!
MOTHER: I hear he's accomplishing great things in the prefecture!
LAOLAO: He puts food on the table, that's it.
MOTHER: Poor Laolao, it's only having struggled most of your life that you've obtained happiness in your old age.
LAOLAO: [*In a slightly wavering voice*] Isn't that the truth? I was widowed at nineteen and have remained a widow to this very day. Life has not been easy. [*Her eyes fill with tears.*]

MOTHER: This is truly what is called sweetness follows bitterness. Now your house is filled with sons and grandsons, and there is no greater happiness than that.

LAOLAO: Only those who've plunged to the bottom of the sea know its coldness. You've experienced it yourself, so you understand the price I've had to pay for my happiness. Actually, what is most difficult is not widowhood, but having nothing to dedicate oneself to.

MOTHER: But surely you dedicated yourself to your son! Can you imagine how a widow with no son must suffer?

LAOLAO: Of course. When your son is young, he still has room for you in his heart, indeed his heart has room only for you. But as he grows up day by day, his heart also swells, and he begins to feel his heart is too barren with just his mother in it. He won't be happy until he's packed it full.

MOTHER: [*Shudders*] But surely his mother always occupies the center of his heart.

LAOLAO: As she should. But being stuck in the middle is plenty uncomfortable.

MOTHER: What an appalling thought!

LAOLAO: It's not so bad. Fortunately, while such suffering is hard to bear, soon there is a great elixir to alleviate the pain: waiting for the grandsons to be born so our love can be transferred to their tender hearts.

MOTHER: Thank goodness! But when the grandson grows up, somebody else will come along and squeeze us out!

LAOLAO: You'll be old and muddled about everything by that time, so what's there to fear about that?

MOTHER: Still a discouraging thought!

LAOLAO: Those of us fated to be widows have no choice but to swallow our cup of bitterness to the last drop.

MOTHER: Laolao.... [*Covers her ears, then silently sobs*]

LAOLAO: [*Tears flowing*] I've been through it so I understand your sorrow. But you must remember: happiness in old age is won only through struggle.

MOTHER: Laolao ... my heart can't find another home again....

LAOLAO: Don't be sad. The ways of the world are inevitable. Submit to the will of Heaven. Besides, we widows not only have to carry on the family line for our husbands, we also have to set our eyes on honor in old age. Our choices are suffering and sacrifice. What we value is always out of reach. We might as well give in when it comes to matters of the heart. My own life's achievement is in having conquered mine. That white stone chastity memorial archway at the entrance to the village is a war trophy for a lifetime's battle between me and my heart.

MOTHER: Laolao, are you saying that those of us who have resolved to remain widows must consciously slay our own hearts?

LAOLAO: That has basically been my experience.

MOTHER: Over the past ten years or so I have felt quite content in rechanneling the love I had for my husband to my son. Fortunately, my son is still young, and although he is a little preoccupied with the question of his career, he has no other wild thoughts. Right now I can't stop worrying about his illness, how could I worry about anything else!

LAOLAO: His illness is upsetting. But as far as I can see, it isn't all that serious. If he could just relax, he'd be all right.

MOTHER: Laolao, do you think he has consumption? I'm afraid that working in the prefecture would tire him out too much.

LAOLAO: No, I don't think that's it.

MOTHER: I hope not. But the way it drags on like this . . . [*Voices come from outside.*] They must be back. [*Gets up to look. The Serving girl leads the Matchmaker in.*] Oh! Mrs. Li's here. Please come in.

MATCHMAKER: Oh! Laolao's here too. You must be in fine health to be out paying visits at your age!

LAOLAO: I'm in poor health! How are you, Mrs. Li?

MATCHMAKER: Aren't we poor folk always the same! [*To Mother*] Greetings to your honorable family! Where have the Young Master and Young Miss disappeared to?

MOTHER: They went out to play in the garden. How has everything been, Mrs. Li?

MATCHMAKER: Fine, thank you. I hear that the Young Master has not been well these past few months. Is he any better now?

MOTHER: He is feeling slightly better today, thank you.

MATCHMAKER: The Liu family sent me to ask after him and to bring you some fruit, which I left outside. Please inspect it.

MOTHER: They shouldn't have. Please thank them for me.

MATCHMAKER: [*Suddenly sees the sash*] Oh, what a lovely sash! Did Miss Lan embroider this? Aren't those the lovebirds at Clear

	Water Pond? Her embroidery is so precise and exquisite! Madame, look at what fine work your future daughter-in-law does! Laolao, we matchmakers don't lie!
LAOLAO:	Wonderful. You will be rewarded with ten extra years of life for making such a fine match.
MOTHER:	Her embroidery isn't bad, but her theme isn't very tasteful.
MATCHMAKER:	[*Laughs heartily*] Birds frolicking in the water make quite an amusing scene!
LAOLAO:	Girls often enjoy embroidering birds and natural landscapes. There's nothing offensive about it.
MATCHMAKER:	That's right! When we were young, who among us didn't adore embroidering mandarin ducks? Madame, you've forgotten young women's favorite hobbies!
MOTHER:	[*With a change of heart*] That's true, we too used to love such things when we were young.
LAOLAO:	These days belong to the younger generation. It's time for us to sit back and watch.
MATCHMAKER:	Our show is over, now it's time to get off the stage and watch the young ones perform.
LAOLAO:	How old is Miss Lan?
MOTHER:	She just turned seventeen.
MATCHMAKER:	[*Laughs heartily*] The springtime of her youth! Madame, why haven't you already married her into the family so you can enjoy playing with your grandchildren in your old age?
MOTHER:	How can you bring up marriage when my son is critically ill?
MATCHMAKER:	It seems to me that we should try to drive away his illness with a "joyful celebration."[1] The year before last, the Young Master of the Li family was just like your son. He was so sick for three or four months that he couldn't get out of bed; but as soon as he got married and the little bride moved in, his illness just disappeared. The darling grandson is already a half a year old.
LAOLAO:	There's truth to what Mrs. Li says. A young man's illness can always be cured by getting married.

---

1. According to traditional belief, weddings were auspicious events that could counteract a person's bad luck, in particular illness.

MOTHER: [*Downcast*] He's all I have. I wouldn't mind if it cured him, but what if something happened to him?
MATCHMAKER: You can worry all you like, but such celebrations always do the trick. The Liu family was anxious when they heard that your son has been sick, so they sent me over to see what you think about spiriting away his illness through marriage.
LAOLAO: Judging from your son's expression just now, he would be cured instantly.
MOTHER: What expression, Laolao?
LAOLAO: When I was laughing about how he and Miss Lan were a match made in Heaven, his ears turned completely crimson.
MOTHER: It wasn't just youthful shyness?
LAOLAO: There was a certain joy in his embarrassment!
MOTHER: [*Trembling slightly and biting her lip*] Really?
LAOLAO: You didn't notice?
MOTHER: [*Recalling Zhong's words, speaking as if to herself*] No wonder . . .
MATCHMAKER: No wonder what?
MOTHER: Nothing . . . so, spiriting away his illness through the marriage is the best cure?
MATCHMAKER: And the sooner the better! The Lius have already prepared the dowry.
MOTHER: They may be prepared, but we're not.
MATCHMAKER: [*Charming laugh*] It's simple! Your honorable residence has plenty of gold and silver; all you have to do is get it out and spend it.
MOTHER: Let me think it over . . . we must take this seriously. Besides . . . [*A peal of laughter can be heard.*]
MEI: [*Enters, beaming with a smile and carrying a bunch of peach flowers. Zhong follows, smiling.*] Ma, just now when I was saying how much these peach blossoms look like Sister-in-Law, Brother started hitting and tickling me . . . [*Sees the Matchmaker*] Oh! Mrs. Li. . . .
MOTHER: Hurry up and pay your respects.
[*They greet the Matchmaker.*]
MATCHMAKER: So! Who says the Young Master is sick? With this smiling face, he looks every bit the bridegroom!
ZHONG: Enjoying the garden with my sister has cheered me up.
MEI: [*Laughs*] He raved about the peach blossoms on every tree he saw. I joked that he was thinking about Miss Lan and so

he started tickling me to death. He also swore at me and said that he wants Ma to betroth him to Miss Lan someday soon so she can help him tickle me.

MATCHMAKER: [*Laughs heartily*] Miss, someday soon you'll be helping Miss Lan tickle him.

MEI: [*Innocent and lighthearted*] Fine! Fine! Mrs. Li, hurry and help marry her into the family. I want revenge! Laolao, you come over too and help them get married!

LAOLAO: All right, I do want to attend the wedding banquet.

MEI: Ma, can we do it soon? I really do want to get Brother back.

MOTHER: [*Can't help laughing*] Stupid child! Are you getting a sister-in-law just so you can get revenge?

ZHONG: [*Secretly smiling*] See, Ma won't help you!

MEI: Someday soon, I'm sure Sister-in-Law will help me!

MATCHMAKER: [*To Laolao*] See how lucky this lady is! Having the two of them in one family is already plenty lively.

LAOLAO: If the bride arrives soon, they'll be even more lively.

MOTHER: And more naughty!

MEI: It depends on how you look at it. Ma, we are bound to be naughty when we are having fun. Being naughty is fun.

MATCHMAKER: It's true, if they weren't naughty, Madame, you wouldn't be happy. What fun would it be to sit around doing nothing all day? [*To Zhong*] Young Master, what would you think if your mother married you to Miss Lan as a way of curing-illness-through-a-wedding?

[*Zhong stares at his mother, but doesn't dare respond.*]

MEI: [*Joyful*] Hooray! Mrs. Li, is this what you came to talk about?

MATCHMAKER: [*Smiles*] Yes, to discuss this very matter. [*To Mother*] Madame, since everyone is happy, let's set a date!

LAOLAO: The fourteenth is an auspicious day. The Young Master of the Wang family is getting married on that day too.

MATCHMAKER: Today is the eighth, so that leaves six days. Madame, is that enough time?

MEI: We can manage! Ma, if Brother and I help, we'll have plenty of time, won't we? [*Zhong looks shyly at his sister.*]

MOTHER: [*To Zhong*] What do you think? They all say that the wedding will cure your illness.

ZHONG: [*Smiles slightly and lowers his head in embarrassment*] As you wish . . . as you wish, Mother.

MOTHER: [*Resolutely*] Fine. Marry her over. Get this thing over with!

MEI: [*Jumps up and claps her hands*]: The fourteenth! The fourteenth! We still have six days to go! Brother, prepare to be tickled by Sister-in-Law and me! Ma, I ought to hurry and make some embroidered clothes! Laolao, bring Little Hua over to play when you come for the wedding banquet, won't you?
LAOLAO: I will!
MATCHMAKER: It's the brother who's getting married, but the sister who's happy. How funny!
MEI: Brother is happy deep down. [*Points to him*] Don't be shy!
ZHONG: [*Chases her and hits her*] You're such a terrible sister!
LAOLAO: How amusing!
MOTHER: Mei, don't tire your brother out.
MATCHMAKER: Splendid! Madame, I'll go back and report the news. [*Gets up*]
MOTHER: Please convey our respects to the Liu family. Tomorrow we'll send over the betrothal gifts and announce the auspicious date.
MATCHMAKER: Fine! Good-bye!
LAOLAO: On the fourteenth, be sure to have plenty of wedding wine.
MATCHMAKER: We'll have a few cups together, Laolao! Good-bye! Good-bye everyone!
MOTHER: Mei, go upstairs and bring down two baskets of tangerines for Mrs. Li! [*Mei exits happily.*]
MATCHMAKER: Don't stand on ceremony! [*Exits. Mother follows.*]
LAOLAO: Young Master, you look so much happier already!
ZHONG: I wasn't that sick to begin with, Laolao.
LAOLAO: It really is the right time for you to get married. You are very lucky, everyone says that Miss Lan is extremely bright and clever!
[*Zhong smiles with embarrassment.*]
LAOLAO: But, Young Master, in the future you and your wife must be particularly respectful toward your mother!
ZHONG: Of course!
LAOLAO: Widowed mothers especially need a filial son and daughter-in-law.
ZHONG: Of course we'll be filial.
LAOLAO: I'm sure that Miss Lan is a virtuous woman.
ZHONG: That I don't know yet.
LAOLAO: Well of course she is.... Fine! Best wishes on giving your mother a few grandsons soon!

ZHONG: [*Shyly*] Thank you for your blessings. [*Mother enters.*]
LAOLAO: Madame, I must be going too. Congratulations on the wedding, you've got a lot to do. On the fourteenth, I'll certainly come here for your wedding rather than go to the Wangs.'
MOTHER: By all means, though I hope you won't mind our humble wine! But stay, let's keep chatting!
LAOLAO: No, I can't stay, it's getting late. Is my servant waiting downstairs?
MOTHER: She's sitting in the back room.
ZHONG: Let me help you out. [*They exit. The stage is empty momentarily. Presently, Zhong returns, picks up the sash, and kisses it fervently.*] My . . . my . . . only six more days, and you will be in my arms! Six days! Six days! Hurry! . . . Oh! [*Feels his forehead*] What's happened to my illness? So I wasn't sick after all. I was just thinking about you [*To the sash*] . . . too much. Ha, ha, ha, ha. [*Mother enters.*]
MOTHER: [*With a hint of sadness in her happy expression*] What are you laughing at?
ZHONG: [*Embarrassed*] Nothing! Laolao is very funny.
MOTHER: Son, are you happy that you're about to get married?
ZHONG: [*Bashfully*] Not especially. Ma, how about you?
MOTHER: Of course I'm happy, as long as you're happy. [*Her voice wavers slightly.*] Have I any other goal in life besides your happiness?
ZHONG: Ma! . . . You're the kindest mother in the whole world.
MOTHER: [*Reaches out affectionately toward him*] My son. . . . [*With grief and joy*] I . . . I . . . con . . . gratulate you . . . the son I've had under my wings for twenty-two years is now about to fly off. . . .
ZHONG: [*Moved*] Ma, where would I fly to? Won't I always fly back into your arms? Ma, why are you getting so upset?
MOTHER: [*Laughs and cries*] Yes . . . yes . . . I ought to be happy. Your father died a long time ago, leaving me to struggle to keep the family line going, so shouldn't I be happy? But . . . but . . . I don't know why. . . . I am very happy! My son! Let me look at your hair! Is it still the same?
ZHONG: [*Kneeling, he lets her stroke his hair*] Ma! Your joy has turned to sorrow! I can see tears in your eyes, tears of joy. Why don't you let them flow?

MOTHER: [*Smiles*] Why would I have tears in my eyes if I am happy? No... yes... I am happy! Son! Your hair is so beautiful and sleek. I want to stroke it forever and ever....
ZHONG: Of course forever! What could be more permanent than the love between mother and son?
MOTHER: I want us to be like this forever.
ZHONG: Of course we'll be like this forever.
MOTHER: [*Strokes his hair with both hands, her eyes raised in prayer*] If only our life could be like this forever....

Act II

A few years later. The season is late summer or early fall. In a small wing room at the Jiao residence; on the matted floor are placed a low, dark-red bench and a small table with a tea set. There are doors on both the anterior part of the right wall and on the right-hand side of the back wall. Bamboo curtains hang from the doors.

When the curtain rises, Lan, dressed simply and with an appealing purity, is sitting in front of a spinning wheel working. As the machine hums, she accompanies it softly with a song. The more she sings, the more animated she becomes. For an instant, it's as though her spirit has been carried away by the tune. The machine stops and she looks like she is dreaming. Suddenly, she comes to, and begins spinning the wheel quickly.

LAN: Oh! Still not fast enough. [*Looks at the unspun cotton in the basket*] I'll never finish spinning this spool of yarn today. Even if I kept spinning until the fifth watch I still wouldn't get it all done. [*Again spins diligently. After a few minutes, she can't refrain from starting to sing leisurely. When she comes to a pleasing section of the song, again the hum of the machine stops and the dreamlike expression reappears on her face. Mother suddenly lifts the curtain of the main entrance and enters. Lan is panic-stricken.*]
MOTHER: [*Angrily*] What do you think you're doing? Is this your idea of spinning?
LAN: Ma, are you feeling hot? Would you like a cup of iced tea? [*Gets a cup of tea from the table and brings it to her*]
MOTHER: [*Takes it and finishes it in one gulp*] This iced tea is delicious, pour me another cup.

LAN: [*As though she has been pardoned*] Ma, why don't you have another big cup? Getting up after an afternoon nap always makes one thirsty. [*Swiftly pours another big cup*]

MOTHER: I was only going to lie down and rest for a while, but this hot weather put me to sleep the minute I lay down.

LAN: It's best for older people to get extra sleep when the weather is hot. Ma, I'll go fetch a basin of hot water for you to sponge off your face with. [*Exits*]

MOTHER: [*Yawns*] It's nearly the beginning of the ninth month. How can it still be so hot? It's so humid! [*Walks over to Lan's spinning wheel and inspects the yarn and cotton still remaining in the basket*] She still has this much left to do! How will she ever finish it today! That lazy girl!

LAN: [*Carries in the water and places it on the small table*] Ma, why don't you rinse off your face. I'll fix you some noodles. Is Sister-in-Law awake yet? Shall I make two bowls?

MOTHER: [*As she washes her face*] She is still fast asleep dreaming! Wake her up after you've finished making them. Sleeping too much in the daytime isn't good for her.

LAN: Fine. I've already boiled the water, so the noodles will be ready in no time. But I'd better wait and let her sleep—she'll be uncomfortable if she hasn't had enough sleep. Is that all right?

MOTHER: Well, all right. Bring my noodles now.

LAN: I'll bring them right away. [*Exits*]

MOTHER: [*Sits down on the couch*] This girl certainly can fool people! The worst is that she has completely beguiled Zhong, to the point where he doesn't even know his own mother anymore.... Laolao was so right, our hearts always get squeezed out by somebody else! Terrible! Terrible! [*Puts her hand on her heart*] Oh, heart! Be patient. Didn't Laolao triumph through patience? Laolao, fortunately you warned me about how painful this would be, otherwise my suffering would have killed me! [*Lan enters, carrying the bowl of noodles.*]

LAN: Ma, here are your noodles! [*Mother tastes them and thinks the flavor is bad.*]

MOTHER: [*Irritated*] What did you do to these noodles? These are noodles? This is inedible! Take them away!

LAN: [*Takes the noodles nervously*] Ma, if these taste bad, let me go and make you another bowl, all right?

MOTHER: I don't want any more; you think we can afford to let you waste so much?
LAN: [*Takes the bowl with trembling hands*] Shall I make you a bowl of dumplings?
MOTHER: [*Angry*] I said I'm not having anything. Take it away. [*Looks at the spinning wheel*] Move this spinning wheel into your room; you'd better finish weaving that spool of yarn today. [*Lan first removes the bowl of noodles and the water basin, then exits with the basket and the spinning wheel, looking miserable. Mother takes out her handwork from the drawer of the small table and sits down to embroider a pair of men's slippers. Her expression is sad, and she occasionally sighs or groans. Mei, now seventeen or eighteen, tiptoes in holding her breath and gently covers her mother's eyes. Mother angrily throws off her hands.*]
MOTHER: Mei, you are old enough now to behave properly.
MEI: [*Smiles*] Ma, can't you still have fun when you're grown up?
MOTHER: You should act your age! Do you think you are still a small child?
MEI: Don't Brother and Sister-in-Law often fool around? I don't believe that once you're old you can't be naughty anymore.
MOTHER: You insist on modeling yourself after that disgrace rather than learning from good examples.
MEI: I don't think she's disgraceful. This is called being happy in life. What good is it to pull a long face all day long? [*Falls silent, thinking*] . . . Ma, you've been far too depressed these past few years. Why aren't you happy like you used to be, why don't you play with us anymore? It's the same with Sister-in-Law. Whenever Brother isn't at home, she just works with a long face. When Brother's not here there isn't a bit of joy at home. Sister-in-Law plays the lute so beautifully, but when Brother is not around, we don't get to hear a single note. Whenever I ask her to play, she says that her spinning is more important and that if you hear her, you'll curse her. Ma, why do you always curse her? She's scared to death of you!
MOTHER: What nonsense! She, terrified of me? It wouldn't be so bad if she were scared of me! I don't know how your brother can care for such a demon-woman!
MEI: Demon! Ma, now you're exaggerating. I think Sister-in-Law is exceptionally talented. If I were Brother, I would be totally in love with her too.

MOTHER: [*Raises her hand to slap Mei but misses*] You worthless girl, I will not love that demon and there's nothing you can do to make me! ... Fine! You go ahead and learn her ways, but don't blame me when no one will marry you.

MEI: [*Ashamed*] Ma, you say such silly things! I won't leave you as long as I live.

MOTHER: If you don't ever want to leave me, you'd better learn to behave properly, and I won't permit you to fool around with your sister-in-law all day long. I'm telling you, a woman's virtue is more than being seductive and serving her husband. The less talented a woman is, the more virtuous she is![2] Why does she have to show off how intelligent she is all the time, and fuss so much over her clothing? Just because she can curry favor with her husband, does that mean she's better than everyone else? Look at how serious and respectful the young lady of the Dong family looks. Who doesn't praise her?

MEI: Stop! Stop it. Sister-in-Law's looks alone suffice! Ma, it seems to me that it's only the ugly ones who have to be so polite and proper in order to make up for their natural deficiencies. Someone like Sister-in-Law, who is smart and clever and beautiful, doesn't need any help. Anyway, she is never impolite to you, so I don't know why you find her so annoying. Would she have to have been born ugly and stupid for you to like her? I'm afraid if she had been, then she wouldn't have pleased Brother. I doubt there is anything more difficult in the world than being a daughter-in-law.

MOTHER: [*Angry*] What kind of ghost did you bump into today that's made you use that tramp of a daughter-in-law against me?

MEI: I see how you worry all day long and how pained you are; Sister-in-Law often cries in secret as well. How did such a good family come to be so hostile? I just hope that Mama will be a little nicer to Sister-in-Law in the future.

MOTHER: Isn't it enough that she has taken my son? What's the use of being nice to her? I've already given her all that I have. [*Her*

---

2. The mother is quoting a saying about women that gained currency in the late Ming, an anachronism on Yuan Changying's part since the play is set in the much earlier Han dynasty.

eyes fill with tears.] What more does she want? But what does this have to do with you anyway? Why must you stick up for her? It's none of your business! In the future, I forbid you to mention that whore to me again!

MEI: Ma, don't be so cruel. You should be more lenient. [*Looks at the slipper her mother is embroidering*] Ma, you've stitched the wing wrong. It looks as though it's broken.

MOTHER: [*Looks closely*] I have sewed it crooked. My eyes are no good any more! On top of that, you've gotten me agitated with your quarreling.

MEI: [*Sighs*] My dear old mother, going to such trouble! Is Brother short on slippers to wear now that he has Sister-in-Law? Why don't you give your old eyes a rest?

MOTHER: [*Rips the slipper in two and throws it on the floor*] Sooner or later, we all end up as white bones buried beneath a mound of yellow dirt! I'm old! So I'm useless, am I? Should I let you young ones bully me? I . . . I . . . I'll show you! Hurry and call that hussy Lan out here for me! Go on! Hurry up! [*Mei, who has been standing to one side in fear, kneels down, aware that something is wrong.*]

MEI: Ma! Ma! It's my fault for talking too much. Please don't take it out on her.

MOTHER: [*Can't contain her anger*] Go on! Hurry up! This has nothing to do with you. She's been working on one spool of yarn for three days; I want to ask her why. The noodles she just made were bitter and salty; I want to ask what she meant by that! I seldom curse her, but you always say I'm cursing her. I'll show you what real cursing is! Go! Hurry and go! [*Mei is still hesitating when the Servant girl runs in, laughing breathlessly.*]

SERVANT: Madame, the Young Master has returned.

MOTHER: If he's back, then where is he?

SERVANT: He's in the Young Miss's room. I saw the two of them from the window. The Young Miss fell into his arms crying, and now he's hugging her and kissing her passionately.

MOTHER: Nonsense! Get out of here! [*Insulted, the Servant exits. Mother is increasingly infuriated.*] Go at once and bring that pair of dogs to me! Has the light of day ever seen such a discourteous son and daughter-in-law? Go! Why don't you hurry up? [*Mei exits, tears welling up in her eyes.*] We all end up as white bones buried in a mound of yellow earth! I'll carry this out no matter what the consequences. Am I the only one who must suffer? Shouldn't others suffer too? Poor me, my hard fate . . . day and night . . . suffering. The son I have brought forth now only has eyes . . . for her! Is this not the greatest insult? [*Her anger turns to sorrow.*] My husband! When you closed your eyes, why . . . why didn't I want to go with you? Because there were the sounds of his crying . . . that alarming sound called me back . . . amid his sad cries, I heard my life's calling. My bitter life over the past twenty years was all for him. I endured it all for him. So now, now how can I let her, that whore, snatch him away? Heavens! If Heaven had eyes, it wouldn't permit such . . . such an injustice! In the past few years my heart—this widow's heart—has been smashed into a thousand tiny pieces and thrown to the dogs and pigs as gristle for them to gnaw on! Is this possible? Gods of Heaven and Earth! You allot us mothers every hardship. We suffer and we endure, yet what is our reward? The reward is that our sons get snatched from our bosoms and tossed into somebody else's! Is this fair? If there is even a little justice on Earth, why aren't we allowed to keep this one speck of happiness that we have amid all our pain? And if your laws and commands really are so inequitable, why shouldn't the mothers of this world revolt? I . . . I dare to be a traitor against Heaven! Anyway, we all end up as white bones in a mound of yellow earth! I will carry this out no matter what the consequences! [*Mei enters, leading in her brother and sister-in-law.*]

ZHONG: To the everlasting happiness of my mother! [*Stands solemnly at one side*] Your son has returned home.

LAN: [*Kneels down. She looks graceful, gentle, modest, and frail, like a bough of pear flowers in the spring rain.*] Mother, what instructions do you have for me?

MOTHER: [*To Mei*] Get out! [*Not daring to disobey, she exits quietly.*] You two unfilial children, how dare you behave so presumptuously?

ZHONG: [*Kneeling*] What error have I committed? Please, Mother, inform me.

MOTHER: You still have the gall to ask? You studied the Confucian rites, did you not? Where does it say that when returning home from afar you should first not go to honor your parents, but instead sneak off and linger in your wife's room?

ZHONG: Please don't be angry, Mother. I didn't intend to put you after my wife, but the truth is that I was careless riding my horse, and got my clothes dirty. I didn't dare come and see you before I changed them.

MOTHER: How dare you utter such nonsense! Before, when your clothes got dirty, who changed them for you?

ZHONG: The past is better than the present. I wouldn't dare burden my mother now that I have a wife.

MOTHER: Rubbish! Does having a wife mean you should kick your mother aside? [*To Lan*] You, miserable woman, know nothing about proper behavior; how dare you sabotage the affection between mother and son!

LAN: I wouldn't dare.

MOTHER: [*Spilling over with anger*] You wouldn't dare! An unequivocal "I wouldn't dare"! Yet, today you loafed about, and tomorrow you'll take it easy. You change your clothes several times a day, you cake your face with powder and paint, you deck yourself in reds and greens, all in order to make yourself an alluring woman. What is it all for? It takes you ten days to sew one piece of cloth, and three days to spin one spool of yarn. What does this mean? Such improper feminine conduct, yet you still won't admit your mistakes? The noodles you just made were bitter and salty, what did you mean by that? Your husband has returned from far away, how dare you detain him in your chambers instead of sending him to pay respects to his own mother? This is what you mean by "I wouldn't dare"? You unreasonable and unfilial woman, I have nothing more to say to you, so get out of here, go back to the Liu family. My family won't tolerate a woman like you. Get out at once. Go straight back to your own family! [*Lan exits, weeping.*]

ZHONG: [*His head bowed, crying*] Ma, why must you be so cruel? If something is the matter, explain it to me. Ever since I got married, I have been in good spirits and my health has steadily improved. I assumed this made you happy. Now, to my astonishment, you suddenly send my wife back home after we have been together for only a few years. How can I bear it? Moreover, there's nothing improper about her behavior. Why are you being so unforgiving?

MOTHER: Why are you always so concerned about her? An overbearing woman like her has absolutely no regard for propriety. I have been angry about this for some time. Now I am determined to get rid of her. Have you any more to say? The young lady of the Dong family is unsurpassed in her virtue, exactly to my liking. I'm sure I could succeed in getting her to marry you. Does a top-rate man like you have to suffer with an unsatisfactory woman? You just wait until I've driven that woman out and then I'll try.

ZHONG: If you insist on driving her away, I swear I will never remarry. And don't say I didn't warn you.

MOTHER: [*Furious*] How dare you be so brazen! How dare you defend her to my face? My ties to her are already broken, there's no changing that. Quick, get rid of that whore! I won't allow you to delay one more instant! Oh! Heavens! My husband! [*Covering her face, she runs out sobbing. Zhong lies prostrate on the floor, weeping silently. Lan, with a tear-streaked face, tiptoes in hesitantly. Seeing Zhong, she collapses and embraces him as she cries.*]

ZHONG: [*Tries to speak but is choked with tears. After a long time he speaks sadly*] You, you'd best go back home for the time being! You know my feelings for you, but how can I defy my mother's authority! Go back for now and wait for me to go to the prefecture to sort out some unfinished business, then I'll come and get you. I'll come and get you soon.

LAN: [*Weeping*] You. . . . Why must you bring up this plan again! When the spider's thread snaps, can the spider continue to spin its web? When water spills, can it be collected again?

ZHONG: But does a delicate spider's thread ever break? And does calm water ever spill?

LAN: [*With grief and indignation*] It is fate, what can we do about it?

ZHONG: [*Determined*] Naturally, I have my ways.

LAN: But your way is to defy your mother's wishes! Heavens! When we first got married and I came to your house in a decorated sedan chair accompanied by musicians, who didn't admire and envy me! How humiliating it is to be driven from your house today! But this is fate. I don't think I've done anything wrong . . . it's just fate!

ZHONG: Don't be sad. Everything will work out. Mother can force you to leave, but she can't force me to marry someone else. You had best set your mind at rest and go back home for the time being. My heart and soul are eternally yours.

LAN: And I feel only gratitude toward you for your affection.
ZHONG: After I've finished up at the prefecture, and Mother's anger has cooled off, I will come get you. I swear I will not fail you.
LAN: Your noble affections are etched firmly in my mind. I hope you will come for me the moment you've finished your work.
ZHONG: I promise to come for you. Our love is unswerving; mine like a great rock, yours like a reed.
LAN: Reeds are as durable as silk!
ZHONG: Rocks never move!
LAN: But my own father and elder brothers are cruel. Even though I am willing to wait for you, I'm afraid in the end it won't be my decision that counts. What shall I do if it comes to that?
ZHONG: [*Resolutely*] Don't worry, I'll come for you soon! Lan, my love, as long as your heart is as firm as stone and your will like iron, then our love and affection will remain unchanged even if Heaven and Earth collapse.
LAN: My heart is as firm as stone and my will like iron, but how can we withstand the ravages of fate? Zhong, I can't live anywhere except by your side.
ZHONG: And I don't want to live except by your side. Every night at the prefecture, I used to dream that I was with my sister out picking peach blossoms. Each bough looked like you, and when I would look again, it really was you. But when I would go to take you in my arms, it would still be a cold branch of peach blossoms . . . [*Passionately hugs her*] My dear peach blossom, you alone are a blossom with real flesh and blood, with a soul! My flower! [*Kisses her on the lips*] My divine flower, how can I bear to part with you? How can I lose you? You are mine, mine forever. Who would dare take you away from me?
LAN: [*Mesmerized*] My dear, I am yours, I am yours forever. Ever since this bough of peach flowers produced buds, hasn't it always radiated for you? But just when they were about to blossom and bear fruit, unexpectedly right in the middle . . . in the middle. [*Crying*]
ZHONG: Don't be sad! No matter how fiercely the eastern wind blows, it can't sweep our affections away. Our parting is only temporary, that's all. We will soon meet again. But, my peach blossom, don't flower anywhere else. When I'm not with you, contain your splendor, wait until spring to bloom again.

LAN: Where will the beholder of flowers be in the spring?
ZHONG: I promise I will be with you. I will not forsake you.
LAN: Then, even if the seas run dry and the rocks crumble, this flower will open only for he who admires it.
ZHONG: I pray you always remember these words.
LAN: I pray you do not delay in coming for me!
[*Mei pokes her head in through the curtain and speaks softly.*]
MEI: Brother, Sister-in-Law, what happened? What is going on?
ZHONG and LAN: [*In unison*] Come in, come here, Mei!
MEI: [*Enters*] I saw Ma let loose a flood of tears and run to cry on Father's grave. I didn't even dare ask her about it. [*Lost in thought with a guilty expression*] ... Actually, it's all my fault. I was trying to encourage Ma to be a bit kinder to Sister-in-Law. Who would have thought it would only make her angrier?
LAN: How could we blame you? I hate myself for not being more virtuous and pleasing Mother. Did you know she is going to send me back to my own family? Sister, what ever shall I do? [*Sobbing*]
ZHONG: Don't worry!
MEI: [*Stunned*] What? She's making you return to your own family!
ZHONG: Don't worry, I'm going to bring her back to us again.
MEI: Mother has gone mad! How can she do such a thing? I simply don't understand why she dislikes Sister-in-Law so much. What is the reason?
ZHONG: Only Heaven knows. In the past few years, Mother's temper has gotten worse and worse! Ever since your sister-in-law moved in, she hasn't unknit her brow for a single day. Right before I got married, she often cried for no reason at all. It really is sad—have you seen how haggard she has become?
LAN: It's all because I'm not virtuous enough.
MEI: How good do you have to be? I think it must be some sort of illness, otherwise I can't figure out where that temper of hers comes from. Before, our family was so happy. She was full of joy and laughter. But in recent years, she's always crying by herself, like an abandoned orphan. It really is sad how lonely she is! [*Lan cries.*] Sister-in-Law, you mustn't worry. Go back home for the time being. I'll try to persuade her. I am sure she'll have a change of heart. If she thinks she can find another daughter-in-law like you, it'll be like grab-

bing for the moon's reflection in a lake. She's doing this in a fit of anger and she'll certainly regret it later!

ZHONG: Mei, your sister-in-law and I have taken a vow! In this lifetime she won't serve a second husband and I won't take another wife. We will remain faithful to each other even if the earth cracks apart and the sky collapses. Make sure you impress this upon Mother when you try to persuade her.

MEI: Of course. But she might not listen to me! It's best to have the venerable Laolao come to convince her. I sent someone to fetch her when I saw how angry Mother was. I am sure the old lady can bring about a reconciliation. I don't think she'll be long. Go back to your room for now and tidy up. Nothing would be better, of course, than if Laolao could make peace among you all today; if not, as unfair as it is, Sister-in-Law will have to go back home temporarily! Then we will come up with a new plan. Mother has truly gone mad, kicking Sister-in-Law out like this for no reason. [*Footsteps outside the door*] That must be Laolao now. Brother and Sister-in-Law, go back for now and tidy up! Wait until I have explained the whole story to her.

ZHONG: You are such a good sister. We used to consider ourselves lucky, but now we've suddenly become the most unlucky of children.

MEI: Brother, you never complain when Mother punishes you. You are truly a filial son, and as your sister how can I not do my best to help you?

LAN: Sister-in-Law, we've put you to such trouble! Someday I will try to repay you!

MEI: It's good of you to say so, but I don't want anything in return. I just want to repair the mess I've made. Good-bye!

ZHONG and LAN: Don't say good-bye yet! [*They exit hand in hand from the side door, as the Servant girl enters from the door at the left leading Laolao. She is still as robust as before, only she is now somewhat older.*]

MEI: Laolao, you're here, please come in!

LAOLAO: Young lady, what have you called me here for? Where has your mother gone?

MEI: Laolao, my mother has gone off to cry at my father's grave.

LAOLAO: What is she crying for?

MEI: It's a long story. Please sit down and let me start at the beginning. [*Helps her sit down and moves over a small stool for her-*

	self. To the Servant girl:] Bring in some tea and fruit for Laolao [*The Servant girl nods and exits.*] Laolao, our family has been so unhappy these past few years. Surely Laolao has heard that Mother is not satisfied with Sister-in-Law?
LAOLAO:	I have heard, but I don't know the details. Your sister-in-law seems fine. Why doesn't she please your mother?
MEI:	This is precisely my question! With your age and experience, you must have some understanding of the reason why.
LAOLAO:	Well! First tell me everything that has happened.
MEI:	It all happened this afternoon.
LAOLAO:	Is it serious?
MEI:	Mother is forcing Sister-in-Law to go home to her own family!
LAOLAO:	Oh! How did it come to this?
MEI:	I'm afraid this idea has been stewing in her head for some time. Ever since my brother married Lan, there has hardly been a single day when Mother did not go off and cry in secret. When a family gets a daughter-in-law like Lan, and sees how compatible the couple is, it ought to be a happy thing. But for my mother it has been the exact opposite. Every time she sees how harmonious and happy they are as husband and wife, she gets angry and . . . I don't dare say how she treats Sister-in-Law. In short, she can't stand the fact that Brother loves Sister-in-Law. What does this all mean?
LAOLAO:	Young lady, you have never been through this sort of experience, so how could you possibly understand? Have you ever really wanted to be with someone?
MEI:	Once, I really liked a younger cousin of mine.
LAOLAO:	Did she like you?
MEI:	At first she adored me but . . . [*Her voice wavers slightly*] but now she ignores me. Laolao, just talking about it makes me sad! Before we often played together, and I always let her have her way. She doted on me. But in the past few years, she's been in school and made a lot of new friends, so she's forgotten about me.[3] Whenever I think about going to my aunt's house to visit her, my mother says that I'm grown up

---

3. The reference to the schooling of Mei's younger female cousin is another anachronistic detail, since during the Han dynasty it would have been highly unusual for a girl to attend school.

now, and that I shouldn't fool around with my cousins anymore. Each time I hear how close she is to other people, I feel indescribably sad, as though there were something sour clogging my heart, making it hard for me to vent my feelings of resentment.

LAOLAO: Do you know what this kind of sorrow is called?

MEI: People call it ... [*Her face turns red to the ears.*] But what does this have to do with my mother not liking Sister-in-Law? Are you saying that Ma is ...?

LAOLAO: It's very hard to say! In any case the bitterness is the same. It's not that I want to speak badly of your mother. I too have tasted this bitterness. After our husbands die, we widows pour all of our affection on our children. Our sons and daughters become our soul mates. But then suddenly, they love somebody else! It is as difficult for us as it is when your cousin ignores you! Our lonely hearts are pushed away from our sons' affections by our daughters-in-law, and there is no place for us to turn. Young widows are the most wretched. Once we get older, however, things become less clear, and it's as though the blood in our hearts has become cold or has dried up and has no need to gush into somebody else's heart.

MEI: Laolao, what you say is unpleasant to hear, but to the point. My mother's love for Brother is excessive.

LAOLAO: How could your brother have grown up and become a man without your mother's loving care? If there were no motherly love in the world, I think humanity would have long since perished.

MEI: How true. But other mothers are happy to see their sons love their wives. ...

LAOLAO: How would you know anything about a mother's happiness?

MEI: It seems that way on the surface!

LAOLAO: You only see the surface! In their heart of hearts, how many mothers and daughters-in-law are at peace with each other? As for those mothers with many children, or with husbands, it's a different matter. In short, as long as there is some place for our hearts to go, they will behave. ... Your poor mother! I knew she was suffering, but I always hoped she would have the strength to control her feelings!

MEI: Let's not talk about her anymore. How are we going to resolve this matter?

LAOLAO: Let me try to convince her.

MEI: Thank you for going to the trouble! [*The Servant girl brings in the tea and fruit. To the Servant:*] Has Madame returned?

SERVANT: She just got back. She's washing her face in her room.

MEI: Go ask her to come here and tell her that Laolao has come to visit her. [*Servant nods and exits.*] Laolao, please have some!

LAOLAO: I'm not hungry, thank you! Your poor mother! I do understand her sorrow. [*Weeps*]

MEI: [*Tragically*] Laolao, tell me how you overcame these emotions.

LAOLAO: What other way is there besides endurance? I'm telling you, if all the tears I have swallowed ever came pouring out, they would flood the village's memorial archway!

[*Mother enters with a sad pale face.*]

MEI: Ma, Laolao has come to visit you.

MOTHER: [*With a strained smile*] How nice of you to come over, Laolao. We don't deserve your visit.

LAOLAO: I was just passing by, so I thought I'd stop in and see you.

MEI: Ma, I'm feeling a bit cold. I'll be right back as soon as I change my clothes.

MOTHER: Fine, go on. [*Mei exits.*]

LAOLAO: Mei was just saying that you weren't feeling well today. Are you any better now?

MOTHER: It's not that I don't feel well. That son and daughter-in-law of mine infuriate me. Laolao, to your knowledge, has there ever been such a son and daughter-in-law? When my son returned home from the prefecture, instead of first coming to pay his respects to me, he snuck into his wife's room to shower his attentions on her! When I asked him the reason for his disrespect, he made up some story about falling off his horse and getting his clothes dirty. Tell me in all fairness, is he or isn't he unfilial? [*Lost in thought, changes her tune*] Actually, Laolao, my son's not to blame for this. I know that his unfilial behavior toward me in recent years is all his wife's doing. Oh! Once a family gets such an unvirtuous daughter-in-law, it's done for. But I won't let her ruin the family that I have so painstakingly created. I have ordered her to return to her own family at once; we cannot tolerate such a discourteous daughter-in-law. Laolao, do you think I should have to put up with her?

LAOLAO: Madame, one can always be more tolerant! Young people are often inconsiderate. We parents can only cope by forgiving.
MOTHER: I've been forgiving enough. Now I've come to the end of my patience.
LAOLAO: I have also suffered like you, and am I not still putting up with it? Look at how I am with that daughter-in-law of mine.
MOTHER: How can you compare your eldest daughter-in-law with this imbecile of ours! Your daughter-in-law is a virtuous woman, everyone in the village praises her.
LAOLAO: The more she is complimented, the more she angers me. How often I cry in secret to relieve the grief and indignation that fill me! I'm urging you to be patient. It's easy to make rash decisions in a fit of anger. But after your anger has subsided, you'll regret it. You should have mercy on them this time! Your poor son. Forcing them apart like this!
MOTHER: But they were so unfilial! There are times when I simply can't take it anymore. Laolao! [*Sadly*] I don't know how many times I have hid and cried over these past few years! You told me before about the lifelong hardships of being a widow, but only now do I understand what you meant! If my husband were still living, would I mind my son and daughter-in-law? Even if I did, I would have someone to back me up. Now I am so utterly lonely. Even my little Mei doesn't understand me. Why do we even have children?
LAOLAO: Madame, we must have children, even if they are naughty! Forgive them this time, all right? Suddenly forcing Lan to return home like this will make her lose face!
MOTHER: She should lose face, that ill-bred creature!
LAOLAO: Young people can't help making a few mistakes. Forgive her this once!
MOTHER: I appreciate your kind advice, and I'm naturally embarrassed not to do as you say, but it's simply impossible to forgive her!
LAOLAO: Forgive her! Forgive her! A parent's tolerance ought to be as great as the earth and as wide as the sea! The less trouble in life the better.
MOTHER: Since you have interceded on her behalf, I guess I will forgive her this once.
LAOLAO: Now that's being a merciful mother!
MOTHER: Thank you, Laolao.
[*Mei enters with more clothing on.*]

LAOLAO: Young lady, your mother has forgiven your brother and sister-in-law this time. In a minute you can go tell them to come kowtow and apologize.

MEI: [*Joyfully*] Really, Ma, you forgive them? Why don't I go get them right away?

LAOLAO: Wait until I leave.

MEI: Thank you for interceding, Laolao. Of course they will want to thank you themselves.

LAOLAO: That won't be necessary! I have things to do at home today. My grandson isn't feeling well, so I'm anxious to get back and see him.

MEI: Then tomorrow they'll go to your honorable home themselves to express their gratitude.

LAOLAO: We'll talk when they come to my humble abode, though I don't deserve any thanks. Well! I'm going. I'll see you tomorrow.

MOTHER: Thanks so much, Laolao. [*Mother and daughter help her out. The stage is momentarily empty, then the mother and daughter re-enter slowly.*]

MEI: [*Apprehensive*] Ma, I'll go get them, all right?

MOTHER: [*Listlessly*] As you wish . . . [*Before she finishes speaking, the desolate and anguished sound of a lute can be heard, like the accusatory and sorrowful cries of a dying deer or the mournful calls of a night oriole, leaving both mother and daughter spellbound. Mei bursts into tears. Mother is at first resentful, then grave, and finally angry like crashing waves or blazing flames. She dashes around the room madly, muttering to herself.*] That whore is bewitching him again . . . that whore, that hussy, what is she doing? No . . . no, I cannot stand her! My heart! [*Beats her chest in anger*] Go ahead and break! Break into so many fragments! No . . . no . . . I cannot stand her! Either she goes or I go . . . I can't . . . I can't . . . I can't listen to such poisonous sounds. This is . . . this is the sound of death . . . Oh! Heavens! [*She lowers her head to strike it against the wall but Mei holds her back. A string on the lute suddenly snaps and the music stops.*] Death! This is death! Ha! Ha! [*Her anguish turns into hysterical laughter.*]

MEI: [*Panicked*] Ma, what's wrong? Mother? Breathe! Breathe! Getting so angry isn't good for you!

MOTHER: [*Cries*] My husband! Why didn't you take me with you . . .

MEI:	[*Cries with her*] Ma, Ma, don't be so sad, don't cry.
MOTHER:	I would rather die! Mei, I would rather be with your father!
MEI:	Ma, Ma, then I'll die with you! We'll all die!
MOTHER:	[*Suddenly extremely angry and irritated*] Die? Die? Why should the three of us, mother, son, and daughter, die because of that whore? This is unheard of. Ha! The old man in the ground would weep! He would curse too! His tears of anguish would wash away his skeleton! Life is not so simple. Out, Mei, I want that damned girl out of here at once! [*Mei watches her with a pained expression.*] Go on, why haven't you left? [*Raises her foot as if to kick her*] If you don't obey my orders I will kill you! [*Terrified and resentful, Mei exits.*] Heavens! Anyway, we all end up as white bones beneath a mound of yellow earth! I will do this no matter what.

Act III

A few months later, at the end of autumn. The setting is a mountain road between the Jiao and Liu family residences. The road spans the front part of the stage. In the background are lonely, overgrown autumnal mountains. Next to the road, there are some smooth rocks in the wild grass that travelers use to sit and rest on. When the curtain rises, there is a hazy autumn sun in the western sky that casts light upon the ground. However, in the northeast corner of the sky, dark clouds are amassing like bandits lurking in a dense woods, waiting until the sun goes down before rushing out to menace the travelers passing by.

As the curtain rises, the elderly LAOLAO is hobbling along the right-hand side of the stage, supported by a twelve- or thirteen-year-old girl. She sees the rocks along the side of the road.

LAOLAO:	Oh! Hua, let's rest here a moment. My legs ache from walking. How lovely and smooth this rock is, perfect to sit on. [*Sits down*]
HUA:	Fine! Laolao, you sit here a while! We'll go look after you've rested up. We're only a few steps from Clear Water Pond now. See . . . [*Pointing to the left*] there by the mangrove tree? A pair of mandarin ducks is dying under that tree. Laolao, how sad they are, with barely a breath of life left in them.

LAOLAO: [*Shields her eyes and looks*] You're right. That's the old mangrove tree. Is that pair of ducks really going to die? How pitiful! Hasn't anyone noticed? Why haven't you gone to tell the Lius?

HUA: They're so busy, it's a madhouse over there. Who has time to think about taking care of those pathetic birds?

LAOLAO: Miss Lan is fond of that pair of birds, so why don't you tell her? They'll live if she takes them back home to take care of them.

HUA: Miss Lan can't even stop crying, let alone think about those birds. Yesterday, her mother and brothers forced her to sew all day long to get ready for her betrothal tomorrow!

LAOLAO: [*With tears of pity*] Poor Lan, such a cruel fate!

HUA: Laolao, she and Zhong got along so well, why did her mother-in-law kick her out?

LAOLAO: Because Mrs. Jiao didn't like her.

HUA: Why not? Just because Mrs. Jiao didn't like her, she can't be Zhong's wife?

LAOLAO: Yes! Mrs. Jiao didn't like her, so she couldn't be Zhong's wife anymore.

HUA: But why?

LAOLAO: Because Mrs. Jiao is Zhong's mother.

HUA: Oh, I get it. A man can't marry anyone his mother doesn't like, right?

LAOLAO: Exactly. But that's life.

HUA: Life certainly is strange. Is it the same when a woman gets married?

LAOLAO: It's the same for everyone; for you too when you get married.

HUA: [*Embarrassed*] Laolao, you're tired, please rest here. I'm going to go see if the mandarin ducks are dead or not. I can't stop thinking about them.

LAOLAO: All right! I don't feel like walking anymore. You go take a look. If they're not dead yet, tell somebody at the Lius' that we are taking them home with us to care for, and that we'll bring them back to the pond later. Be careful not to fall in the pond, the water's very deep.

HUA: Don't worry! Laolao, whenever I go there I only play under the trees along the bank, never next to the water.

LAOLAO: Good child. Go on, but hurry back.

HUA: Fine! [*Walks quickly to the left, then starts running, nearly colliding with the Matchmaker*] Oh! Pardon me! Mrs. Li, my grandmother's over there, why don't you go over and have a chat with her. I'm going to look at the ducks.

MATCHMAKER: Okay! Run along then. Young ladies always love looking at mandarin ducks. [*To Laolao*] Laolao, isn't that so?

LAOLAO: Hua said those ducks look like they're about to die and pestered me into coming to look at them. But I'm so tired I can't walk any farther. She'll have to go on by herself.

MATCHMAKER: What? That pair of mandarin ducks at Clear Water Pond is going to die?!

LAOLAO: Hua says they are lying there under that maple tree barely breathing!

MATCHMAKER: Laolao, this is a bad omen! Do you still remember the sash that Miss Lan embroidered for the Young Master Jiao?

LAOLAO: I do remember! She embroidered a picture of these ducks on it!

MATCHMAKER: Now the ill-fated Lan is being forced by her older brothers to remarry.

LAOLAO: The poor child! Weren't you the one who suggested the match?

MATCHMAKER: Laolao, I don't have anything to do with such evil business anymore. That high-ranking family she is being married into this time has so much money and power! There are dozens of betrothal gifts for her!

LAOLAO: Lan won't care whether there are dozens or hundreds of gifts. How can a tender flower stand up to the ravages of so much wind and rain!

MATCHMAKER: I hear that she hasn't stopped crying since she came back home. Her brothers and mother even made her sew her own betrothal clothes. Everything comes down to fate in the end. When I introduced her to Young Master Jiao, I thought, here was a match made in Heaven: such a talented lad, such a beautiful lady, what better match could be made? But now look at how it has turned out! I never want to have anything to do with matchmaking again.

LAOLAO: You're not to blame, Mrs. Li. How harmonious does a couple have to be?

MATCHMAKER: It's all because they got along too well!

LAOLAO: It's not unusual for a daughter-in-law to fail to please her mother-in-law. We should just pray that when Lan marries this time around, everyone will be satisfied.

MATCHMAKER: I heard that she and Young Master Jiao swore that neither would ever remarry.

LAOLAO: It's true. The day she was forced back home, our Hua saw Zhong accompanying her cart on his horse. On the way, he got off his horse and cried with her in the cart. I felt so bad when I heard about it. But his mother is quite pitiful herself. Bringing up her only son all by herself, and now she thinks he's being unfilial to her.

MATCHMAKER: Master Jiao can hardly be considered an unfilial son.

LAOLAO: Matters of the heart are always subjective. If she thinks her son is unfilial, or her daughter-in-law is unfilial, then that alone is enough to make her suffer. But really, what young man doesn't feel attached to his wife?

MATCHMAKER: I heard that Zhong has already received the news of Lan's betrothal, and that he's on his way back to put a stop to it.

LAOLAO: I'm afraid he won't get here in time, since the wedding takes place tomorrow morning.

MATCHMAKER: Perhaps there will be less of a scene if she's already gone and they don't see each other.

LAOLAO: Supposedly it's an auspicious day, but stormy weather's ahead. The poor young couple!

MATCHMAKER: Laolao, you are always so compassionate!

LAOLAO: I don't know why, but I feel bad for all three of them, the mother, the son, and the daughter-in-law.

MATCHMAKER: Actually, Mrs. Jiao is the heartless one.

LAOLAO: Mothers also have their sufferings! Mrs. Li, your son is still little, and Mr. Li is still living. You haven't experienced what it feels like to suddenly be left out in the cold after having been a mother in control of everything.

MATCHMAKER: Laolao, hearing you say this makes me nervous about choosing a daughter-in-law.

LAOLAO: There's no need to be afraid! You have a husband. You can't put yourself in a widow's place. What's more, it all depends on one's nature. If one is gentle or selfless, then seeing one's son love his wife is the happiest thing.

MATCHMAKER: That's the way it should be. Otherwise, it would be humanly impossible for anyone to be a daughter-in-law.
LAOLAO: Ai! It is impossible for so many of them.... [*Hua runs in with a long face.*] Hua, what's the matter? What are you crying for? What about the ducks?
HUA: [*Moved*] The mandarin ducks ... they're already ... dead! Laolao, it's so pitiful they've died! What a sad pair! Both of them are dead!
LAOLAO: They've died! How sad! [*Crying*] I used to come to see them almost every day in the summertime!
HUA: Such a lovely pair! Now they're dead!
MATCHMAKER: Did you tell the Lius or not?
HUA: I told them. Lan's brother picked them up and tossed them into the pond without even a trace of remorse. When he saw me crying, he said I was a stupid child and that there's no point in crying over a pair of dead ducks. I really hate Lan's brother, Laolao, he's so heartless!
MATCHMAKER: There's no need to hate him! He'll buy another pair tomorrow for the pond, that you can see every day. How's that, young lady? [*Smiles*]
HUA: I don't want him to buy more! Hateful man!
LAOLAO: [*Softly*] Hua, don't curse others.
MATCHMAKER: The child has a compassionate heart. How endearing! [*It is near dusk, and the golden rays in the western sky suddenly disappear, leaving behind only a few purple clouds. A slight breeze comes up announcing the imminent arrival of the spirit of night. The dark-faced, stern Knight of the Northeastern Sky is about to demonstrate his skills. The three of them shiver.*]
LAOLAO: Hua, let's go home. It's already getting dark.
MATCHMAKER: It is time to go. Laolao, don't catch cold.
HUA: [*Softly*] Laolao, Zhong has returned already.
LAOLAO: How do you know?
HUA: Just now as I was going to the pond, I saw him hiding behind the bushes. As I ran past he signalled to me, so I went over and he wrote a message for me to pass on secretly to Lan. After I saw that the ducks had died and went to tell the Lius, I slipped her the note.
MATCHMAKER: Really? In that case, there's going to be quite a scene to watch.

LAOLAO: [*In a trembling voice*] If there's a scene, don't get involved. . . . Pitiful! Pitiful! [*The sky has become completely dark. Mei dashes in.*] Oh, Mei, what are you rushing about here for?

MEI: [*Flustered*] It's terrible! My brother has come back after learning that Lan is getting married tomorrow. He's already had a fight with Mother. Ma cried herself into a half-dead frenzy, and he stormed off. When Ma finally came around, she told me to come find out where he's gone. Laolao, have you seen him?

HUA: I saw him in the grove behind the Lius' house.

MEI: Good! I'll go look for him. Laolao, Mrs. Li, please excuse me. [*Exits*]

LAOLAO: Don't rush. Persuade him calmly.

MEI: [*Her voice trails off*] Okay, okay!

MATCHMAKER: Who knows what kind of commotion will come of this!

LAOLAO: I pray the gods will bless and protect them!

MATCHMAKER: What a pity!

LAOLAO: May every god bless and protect them! [*As they all think to themselves for a moment, a tragic silence fills the stage. Then the three slowly part. Laolao puts her hand on Hua's shoulder.*] Good-bye, Mrs. Li!

MATCHMAKER: Good-bye, Laolao! I pray the gods protect them and there's no trouble! [*Exits slowly*]

HUA: [*Sobbing*] The poor ducks are dead!

LAOLAO: [*Exits supported by Hua*] May the gods bless them! May the gods bless them!

[*The stage is empty momentarily. A gloomy and piercing-cold wind blows, and dark clouds fill the sky. Moonlight streams in from the breaks in the clouds. Suddenly, from the mountains at the rear, Zhong and Lan come into the darkness amid the cold wind, embracing. They walk to the side of the road and sit down together on the rock.*]

LAN: [*Mournfully*] What do you want me to do? My brother is forcing me. How can I refuse? Once a woman marries, she is not supposed to eat her own family's food again. Can a lowly woman like myself dare say "no"?

ZHONG: A reed is as durable as silk, but has the silk grown so fragile? [*Slightly irritated*] Of course! Who wouldn't want status and wealth if it were handed to her!

LAN: Zhong! [*Cries*] How can you be so sarcastic? Have I been so unfaithful?

ZHONG: You have been unfaithful under pressure.

LAN: So what would you like me to do now? Run away? How can we escape the powerful clutches of the Prefect? Wouldn't he order a search? After spending so much on the betrothal gifts, do you think he would just give up and let me go?

ZHONG: [*Stands up, angry*] If you were pressured, would you become a thief? Would you become a prostitute? A murderer?

LAN: [*Also angry*] If I did become a thief, or a prostitute, or a murderer, what would you do about it? What would you do about it? [*Leaps up and is about to dash away*]

ZHONG: [*Grabs her tightly*] If you became a thief, I'd help you hide the cache! If you became a prostitute, I'd find customers for you! If you went to kill someone, I'd sharpen your knife! My . . . My Lan, if you went to Heaven, I'd go to Heaven. If you went to hell, I'd go to hell! I . . . I will never . . . be able to leave you. Your flesh is mine! Your soul is mine! All that is yours is mine! . . . Mine! [*Kisses her passionately.*]

LAN: Heavens! [*She is nearly choked by his tight embrace and passionate kisses.*] I'm yours . . . yours . . . take me away . . . take me . . . take me to the end of the sky, to the edge of the Earth!

ZHONG: [*Excited*] I will take you to a land filled with peach blossoms. I will take you to a village of almond flowers! There, to a place where spouses who love each other, spouses whose bones and flesh, and hearts and souls are fused as one, embrace each other forever . . . forever!

LAN: [*Delirious*] I am willing to ascend towering snow-peaked mountains with you to inhale icy wind and freeze in your arms! I am willing to descend to the depths of an abyss to drink from icy springs and die in your arms!

ZHONG: I want to carry you, intoxicated, into the golden luster of the evening sunset. I want to hold you as we float on warm afternoon waves. There . . . there we could live forever!

LAN: I am willing to kiss you to death in the fiery white flames of the sunlight! I am willing to be purified with you in the mouth of a blood-red volcano!

ZHONG: Flesh and bones, blood and soul, forever, forever fused as one!

LAN: Just like the pair of mandarin ducks of Clear Water Pond who died with their necks entwined in the quiet current!

ZHONG: [*Releases his embrace*] What? That pair of ducks at Clear Water Pond is dead?

LAN: They died beneath the mangrove tree. My brother picked them up and flung them into the deep end of the pond! They sank into the pure silent stillness!

ZHONG: [*Takes out the betrothal sash from his pocket, looks at it under the faint moonlight. Lan leans forward.*] It's no wonder that before they died, this sash had become so completely tattered.

LAN: All mandarin ducks have to die!

ZHONG: In death there is eternal life! In death there is pure love. [*The two embrace and gaze up at the moon, which sneaks out from behind the dark clouds, suddenly making it clear and beautiful. A mysterious and strange expression comes over their faces, like the strange joy of a martyr who looks toward Heaven right before the end. The sash falls silently to the ground.*]

LAN: [*They embrace*] Let us live forever! Let our love remain forever untarnished!

ZHONG: Like the lovely ducks.

LAN: Exactly. [*The moon is once again covered up by the dark clouds, and the cold wind suddenly sighs. They hear the far-off voice of Mei as they embrace in rapture.*]

MEI: [*Distant cries*] Brother! Brother! Where are you? Mother is looking for you! Mother is looking for you!

ZHONG: It's Mei, Mei is coming. Let's go!

LAN: Where to?

ZHONG: To the edge of Clear Water Pond! To look for the mandarin ducks in the pond!

LAN: To the edge of the pond! To look for the mandarin ducks in the pond! [*They dash out. Mei comes staggering down from the mountains.*]

MEI: Just now I thought I saw two shadows, where have they disappeared to? [*Looks around. Suddenly she hears mournful cries from the right.*] Who's that? Is it not Mother? Ma, is that you? [*Mother comes limping in, in black clothes and disheveled hair.*]

MOTHER: It's me! Mei, you still haven't found your brother?

MEI: [*Sadly*] No. Why are you limping like that? [*Helps her sit on the rock*]

MOTHER: [*Rubs her knee*] I fell down! It's terribly painful! [*Mei kneels down to rub it.*] Go on! Go on! Go find your brother. Something must be wrong if he hasn't come back at this hour!

MEI: Just now I thought I saw two shadows here, but when I came over they disappeared somewhere.

MOTHER: [*Agitated*] Then they can't be far, they must be somewhere nearby. Go on, go look for them by the Lius' house. I'll sit here and wait for you! [*Mei runs off to the left, panicked. A gust of cold wind blows in, and the mother shivers. The faint moonlight reveals Zhong's sash. She snatches it up like a hungry cat catching a rat, and bursts into tears.*] My son! Son! How did your sash get here? [*She cries as she holds it tightly up to her chest. The cold wind blows even more fiercely, blowing her long grey hair in all directions. Sitting there in the dark night, she looks like a forsaken ghost without a soul. She shivers.*] It's so cold! So cold! My son, why haven't you come back home yet! . . . [*Tilts her head and hears Mei crying in the distance*]

MEI: Oh no! Help! Help! [*Her voice gradually draws nearer.*] Help! Oh! Oh! My God . . .

MOTHER: [*Extremely frightened. She tries to get up.*] What? Mei, what is it?

MEI: Ma! Ma! It's terrible!

MOTHER: [*Cries anxiously*] What? What?

MEI: [*Enters, in a frenzy*] Ma! It's terrible! A ghost! Two ghosts!

MOTHER: What ghost? Tell me! Hurry and tell me!

MEI: Brother's ghost! Sister-in-Law's ghost! They have turned into ghosts!

MOTHER: Nonsense!

MEI: [*As though she hasn't heard her mother's curses. Opens her eyes and mouth wide*] Two ghosts! Two ghosts! They were embracing each other under the old mangrove tree, hugging each other like this. [*Demonstrates*] They jumped into the pond with a splash . . .

MOTHER: [*Looks up with blanched face and screams*] Heavens! What could they have . . .

MEI: [*Chants monotonously to herself*] Then they surfaced! They jumped in the pond with a splash. Then they surfaced! They jumped in the pond with a splash. Then they surfaced . . . [*Hypnotized by the monotonous, depressing tune*] they surfaced and then they jumped in the pond . . .

MOTHER: Heavens! Help! [*Shakes Mei*] Go, go and cry for someone to rescue them!
MEI: [*Snaps out of it and a mournful sound emanates from her whole body*] Oh pain! Oh agony! Brother! Sister-in-Law! How could you have committed suicide?
MOTHER: [*Panicked but still unable to move*] Rescue them! Quick, go and call someone to rescue them!
MEI: [*Runs off wildly to the left*] Rescue them! Rescue them!
MOTHER: [*Ignores her hurt leg and wildly pulls herself up*] Rescue them! rescue . . . [*Rushes forwards but falls. For an instant she seems to have died. Everything is deathlike; the universe is filled with the stillness of death. Even the wind has been subdued by the power of death. A moment later, the moon suddenly appears and the mother shudders slightly. She struggles to get up from the overgrown grass and snatches up the sash as if mad, or in a trance. An expression of kind motherly love suddenly appears on her face. A bunch of dry grass happens to be nearby. She smiles, gathers it up, and ties it with the sash.*] My darling, see how pretty you look! Your aunt sent this to you yesterday, for your birthday. Good baby, how pretty! [*Holds the image of her son and strokes the top of the grass*] What beautiful hair you have! Just like your father's! [*Kisses it*] How fragrant! How fragrant! Oh, my baby is unhappy! He wants some milk! [*Starts to unbutton her clothing, but opens only her outer jacket*] Here! Here! Drink some milk. [*Holds the dried grass up to her breast as though she is nursing it*] Isn't a mother's milk good! There's a dear, my darling! [*The moonlight illuminates the sky. She is startled. She looks closely at the dried grass and then suddenly throws it away from her, crying out in shock.*] Whose son is this? This is rice straw! My son! My son is dead! My son is dead! [*Covers her head and wails. At this point, a fierce gust of wind blows her disheveled hair like the tattered flag of a defeated army, surrendering to an invisible enemy. The mournful sound of the wind is like the wailing of defeated soldiers. Amid the sounds of wailing we can still hear the sounds of the mother's grief.*] My son! My flesh! . . .

12

Xie Bingying

Xie Bingying (1906–)

Xie Bingying was born in Hunan in 1906 into a strict Confucian household. Her mother was determined to raise Xie according to the orthodox standards of feminine behavior and insisted that she study the Confucian classics for women, learn the art of needlework, and have her feet bound. According to Xie Bingying's self-description in her *Autobiography of a Girl Soldier* (1936), however, she was a born rebel and defied her mother's authority at an early age by demanding to be allowed to attend the local boys' school. Later, after staging a hunger protest, she again overcame her mother's objections and won permission to continue her education at a girls' school. One of the first things she did upon arriving at her new school was to unbind her feet. The conflict between Xie's desire for personal autonomy and her mother's pressure on her to conform to more conventional female roles continued to be a source of frustration and anxiety as Xie grew older, and is an important theme in her autobiography.

As a student, first at a Norwegian missionary school and later at the Hunan Normal School for Girls in Changsha, Xie Bingying came in contact with the literary, intellectual, and political trends of the New Culture movement through the vernacular journals then circulating among Chinese youth. She was an avid reader of translated Western fiction and the new Chinese fiction—her favorite writers included Zola, Wilde, and particularly Goethe, whose *The Sorrows of Young Werther* she read many times, as well as contemporary Chinese writers such as Yu Dafu and Bai Wei.

Like many students of her generation, Xie Bingying became enthusiastically involved in the anti-imperialist protests of the early 1920s and was eventually expelled from one school for her political activism. In 1926, when the revolutionary base in Hankow set up by the Guomindang and Communist alliance began rallying Chinese youth to join the revolution, Xie responded by enrolling in the Wuchang Central Political and Military Academy. Shortly thereafter, she was selected as one of just twenty women to accompany the army on its first major expedition into Henan province. Although Xie's bold decision to enlist in the army was motivated by her patriotic convictions, it was also related to her ongoing struggle with her traditional family. By joining the army, she found a way of avoiding the marital arrangement awaiting her at home.

The diaries and letters Xie wrote during her exhilarating experience as a woman propagandist on the Northern Expedition were initially published in 1927 in the Wuhan *Central Daily Newspaper* and published the following year in book form under the title *War Diary*. This book was reprinted nineteen times and was soon translated into numerous foreign languages; the excerpts featured here are taken from the 1930 English translation by the prominent bilingual writer and intellectual Lin Yutang. Heralded by critics as marking a whole new style of women's writing, *War Diary* was praised for its straightforward, unadorned quality of prose and its passionate, revolutionary outlook.

Although Xie's first book brought her instant literary fame, neither her revolutionary goals nor her personal objectives were so easily achieved. In 1927, when internal struggles within the ranks of the Guomindang led to a massive crackdown against the party's "radical elements," Xie's brigade, which had been involved in mobilizing rural women, was disbanded and Xie was forced to make a hasty retreat back home. For Xie this was a traumatic turn of events, not just because she was now marked as a politically suspect "radical," but because it meant having a showdown with her parents over the touchy subject of her marriage. Despite being kept under lock and key at her parents' house, Xie ultimately prevailed, making a narrow escape just days before the wedding ceremony was to take place. The personal freedom she gained, however, came at a high cost: her "wandering years"—as Xie and many other young women in similar circumstances referred to the uncertain periods following their courageous revolts against traditional families—were filled with financial hardship and emotional turmoil.

Xie Bingying was a prolific writer, no doubt in large part because she relied heavily on her income from writing to support herself. In addition to the critically acclaimed *War Diary* and her 1936 autobiography, she published numerous short stories, novellas, essays, and works of reportage during the 1930s and 1940s. Two topics in particular dominate her writing: women's rebellion against traditional social practices and China's national liberation struggle. In 1937, when Japan invaded China, Xie Bingying once again became personally involved in the war effort, this time leading a troop of nurses to the front. In 1938, she published the *New War Diary*, in which she records the resilience of Chinese soldiers in their resistance against the Japanese. After moving to Taiwan at the end of the Chinese civil war, she turned primarily to research in the fields of Buddhism and children's literature.

Excerpts from
WAR DIARY
(1928)

I suppose you must have received the unfinished letter that I sent on the morning of the twenty-sixth from Puqi. That morning we started out at six. Oh, the serene beauty of that calm, starlit sky, the waning moon, the wafts of morning air, mingled with the sounds of the babbling brook. All was still beneath the beautiful dawn! I still remember how, before we set out, I was sitting on the fine sand where my battalion had encamped, scribbling a few lines to you on a sheet of letter paper against my knees, though I have now forgotten what I wrote. Mr. Fuyuan,[1] I have forgotten all those fine, elegant expressions, for now I have nothing but ardent revolutionary feelings and a fervor for battle. I can no longer compose elegant essays or sentimental poetry. As I told you before, I will have to wait until the revolution is over to resume my former literary life.

---

1. Sun Fuyuan was an important editor who had been an active promoter of new literature since the early May Fourth Movement. Xie Bingying's letters from the Northern Expedition were first published in the *Central Daily Newspaper*.

I am delighted by the singing birds and the blooming flowers along the way, since I have not seen such sights for six months. But I mustn't digress; I have important news to report. I rode on horseback for over twenty *li*. Moreover, I rode the Major's horse, which is known to be skittish. At one village about six *li* from Jiayu, my horse had a run-in with some cavalry horses after they had charged at us. One of my comrades was so frightened that she fell off her horse with all her equipment. It scared the living daylights out of me. Many fellow cadets turned back to look at me and smiled, but of course all I could say was, "Who me? I'm not a bit afraid. Not a bit!" I am really not afraid of death. But it would be a disaster if I got hurt falling and couldn't walk. Well, Mr. Fuyuan, here I go talking too much again.

I arrived in Jiayu ahead of the others. I had to go up and down the street in order to locate our living quarters. "Here comes a woman soldier! Here comes a woman soldier! A woman soldier on horseback—could she be the commander?!" Such cries brought even the young ladies secluded deep in their chambers out on to the street to gawk at me. As I was surrounded by the crowd, all I could do was whip my horse and hurry on. I was truly afraid I might fall, since I had never ridden before in my life. You can imagine my embarrassment.

When I reached the church, I decided to dismount. I had been informed that we would be staying in a foreign building, so I guessed this must be the place. A crowd of several hundred people had followed me there. Some addressed me as "Old General," some as "Lady Teacher" or "Lady Commander." There was even one child who called me "Lady Generalissimo." Pouring with sweat and my face burning hot, I had no idea what to do. I realized that to them, I was like a curiosity in a peepshow, or rather, some monster of the modern age. Men and women alike stared at me from head to toe; I believe some of them were even counting the number of hairs on my head. An old woman with a walking cane said to me, "I have lived more than eighty years and I have never seen a woman in a military uniform, or with feet as big as yours, and no hair! Ha, ha, ha!" She laughed her head off, and I joined in laughing with the others!

Another forty-odd-year-old woman came and offered me tea, for which I was very grateful. She said something painful—but then again not that painful—to me: She said, "If an energetic young girl like you died on the battlefield, what would your parents do?" To which I calmly replied, "Madame, don't be sad. I am prepared to die on behalf of the revolution and the people. As for my parents, of course I couldn't bear to leave them, but we don't mind, since the revolution always requires the sacrifice of a few for the benefit of the many." Some of them nodded their heads as if in admiration of my bravery; others made a sign to the woman as if to reproach her for having mentioned the topic altogether. Still another group of old people seemed to be saying, "The poor young child...."

We stayed in the Roman Catholic Church. There are old, tall trees here, a carpet of soft green grass, whistling pines, and sweet chirping birds, and—well, I needn't go through the whole list of nice things. I would go so far as to call it the Peach Blossom Spring, but could even Peach Blossom Spring compare?[2]

Alas, after just one good night's rest and recovery from a hard day's work, today (the 27th) we start again for Tangjiazui, fifteen *li* from Jiayu. Reluctant as I am to leave this place, my heart leaps at the idea of going to the countryside, since the revolutionary army is the army for farmers and workers, and since we want the army to become one with the peasants.

And so we left and now have already arrived in the countryside, where the roosters crow and the dogs bark! The poor peasants, how frightened they must have been of the soldiers of S——; at first, they fled at the sight of us!

The place we stayed today was the most horrid, yet happiest, place since the beginning of our expedition. Although we slept on the ground in the straw like little pigs in a sty, were plagued by mosquitoes, got our clothes soiled with foul-smelling chicken and cow dung, and saw and smelled filth beyond anything we've ever before experienced, our material suffering was transcended by our spiritual elation! The joyous conversations I had with the common people made me completely forget my fatigue and discomfort. All six of us female cadets wanted to talk with the peasants, but unfortunately they only understood Hubei and Hunan dialects, so my four comrades from the north have gone off to bed, bitterly disappointed.

When I see the honest, simple, and hardworking peasant women, a feeling of happiness surges from deep within me. I was eager to talk with them, and told them how I knew how to harvest wheat, pick beans, and transplant and sow saplings from when I was a little girl. When I saw their sincere attitudes, I was reminded of the deceptive ways of city folk. In

---

2. Peach Blossom Spring, described in the preface to Tao Yuanming's poem of the same name, is one of the most famous literary utopias in the Chinese tradition.

short, I love the countryside: true, I love its natural beauty, the birds and flowers, but its greatest significance lies elsewhere.

Dear Mr. Fuyuan, the bound feet here are insufferable. The smallest ones measure only two inches, but even the biggest ones are no more than four inches. Once, I was sitting in a meadow writing letters when a group of women came and started chatting with me, so I put down my pen and began lecturing them about unbinding their feet. One well-to-do middle-aged woman who had three-inch "golden lotuses"[3] laughed at me: "Your feet are enormous. Don't you get your shoes mixed up with your husband's?" At this, all the soldiers, captains, and peasants who were standing around burst out laughing. They laughed so hard that even a brave young girl like myself began to blush.

There was one company captain who wanted to cut their hair for them, and told them, "Your husbands won't be able to pull your hair when they beat you if your hair is short." They all agreed, and added, "True, and if we unbound our feet we'd be able to beat them up." Even though they are fully conscious of the agonies of foot binding, they all say that having "big feet" would waste too much cloth. We responded by asking, "With bound feet, don't you need cloth for the countless layers of bindings?" But obviously, they don't bind their feet to save cloth!

The First and the Third Battalions hired some big river boats, all together sixteen in number, and we all showed our "grit" by becoming boatmen and oarsmen ourselves. We rowed and punted—indeed, I would say we soldiers, men and women alike, made rather respectable sailors.

The whole time we were on board, I could hear the rippling of the river mingled with the clear melody of the "Green Hills and the Blue Waters" and the husky strains of the *Internationale* off in the distance. Most of us kept quiet, some reading, others napping.

Here's something interesting. All along the banks, there are young maidens and old women who work the pedals of the draining wheels with their tiny bound feet. Sometimes, they would start competing with us: the more they accelerated, with their little feet rapidly treading the pedals of the wheels, the more we passengers on board would clap our hands; and the more we clapped, the faster they would go; sometimes, I imagine, our clapping and laughter was so loud the river echoed. I cannot help thinking about all the misery their small feet must cause them, especially while

---

3. A traditional euphemism for bound feet.

engaging in such strenuous labor. Dear Mr. Fuyuan, I regard foot binding as a great misfortune of our sex and consider it a terrible disgrace that even today, in the era of women's emancipation, there are those of our sex who are still willing to be like the slaves of the eighteenth century. While in Fengkou, Comrade Xu Zhaoming (an advisor with the First Battalion) and I saw a pair of feet that were actually only a little more than an inch long, while two-inch feet were quite common. My young friend Jili wrote me today and said, "I absolutely refuse to believe that two-inch feet exist. Even the ancient books speak only of the 'three-inch golden lotus,' and since people no longer believe in ancient ways how could this custom have 'improved'?" Naturally, I have no way of convincing him, short of bringing him here to see them with his own eyes, or perhaps finding someone to confirm my statement when I return to Wuhan.

During this journey (though, in fact, it might have happened anywhere), we two—Hui and I—have had two amusing experiences. One of these was when we went on shore to look for an outhouse. At a little stand, I took a young girl by the hand and asked her to show me the way. After she took one look at me, she was nearly scared out of her wits and tried to run away. But her father immediately assured her, "Don't be afraid. They're female soldiers. Take them along!" Ha, ha! Dear Mr. Fuyuan, why do they fear male soldiers but not female ones?

The other incident has to do with the question of our *laoban*. No matter where we go, the old women, upon learning our age, proceed to ask, "But where are your *laoban*, your husbands? Aren't you married?" When we shake our heads, some of the more clever ones remark knowingly, "They are afraid that marriage will tie them down and prevent them from coming out to fight. They're all still virgins." True, I think to myself, we are still virgins at our age; but the ones to be pitied are your daughters, who have become the slaves of other families at the age of seven or eight. But I keep these thoughts to myself.

Sometimes, when we get irritated with all their questions about marriage and husbands, I tell them bluntly, "Nowadays, our sole concern is the revolution. We don't want any husbands." One day, when we had nothing better to do, we came up with the following plan: If anybody asks Hui about her husband, she will simply point to me in response, and should I be the one asked, I will point to her and say, "That's him." So the trap is set, and woe unto whoever comes our way!

Yesterday, when I was over at the political department, they told me a funny story. Once there was a propaganda corps—four young men and four young women—and while the eight of them were eating together at the mess, an old woman standing nearby asked one of the women, "Which one is your husband?" Oh, how they laughed at the old woman's remark! Dear Mr. Fuyuan, why can't they get these ideas out of their heads? Why are they so worried about us and our husbands?

The streets of Xindi are just as crowded and busy as those of Wuchang, but I have only seen a few stray rickshaws, and only the bigger stores and foreign buildings have electric lights. Shopping is very convenient here, more so than in any other place we've been. There is one thing, however, that bothers me: it is that nine out of ten families living in the Xindi area run brothels. Whenever the young prostitutes, who dress up in provocative clothing, see someone approaching from the Niangniang Temple direction, they rush out to greet him. In the afternoon two days ago, I was wearing a very charming foreign suit (I had borrowed a gray checkered suit from Song, who's on the military staff, since I had nothing else to change into while I was doing my laundry) and was coming down toward the political department with Comrade Ciyu, when they accosted me, one after another, apparently mistaking me for a man. Oh, how sorry and how angry I felt that such boisterous young girls have ended up on the streets, to suffer a life of depravity! But is it their fault? Haven't they been driven to this by poverty, and is it not the lure of money that has led them to this? My dear comrades of the revolution, we cannot afford to condemn them for being shameless and lacking morals, we can only lay blame on the present economic system. If we wish to save them and cleanse them of their shame and their crimes, we must overthrow the unjust economic arrangements of the present. If we want to emancipate them and enable them to return to life as normal human beings, then we must go forward in the spirit of firm determination and dauntless courage and fight against the old society! Let us fight with all our power and struggle to the end!

Translated by Lin Yutang, with slight modifications

13

Ding Ling

Ding Ling (1904–1986)

One of the most famous twentieth-century Chinese women writers, Ding Ling (pen name of Jiang Bingzhi) was born in Hunan in 1904. Her mother, a remarkable woman of Qiu Jin's generation, took Ding Ling with her when she enrolled in a newly established women's academy, and it was there that Ding

Ling spent much of her early childhood. Following her mother's example, Ding Ling herself revealed a highly independent nature as a young girl; for instance, she acted as a student leader in demanding coeducational opportunities and bobbed her hair in defiance of school regulations.

In 1920, Ding Ling left Hunan to join the many other young intellectuals assembling in the cosmopolitan city of Shanghai (and to avoid an arranged marriage). There, she was enrolled briefly at the People's Girls' School, a progressive institution run by the early feminist socialist Wang Huiwu, but spent most of her time leading a bohemian lifestyle, and dabbling in anarchist politics and modern art. In 1924, Ding Ling moved to Beijing with the intention of attending Beijing University, but instead ended up befriending two struggling young writers, Shen Congwen and Hu Yepin, a poet whom Ding Ling eventually married.

The three followed the massive relocation of cultural and intellectual activity in the late 1920s to Shanghai, where Ding Ling hoped now to pursue a career as an actress in the rapidly expanding film industry. This plan failed but provided her with material for her first work of fiction, "Mengke," a novella published in late 1927. It was her second story, "Miss Sophia's Diary," however, written just a few months later, that created a tremendous sensation in the literary world and established Ding Ling as one of the foremost women writers of the day. This story, which boldly explores the psychosexual turmoil of the modern urban woman, was considered a major breakthrough in women's writing for its candid depiction of "feminine" psychology. The majority of Ding Ling's early short stories focused on similar themes and were extremely popular with readers.

In 1931, Hu Yepin, who had become increasingly involved in left-wing politics, was arrested by the Guomindang and executed along with four other writers, an event that shocked the intellectual world and fueled the growing left-wing opposition to Chiang Kaishek's regime. For Ding Ling, the loss was devastating and influenced her own decision to embrace leftist politics. In 1931, she joined the League of Left-Wing Writers and soon became the editor of its literary journal, *The Big Dipper*. The following year, she joined the Communist Party. Although her writing had already begun to move away from the highly subjective narrative focus of her earliest fiction, she now dedicated herself seriously to the program of revolutionary writing. Her 1931 story "Flood," for instance (which was also praised as a breakthrough text—this time, in socialist realism), used innovative descriptive techniques to portray the peasant masses facing a calamitous natural disaster.

In 1933, Ding Ling was suddenly arrested by Guomindang authorities, and when rumors of her execution circulated in Shanghai, cultural circles went into mourning. She had actually only been placed under house arrest, where she remained until managing, somewhat inexplicably, to escape to Yan'an in 1936. By now considered a prominent cultural figure, Ding Ling was assigned numerous top positions at Yan'an: she served as vice-director of the Red Army Guard Unit, led an agitprop drama troupe to villages in Shanxi and Sha'anxi provinces to mobilize peasants to resist the Japanese invasion, and for a time edited the literary supplement of the main Yan'an publication, *Liberation Daily*. Ding Ling's views on art and literature did not always sit well with Party leaders, however, and during her Yan'an decade (1936–46) she found herself the target of criticism at various points. In 1942, her forceful critique of the discrimination against women at Yan'an became the subject of controversy and helped prompt Mao's famous "Talks at the Yan'an Forum on Literature and the Arts."

Ding Ling nevertheless continued to write and, shortly before the founding of the People's Republic of China in 1949, completed a major socialist-realist novel, *The Sun Shines on the Sanggan River*, one of the best examples of that genre. During the antirightist campaign in 1957, however, she once again became the center of criticism and ceased writing for twenty years.

"Day," the story translated here, was first published in the short-lived journal that Ding Ling, Hu Yepin, and Shen Congwen jointly founded in 1928, *The Red and Black Monthly*. A transitional work, written when Ding Ling first began experimenting with a more socially oriented narrative point of view, "Day" highlights the meaningless existence of a young woman living in Shanghai. While the heroine, Yisai, is similar in many respects to characters like Sophia in "Miss Sophia's Diary," the panoramic vision of the city at the beginning of the story provides a very different narrative frame from the intensely subjective focus of Ding Ling's first short stories.

DAY
(1929)

Daybreak.
This is a bustling metropolis, a semicolony, a space populated by people of different races living under the jurisdiction of a few imperialist nations. Thus, when the first rays of light reflect off the surface of the Asian seas, the myriad splendors illuminated beneath the same clear sky are not at all alike. In some sections, there are mansions that tower dozens of meters high, standing there tranquilly with their tapered roofs set off against the blue-and-white horizon like in a cubist painting—thin smoke from the chimneys adding an extra touch. Inside each of those square houses, handsome red lamps have just been turned off and the fine sherry glasses and cigarette ashes of a drunken party clutter elegant tabletops. Cushions from plush chairs are strewn about in all directions; the people, exhausted, have stretched out their delicate limbs on soft satiny comforters made from raw materials from the East and with labor from the West. These comforters crisscrossed the seas and passed through the hands of people of different colors before coming to furnish this room;

all for the enjoyment of a few fat-bellied Asians, hat-sporting Caucasians, drunken soldiers from distant lands, and heavily made-up ladies.

Along the wide stretch of road where the light is obstructed by the tall mansions, there are young women walking the streets in search of customers, sighing as they swing their hips. When day breaks, they trudge back dejectedly along the dimly lit road to their own cramped quarters.

In another part of town, buried beneath a jungle of big black smokestacks, is a dense tangle of dilapidated shanties, home to tens of thousands of Asians. At this hour, they are just getting out of their beds, from beside their undernourished wives, and use the coarse blue sleeves of their work clothes to wipe the filth from their faces. Their hair is unkempt, their shoes are tattered, and their toes poke through the holes in their socks. They all scurry out the door and rush down the mucky road alongside the putrid canal toward the factories that exploit the labor of these working masses. The canal is jammed with boats on which the conditions are still worse. A few of the lucky ones join the throngs on the banks and, with empty bellies, head for the early shift at the factory. The shrill whistles of hundreds of factories built by Caucasian and Asian capitalists, including some of our very own greedy Chinese, blow simultaneously and the gates of the factories open wide as the filthy swarm pushes its way in. There is an even filthier crowd of workers who have just been let out the gates and who have not had a wink of sleep the whole night, since taking up where the day shift left off; together these men keep the machines in perpetual motion, day and night. Even amid the excessive noise and commotion of this part of town one can hear the wails of hungry children. Who here can admire the splendor of the morning sun and the drifting clouds, when shadows stretch down from the chimneys and thick black smoke races along the ground and colorful patterns float on the putrid canal as it catches the light of the sun? The lives of these people are wretched and their minds are numbed; they are stripped of all hope and ideas as they eke out a living from one day to the next. Why don't these people, if not for themselves then for their posterity, think of a way to put an end to this, to temporarily halt their back-breaking labor and take up a different kind of work?

In other parts of the city, things have also begun to liven up: the ships are preparing to set sail, and the dock workers who load the cargo are shouting. The trams have started running and are filled with hordes of bustling passengers. In short, this is a metropolis: there are no golden-feathered roosters to announce the break of day here. You can't see any simple peasants coming out of their thatched huts to prepare their farm tools, nor can you see ruddy-faced maidens herding their sheep. You can't hear the endearing clamor of farm animals or any of those lovely little birds that chirp happily to welcome the light of the dawning day.

In yet another part of this metropolis, there's a section where, in spite of being under Caucasian jurisdiction, only Asians live because even the most impoverished foreign nationals refuse to. Huge red residential structures have been precariously erected up and down every street. More than one hundred families live in each, and the size of each family is absolutely shocking. When the first faint rays of dawn brighten the windows of one of these homes, Yisai, who hasn't been asleep for long, wakes up. She is a woman in her twenties who lost her innocence long ago; her face, for lack of exposure to the sun, has turned from yellow to an unhealthy shade of pale white. She has not been roused from her dreams by the sun shining down upon the earth or by the lovely clear morning, nor have her eyes been opened by the dawn breeze carrying in the scent of damp grass. It is a habit, an unfortunate habit, but she never sleeps soundly and even the slightest noise wakes her. For instance, the child crying next door or the mah-jongg tiles being slapped on the table a little too heavily in the room across the hall—all minor noises that wouldn't bother an average person—are enough to disturb her. But at this early hour every day, it is the sound of the garbage carts in the street down below, their iron wheels clanking over the pavement, that wakes her. A metal cart turns down the street, the man pushing it shouting loudly. The landladies and servant girls in each family then hurry out from their dark beds beneath the stairwells. A thick pungent odor rises, spreading up along the high walls and into the congested apartments, as hundreds of housewives scrubbing hundreds of wooden buckets with bamboo brushes create a cacophony of random swishes and splashes of water that shake the thin walls of each apartment. Each morning, Yisai is startled awake by the sounds of chamber pots being emptied and cleaned, and every morning it irritates her.

The sound of the cart gradually fades into the distance and the women curl back up in their beds to sleep; everything is peaceful once again, except for the occasional honking of automobile horns far away. But Yisai cannot get back to sleep and the sky is already getting light. As usual, she starts thinking of that metal cart, which is by now already long gone: Where do they push that cart? Once they get there, then what? Then she thinks about the family she often sees pushing their cart together; their entire life revolves around this cart, and their children and grandchildren will go on pushing it, never tiring. They have no hopes other than those pinned on this cart, and they have no dreams other than those that have to do with this cart. Yisai looks down at the filthy faces and hands of the people pushing the nightsoil carts. The women have tangled buns at the napes of their necks and their stockings hang loosely about their ankles. They walk at a quick pace but, she thinks, once they get home, they will have nothing interesting to talk about; how dull and stupid their eyes seem; and then they will eat their meals with those dirty hands, and then, and then they will snuggle up and go to bed. What a dreadful life, she thinks. She wishes she could help them in some way, and make them realize that they too are human and are entitled to a more humane way of life. But then she considers all those people who dress so meticulously, with their ignorant ways of thinking and their purely selfish desires—how can you call that a humane life? Everyone squanders their time in this useless, meaningless existence!

She glances out the window—it is a fine, sunny day. Then, seeing the clouds reflected in the windows of the building opposite, she listlessly turns her head away.

She despises this metropolis, but as long as she has to keep on living here she wishes for weather in which she can hibernate, staying locked up inside all day long without feeling anything. She thinks back to the overcast days of winter when the curtains were tightly drawn and she would sit in front of the heater letting her body relax and her nerves deaden in the warmth of the meager fire. This was the best way of making the dreadful time pass. But now the weather has turned too nice, and nice weather does nothing but irritate her because she can't suppress her thoughts of another place that once charmed her so.

Covering her head with the comforter, she tries to go back to sleep, but under the blanket she has started thinking about all sorts of other matters.

The clock next door strikes eight.

Eight o'clock. During the past ten years, hadn't she always been deliriously happy at this time of day, with her arms around friends' shoulders, singing together and shouting as they went to class? But that is all long gone, the bliss of bygone youth! She longs to relive it, rest her hand on someone's shoulder, be among innocent youth, and step enthusiastically into a completely different realm, but. . . . Now she feels even more miserable than before.

With these thoughts racing simultaneously through her mind, she can no longer lie down, so she leaps out of bed with determination. On the street, the commotion picks up. The street vendors cry out in a continuous stream, although some use bells or copper gongs instead. Just counting the peddlers of used goods alone, she can tell from the sounds that there must be at least ten. The children, drawn by the prospect of scraps of food, sit at the back doors, laughing and crying. The ones who achieve their objective are filled with jubilation, while those who still aren't satisfied scream for more.

The maidservant comes in to do a few miscellaneous chores for Yisai. What an irritating face she has! The stupid yet shifty expression on her face often ruins Yisai's daydreams. Yisai patiently puts up with her disturbances, but there is no friendship between them. The more Yisai tries to humor the maid and to melt away her hostile attitude, the more awful she feels. After looking at that pair of unfeeling eyes, Yisai gently beseeches the maid to leave the chores to her; only then does the maid depart, muttering to herself.

Traipsing back and forth across her tiny room at least thirty times, Yisai patiently does her chores, spending two minutes to wash a single teacup. Even though she sighs as she meticulously does these things, it would be difficult to guess that in fact what she really wants to do is smash everything to pieces. But she doesn't have it in her to go ahead and do this, for she knows that boredom will eventually cool down her temper. Aside from the daydreams that comfort her, she doesn't seem to think about anything else; she often slips into a daydream right in the middle of her complaints, and complaints in the midst of her daydreams.

She eats lunch with three of her hypocritical relatives, and soon afterward her friend Weili comes to visit. He is a young man with long hair whose talent is conversation, just as her talent is daydreaming. He often spends his afternoons here, just so long as she doesn't object or interrupt his train of thought or his emotional outpourings. The minute he steps through the door, he bursts out, "My, what a fine day!"

She knows full well that what he says is usually an exaggeration of how he really feels. Laughing, she replies, "Then why aren't you out enjoying yourself?"

He sighs again and says that he isn't in the mood for beauty, then adds, in jest, "And the revolution has still not succeeded."

Tossing his cap down on the bed, he reclines in a rattan chair in front of the desk, with one leg stretched out and the other resting up on the desk, and proceeds to tell her about his recent romance.

It is all so familiar; she understands him too well. And, as usual, he goes on far too long. Does she care? Under his inquisitive gaze, she often nods her head in agreement when in her mind she wants to say the opposite. But she is unwilling to say anything because it is too much trouble to get into an argument. Anyway, she hasn't grown tired of him since he can also be quite charming. In fact, she really ought to appreciate that he often visits her, because the time passes more quickly with someone to talk to.

Yes, she often feels grateful to others for this, but what does she get out of it? What does her time mean? What do her friends have to offer? Under the now-routine cloud of boredom, she once again confirms the hopelessness of her situation. When she daydreams she is capable of ardent emotions. But after talking with friends she realizes her fantasies lack foundation, and for this reason she feels even more depressed and lonely. It often occurs to her that perhaps she would be better off if no one came to see her at all.

Thereupon Yisai, this pale woman, gives a quiet yawn, lifts her head, and leans back against the chair. Weili observes this and promptly stops talking. Looking at her, he asks, "Tired? Why don't you take a rest?"

Yisai is secretly happy that he might leave; but she languidly shakes her head, indicating that she is indeed tired but she doesn't want to say so directly. She never would have guessed, however, that Weili would respond by saying, "Good. You shouldn't sleep during the day anyway, you'll feel dizzy." What's more, he sits back down in the rattan chair, stretches his back, and starts gossiping about their friends.

Shortly, a woman friend who visits every day arrives. She always brings with her an oppressive silence and leaves behind a trace of gloom. She comes in quietly, glances at the long-winded Weili, and gives Yisai a cold smile. When Yisai offers her a seat, she sits down in front of the desk, directly facing Weili.

"How's everything? What have you been up to at home?"

She shakes her head at Yisai in reply. Weili changes the subject and starts expounding on how the Chinese lack expressive abilities and how people ought to be able to thoroughly convey their feelings and how being excessively reserved makes others uncomfortable.

The woman friend knits her brow when she hears this but doesn't speak to him. Instead she asks Yisai a few trivial questions. Afterward, she gets bored and leaves. As she is going, she simply says, "I'll be back tomorrow!"

Dusk finally arrives, a resplendent dusk. Those filthy men in coarse blue clothes are resting their weary limbs and wry smiles flicker across their wrinkled grey faces; busy on the streets, the young girls smile knowingly in the radiance of the evening glow and the electric streetlights. Everything is transformed—the reverse image of dawn. Only the constant confusion along the river and the roar of the traffic confirm the unstopping world.

By this time, the room has become dim and Weili leaves. Yisai lies quietly in bed all alone, her head dizzy, her energy spent. She thinks about nothing but simply listens to the bustling city noises. Not long after, she falls asleep.

Tomorrow, the cycle will begin again.

14

Chen Ying

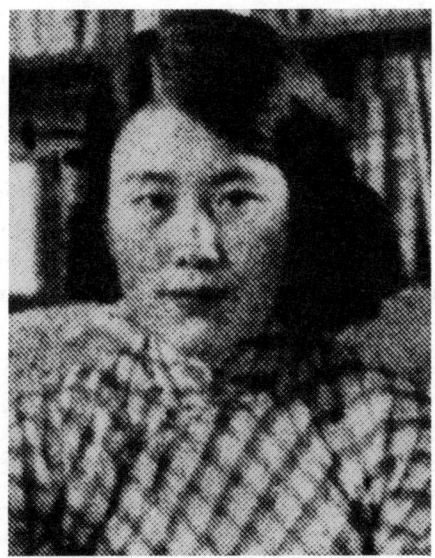

Chen Ying (1907–1986)

Like many women from intellectual families in traditional China, Chen Ying's mother was a learned but illiterate woman. She often recited one of the hundreds of classical poems she had committed to memory to her daughter or asked a relative to read aloud from one of the great works of traditional Chinese fiction and drama. When Chen Ying's father, a late-Qing educator, allowed his daughter to attend a private elementary school in their native Shandong province, he also insisted that she be tutored in the Confucian classics at home. As a pupil at Shandong Number One Girls' Middle School from 1920, Chen Ying continued to build upon her strong background in classical Chinese studies, but she was most inspired by a young teacher who introduced his students to new Chinese writing from Beijing and Shanghai as well as translations of modern literature from Japan, Russia, and Europe.

By the time Chen Ying's family moved to Shanghai in 1924, many universities had opened their doors to women; Chen entered the Chinese department at Shanghai University, a school founded by the Communist Party. Having participated in protests against imperialism since the age of twelve, Chen Ying was no stranger to political activism and quickly threw herself into the hotbed of Shanghai dissident politics. She joined demonstrations for freedom and democracy, distributed propagandist handbills, and helped to organize labor unions in several factories. However, the Guomindang crackdown on Communist sympathizers in 1927 closed Shanghai University and forced Chen to transfer to Fudan University, across town. She curtailed many of her overt political activities and devoted her energies to acting in new-style dramas and writing short stories. By the time of her graduation in 1930, she had already established a reputation as a talented new woman writer.

"Woman" appeared in *Short Story Monthly* under its original title, "Wife," in 1929. It is typical of the stories written by Chen Ying during the late 1920s and early 1930s, in which she focuses on a modern woman's dissatisfaction with the life she has created for herself. In "Woman," a young man describes the ordeal his common-law "wife" goes through in coming to and carrying out her decision to abort an unwanted pregnancy rather than give up her ambitions and become a dissatisfied mother. Chen Ying is often described as a writer of love stories, but the complex emotional experiences uncovered in "Woman" carry deeper resonances than any simple romance. An extremely popular writer, Chen Ying published five collections of writing between 1929 and 1935, including *A Woman Writer* and *Woman*, all of which went into multiple printings.

Despite her youthful success, however, Chen Ying wrote very little fiction during the rest of her life. After a brief marriage to playwright Ma Yanxiang, Chen Ying moved to Beijing where she met and married Liang Zongdai, a professor of French at Beijing University, in 1935. They started a family and, like many intellectuals, moved inland to Chongqing in Sichuan province after the outbreak of the Sino-Japanese War in 1937. Near the end of the war, Chen Ying left Liang and moved back to Shanghai where she worked as a schoolteacher, joining the staff of the Shanghai Experimental Drama School in 1946. Her brother, a Guomindang military officer, persuaded her to move to Taiwan with her family in 1948.

In Taiwan, Chen Ying taught middle school and renewed her literary career as an essayist and translator. Her translations of works by Somerset Maughm, Stefan Zweig, Herman Hesse, and many other Western writers remain in print and are considered classics of modern Chinese translation. Chen Ying moved to the United States in 1972 to be near her children.

WOMAN
(1929)

My wife and I live alone, so whenever I go out, she is left at home by herself. Unfortunately, my work takes me out quite often.

By the time I managed to set out for home that day it was already completely dark out. Thinking of my wife anxiously waiting for me, I rushed straight home, looking forward to her cheerful greeting. But when I pushed open the door, I found the apartment pitch black. Not a single light was on and all was still; it looked as if no one was home. Only after turning on the light did I notice my wife curled up on the bed. She was not asleep, however, and when she saw me come in, she languidly lifted her eyes and forced a smile. I knew right away that she had sunk back into the depression that had been plaguing her recently. Knowing that there was little I could do to comfort her, I just tried to distract her from her worries by talking about all manner of unrelated things and doing my best to avoid touching upon her problem. My wife not only seemed reluctant to say anything, but she also refused to listen to me and stubbornly remained in her melancholic state.

"Don't just lie there, why don't we go for a walk in the park?" I did my best to change her mood, but to no avail. Finally I sat on the sofa and beckoned to her with my arms outstretched.

"I don't feel like moving!" she mumbled as she sluggishly walked over to me.

We sat together on the couch embracing, neither of us saying a word. I was worried about bringing up the subject, but at the same time felt anxious, knowing that it would soon come up anyway. We remained silent, and yet we each knew what the other was thinking.

"Xige!" My wife suddenly called out my name and wrapped her arms around my neck, burying her head in my chest.

"What is it?" I asked, bending my head to look at her face.

"Whenever I think about it, I feel terrible, as if all were lost!"

"Don't say such things. If you loved me, you wouldn't talk like that!"

Her sadness had already had an effect on me, yet I still thought it best to try to avoid beginning this conversation. When I said these last words, she gently nodded her head and nestled closer against my chest in silence, but I could soon feel something wet soaking through the front of my shirt.

My wife and I had fallen in love and begun living together six months earlier. At the time we were intoxicated with love and full of fantastic dreams about our future. We both had literary ambitions, and after beginning our new life together we happily threw ourselves into a frenzy of hard work. We wanted to go on living together and working toward our common ideals forever. Neither of us wanted a conventional married life, so we even fashioned our lifestyle after our romantic school days. My wife wanted to learn to read Russian literature, so she had begun studying with a private tutor. Every evening, I would gaze at her as she sat with her head bent under the lamplight, looking like an innocent little child as she concentrated on mastering her Russian text. She seemed even more beautiful than usual as she sat illuminated by the glow of knowledge. Often I would be unable to stop myself from going over to kiss and embrace her, exclaiming: "I really love you!"

When she wasn't studying, my wife spent most of her time hunched over her desk, writing. Sometimes I would urge her to submit a manuscript for publication in one of the current popular literary journals. But my wife always felt very modest about her own work and liked to say, "Wait until I write a piece that I myself am completely satisfied with, and then I will send it out for publication."

She had a deep respect for literature as well as an almost juvenile love for it. Sometimes when we would reach a particularly happy moment as we discussed our future plans together, she would cheerfully grasp my hands and say, smiling, "That would be wonderful, Xige! We must work hard for that!"

Other times she would excitedly, but still quite timidly, tell me about her own ambitions. She would carefully watch my face as she talked, and if she saw me smile, she would stop immediately and say resentfully, "You're laughing at me! I'm not going to tell you another word."

Happiness of any kind is hard to appreciate when you are in the midst of it. But the indescribable happiness that filled our lives then is not just a rosy memory, for even to us our life together seemed too wonderful to be true.

One day, however, a sad expression appeared on my wife's face. She told me about several changes in her body that made her fear she might be pregnant. After hearing this unwelcome news, I myself shared a little of her unhappiness, but gradually I began to feel that it was not such a terrible thing after all. I tried my best to comfort her, but no matter how hard I tried, my wife was unable to set her mind at ease. At times she would grow angry at my casual attitude. "You're just being self-centered," she would say. "You feel that what's done is done. It has nothing to do with you, so you don't really care." She would blurt out such exaggerations when she was in a dark mood, but of course I always understood and quickly forgave her.

As time passed, what we had feared in abstraction turned out to be reality, and her depression deepened. I told her that since it was now true, even though we hadn't wanted it there was no longer anything we could do about it, so it was not worth getting depressed over. She felt that I didn't understand her or have any compassion for her. Sometimes, either because of me or because of the problem—I was never quite sure which—she would become so aggravated that she would burst into tears. The fact was, she was never easily going to come to terms with the fate that had been dealt her. She would often say to me, "I never even wanted to be a conventional wife, so I can't tell you how much I detest the idea of becoming a mother." My wife had always had so many lofty ambitions that it wasn't hard to understand why she said such things. Clichés like: "It is a natural and spiritual obligation to be a mother" had little impact on her. I tried to comfort her, saying, "Even if we were to have the child, it wouldn't be that much trouble."

"How is that possible? Having a baby automatically transforms a woman into a maternal person. Even now, whenever I think about it I feel disgusted by it, but oddly enough, at the same time I find myself beginning to wonder about the joys of motherhood. It's all too frightening! Women have maternal instincts, so it would be impossible to have a child without becoming a mother."

My wife thus was in a real dilemma. She was in despair, yet somehow found herself happily fantasizing about the future despite herself. One time when we went out, there was a three- or four-year-old child sitting directly in front of us in the trolley car. He was really cute and my wife couldn't keep her eyes off him. Even the slightest movement of the child seemed to interest her. She had an unconscious smile on her face, and every now and then she would nudge me and whisper "Look!"

"It would be fine if we had a baby like that!" I said admiringly, deliberately trying to provoke her.

She didn't get angry, but just smiled mockingly at me.

Another time after returning from a shopping trip, she was telling me this and that about her excursion when suddenly she smiled to herself.

"What is it?" I asked her.

"There were lots of children's clothes there that were really adorable and very inexpensive, only one *yuan* apiece." After saying this, she continued grinning, slightly embarrassed.

"You wanted to buy one or two, didn't you?" I couldn't help but laugh.

"No." She shook her head coquettishly.

"The child hasn't even been born yet and you're already preparing clothes for it!" I teased her.

"Who is it that really wants to start making preparations?" she mocked, throwing me an angry look.

"I know you love children and you would love a baby much more than you love me. I don't want you to have a child, because then you wouldn't love me anymore," I said to her provokingly.

"I don't want a child and I don't love children. I just want to keep on loving you," she said, running over and embracing me.

"No, I'm willing to have a child, that way we'll love each other even more."

"But I don't want to, no matter what happens," she blurted out with determination, falling back into her previous state.

Thus, the conversation abruptly ended.

Imagining what life would be like with a baby often became the focus of our conversation together. In those moments, my wife would appear to forget her usual depression, speaking quite cheerfully with me. But it did little to alleviate her mounting anxiety, and as the extent of her physical changes grew more obvious, she could rarely forget her troubles even momentarily. She grew alarmingly dispirited and refused to do anything. Normally so industrious, my wife stopped going to her Russian lessons and even gave up casual reading. She would often sit alone, despondently lost in thought, not moving for long periods of time. Once in a while when I spoke to her she would lift her head and stare up at me blankly, as if she were thinking about something else and had not clearly heard what I had said. I don't remember when it first started, but her face had grown as dark as the sky on a rainy day. Seeing her this way made me indescribably scared and upset; I began to feel that she was really suffering from some invisible, destructive force.

Thinking that keeping busy might distract her, I urged, "Why don't you review some of your Russian lessons? You don't want to forget everything you've learned."

"Study Russian?!" she exclaimed incredulously, on the brink of tears.

At other times I would try to speak with her about the future—her favorite topic in the past—but now she never wanted to talk about it and even seemed afraid to. She would often cut me off. "Everything is nearly over. What's the point of talking about it?" she would say dejectedly.

Although I myself had never considered the situation to be so tragic, as I watched my wife's misery I came to share in her despair.

My wife seldom divulged her worries. More often she sat alone in a gloomy silence that made her appear all the more mournful and dispirited. One day when she sat brooding like this, she cried out suddenly.

"What's wrong?" I asked, lifting my head immediately to look at her.

She didn't return my look, nor did she answer me directly but went on, lost in her thoughts. Then, hesitating momentarily, she slowly stated, "I want to go to the hospital."

"What? Where did you ever get such an idea?" I asked in astonishment and disbelief.

As if she had long foreseen my reaction, she turned her head to stare at me coldly, letting me know that nothing I could say would dissuade her.

"How could you do such a dangerous thing?" I continued.

"What danger is there? It's no more dangerous than having a natural birth. Besides, you're not saying this merely because you're worried about the danger." These last words came out with a sneer.

"Granted, it's not only the danger involved that makes me uncomfortable, but it's by far the most important reason. Besides, it's just too ruthless."

"It's still nothing more than a lifeless thing, so there is nothing cruel about it. I feel it would be more cruel to throw away my whole future for its sake."

"The way you are talking right now, it wouldn't be right for you to have a child anyway."

"It's just that for the sake of my ambitions, for my future, I can't have one right now."

"You are taking this problem too seriously. I doubt it would really be such a great obstacle for you."

"People's ideas change with their circumstances. If I have the baby, I will fall into the trap of motherhood; the person I am and have been will completely disappear. How can you say that there wouldn't be any obstacles? A trap has been set before me right now and before long I will walk straight into it. How could I be anything other than fearful and resistant? It's certainly possible that had this never happened, I would still not accomplish anything exceptional. But the moment I think that all will soon be lost, then it seems as if I had an amazing future before me which, if I am not resigned to fight for, will never happen."

"When the child is born we'll find somebody to take care of it. Then wouldn't you be able to go on living like you do now?" All I could do was offer my assurance.

"I think that is irresponsible. It wouldn't be right and it would be impossible; maternal love can't be so easily suppressed. If I were to become a mother, I would put all my energy into raising my child, and any aspirations I had before would be cast aside." With this my wife lost control and broke into tears of despair.

"But since it is already too late, isn't it best just to let nature run its course?" I said gently.

"Why should we give up and surrender to nature when we don't want to?" My wife's desperation had turned into obstinacy once again.

"But . . ." For a moment I was at a loss for words.

"At any rate, I have already made up my mind to do it," my wife said, more firmly.

"You can hate me or curse me all you like, but I beg you, please don't say such things!" The more I went on trying to dissuade her, the more resolute her decision became, so I tried appealing to her emotions instead.

"Doesn't it pain you to see me suffering like this day after day? Doesn't it upset you to think about a future in which all my former aspirations have turned to nothing and I have become someone I never wanted to become? Whenever I think about it, my future seems completely bleak as

I get closer and closer to that dark, ominous place; everything will be over." She grew distressed as she spoke and began crying again.

"Don't be this way. I don't feel good about it either. Go ahead and do as you wish." Deep in my heart I knew that I could no longer bear to oppose her, yet when I held her and consoled her I nearly cried.

"Don't just say that to humor me!" Almost begging, she lifted her tear-filled eyes and looked at me sadly.

"Really, I'm not just saying it." I tried to assure her of my sincerity.

"Then when should we go?" she asked, not daring to believe me, yet at the same time knowing that she had to trust me.

"This can't be done too hastily. First let me look into it, and when I find out which hospital is reliable, then we'll go. All right?"

"Do it as soon as possible. Now that we have made the decision, I don't want to prolong my unhappiness any longer." She sensed that my promise was nothing more than a few false words said to appease her for the moment, yet she did not want to come out and say she didn't trust me, so she kept on imploring me to make the arrangements quickly.

Perhaps to give me some time to do what I had promised, she didn't bring the matter up again for several days. Yet still her mind was not at ease. In fact, she appeared to be unusually nervous. Sometimes she would stare at me and her silent expression made me feel as if she were questioning and pleading with me. I felt so much pressure that I didn't dare look back at her.

As I watched my wife grow weaker by the day, my own pain in trying to deal with this alarming situation surpassed even hers. I never acted on the promise I had made to comfort her, nor did I come up with any alternative solution. My guilt deepened as I watched her so helplessly putting her trust in me and waiting, and I felt very confused. I knew that she had good reason to be depressed and that her fears were well founded, and I wondered at times if perhaps going ahead with her plan wasn't the right thing to do after all. I couldn't resolve this question. Would a woman whose aspirations went beyond the norm of simply being an obedient wife and good mother really be harmed by fulfilling her supposedly natural obligation to bear offspring? I thought of all the women I knew who were as ambitious and enterprising in their youth as any man, but who after getting married and becoming mothers shed all their youthful hopes as though merely stripping off an outer shell. They turned into completely different people. It was no wonder that my lovely wife was scared and struggling against the possibility of suffering a similar fate. I was well aware of the contradictions that arise in people's lives under the present social system, but what could I do that would be best for my poor wife?

The moment I arrived home that day, the atmosphere in the room told me that my wife had been thinking about it again. She remained silent at first, but finally she broached the subject. "I don't want to talk about it," was all I could say as I tried to avoid the topic. But my wife seemed determined, and no matter how uneasily I acted, in the end she said the words I feared she would.

"What about the hospital?"

"This isn't the kind of thing that can be decided overnight. It's quite a lot of trouble," I lied once again.

"But it isn't something that can be put off easily either!" My wife's expression was extremely anxious as she spoke, but still she appeared more sad than worried.

"Of course I am aware of this. I will definitely take care of it soon," I said once again in earnest.

My wife was left repeating her pleas over and over again.

All our beautiful dreams had been shattered; the sweet life we had once shared seemed to have taken place in another world. Even though each day was so gloomy, the time passed surprisingly quickly. The extreme heat of summer gradually turned into the milder weather of autumn, but my wife's burning distress did not cool. On the contrary, like an illness taking a turn for the worse, her mood was so vile that her temper grew violent and she became extremely irritable, showing no patience with me. At times she would even say impulsive things like, "If there is no way to solve this problem, then I would rather just die. Death is better than not living life freely."

Finally my wife lost her trust in me and secretly took the matter into her own hands. Without telling me, she went ahead and made arrangements with a reliable hospital recommended by a girlfriend. Faced with her staunch determination and the finality of her action, I could say little other than, "Well, we'll go then." Afterward, I went myself to see her girlfriend and questioned her about all the details. We left for the hospital that very afternoon.

When I walked in the front doors of the hospital I felt as if something cold were piercing my heart. From the color of my wife's face I could tell that she felt somewhat strange too, but steadfast in her determination, her expression remained calm. It was a large, well-equipped hospital so I felt that it would be unlikely that the doctors here would be unreliable—a thought that comforted me slightly. In the waiting room we met with the doctor who had been recommended by her friend. He was a middle-aged man with the gentle and dignified manner typical of doctors. He appeared to be very kind, but inexplicably I was unable to say a word to him. As he had been introduced to us through a friend, he already understood our situation; in a rather overly routine way he only asked my wife a few questions about her health before leading us upstairs to an examination room. The room on the second floor was large and tidy; everything in it was completely white, giving it a sterile air. Soon after we entered, a nurse carrying white bedding came in and placed it on the bed.

"Am I going to be staying here tonight?" Having assumed that we had come only for an examination today, my wife sounded slightly alarmed.

"Yes, that way we can begin administering the medicine immediately," the doctor answered with a smile.

"Will you need to operate?" I asked nervously from the side.

"Perhaps not," the doctor responded nonchalantly, and left the room.

My wife and I were then left alone in the whiteness, and for a time neither of us said a word as we sat in silence on the freshly made bed.

"Are you going home?" my wife asked me suddenly.

"I can't stay here, of course. Don't be afraid, I'll come to see you every day." I did my best to reassure her calmly.

"It's not that I'm afraid." Finally my wife could no longer maintain her composure and she fell into my arms crying.

"Don't do it, let's go home, okay?" I don't know why it had taken me so long to say this.

"No," she answered, lifting her head, her firm resolve returning.

Outside the sky grew dark as dusk arrived and turned to night while my wife and I continued to sit there, unable to think of anything to say; in my mind, however, my thoughts were racing chaotically. After a while I could stand it no longer and finally managed to get out the words "I should go."

"Stay a bit longer," she begged me, but still there was nothing to say.

After a time she burst out, "Go on home." And yet I couldn't get myself to leave right away. As I lingered she became extremely agitated and urged me repeatedly, "Hurry up and get going!" There was nothing I could do but force myself to leave quite uneasily. I am certain that as soon as I went out the door the tears she had been fighting back started flowing.

I walked home in a daze. I was so confused that I did not know what to think about and I felt even worse once I arrived. A few hours earlier this had still been our cozy little home, but now it had become frightfully barren. Everything seemed lifeless now that my wife was gone. A bouquet of some kind of white flower buds that she had just brought home that morning stood in a vase on the table. We had never expected that she would be staying at the hospital so quickly and the thought that she would not be able to see the flowers bloom only compounded my escalating sense of loneliness. I thought of her in the hospital at that moment, perhaps already undergoing the operation. In her pain would she still think of me? Uneasy thoughts overtook me as I lay down on the bed, completely unable to fall asleep. Every time I began drifting off, I would suddenly be startled awake.

I was all set to visit my wife very early the next morning when I realized that the hospital would probably not be open yet. I tried to be patient and wait a bit longer, but when I finally went out on the street the yellow rays of the morning sun had just barely reached the tops of the buildings. Although the cold winds and falling leaves of autumn had not yet fully arrived, on this clear morning the sidewalks along the road already felt desolately autumnal. The streetcars were running, but there were hardly any passengers and my mood darkened. As I rode in the chilly streetcar, I contemplated how people continuously search for happiness, and yet life remains more full of sadness than ever. I walked straight up to the door of the tall hospital building and stared up at it before snapping out of my daydreams and gathering my thoughts.

Reaching the door of my wife's room upstairs, I seemed to hear a low moaning sound coming from within, but when I gently pushed open the door, it disappeared. The air in the room was as silent as the surrounding whiteness. Everything remained exactly as it had been when we first entered the room yesterday, only now my wife's pale face lay on the white pillow of the slightly raised hospital bed. She looked like she was sleeping. Fearing I would wake her, I tiptoed in, but my wife had already opened her eyes wide in surprise and seen it was me. Instantly her expression grew agitated, and she drew her arms out from beneath the blanket and held them out to me. I went over and embraced her tightly as she firmly buried her head in my chest without saying a word. Afraid that she was overly excited, I wanted to calm her down a bit, so I just stroked her hair in silence. Suddenly I felt my wife's shoulders begin to tremble, and only then did I hesitantly lift her head to discover that her face was already streaked with tears. I asked her right away, "What is it?"

She held me even tighter and cried, still not uttering a word. Only after I urged her over and over again did she finally blurt out, "I feel so sad."

Strangely enough, this outburst made me feel relieved and gradually I became more relaxed. She calmed down a bit as well, but before the tears on her face had dried, she suddenly broke into a smile.

"Did they give you the medicine yesterday?" I asked.

"Yes. Yesterday when I saw the nurse carrying in a tray of knives and scissors and things and the doctor took them and was about to begin, I really felt scared. I closed my eyes tightly, gritted my teeth, and prepared for the pain. My back broke out in a cold sweat, but then I did not feel a thing and before long it was over." In a playful tone my wife related the story of how happy she was that it had been so painless. I was relieved that my own terrible worries had been unfounded.

"You didn't ask whether they would have to operate when it started coming out?"

"I did, and he said that after administering the medicine inside, it comes out by itself and there is no need for an operation," my wife told me quite cheerfully.

"When did he say it could come out?"

"Probably tomorrow or the day after."

"Then take care of yourself and keep still. How do you feel now?"

"My stomach hurts a little."

"And yet you were still crying like that just now? It can't be good for you, from now on you must not do that!"

"Okay!" she answered, like an obedient little girl.

"Tell me, why were you so upset just now?" I asked her, smiling.

"I don't know why, but when I saw you I just felt like crying," she answered, laughing in embarrassment as she leaned her head on me.

"How come you feel like crying when everything is going so well? You really scared me just now. How do you think I felt?!"

"I missed you so much that as soon as I awoke at sunrise, I began to wait for you. Then when I saw you come in, I don't know why, but I just felt like crying."

"From now on don't be like that. If you do, then I won't dare come anymore."

"All right, I won't cry," she agreed, glancing up at me quickly.

Although she lay in bed like a sick patient, my wife's spirit was livelier and happier than it had been in months. It was as though her problems were already completely solved, and she could not help telling me about all the things we would do after she got out of the hospital, even bringing up plans for the very distant future. It was odd, though, for seeing my wife in such a happy mood hurt me strangely.

After a time, I had to leave for the office and my wife looked at me helplessly. She did not try to stop me, but just told me repeatedly to come back soon. When I got to the office I didn't feel quite as uneasy as the night before, but I still didn't feel completely relieved either. I kept thinking about how high her spirits had been when she saw me that morning, how sad she might have felt after I left, and how she was now waiting for me to come back.

It was four in the afternoon by the time I left the office. I rushed to the hospital and when I pushed open the door and went in, I deliberately hesitated for a moment, hoping that she would call out to me so cheerfully and beckon me with her arms outstretched as she had that morning. But when my wife saw me come in this time, she only smiled at me momentarily before letting her gaze drop down lifelessly once again.

"What's wrong?" I went to her side and asked.

"My stomach hurts."

"How badly?"

"Terribly, in spasms."

"Has the doctor been in?"

"He was here and said not to worry."

"It's probably going to come out soon. Don't be afraid, just be patient and it will soon be over."

"Yes." She nodded her head slightly in reply.

As I was saying this, my wife's expression grew tense, her eyes shut, and she seemed to be grinding her teeth; she looked as though she were trying her best to hold something back but couldn't, until finally she turned over in the bed and cried out, "Aiya!" Her hands grasped the sides of the bed, holding them tightly with all her bodily force.

"Your stomach hurts?" Frightened, I stood up, not knowing what to do.

My wife didn't seem to have heard what I said, but just went on crying in pain more and more intensely. The sound was so penetrating it made me crazy.

"Let me go get the doctor."

"No." She contained her pain and stopped me abruptly. Gradually her shouts subsided and her furrowed brow relaxed, but even though she was calm again, she was not exactly completely at ease. Her face had become pale and her eyes remained closed; her head rested listlessly on the pillow, perfectly still, as if she were asleep. I then noticed that her forehead was covered with large beads of sweat, and I wiped them off gently, my hand feeling the damp coldness of her skin. She looked unusually weak and I did not dare to say anything to her.

"Xige! It really hurts terribly." She rolled on to her side.

"It must be about to come out. Bear with it a bit longer." This was the only comfort I could offer.

Her eyes closed again and she fell silent.

Before long, she appeared to have recovered some of her strength, and she opened her eyes wide and asked for a drink of water. She seemed to want to say something, but her gaze and her voice did not return to their usual liveliness and her earlier cheerfulness had vanished altogether. Even when a smile appeared on her pale face, it only revealed all the more how miserable she felt.

"Are you starting to regret it now?" I asked her, smiling.

"Wouldn't it have been just as painful if I had gone ahead and had it?" she snapped back, annoyed by my question.

"Yes, childbirth is always painful."

"Why does it have to be painful? It doesn't seem natural," she said, as if asking herself.

"It's painful in order to show how serious a thing life is!" I said, trying to follow her train of thought.

Every time a contraction overcame her I was at a loss what to do and just stood there nervously. In her pain, my wife kept calling out my name over and over. What an unbearable sound! Was she crying out like this because she hoped I could alleviate her suffering? Maybe my standing in front of her so tensely, even if I could do nothing, might comfort her a little. I also thought about how awful it would be if I hadn't been here when the pain came, and I felt dissatisfied with the lack of sensitivity in the treatment provided at this hospital. The nurses did nothing more than come in like robots to take her temperature or indifferently ask her a few questions; they never tried to comfort the patient at all.

I said to my wife, "Why doesn't a nurse come to take care of you? If I weren't here, what would happen when you were having a contraction?"

"But I don't want them to stay with me. Seeing them won't help me when I'm in pain. Sometimes I can think of things to distract myself, but if they were in here it would just be annoying."

"What kinds of things do you think about?"

"I think about what I will do after I leave the hospital. Knowing that I will get back everything I lost makes me feel much better. The moment I think about how I will be my old self again, I'm really happy and I feel free to go ahead making plans for the future."

Hearing her speak so passionately, I recalled the hopelessly depressed state she had been in before and I was extremely touched. What could be more moving than a person thinking so desperately of the future in order to lessen the pain of the present? This thought came to me as I contemplated my wife looking forward to life with such intensity.

Finally I could no longer stand by and watch my wife suffer wave upon wave of such terrible pain, and I went to get the doctor.

"She's in such agony, don't you think it's about to come out? Please have a look, doctor."

"It couldn't be coming so soon. Let me see..." The doctor spoke calmly, and taking the stethoscope from the nurse, he placed it on my wife's abdomen and listened quietly for a moment before saying, "Not yet."

"When will it most likely be?"

"Tonight at the earliest," the doctor said and walked out nonchalantly.

How will my wife be able to stand it for that much longer? The doctor's words only served to increase my own anxiety. My wife's condition remained unchanged right up until the time I had to leave. Back home, I seemed to be hearing her painful cries all night long. At moments I would wonder whether her pain had already subsided, but then would fear that this was just wishful thinking. The next day when I went to the hospital, her condition had changed little although the situation appeared to have grown more tense, as two nurses now stood watch before my wife's bed.

"It hasn't come out yet?" I asked in a whisper, since my wife looked like she was asleep.

"Soon," one of the nurses answered in a low voice.

Suddenly my wife's eyes flew open, and catching sight of me, she forgot the presence of the nurses and grasped my hands tightly, not saying a word as her tears began to fall. But just as I was about to speak, she let go of me and began writhing in pain again. The nurses held her firmly to keep her from turning over and ordered her, "Don't move!" My wife could do nothing but rock her head back and forth on her pillow wildly. The degree of pain had increased since last night, and the time between contractions shortened so much that even when the pain stopped, there was hardly time to say anything before it began again.

"It's going to come out soon. Please go out and wait for a while," one of the nurses said to me.

Just as I was about to go out, my wife sat up with a start and grabbed hold of me screaming hysterically, "Don't leave me, don't leave me!" Only when the pain began again did she release me.

"But there's no harm in letting me stay, is there?" I pleaded with the nurses.

The two nurses only glanced at each other in embarrassment, which I took as an expression of silent consent. I then sat next to my wife and took hold of her icy hands.

The nurse told my wife to draw her legs up on the bed. She tied a piece of cloth to the bed frame behind my wife's head, telling her that holding on to this when the pain came would help her push harder. When the next contraction arrived, my wife obediently raised her hands above her head to grab hold of the cloth and drew her feet up on the bed, exerting all her energy. After the nurse told her again to keep quiet, my wife only let out a scream when she was absolutely no longer able to restrain herself. But just as quickly as she let out the scream, she shut her mouth again tightly. Every muscle in her face was tense and trembling; I had never seen a more pained expression. She appeared to be completely unconscious of what was going on, yet obediently followed whatever the nurses instructed her to do. The unyielding expression on her face was astonishing. With every contraction, one nurse pressed down on her abdomen with her hand and sternly urged her, "Push! Push!" Some water would pour out from below and all of us would hope that "this time it will come out," but the contractions were stubborn and once the pain climaxed, the contraction stopped with no outcome. I felt almost disappointed each time I saw my wife's body suddenly go limp and still after having pushed with all her strength. When the contraction stopped, my wife was so tired she hardly seemed to have the strength to breathe. The color had completely drained from her face and lips. Large beads of sweat formed on her forehead and her hair was thoroughly soaked. She looked like she had no more strength left, but when the next contraction began, she would somehow muster energy again. But it was never with any result.

"I don't have any more strength left! I want to sleep!" My wife spoke deliriously, as if unconscious. She called out listlessly, and seemed to be completely exhausted and nodding off. But the contractions were coming in quick succession so it wasn't easy to have a moment's rest.

"How can this be right? I don't have any strength left! Will they have to operate?" my wife said, beginning to panic herself.

"Don't worry, it will come out soon," the nurse said encouragingly in an effort to comfort her.

"Shouldn't we ask the doctor to come in?" I sensed that my wife really did not have the strength to go on, and I was growing alarmed.

"Don't worry, it will come out. The doctor is operating on someone else at the moment."

The next contraction arrived and this time it was especially prolonged. My wife continued to struggle, but she was having to do her utmost to keep it up, and I was certain that she would faint. The nurse looked on nervously and then suddenly urged on my wife sternly: "Okay, quickly, push again!" I looked at my wife's face and thought that she would not be able to do it, but unbelievably, she pushed with even greater force. As she was pushing with her last bit of might, her body suddenly collapsed, and the fetus appeared from between its mother's legs. The nurses said happily, "Good, good," as they deftly went about taking care of things. I too felt an incredible sense of relief, as if suddenly letting out a deep breath I had been holding for too long. My wife, whom I expected would fall straight asleep from exhaustion, opened her eyes wide and smiled at me calmly. I could only hold her hands tightly, not knowing what to say.

As the nurse was placing it in a pan, she suddenly said, "Oh, it was a boy."

"Please bring it here for me to see," my wife said, raising her head.

The nurse carried the pan over, and in a pool of blood was a nearly completely formed body of a baby. A cold chill swept through me, and I could not look at it closely. My wife too lay her head back on the pillow. After the nurses had cleaned up everything properly, they said a few words to my wife and then went out. I gratefully thanked them. "I'm sorry we caused you so much trouble."

Left alone, my wife and I embraced in silence, our relief disturbed only by the impression left by the awful sight of the baby. My own emotions were in turmoil. Suddenly my wife stared at my face for a moment and said, smiling, "The baby really looked like you."

"I'm too upset. Please, let's not talk about it." I rested my head on my wife's chest, feeling so overwhelmed that I nearly broke into tears.

My wife immediately fell silent. I quickly realized that I should not let her get too excited since she was so exhausted.

"Aren't you tired? Why don't you go to sleep for a while now?"

"I don't understand why, but for some reason I don't feel the least bit sleepy."

Her mind was awake but her body was worn out, and before long my wife quietly drifted off to sleep with a tired but contented smile on her face. Like a mother watching over her child, I happily prayed in silence that she would sleep more, but at the same time I waited for her to wake. Although I sat there alone, I did not feel the least bit lonely.

At dinnertime my wife said to me suddenly, "Now I understand why childbirth is so painful. When a person is in extreme pain and the pain vanishes instantly, nothing can be more joyous. And if a new life suddenly appears beside you as well, there is no comparable happiness—how fascinating the mysteries of life are." My wife seemed to be saying these last words to herself, and she went on smiling even after she finished speaking.

For a time I didn't know how to respond as I thought to myself, "Is my wife feeling somehow empty now?" Her reflections were not simply those of a fickle soul, however, but more likely arose from the mysterious essence of feminine nature.

Although my wife was very weak after the delivery, she did not feel unhealthy. She would often say to me quite cheerfully, "My health is even better now than before. All those little annoying illnesses are gone, and my appetite is back." But unlike her health, her spirit did not seem to recover, and instead of feeling happy she became consumed by a new series of anxieties. Every time I went to see her she would hug me warmly as if she were extremely happy, but then a moment later, as if greatly hurt, she would begin to cry for no apparent reason. "What's wrong?" I would implore, but then she would have even more trouble holding back her tears.

"What is making you cry?"

"Nothing, don't ask me that!" she would say, looking so embarrassed that if I persisted, her crying only became fiercer.

It was a few days since the birth, and already she had begun asking when she could be discharged from the hospital. Upon hearing answers like "at least another week," she responded all the more despondently, "How can it possibly be that much longer? I don't even want to stay here one more day!" Sometimes I would try to talk with her about what she would do after getting out of the hospital—a topic that used to make her so happy—but she no longer seemed interested. She would just reply "okay" or "whatever" with cool indifference to anything I tried to discuss with her. There didn't seem to be anything she wanted to talk about. She was easily upset and wept without provocation; sometimes it even looked as though she had been crying for hours before my arrival. One day as I was about to leave after a visit, she suddenly produced a letter, which I don't know when she could have written, and handed it to me, saying, "Read this when you get home." I tore open the letter and read it on my way there:

> Xige,
>
> I myself am at a loss to understand this pain, so it must make you feel even more exasperated. I know this and yet there is

nothing I can to do to stop it; perhaps this letter will help you understand.

The hospital is such a frightful place, everything here makes me feel miserable. All kinds of sad, unknown emotions have overwhelmed me at once, and try as I may, I cannot rid myself of them. I think that I might feel better if I could leave this place. I can hardly bear it for even one more day!

Happiness always remains in the realm of the imagination, while in reality all is void. I know that just getting out of the hospital will not make everything all right as I often say it will, but I can't help hoping for this. People are endlessly searching and hoping even though all they find in the end is emptiness.

If you knew how I was suffering right now, then you would not continue to urge me to stay here. But you certainly can't know, since even I myself am at a loss to understand it.

I could sense that my wife was suffering, but how she had gotten this way I could not comprehend. At this point I felt that keeping her in the hospital wasn't likely to benefit her health any longer. So after a few more days—a week after the birth—I got the doctor's permission for her release from the hospital the following day. When my wife heard this news she immediately perked up, becoming so happy that she wanted to jump out of bed and get dressed right away. No matter how I urged her, she refused to listen, saying that she wanted to go downstairs and walk around a bit to see how it felt. I could only stand behind her as she unsteadily made her way, step by step, over to the mirror, where she paused for a moment and said with surprise as she gazed at her reflection, "What a state I'm in!" Indeed, my wife did look even thinner now that she was out of bed. She pulled at her clothes and looked in the mirror again; they were really much too big for her now. She wrapped them around her, gazing at herself in the mirror again and again, extremely pleased to see that her body had returned to its former slender shape. Only after I had urged her several times did she finally return to her bed, but she was unwilling to lie down. As I left, she instructed me to bring her clothes and makeup the next day, saying, "I am so happy to be getting out tomorrow that I want to make myself up a bit." Having something to look forward to and daydream about again, my wife became very happy.

Since my wife had been in the hospital, our home had become practically uninhabitable. I only went back there to sleep at night and was never in the mood to tidy up, so a thick layer of dust covered everything. Now that my wife was coming home the next day I had to do some cleaning. I spent the whole evening sweeping out the desolate rooms. Only now did I see that those nameless white flower buds that my wife had bought the morning before she went into the hospital had already bloomed and withered unnoticed in the vase. I was about to throw them out when suddenly a strange feeling came over me and I left them as they were.

When I arrived at the hospital the next day, my wife was already waiting for me, her hair combed neatly and her face powdered. Seeing my wife made up like this after having been in bed for so many days, I thought she looked especially beautiful.

"Oh, you've already made yourself up. Where did you get the makeup?"

"Since it was taking you so long to get here, I didn't want to waste any time when you finally did, so I borrowed some from the nurses."

As she spoke she changed into the clothing that I had brought along for her. She looked as happy as a little girl preparing to go out and play.

Taking my arm and walking unhurriedly out the door, she could not conceal the smile that appeared on her face. She grew even happier the moment we got home, like she was returning to her mother's bosom for the first time after a long separation. She looked very tired, but she would not go to bed and rest. Instead, she insisted on sitting on the sofa as if she were fully recovered and kissing me warmly. Her excited state lasted until the next day, when she gradually calmed down and quietly returned to bed. But my wife's mood was unstable; if she was not extremely excited, then she was abnormally melancholy, frequently falling back into her deep, brooding state.

Finally my wife noticed the vase of forgotten flowers that I had nearly thrown out the day before.

"Why are those flowers still here?"

"Because they are a commemorative marker, you bought them the day you went into the hospital."

"It certainly must have crossed your mind that these flowers would only become a memorial if I had died."

"Why would you say something like that?"

"Don't get mad, I was just joking!"

She smiled as she said this and seemed very cheerful, but she soon grew weary again. I then went to do some writing at my desk while she lay quietly on the bed. A serene atmosphere pervaded the room. Before long my wife suddenly said, as if she were trying to comfort herself, "If I had brought home a baby from the hospital, I don't think it would be this quiet."

"But that would have been fun too," I said, trying to draw out her real meaning.

"Nothing is ever easy. On the one hand it would have been fun, but on the other it would have been a lot of trouble," she said, sounding like she was no longer so resolutely opposed to having children.

"Next time let's have a child. This has made me too sad," I said.

"I don't know what it is, but whenever I recall his face, I think that it was very handsome. Really, he looked just like you." Smiling, my wife pretended as if she were speaking very casually.

She was not interested in any other topic of conversation, only becoming strangely excited when we talked about this one subject. She would seem to be smiling slightly while still subconsciously suppressing her own true feelings. She often said to me as if in jest, "Are you thinking about that baby again? Why don't you go get him? I'm sure he is still at the hospital." Or, "You want a baby, don't you? You're still so young and yet you want a child already?"

Life continued on without a new beginning. My wife's dream of "being a new person after I get better" had, needless to say, long since disappeared. Now she was once again tightly wrapped up in her sadness.

Knowing how my wife liked flowers, one day I brought home those white flowers that she liked the best. "Last time you bought them you weren't able to enjoy them, so I got some for you again."

After putting the flowers in a vase, my wife stared at them for some time. Then, in her old playful tone, she said, "From now on we'll only buy this kind of flower. They'll be a memorial to our baby."

15

Lin Huiyin

Lin Huiyin (1904–1955)

Lin Huiyin (or Lin Whei-yin, as she spelled her name in English) came from a prominent gentry family originally from Fujian province. Her grandfather was a high-level bureaucrat in the late Qing dynasty and her father, Lin Changmin, a graduate of Japan's Waseda University, was a leading member of the constitutional faction in the Republican government who served in many capacities, including chief of the judiciary. Early exponents of modern education for women, Lin's grandfather and father enrolled her in school at the age of four. As a teenager, Lin accompanied her father on a diplomatic mission to England in 1920, where she attended St. Mary's College and became interested in architecture. During her stay, she met distinguished members of British literary circles such as H. G. Wells, E. M. Forster, and Katherine Mansfield, as well as Xu Zhimo, then a student at Cambridge, who was to become one of China's most acclaimed modern romantic poets. Xu fell madly in love with the seventeen-year-old Lin, but her father disapproved of the match and took his daughter back to China in 1921, where she soon became engaged to Liang Sicheng, the son of China's most famous early political reformer, Liang Qichao.

In the fall of 1924, Lin Huiyin and Liang Sicheng traveled to the United States to pursue their mutual interest in architecture. Liang enrolled in the architecture program at the University of Pennsylvania, but Lin had to matriculate in the fine arts program as the architecture school did not yet accept women. After graduating in 1927, she studied set design at the Yale School of Drama. Liang and Lin were married in Canada in 1928 before returning to China, where Liang took up a post as the head of the architecture department at Beijing University.

Throughout the 1930s, Lin raised a family, taught architecture, designed buildings, and went on architectural surveys throughout China, yet still managed to find time to leave a mark on modern Chinese literature with her experimental poetry, essays, and short stories. Her 1934 short story "Ninety-nine Degrees," considered an outstanding example of neoimpressionist-style modern Chinese fiction, employs a brisk stream-of-consciousness narrative. But it is Lin Huiyin's poetry that solidified her reputation as a modernist writer. Although women wrote and published large quantities of poetry in the 1920s and 1930s, Lin is one of the few whose works were collected and preserved. The three poems presented here, published during the 1930s in *Dagongbao* and a poetry anthology produced by *Crescent Monthly*, demonstrate Lin's fresh and direct free-verse style, in which she transforms a moment of perception into a crisp colloquial poem.

After living in Chongqing for a period during the war, Lin Huiyin and her husband returned to Beijing and began work on their groundbreaking history of Chinese architecture. After the Communist victory in 1949, Lin became a professor of architecture at Qinghua University. In addition to helping to design the flag and national seal of the People's Republic of China, Lin and Liang worked tirelessly together to preserve the architectural beauty of old Beijing. The new government rejected their plan to turn portions of Beijing's spectacular city wall into a public park, however, choosing instead to tear it down to make way for new construction. Lin also helped to design several of the monuments now standing on Tiananmen Square. Lin Huiyin published little after the 1930s, but poured her creativity into architectural design work and teaching until her death in 1955.

THREE POEMS BY LIN HUIYIN

Still

You spread out like a pool of water below the clouds,
Clear as a cool mountain stream.
You let me circle the wooded shoreline searching for your
    wellspring.
But still I am suspicious
Of your every reflection!
You unfold like the petals of an enormous flower,
Each one more brilliant and fragrant than the last.
The warm enticing fragrance comes in with the evening chill.
Spring teases with its flowers,
Stealing away one's heart.
You study leaf after leaf of a book blown open by the wind,
Uncovering your every thought, every corner of your heart.
You stare off, I go on talking,
But still I don't answer, a vast expanse of silence
Forever guarding my soul.

1931

On the Gate Tower

What did you say?
About ducks, the sun,
the moat below the gate tower?
Me?
I was just thinking,
It wasn't that I didn't hear you.
I was thinking about . . .
the past . . .
That's right,
it was autumn then too!
You have been there as well,
no? That little forest?
Don't you remember?
The mountain cave, the leaves as red as flames?
The reflection,
floating upside down upon the lake?
The quiet?
And the sky!
(It's just as blue today, look!)
The white clouds,
billowing like smoke.
Who's talking too much again?
You prefer this gate tower,
the ancient tombs, the solemn dirges,
wildflowers blooming on vines.
Fine, I won't speak more
of the past. I'll think only of
us here on the gate tower,
today. . . .
White doves,
(did you know that they were white doves?)
flying before us.

1935

Sitting Quietly

Winter comes for its reasons,
Cold like a flower.
The flower has its fragrance, the winter its memory.
The shadow of a withered branch, grey and thin,
Traces a stroke across the late afternoon window;
The winter sunlight fades, gradually setting....
Just like that,
As if waiting for a guest to talk with,
I sit quietly sipping my tea.

1937

16

Bing Xin

Bing Xin (1900–)

Bing Xin (born Xie Wanying) was the daughter of a Qing Imperial Navy officer and spent much of her childhood by the sea, first in Fujian and then in Shandong province. Tutored at home in Chinese literature and poetry, she was a voracious reader and began composing her own stories and poems as a young girl. In 1914, her family moved to Beijing and Bing Xin enrolled in the Bridgman Academy for Girls, a school run by Congregational missionaries from the United States. After graduating in 1918, Bing Xin entered Peking Union College for Women, also an institution established by American missionaries, which later became part of Yanjing University. Although originally planned to study medicine, Bing Xin became so absorbed in the student politics and intellectual debates surrounding the May Fourth Movement of 1919 that she decided to switch her major to literature.

A cousin helped Bing Xin publish her first article in Beijing's popular daily *The Morning Post* in 1919 and the positive response she received to her work encouraged her to produce a steady stream of essays and short stories in vernacular Chinese. Her first short story, "Two Families," appeared in the literary supplement of the same paper in late 1919 under her new pen name Bing Xin, or "pure heart." While pleased to see her new name in the newspaper, she was less thrilled to find next to it the word "Miss"—a gendered appellation that she and other women writers felt marked their work as inferior to that of male writers. Thereafter her readers knew her as Miss Bing Xin, easily the most famous woman writer of the early May Fourth period.

Bing Xin also achieved renown at a very young age for her poetry, particularly her short poems on natural and sentimental themes. Her collections, *Myriad Stars* and *Pure Water*, inspired by the work of the Indian poet Tagore who had recently visited China, were published in 1923 and sparked a fad for short, free verse poetry.

Upon completing college in 1923, Bing Xin received a scholarship to pursue graduate studies in literature at Wellesley College in the United States, where she received a master's degree in 1926. Although she was plagued by illness during her time at Wellesley, it was there that she began to write "Letters to Young Readers," a series of short essays for children published regularly in *The Morning Post*. Included in elementary school readers since the 1930s, these descriptive, lyrical pieces established Bing Xin as one of China's most beloved children's writers.

After her return to Beijing in 1926, Bing Xin taught literature at several universities in Beijing and married sociologist Wu Wenzao in 1929. Her literary output dropped off noticeably as she raised three children and accompanied her husband on numerous moves during the Sino-Japanese War of the 1930s and 1940s. "Our Mistress's Parlor" is a bitingly sarcastic portrait of a cosmopolitan "new woman" and her "salon" in Shanghai of the 1930s. First published in *Dagongbao* in 1933, "Our Mistress's Parlor" reveals a side of Bing Xin that challenges her later image as a poet and children's writer, and illustrates how she continued to develop her skills as a literary stylist long after the May Fourth period.

Abroad during the Communist revolution of 1949, Bing Xin and her husband surprised many friends with their decision to return to the newly founded People's Republic of China in 1951. During the next decade, she served on numerous government-sponsored cultural committees, traveled abroad on official delegations, and was a delegate to the National People's Congress. She also republished many of her earlier writings and wrote several more volumes of children's literature. For many children growing up in China during the bleak years of the late 1950s and 1960s, reprints of Bing Xin's letters about her travels and observations were coveted reading materials. This, in addition to her indefatigable work on behalf of Chinese women, has made her one of China's most well-known and admired writers.

OUR MISTRESS'S PARLOR
(1933)

The setting: a perfect sunny spring afternoon in Beiping.[1] The place: our mistress's parlor. We shall call it our mistress's parlor because, of course, our master has a parlor of his own, although guests seldom gather there.

Our mistress likes to think of herself as the hostess of one of the "salons" of the day; her guests do too. Whenever local artists, poets, or people from other walks of life have a free afternoon to drink a strong cup of tea or coffee and smoke a few fine cigarettes, sit on a warm comfortable sofa and see a few friends, or have a tête-à-tête with an attractive, articulate person, then without delay they grab their hats and walking sticks and stroll or catch a ride to our mistress's parlor. One can find whatever one's heart desires here.

Directly facing the parlor is a semicircular alcove, the top half of which is a large window draped with light yellow gauze curtains. A deep purple lilac tree is in full bloom outside the window, and a golden canary

---

1. Present-day Beijing.

is singing happily inside a copper wire cage hanging just inside. With the sun pouring past the purple blossoms and through the light yellow gauze and the shrill song of the bird in the air, everything appears bathed in a beautiful softness and hue. A small desk and a swivel chair sit before the window. The desk is topped with a thick sheet of glass covering a bird-and-flower painting done by our very own mistress. There is a large inkwell and a white porcelain brush holder with several writing brushes in it on the desk alongside a roll of white calligraphy paper.

Frames hang here and there on the walls, most of which contain portraits or photographs of our mistress. There's no doubt that our mistress was something of a social butterfly in her day and quite a tender beauty at the age of fifteen or sixteen! Several of the photos are mementos from her youth. One of them directly faces the sofa so that whenever a guest sits down he is confronted by a nearly life-size photograph that takes up almost half the wall. She sits on a flight of stairs, bright-eyed and smiling shyly; a long branch of peach blossoms hangs above her on the stairway; and everything from her cloudlike hair and sleepy eyes to the line of her scarf and even the pleats in her clothing exudes a certain virginal charm. According to our mistress, this picture was enlarged from a tiny two-inch photograph that was taken when she was a middle-school student. On a nearby bookcase stands a small stone bust of our mistress, her torso leaning forward and her head tilted, which was made by a French sculptor. Another photo in an oval frame sets off her oval face, and her waves of hair and knit brows recall the famous line of verse "long brows fill the mirror with melancholy." Beside the bookshelf hangs a portrait of our mistress and her young daughter, their jadelike arms wrapped around each other's necks as in a famous European painting; their faces and eyes are nearly identical. There are also a number of theater and bridal portraits of our mistress alone—she rarely has her picture taken together with her husband, at least as far as we know. Naturally, our master can not be placed alongside our mistress because in the eyes of her guests he's common and vulgar. Who wouldn't sigh in admiration for our mistress or moan in disgust at the sight of our master?

A fireplace occupies the north wall; it is flanked by tiny windows below which are bookshelves lined with neat rows of hardbound collections of foreign literary classics. There is one yellow-bound set with gold lettering that from afar is often mistaken for the complete works of Shakespeare, but is actually a collection of Thomas Hardy. Our mistress laughs contemptuously and says, "Shakespeare? Who has the patience to read that old stuff!" The person asking will then blush with embarrassment. Next to it on the shelf are the poems of e. e. cummings and novels by Aldous Huxley, but the inquirer, having certainly never heard these names before, dares not look any further.

Tall French windows adorned with long flowing curtains of pale yellow silk form the south wall of the room. Through the curtains one can vaguely make out a weeping willow tree that is beginning to fill the courtyard with new green leaves. Several decorative stones are piled below the tree, and the cracks between them are alive with tiny flower buds on the verge of blooming. Facing the window is a huge green-upholstered sofa and next to it stands a large lamp with a fringed yellow silk shade. On a mahogany stand nearby is a great brass platter bearing a carefully arranged tea set, and next to it sits a small tiered tower of serving platters filled with an assortment of savory treats.

Covering the floor is an exquisitely detailed carpet in the Imperial Garden style. Placed in the center of the carpet is a very low, round table holding a large bowl filled with peonies. Arranged around the table are three or four small stools and a number of soft pillows for the artists and poets to lounge or sit on.

Our mistress flutters lightly through the door, still hurriedly fastening the buttons under her collar. She is wearing a plain, light green, crepe-lined gown with jade buttons and bordered with three thin stripes of dark green satin, nude stockings, and deerskin high-heeled shoes. Her hair, parted in the middle and half covering her ears, is held back loosely on her neck with a bone pin. Her sleeves are very short and reveal her smooth arms. A jade bracelet hangs on her right wrist and a diamond ring and a band of green jade adorn the ring finger of her left hand. She has a tranquil look on her face and, as if she had not fully awakened from her midday nap, her eyes are moist and her cheeks faintly flushed. Time has painted two faint black circles under her eyes and her face is no longer as full as in the photographs, nor is her waist as supple as at "exuberant eighteen"!

Looking about her, our mistress calls out "Daisy" and a young maid of seventeen or eighteen with dark brows, large eyes, and a very pale face and rosy cheeks comes into the room. The guests all adore our Daisy. Often when they are all seated around the room comfortably and listening to a poet recite a lengthy verse, Daisy will slip into the room wearing her black high heels, black silk stockings, a black silk dress with a stiff white collar and sleeves, and a snow-white apron tied about her. Her thick black hair is always cut in a neat bob that just brushes over her brow and eyes. She will carry an incense burner or a plate of medicine and gently place it on the table, or else she'll lean against the back of the chair to whisper a few words in our mistress's ear. Our mistress will then nod her head and smile slightly. The quaint scene always momentarily distracts those listening to the poetry recitation.

Daisy is the servant girl who came with our mistress when she was married. Although our mistress raves on and on about women's rights and absolutely deplores the buying and selling of women, when it came to getting Juhua as a dowry present, she didn't utter a word of protest. Juhua is Daisy's real name, but our mistress thought it was too common and thus began calling her Daisy. After her name was changed, Daisy even began to pick up a few words of English. Whenever a new European or American artist arrives in Beiping and calls on our mistress to invite her out somewhere, Daisy answers in very polite and clear English: "*Mrs. is in bed, can I take any message?*"[2]

Our mistress says: "Look at yourself, you still haven't changed your clothing! And change Binbin's dress as well. When the guests arrive bring her out for a cup of tea." Daisy nods and leaves the room.

Binbin is none other than the little girl in the painting clasping her mother's neck. She was born in Italy. Our mistress and her husband, a well-to-do banker, went on a honeymoon that lasted nearly two years. In order to make his young wife happy, our master dallied about everywhere with her. Although he himself was not the least bit interested in the things his wife enjoyed, he never dared to suggest that they should return home. At every gathering and banquet along the way, our mistress would throw herself into spirited discussions with others while her husband merely sat impassively to the side and listened, sometimes even nodding off. Whenever he did so, our mistress would shoot him a tender but angry glance, and he would wake suddenly from his doze and look about sleepily. Occasionally others would laugh at him in spite of themselves. It was then that our mistress began to regret her choice; if it hadn't been for all the comforts and conveniences he supplied, he might no longer be our master! But although her husband will never resemble a real lover, our mistress enjoys the luxuries he provides. To her most loyal admirers, our mistress will woefully list all of her husband's shortcomings, but in large crowds, she merely cringes indifferently over them.

---

2. Original in English.

Before Binbin was born, our mistress dreaded the thought that her daughter might resemble her father. But thank goodness, from the day of her birth she looked like a miniature replica of her mother! Our mistress was pleased beyond words, but due to the inconvenience of taking care of her abroad, she whisked her back to China.

Binbin has long lashes, huge eyes, a high nose, and a tiny mouth, so it's no wonder that when anyone sees her they praise our mistress for bringing home a tiny piece of Italian scenery. Although she does possess a bit of her father's dullness, at five Binbin is already very skilled at acting sweet and agreeable. Unfortunately, being an only child herself, our mistress has taken center stage her entire life, and so even though she loves Binbin dearly, the little girl will never occupy more than a small corner of her life.

There's a scene in a famous Peking Opera in which the character Three Pocks dresses up as Duke Gong, taking on a majestic air the moment he puts on his red face makeup.[3] The servant boy who leads his horse and walks ahead of him always wears a plain green gown to set off his master's ornate attire. Whenever the Duke lifts his pointy boot, the servant boy turns ten somersaults in a row. Our Binbin is a bit like that servant boy....

Far off the doorbell rings several times, followed by the tread of footsteps in the outer courtyard and Daisy's voice announcing, "Mr. Tao has arrived." She opens the door, bows slightly, and shows the guest in.

Our Mistress has already glanced at herself in the mirror in the corner of the room and turned back to recline across the sofa, leaning on a bent elbow, daintily crossing her legs, and lifting her head with a smile—a pose that is once again reminiscent of a European painting.

Mr. Tao is a scientist. And like most scientists, he's not very skilled at making conversation and is invariably rather awkward and untalkative, particularly in the presence of women. He's an old acquaintance of our mistress. The curtsy she gave him once at a New Year's ceremony when she was still sweet sixteen and Mr. Tao was just twelve or thirteen left an indelible impression in his mind. To be sure, our mistress does not shy away from men, but Mr. Tao has never managed to take advantage of his numerous opportunities with her. Whenever he sees her he just blushes and mumbles a few words, and when our mistress is laughing and chat-

---

3. In Peking opera, the character Duke Gong is often identified by his red face paint.

ting in a group, he steals away to some corner to quietly admire her appearance, her voice, her smile—everything about her. At first our mistress simply laughed at him, but later she began to despise him and never had a nice word for him. Recently, however, as Mr. Tao has remained just as faithful to her as in the past despite the slipping away of her youth, our mistress always devotes a few moments of kindness to Mr. Tao before the rest of the group arrives.

She smiles at him and says, "Please sit down. How is your experiment going? Are you still promoting science as a means of saving the nation?" As usual, Mr. Tao can only stammer out a muddled answer before placing his hat on his knees and sitting back very stiffly in an armchair in a corner of the room. His heart pounds wildly in this singular moment of dread and ecstasy.

On seeing that, as usual, Mr. Tao is unable to say anything, our mistress sighs in ridicule and disgust as she stands up listlessly. Binbin has just come running in, her thick mane of black hair flying about her shoulders. She is wearing a green dress topped with a delicate white sweater, white stockings with light green trim, and black patent leather shoes. The green of Binbin's dress matches perfectly the colors in our mistress' dress and bracelet. Daisy knows how to dress Binbin to coordinate with whatever our mistress is wearing.

Seeing Binbin come in, Mr. Tao feels much more at ease and quickly stands up and goes over to shake her hand. Our mistress sits down and, brushing back her hair, says, "Binbin, why don't you play with Uncle Tao. Uncle Tao researches chemistry all day long; ask him whether liver or spinach have any vitamin A, B, C, or D? I'm always trying to get you to eat these things, but you never listen...."

From outside Daisy calls in "Miss Yuan is here." Our mistress smiles happily and stands up.

Miss Yuan is a painter and a poet, as well as our mistress's only female friend and the only female guest at this "salon." Of course Miss Yuan is not the only female painter or poet around, but she is the only one for whom our mistress ever has a word of praise! Although our mistress is herself a woman, she doesn't especially like women. She feels that Chinese women are particularly old-fashioned, particularly trivial, and particularly pretentious. Although there are many female painters and poets who, like Miss Yuan, are not old-fashioned, trivial, or pretentious, they never enter our mistress's sight and their names never cross her lips. This does not mean, however, that she is not aware of their existence.

Our mistress claims that only a woman can really understand other women. Therefore, she often describes in great detail the numerous weak points she sees in other women, although she has never once criticized Miss Yuan. Our mistress is the first to sing her praises to her guests, to defend her, or to call her a natural, unaffected, and genuine beauty!

People have come up with various theories as to why our mistress likes Miss Yuan. First of all, some think, it is because according to our mistress herself, any woman who does not have female friends is not psychologically normal. And there's also the fact that when she attends parties, a woman who laughs and talks only with men soon finds other women whispering about her. Although our mistress may have been proud of this when she was younger, in recent years it has made her rather uncomfortable. The second theory is that the two women complement each other. Standing side by side, our mistress and Miss Yuan serve as foils to each other: Miss Yuan's chubbiness makes our mistress look all the more slender, and our mistress' jadelike skin appears fairer next to Miss Yuan's dark complexion. The "salon" guests would naturally appreciate the aesthetics of this. The third theory is that their friendship is based on genuine mutual feeling: Miss Yuan fell in love with our mistress at first sight and when she speaks of our mistress her whole body trembles; our mistress is her ideal of beauty. In return, our mistress says that Miss Yuan is a beauty as natural as a fresh forest breeze. The more they talk, the more congenial they find themselves, and their friendship has endured....

Miss Yuan, her chest held high, storms in through the door like a whirlwind, plops herself down on the sofa with a great sigh, tosses her grey georgette scarf aside, and pulling out a yellowing handkerchief wipes the sweat from her brow. She is wearing a long grey serge-lined gown that hangs below her knees, orange silk stockings that sag around her two thick legs like bean-curd skins, and a pair of flat, round-tipped yellow leather shoes. Her hair is cut very short and combed back. Perched on her flat nose is a pair of glasses (for her nearsightedness) with lenses as thick as the base of a bottle. But of everything about her appearance, the thing that most marks her as an artist is the dreamy, faraway look in her eyes.

Smiling contentedly, our mistress sits down at Miss Yuan's side and says, "Now calm down and tell me, which critic are you angry with today?" Miss Yuan takes a deep breath and blurts out, "What critic? It was a bunch of fools! Just now, in a sudden burst of inspiration after lunch, I ran to Tiantan Park to do some painting before even washing up. But just as I finished arranging my things and picked up my brush, the place was overrun by a huge group of soldiers. At first they simply watched from a distance, but as they moved in closer I could make out their vulgar remarks and gestures, and the stench of garlic and sweat was enough to make a person sick. The more I painted the less I could stand it and finally I hastily packed up my things, grabbed my paintbox, and left, but their idiotic laughter followed me all the way to the gate! Isn't that infuriating? All of my inspiration was simply driven away!"

Our mistress laughs. "They're just proletarian admirers, you should have welcomed their criticisms! Now have a rest. Did you bring along that painting of Jade Spring Mountain Pagoda? Let's put it out for everyone to enjoy."

Mr. Tao and Binbin look over at them blankly.

Our mistress calls to Mr. Tao, "Come over here and chat, you need a friend who is exactly the opposite of yourself: an artist, a woman, and a candid talker . . ." As Mr. Tao awkwardly begins walking over to them, a large group of people enters the courtyard. Our mistress and Miss Yuan both turn their heads, and Mr. Tao, holding Binbin's hand, hastily slides past them and goes outside.

The whole party crowds into the room. At the head of the group is a poet who calls to mind the old couplet: "White cloak fluttering in the wind, he cuts a slender and delicate figure." His hair is shiny and slicked down flat at the sides; he has a pale complexion, a high nose, and very thin lips. His manner is unaffected and full of emotion—that of a born "ladies' man."

The poet bows slightly, takes our mistress's hand, and daintily presses it to his lips, saying, "Madame, no matter when I meet you, it's always like seeing a brilliant cloud . . ." Our mistress smiles a bit, draws her hand back, and extends it to the professor of literature behind him.

This professor is about forty years old, with two short strokes of a moustache and a youthful look to him. He quickly exclaims, "It's been such a long time, Madame, how do you do?"

The philosopher, with his hands behind his back, leans over and carefully examines the books on the shelf, drawing out a translation of Schopenhauer's *On Women*. Just as he is leafing through it, the poet comes over quietly and suddenly claps him on the shoulder. With a laugh, the philosopher shuts the book and turns around. He is a tall, thin man with deep eyes, a high forehead, and sloping shoulders. His complexion is so jaundiced that people who don't know him often mistake him for a heavy smoker.

Our mistress, who is now greeting a politician, turns her head to look and says unhappily to him: "Really! Why did you disturb him? This is a free space, everyone can do whatever they choose to." Apologetically, the philosopher bows and laughs, saying: "I'm just a hopeless bookworm! Wherever I go the first thing I must do is look over other people's books!" Nearby, the poet snickers.

Our mistress turns back to the politician. "What more can you people do to stir up public opinion? Recently the city government has become more and more atrocious. As if people getting sick from public drinking water weren't enough, the other day Miss Yuan and I went to Jade Spring Mountain Pagoda to do some painting, but the car ride was so unbearably rough we nearly died before getting there! And yet a patrolman still had the gall to stop us and ask whether we had paid our automobile tax or not! I asked him 'Where does all of this tax go? Just look at how perilous this road is!' Indeed, you 'politicians' won't let us speak our minds!" Having blurted all this out in one breath, our mistress turns to light a cigarette and sits down, addressing Miss Yuan. "Wouldn't you agree?"

The politician, who is a tall, well-built young man with a large round face, bows and says with a smile, "Well then, allow me to offer an apology to our mistress on behalf of the municipal government! That highway is truly terrible. But wait until I become mayor, then have another look. Don't forget that our party is still not in power!"

Everyone laughs and even our mistress lets out a little chuckle before turning her head and calling out, "Daisy, the tea!"

Daisy gracefully enters the room on tiptoes, carrying in the tea service followed by a tray of cakes. Outside the door two servants in long white gowns and black satin padded vests silently help her to pour the hot water.

Our mistress walks over to the literature professor with a teacup in her hand. He and Miss Yuan are discussing the recent painting exhibition at Beihai Park. When the professor sees our mistress, he quickly stands up, clutching his napkin. Our mistress laughs, saying, "Don't get up, I only wanted to ask you one question. How is that poetry professor I recommended to you?" She sits down on the edge of Miss Yuan's chair.

The literature professor continues to stand and replies with a smile, "When have you ever recommended someone inappropriate? He might be young, but he certainly has a way with words, and he's quite amusing; the students in his classes will never nod off. But apparently his health is not very good, for I often see notices of his absence posted on the bulletin board." Miss Yuan suddenly lets out a laugh: "Are you talking about Little Shi? Sick? I see him nearly every afternoon in the park strolling about with a real looker of a girl."

Our mistress flinches slightly and then says with a serious expression, "Actually, I am not very well acquainted with him. Last year he appeared at my door with a letter of introduction and a book of his poetry. Seeing that he didn't write badly, I let him read here several times. Soon he confided to me that he was broke, so I thought that perhaps your literature department could easily take on such a person. I never dreamed that..." Our mistress shakes her head, stops speaking, and stands up and walks slowly over to the window where she lingers, fingering her teacup. In a preoccupied tone, she calls out the window, "Binbin, come inside."

Binbin, her hands tugging at her blouse, bounds gaily into the room and goes to her mother, lifts her head, and says, "Mama, Uncle Tao said to tell you that he had something else to do, so he left. He's going to take me to the park tomorrow morning." Our mistress breaks her silence and says with a smile, "Well, I guess he has time for such things.... Binbin, look at all these guests, you haven't even said hello!" Binbin turns to everyone, smiles, and says, "Hello!"

The poet sitting at the desk turns in his chair, a cigarette dangling in his right hand, and beckons to our mistress with his free hand. "Mei, this painting under the glass is a new one, isn't it? Your brushwork is getting more and more exquisite." Taking Binbin's hand, our mistress walks over to the desk and replies, "Tutor Jin comes every other day and he pushes me terribly, but I just go through the motions. By the time spring arrives, my wrist aches so that I grow quite impatient."

The philosopher is still reading *On Women*, but hearing our mistress's words, he closes the book and laughs. "Madam, I think you drive yourself too hard. Your health has never been good, but you always want to try and master everything. As I see it, a woman should read a bit, take care of her children..." Our mistress begins laughing and says, "You read a little of Schopenhauer's *On Women* and start insulting women! What should a woman do? Read and take care of children—is that one's life's work? You had better put aside Schopenhauer and take a look at Bernard Shaw. Old Bernard uses the female heroine of his play *Saint Joan* to chide men like you who say women should do housework. As Saint Joan says, 'There are plenty of other women to do it; but there is nobody to do my work.'" She turns her head and asks the literature professor, "Isn't that right? Didn't Shaw write that?" The literature professor hastens to reply "Yes." Apparently finding this exchange very amusing, the philosopher bursts out laughing.

Binbin wrestles her hand from her mother's, and pulls Miss Yuan out to the courtyard again. The politician and the literature professor go out as well and quietly chat under the tree.

The small courtyard gate opens and someone with a head of shiny blond curls trimmed short around her ears and neck comes in. A small woolen cap is perched askew upon her curls like a piece of melon rind. She is dressed from head to toe in light brown. A dark brown summer coat is draped over her right arm, and in her left hand she carries a pair of tan leather gloves and a dark brown leather purse. There is a spring air about her and a smile on her face, her deep blue eyes sparkle and a dimple peeks from her right cheek.

As if a bright light had suddenly appeared before them, everyone cries out at once: "Lucy, how are you? When did you arrive?" Lucy heads for the literature professor and grasps his hand, laughing. "I arrived on the 11:05 express today, dropped my bags off at the hotel, and went straight out to look for you. I finally managed to find your home, but your wife told me that you went out after lunch. She didn't say where you went, but I guessed that you must be here. Look how you've worn me out!" Still laughing, she goes over to shake the politician's hand, then turns to Binbin and says in not quite fluent, but yet witty Chinese, "Hello, Binbin, how you've grown! Where's your mother?" She glances at Miss Yuan as she speaks, but not recognizing her, turns back to the politician.

At this point, the philosopher comes out as well. The poet has just pulled a roll of paper from his pocket and spread it out on the table, and is bending over it with our mistress and reading it in a hushed tone. He smiles as he hears the gate, then lifts his head and stands up. A wide grin appears on his face immediately. He is just about to call out when he turns back to our mistress, who is also looking out the window, her brow knit slightly. He restrains his smile and pats our mistress on the shoulder lightly. "Mei, please continue reading while I go out to greet her." Saying this, he steps outside and at once the courtyard is filled with voices.

Miss Yuan comes back inside; seeing our mistress, her head in her hands as she sits reading poetry, she leans over to her ear and asks softly, "Who is that foreign woman?" Our mistress rolls up the poetry manuscript as she stands and stretches her waist, saying nonchalantly, "Lucy Key, an American artist of sorts, a merry widow. The year before last she came to China with her husband and, not wanting to leave, she stayed on by herself. She only returned to America when her husband died last winter, and though it hasn't been very long, she's already back again. I can't stand her. She flits about like a sparrow, chattering on endlessly! I often say, her husband was a great sugar merchant who wanted to monopolize the entire sugar trade, while she goes about monopolizing everyone's conversation!" Miss Yuan grows quiet, sits down, picks up her cup, and sips her tea.

Before Miss Yuan, Lucy was our mistress's only woman friend. Two years ago, the day after Lucy arrived in Beiping, the literature professor took her to visit our mistress and they hit it off splendidly. After that, our mistress told everyone how clever and polite Lucy was and Lucy told everyone that it would be a great loss if any foreigner came to Beiping without meeting our mistress. Thereafter the two got together whenever possible, but after a few months their relationship gradually cooled. Some said that it all started when the guests of our mistress's parlor performed *The Merchant of Venice*. Our mistress played the part of the young miss and Lucy played her serving girl. After the first performance, our mistress saw the review in the paper. It said that everything about Lucy, from her voice to her expression to her gestures, was unrivaled. It was a real case of the guest usurping the host's role. At the time our mistress didn't say anything about it, but from then on Lucy's name was often missing from the guest list.

Daisy comes in lightly, stands by our mistress's chair, and whispers to her, "Madame, Mrs. Key has been here for some time, she's in the courtyard talking." Our mistress raises her brow, saying, "I know, and she hasn't even been invited in yet! Please call Mother and see if the front box for this evening's performance has been reserved or not. I might go over in a bit." Daisy nods and slips out quietly.

The poet pulls Lucy inside and the whole group follows. Lucy is chuckling as she pushes off the poet's arm. "Please let go, I have not yet seen the hostess." Smiling, our mistress stands up and extends her hand, saying, "I know you didn't come to see me, so I didn't go out to greet you." But Lucy is already turning her head toward Miss Yuan and asking her with a smile, "Who is this? Someone please introduce us." The poet hurriedly complies: "Allow me, this is Miss Yuan, an artist and a poet . . ." Lucy immediately puts out her hand to Miss Yuan. "Pleased to meet you. You're reciting your poems today, aren't you? I feel lucky to be present on such a grand occasion." Miss Yuan clasps her hands together and stammers, "No, no, I'm only here to listen to poetry today." She points to the poet. "He's the one who has a long poem he's going to read." Lucy has already selected a small chair for herself and, leaning back against the desk with her feet stretched out on the padded footstool, speaks merrily. "Come, come, read it for me and let me cleanse myself of the dust of travel." She lights a cigarette and closes her eyes affectedly.

Everyone scatters to find seats and the room suddenly falls silent. Our mistress is still half reclined on the sofa. The poet pulls over a footstool and sits down by her side, his hair brushing the tips of our mistress's shoes. He takes his manuscript from our mistress, unrolls it, lifts his head and smiles at her, and then turns to the others. "I am going to display my incompetence. This poem is entitled, 'For . . .'" and he reads:

> For —
> In a dream last night I ascended a tall peak,
> Below not a single light, above not a single star,
> I felt only you by my side,
> Cold was your hand, beating was your . . .

Suddenly, Lucy's eyes fly open and she laughs so hard that her chair nearly falls over. Gesticulating wildly with her hands, she says, "There's no need to read on, let me recite the rest: beating was your heart. 'Star,' 'heart'—what a talent for rhymes you have . . ." Her shrill laughter breaks the silence of the room and everyone chuckles. The politician howls with laughter as he stands up and, pointing at Lucy, shouts, "Order! Order! What a mischievous creature you are!"

Only Miss Yuan does not laugh but looks over at our mistress, who is just about to speak when the poet, who has already rolled up his manuscript with a laugh, crawls over from beside the sofa to Lucy's chair and taps her on the head with the roll of paper, saying, "What a person you are, upstaging me like that!" Lucy, who is still laughing with a cigarette in her hand, straightens her hat and says, "Be careful, you, this is a new hat!"

Standing at the door, Daisy announces, "Miss, the call went through. Your mother would like to speak with you." Our mistress furrows her brow and replies, "Tell Binbin to get it, I don't have time." She stands up and walks over to the philosopher. He does not get up but sits still and simply smiles, and nodding his head in the direction of Lucy, whispers, "A woman, thoroughly a woman, isn't she?" Our mistress instantly breaks into a warm smile and sits down beside the philosopher.

Binbin comes into the room and skips gleefully over to her mother. "Mama, Grandma says the box has been reserved and there are some people over there who have invited you to dinner. That famous actor Yang Xiaolou is playing the monkey king[4] again tonight. Mama, can I go too?" Saying this, she clambers up on her mother's lap and throws her

---

4. The mischievous hero of the popular tale *Journey to the West*.

arms about her neck, entreating her. Our mistress laughs along with her and pushes her away. "Let go. There's no need for that! If you're good, then Mama will take you with her." Binbin lets go and is about to go out again when she suddenly stops and says with a smile, "I forgot, Grandma also asked me to tell you that a telegram arrived from Changchun saying that Grandpa is not very . . ." Our mistress' face suddenly flushes red and she jumps to her feet, pushing Binbin out of the room. "You must go get ready. We'll go after you finish dinner at home, there's nothing good for you to eat at a dinner party." Binbin skips happily out of the room. Lucy nods and winks at the politician.

Daisy announces from outside the door, "Miss, Dr. Zhou has arrived" and then shows the guest in, turning on the couchside lamp on her way out. Dusk and the faint glow of the lamp make the man coming in look about thirty years old. He wears a Western-style suit, is rather short and plump, and has a broad smile on his face that gives him a trustworthy air. He rubs his hands together as he comes in the door, nodding and bowing to everyone. "Miss Yuan, hello, Mrs. Key, hello everyone. I'm fortunate to have arrived when so many people are here." Our mistress steps forward with a bright smile on her face and shakes the doctor's hand. "But how unfortunate for me that you've found so many people here again, for you'll be scolding me for doing too much entertaining and not resting," she says. Dr. Zhou bends to take a cigarette from Daisy and light it. "Now! Now!" he says, smiling. "It seems I'm always trying to prevent people from seeing each other, but I'm really doing it against my will. As for you, madame, you had a cold just the other day, so you really ought to . . ." The poet walks over laughing and slaps the doctor on his shoulder. "Still singing that same old tune? Sit down and let me ask you, business must be good these past few days with so many people catching colds from the change in the weather. My friends all over town seem to be suffering from colds." Dr. Zhou agrees: "Actually, fluctuations in air temperature do increase the likelihood of contracting influenza." Everyone bursts out laughing and our mistress teases him, "Always the doctor through and through! Saying things like 'fluctuations in air temperature' and even adding on 'increase the likelihood'! What a way to speak!" The doctor bows deeply to our mistress. "The atmosphere of your salon must be catching. It makes even a coarse person like myself add a bit of poetry to his speech!" Lucy, who has just been talking with Miss Yuan, turns around and says with a laugh, "If our mistress is sick, then cure her, but if you get 'infected,' who'll cure you?!" Everyone laughs, and this time even Miss Yuan joins in.

Voices are heard outside the small courtyard and a servant comes to the doorway. Daisy quickly whispers a few words to him. The servant leaves and Daisy turns around, giving Dr. Zhou a smile before saying to our mistress: "The bamboo flute teacher has arrived and asks if Madame will be practicing her *Kunqu* opera this evening or not. I replied that you would not be singing this evening because you still had guests and that even Dr. Zhou was here . . ." The literature professor smiles at Dr. Zhou. "Just look at how you've ruined the party, now our ears will miss a real treat." Dr. Zhou hastily rises to his feet and says, smiling, "I should be going. It looks like I've done it again. All I told her was that if she insisted on studying with him, she should learn to play the instrument; it's less harmful than singing. You all know about her health . . ." The literature professor stifles a laugh and turns to our mistress. "It's up to you, but of course we ought to urge you to put these things aside. Yet we are only human and therefore selfish, and think only of our viewing and listening pleasure . . ." Our mistress smiles slightly and leans toward the literature professor. She is about to say something when Lucy suddenly interrupts from the side, finishing the professor's sentence. "Don't forget her wonderful cooking!" Everyone laughs at first, but feeling that there was something not quite right about it, they quickly stop. The smile leaves our mistress's face and she swallows what she was about to say.

Dr. Zhou pulls out a watch from his waistcoat pocket and takes a look at it, saying, "I really must be going. I actually came out on a house call, but when I saw all the cars at your gate I thought I would step in and have a look . . ." Our mistress smiles. "Is that right? I think you really came to check up on me." Dr. Zhou has already taken his hat. Lucy stands up as well and says, "It's getting late, we should be going too." She looks at the literature professor and the political scientist as she says this, and everyone begins getting up from their seats. Lucy smiles at Miss Yuan. "Didn't you just promise me that you would join us for dinner?" Miss Yuan hesitates, glancing over at our mistress. Our mistress is leaning against the back of a chair, her hand covering her mouth as she lets out a yawn and says casually, "I am going out anyway. Go ahead." The poet quickly comes up from behind and helps Miss Yuan with her scarf.

Lucy smiles at our mistress and says, "I am sorry, I'm taking all of your guests with me, but I know you are going out to the opera tonight and you want to rest before you leave." Our mistress shoots a quick glance at Lucy but doesn't say a word as she turns her head.

The philosopher takes several books from the shelf, piles them together with *On Women*, and tucks them under his arm. He smiles at our mistress.

"Please allow me to borrow these books. I will bring them back some other time." Our mistress laughs and gives the philosopher a look. "First you must bring back all the books you borrowed last time, and then we'll see! I don't believe that I have anything so special on my bookshelf; you probably have these same books yourself." The philosopher jovially replies, "Your editions are much better. I'm a poor man who cannot afford such fine books, so I must take pleasure in your good fortune!"

After gathering up their coats and hats, everyone goes into the hallway. Daisy opens the front door and two servants stand with their hands at their sides on either side of the stairway. Everyone says their thank yous and farewells to our mistress. She seems a bit worn out and only smiles and nods her head as she shows them to the doorway of the little courtyard. The poet calls from behind her, "You all go on ahead first and I'll follow in a moment." Lucy turns her head back. "Don't forget that there is going to be a Spanish dance performance tonight at the Six Nations Restaurant!" Our mistress says to the poet, "You had better go along with them. What are you waiting for?" The poet smiles and doesn't reply as he watches the guests depart.

When the poet comes back in, the parlor has already been straightened up and a pine log is burning in the fireplace. No lights are on in the room. Our mistress is sitting lazily before the dim glow of the fire hugging her knees; she doesn't even lift her head as she hears the poet come in. The poet doesn't say a word but quietly pulls over a footstool and sits down by her side, whispering, "The glow of the fire, you, everything, it's another poem!" She doesn't respond.

There is no sound in the room but the crackling of the fire. Daisy quietly comes to the door, takes a look in, and then silently leaves again.

The poet slowly gets up, goes to the window, and calls to the bird in the cage. "It's too quiet, even this lively canary isn't making a sound." Only then does our mistress glance over at the poet, cock her head, and say, "The canary is no longer happy!"

The poet laughs and walks over to our mistress and sits by her chair, rubbing her shoulder. "Mei, let me go to the opera with you tonight!" Our mistress pushes off the poet's hand and stands up. "That's not possible, there are people waiting for me to have dinner, and besides, . . . besides, there are people waiting for you at the Six Nations Restaurant . . . and there's even Spanish dancing, that graceful Spanish dancing!" The poet gets up as well and moves closer to our mistress. "Mei, you know she invited everyone, how could I say that I wouldn't go? I only vaguely agreed at the time. They won't even notice if I don't show up. Take me with you to the opera. I've been to your mother's before and it's only your cousins waiting for you; it wouldn't be the first time I've met them. Mei, you know I only want to be by your side forever. . . ."

Our mistress doesn't say a thing, but just pulls out a yellow chrysanthemum from the vase on the table with her delicate fingers, lightly brings it to her face, and smells it; there is an air of amusement in her gestures.

The poet lightly touches our mistress's arm. "Do you still need to change your clothes? Go ahead, I'll wait for you here." As he says this, he quietly leads her out of the parlor, and taking a black cloak from the wall in the corridor, he wraps it about her shoulders. Our mistress pulls it closer around her and without turning her head goes to the back of the house.

The poet returns to the parlor, stretches his back, and lights a cigarette. He then turns on a lamp and sits down on the sofa, picking up a book of poetry. As he is leafing through it, he hears a car pull up and then footsteps entering the courtyard. He quickly puts down the book and stands up.

Our master appears at the door of our mistress's parlor. Completely unlike what everyone has imagined, he is not a round-faced, plump banker, but a trim and friendly looking gentleman. His coat is open and he clutches a hat in his hand. Upon seeing the poet, he nods and says, "You're here. And Mei? Is she feeling better? When I left this morning she hadn't gotten out of bed yet." As he says this, he puts down his hat and takes off his coat, hangs them on the wall, comes into the room, and sits down.

The poet takes his seat again. "Mei is fine. She even had guests for tea this afternoon and soon she's going out to the opera."

Just then our mistress comes in, pulling Binbin by the hand. She has changed into a half-sleeve, long black velvet gown dotted with flowers that reveal a bit of jadelike skin between her shoulders. She wears flesh-colored stockings and black satin pumps. Her face is heavily powdered and she has even added a couple of dots of rouge that make her look all aglow. Binbin is wearing a bright red silk outfit with ivory-colored sleeves, white silk stockings, and black patent-leather shoes. When she comes in the door and sees our master, she bolts over to him, hugs him, and cries. "Papa, Mama is taking me to the opera!" Our master doesn't say a word but only puts Binbin on his lap and strokes her hair.

Our mistress still stands there, her hand resting on the back of a chair, and nonchalantly asks our master, "Mother has invited me to hear Yang Xiaolou with her and to eat dinner there as well; will you go with us?" Looking at the poet, our master says hesitantly, "I don't think I will go, you two go ahead. I'm a bit tired today, we had a meeting at the bank all afternoon. Just now Manager Sun invited me to the Six Nations Restaurant to see a Spanish dance performance. I declined thinking that you weren't feeling well; if I went alone it wouldn't be as . . ."

Hearing this, our mistress suddenly looks over at the poet, turns around, and sits down by her husband, leaning against his arm and saying softly, "I didn't really want to go either, but since Mother already invited other people, I felt I had to. But as you have given up seeing Spanish dancing to stay with me, I am willing to give up Yang Xiaolou to stay with you. I'm tired too, let's just stay here and sit by the fire!"

Our master is shocked, she has never treated him with so much warmth! Overwhelmed by the unexpected affection, he is about to say something when our mistress breaks in, "There's no need to try to persuade me, I am definitely not going! I am too tired and I just want to stay home with you!" Saying this, she leans over and puts her head on his shoulder. It looks as if her eyes are glistening with tears.

The poet silently stands up and flicks his cigarette butt into the fire. Our master remains silent as well and pats our mistress lightly on the shoulder. Binbin, who has been sitting on her father's lap, her eyes wide open, anxiously listening to them speak, now slides off his lap and stands before her mother. "Mama, if you're not going, what about me?" Our master lifts his head and looks over at the poet. "Mei is too tired to go. For her sake would you mind taking Binbin?" Before the poet answers, our mistress suddenly stands up and says, "Don't bother him! He has a dinner to go to!" Our master says, "In that case, Binbin won't go either. A child shouldn't stay up so late anyway."

Daisy is standing at the door with our mistress's and Binbin's coats draped over her arm. Hearing the conversation in the parlor, she smiles slightly and comes into the room, leaning over and whispering several words in Binbin's ear. Binbin holds back her tears, hangs her head, and says to her mother and father "Good night," and taking Daisy's hand, leaves the room.

Our mistress then yells to Daisy through the window, "Call Mother back again and tell her that I am tired and not feeling well and won't be able to go. And then tell the kitchen to serve our dinner in here. There's a fire and it's warm."

The poet brushes off the ashes from his clothing and says to our mistress, "I'll be going then. I will see you tomorrow. I have some letters I must write. I am so lazy and my room gets so cold at night that I never feel like writing. My friends are always scolding me for it." Our master stands up and says, "Don't you have a dinner party to go to? Why would you go back to your cold room and write letters? At least stay here and have dinner with us before you leave." The poet, staring at the fire, turns his head and smiles. "I don't need dinner, I'm not hungry. I'm already used to my cold room, like the ancient poet said, 'I've grown accustomed to traveling alone in the cold'!" he says, smiling and reciting the poem softly as he walks toward the door. Our mistress suddenly stands up. She is about to call the poet back, but our master has already shown him out through the door of the small courtyard.

Outside the gate, dusk is falling and the poet calls to a shivering rickshaw puller waiting by the gate and hops in. He stretches out his legs, heaves a great sigh, and calls out, "To the Six Nations Restaurant!"

17

Luo Shu

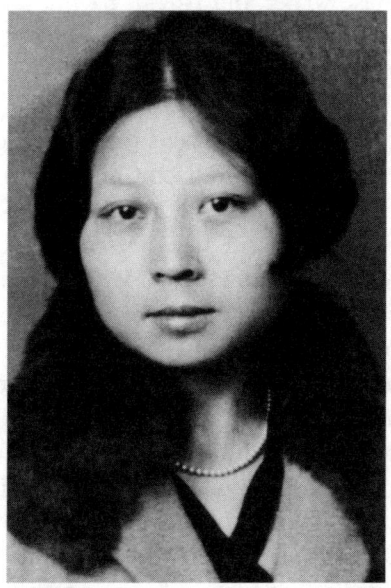

Luo Shu (1903–1938)

Luo Shu (born Luo Shimi) burst onto the Shanghai literary scene with the 1936 publication of the short story "Another Man's Wife." The story's plot—in which an impoverished peasant woman is sold by her husband to another man—had been dealt with before, but critics hailed Luo Shu's vibrant and clear style as equal to the best of the "rural realism" being produced by leftist writers at the time. Luo Shu often drew on her own experiences growing up in the Sichuan countryside and her observations of the peasants who worked at her father's salt mine to produce vivid rural characters like those found in "Another Man's Wife" and "Aunty Liu," the story translated here. Unfortunately, she produced only a handful of works before her untimely death in childbirth at the age of thirty-five. Her fellow Sichuanese writer and friend, Ba Jin, saved Luo Shu's work from complete oblivion by editing and publishing her collected stories and essays in three posthumous volumes.

Luo Shu's writing reflects the influence of her exceptional training in both Chinese and French literature. As a child, she studied alongside her brothers at home and then dressed up as a boy in order to attend a local school. When she grew dissatisfied with the conservative curriculum there, Luo Shu entered a county-level school for girls before enrolling in the Chengdu Number One Girls' Normal School in 1923. She also kept up a lively correspondence with her brother, Luo Shi'an, and his close friend, Ma Zongrong, who had joined the work-study program for Chinese students in France in 1919. Ma Zongrong returned to China in 1928 and immediately asked Luo Shu to marry him. After her high school graduation the following year, the couple set out for France, where they soon married. Ma taught at the Institut Franco-Chinois in Lyon (the same school that woman writer Su Xuelin had attended several years earlier) and Luo Shu studied French there before enrolling in the education program at Lyon University.

Hoping to contribute to China's modernization efforts, Luo Shu and her husband returned to Shanghai with their infant daughter in 1933. Luo subsequently found a teaching position in the agricultural education department of the famed experimental school, the Lida Institute. Friends in the leftist literary circles of Shanghai finally convinced Luo to write down the stories she often told about growing up in

Sichuan. In addition to her short stories, Luo Shu also published several translations of French literature, including works by Romain Rolland. In the fall of 1936, both Luo Shu and her husband left Shanghai for posts at Guangxi University, but soon moved farther inland to their native Sichuan following the Japanese invasion in 1937. Luo Shu devoted herself to writing anti-Japanese "Resistance" literature until her tragic death after giving birth to a son in 1938.

The loss of this promising literary voice is especially felt when reading Luo Shu's haunting descriptions of peasant women suffering in rural China. "Aunty Liu," published first in *Midstream* in 1936, is typical not only of her personal style, but of the realist mode of "native soil" literature favored by leftist writers during the 1930s. What makes Luo Shu's writing particularly successful, however, is her ability to bring the individual peasant woman's personality to life rather than reduce her to a flat or melodramatic stereotype. The protagonist of this story, Aunty Liu, is not an idealized and faultless peasant heroine but a very real woman who, as the narrator comments, "understands life."

AUNTY LIU

(1936)

It wasn't the cowherd singing a folk song as he rounded his cows up the hill or someone in the house speaking loudly to my slightly deaf mother that startled me from my sleep today, but an astonished exclamation, "All grown up!" in a voice that was rough and unfamiliar to me.

A bit annoyed, I decided to find out exactly who was in the room. The moment I opened my eyes, I saw a middle-aged woman in tattered clothes standing before my bed with a flat, pock-marked face under her thinning hair. Her lips were cracked open in a smile that revealed a frightening toothless mouth.

I felt I had seen this unsettling and extremely ugly face before, but I could not remember where. I scrutinized her in silence, trying hard to shuffle through my memory to see if I could recall this person.

She seemed to read my thoughts, for before I could remember she said: "I'm Aunty Liu! I knew you would forget about old Aunty Liu! We haven't seen each other for eight whole years and now you're already all grown up. If nobody told me it was you, I wouldn't dare call out to you if I bumped into you on the street."

"What? Aunty Liu? You're the Aunty Liu who used to take care of me?" I jumped right out of bed, my face flushed red with excitement.

Children often remember insignificant things very easily, but they can be forgetful when it comes to things that they should remember. How could I have forgotten a maid whom I had once loved so dearly? What a heartless little thing!

Yet when I moved toward her, she stepped back, bumping so heavily against the desk that I used when home that she tipped over a vase full of colorful June chrysanthemums standing on it. She hurried to clean up the spill nervously, but I rushed to stop her.

"You . . ." I wanted to say something to put her at ease, but felt quite flustered myself. I really didn't know what to say after that "you." Should I say, "You were once . . ." or should it be, "You are now . . ."? Perhaps what I meant to say was, "You have changed completely."

It was true, Aunty Liu had changed. In the past, she only acted this reserved in front of my father and mother. Why was she behaving this way toward me now? Was I not the child whom she had once loved so dearly and cared for like a tender mother? Yet I knew myself that if she were to sit on a stool and invite me to sit on her lap—so that she could sing me songs that my mother would never sing or tell me horror stories that were supposed to be harmful to a child's soul or have me throw my arms around her neck and plant a kiss on her ruddy, pock-marked face— I would certainly refuse without a moment's hesitation.

She wasn't to blame, nor was I. Time and loathsome conventions of human relations had surreptitiously managed to completely separate us.

We both felt awkward staring at each other in silence, and I searched my mind for the right thing to say to her. Luckily my mother came in just then. She began laughing as she walked through the door and I could tell she was in a good mood that day. "What a hostess you are! Why don't you ask Aunty Liu to sit down?"

I hadn't noticed that I was sitting on the edge of my bed while Aunty Liu remained standing in the middle of the room.

"Look at her. She's even taller than me now," my mother said. Then, pointing to the two braids wound into delicate buns on the back of my head, she remarked, "It's popular for high school girls to do their hair this way now. It's not bad looking, is it?"

It seemed that Aunty Liu hadn't forgotten that when my mother spoke to her, she was expected only to nod her head in response. Yet perhaps she hadn't even heard what my mother was saying, for she was busy scrutinizing me from head to toe. Was she trying to find some trace of the little girl she left eight years ago?

When my mother saw the way Aunty Liu was staring at me, she smiled and said, "I'm afraid you two don't even know each other anymore. One's grown older and the other bigger. Time really does fly faster than the shuttle of a loom." Then she turned to me. "You ought to be happy. Did you ever dream that Aunty Liu could find us here in this remote mountain village? She certainly went to a lot of trouble asking around for us! Do you still remember the day I fired her? She had bought so many fresh water chestnuts and sweet lotus roots for you! I only let her go because she was too fond of drinking."

My mother's bluntness shocked me. I couldn't believe that she would speak so candidly about what she had done to hurt this woman right in front of her.

The mention of the water chestnuts and lotus roots touched me somehow and I wanted only to hide from the fixed attention of my mother and Aunty Liu. A breeze blew in a branch of the palm tree standing outside my window. I tore off a leaf and absentmindedly began shredding it into fine silken threads, scattering them on the floor.

Suddenly I thought of something to say. "How did you find us out here?"

"Just tell me what I can't find along this stretch of road from Huguang to Sichuan!"

Her tongue was as sharp as ever! I was about to ask her some more questions when my mother sent for a jug of wine. She shook the jug before Aunty Liu, saying, "I know that this is what you really love. Go ahead, have some wine in the kitchen. This wine has been well aged in the cellar, so don't drink too much at once. Save some to take home and enjoy it slowly with your family."

When Aunty Liu had left the room, my mother told me that she was now married to a man who owned a small parcel of land in the hills and made his living as a sedan-chair bearer. She hadn't heard where exactly their home was, but she pitied this ill-fated woman.

I didn't know very much about Aunty Liu's life. Someone may have told me about it before, but I had forgotten and only recalled the details after my mother reminded me.

When she was only fifteen, Aunty Liu had been tricked into leaving her family and was sold into a wealthy household as a maid. One night when he was drunk, the master, a man well into his forties, raped her. Later, when it was discovered that she was pregnant, she was driven out straight through the great black doors of his house with the two stone lions standing guard in front. The child was born in a nearby outhouse and died three days later. People say that a good-natured nightsoil collector brushed off the maggots crawling over it, wrapped it up in a torn mat, and buried it for her. After that, she did mending and needlework for other people or stood at the city gates with her hands stretched out to beg from passersby. Sometimes she sold rice gruel in alleyways. I don't know how she finally ended up at our place as a maid. What a great opportunity this must have been for her! What a wonderful life!

If it hadn't been for her love of drinking, my mother would never have dismissed her. Drinking was Aunty Liu's one and only shortcoming. I knew that my mother was a kindhearted person, yet I can still recall the day Aunty Liu left us eight years ago. . . .

I believe it was a summer day like this one. Thunder was rumbling in the distance. I was sitting under the hibiscus tree in the courtyard watching a swarm of yellow ants battle a swarm of black ones. I could hear my mother speaking with a woman behind the bamboo screen and she sounded rather angry.

Just then Aunty Liu came in through the front gate, and it was plain to see that she had been out drinking again. She was holding two thick sections of fleshy lotus root and something wrapped in lotus leaves. It was obvious that the earthen jug hanging from her wrist was filled with wine.

She handed the lotus-leaf packet to me. "I've brought something good back for you. You eat the water chestnuts first while I go and wash the lotus roots and slice them for you."

My mother told me not to eat the water chestnuts.

When Aunty Liu came back to me with a ceramic bowl, the woman who had been speaking to my mother rushed toward Aunty Liu, jabbed at her forehead, and said fiercely, "They don't want you here anymore. Pack up your things and go find yourself another job. I've done all I could to help you, but you keep blowing it! Always thirsty for this horse piss. You asked for it! You brought this on yourself!"

Aunty Liu didn't say a word. She just kept urging me to eat the lotus roots. I could only take the bowl from her and pass it on to my mother, who was embroidering a white silk pillowcase. The reflection of the brightly colored flowers on her face combined with her angry expression made her look far less composed and elegant than usual. She took the bowl and pushed it on the table, shooting me a chilly look. I was already trembling with fear even though I had not done a thing.

I was more worried for Aunty Liu.

Aunty Liu did not come out to serve dinner that evening, and, strangely, my mother did not even bother calling for her. The moment I managed to slip from Mother's sight, I ran to the kitchen. The door was closed and I didn't dare knock. I just peeked carefully through a crack and called out softly to her several times, "Aunty Liu!"

All the servants were seated around the table, a cup of wine before each one. The jug that Aunty Liu had brought home was there as well. They were in the midst of drinking with great gusto and nobody noticed that a child was standing outside the door staring intently at one of them. Aunty Liu's face was very red. Her sleeves were pushed way up her arms; the top of her shirt was unbuttoned and her neck was bared. I had never seen her looking so strange before and I didn't understand why. Later I figured out that since she would no longer be dependent on our family for her meals, she didn't have anything more to worry about. She wanted to free herself from the rules that had been binding her for the past three years. On her final night here, she could finally let herself go!

"Ask someone to put in a good word for you. They might let you stay," someone suggested.

"When you're eating other people's food, you've gotta do as they say—that's just the way it is."

"Forget about it! There's no point in sticking around if they don't want you anymore. When you're working for somebody, you've always got to keep one foot in the door and the other one out. If things are okay, you can step in; if not, you back out. If you don't find work in the east, you move on to the west. As long as a person's got two legs and two hands, he can always find food. I've even been a beggar before, so what do I care?" Aunty Liu replied. Afraid that my mother was calling me, I hurried away.

I tugged at the edge of my mother's dress.

"What are you doing?" she asked.

"Mom... Aunty Liu!" She only understood me after I'd cried out twice.

"I want her to go tomorrow," she said. "I'm worried about leaving you with someone like that. We'll look for another good-tempered woman to look after you." She was talking to me, but seemed to be talking to herself at the same time. "She really is an honest person. It's just that she drinks too much. It's really a shame. I'll give her an extra month's salary and cancel her debts. I'll give her some new clothing as well."

When I woke up the next morning, Aunty Liu was already gone. I didn't see her again for eight years.

I had never expected her to come back. I was happily surprised, but also a little sad. If my mother hadn't dismissed her, she might not have ended up looking so tattered and worn out, but I couldn't place all the blame on my mother.

I hoped my mother would keep her with us.

After Aunty Liu finished her lunch, she came to see me again. "Have you had something to eat and drink?" I asked her.

"Thank you. I've really eaten my fill today. It's been two years since I've had white rice."

"Are you managing all right these days?"

"I'm getting by one way or another. Good days, bad days, you've gotta get through them all. Life goes on."

I was silent for a while, then I explained to her, "I meant, I was asking if you had enough to eat."

"Oh! Enough to eat, you say? He barely makes enough for himself! I've got to cultivate a little patch of rocky land and supplement it by selling a bundle of firewood each day. When there's no firewood, I even do manual labor. Lucky for me I can still carry seventy or eighty catties, no problem."

"Does your husband treat you well?"

"Treat me well? I've had three men since I left your family, and each one of them has beaten me. I ran away and married this man because I was no match for the last one . . ."

"This one doesn't beat you then?" I asked anxiously.

"Huh? What man doesn't beat his woman?" She smiled at me as if to ask, "Doesn't your father beat your mother?" She went on, "When I can't take it any longer or I can't fight back, I always know how to run away."

It had grown rather late, and Aunty Liu prepared to leave. "It's getting dark. I'm afraid it might start raining soon and I've still got five *li* to walk. But after I get home, I'm going to raise two fat chickens and when fall comes around, I'll invite you and the mistress to come over and eat them." Then she shook her head. "But my place is a real pigsty. You won't want to come!"

"Sit for a while longer. There are still things I want to ask you. Are you going to go on living like this? Aren't you planning to look for other kinds of work?"

"What can I do? A beggar like me, even you people wouldn't. . . . Besides, I'm used to living crudely and I'm too clumsy and rough. That's just the way I am. I can sleep wherever the sun sets and I'll never starve to death."

There was little more for me to say.

My mother couldn't persuade her to stay either, so she sent her off with a peck of white rice and reminded her to take the jug of wine home with her.

Not long after, I returned to school in the city. My mother never told me whether she ever went to Aunty Liu's home to eat the fat chickens she had raised especially for us.

When I got back from school the following year, I learned that Aunty Liu had left her husband again and no one knew where she had drifted to.

I believe she is still alive today and I wish her well, for she understands life.

Translated by Janet Ng

18

Xiao Hong

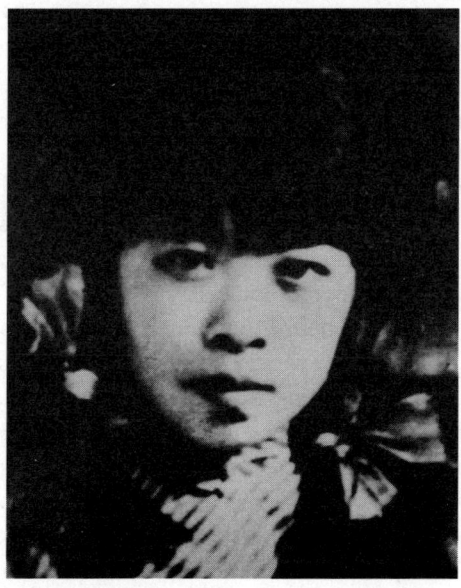

Xiao Hong (1911–1942)

Xiao Hong (born Zhang Naiyang) was the daughter of an affluent landlord from a town outside of Harbin in the far reaches of northeastern China. Although her mother died when she was only nine and her father severely neglected her, Xiao Hong's paternal grandfather loved and encouraged her. He taught her to recite classical poetry and persuaded her father to send her to school. In 1928, Xiao Hong left home to attend a middle school in Harbin, but her father suddenly called her home to fulfill a marriage contract he had arranged. Instead, she ran away and moved in with a young teacher from the school. Both were expelled, and after taking Xiao Hong with him to Beijing, the teacher abandoned her there.

Xiao Hong traveled back to Harbin in 1931, pregnant and penniless. Unwelcome now in her father's home, Xiao Hong wrote a desperate letter to a local newspaper about her predicament. A young writer, who would later take the pen name Xiao Jun, was so moved by her letter that he came to her rescue. The two quickly became lovers and moved in together. An account of their days scraping by on tutoring jobs and an occasional sold manuscript is provided in Xiao Hong's remarkable book of autobiographical essays, *Market Street*. The story translated here, "Abandoned Child," first serialized in the newspaper *Dagongbao* in 1933, has a similar urban setting. Taking place in the squalid parts of a northeastern city racked by disastrous floods, the story also undoubtedly draws upon Xiao Hong's own experience of giving up her baby for adoption in 1932.

The Japanese occupation made life in Harbin increasingly difficult for the young couple, and in 1934 they fled to Shandong province. Both completed novels there before moving on to Shanghai. Xiao Hong's *The Field of Life and Death* (1934), her first and most celebrated novel, is a brilliant exploration of the devastating oppressiveness of peasant life in Manchuria. Shanghai intellectual circles associated with the League of Left-Wing Writers championed this book, along with Xiao Jun's *Village in August* (1935), as authentic voices of nationalist resistance against the imperialist Japanese oppressors. Lu Xun, the "father of new literature," found special promise in Xiao Hong's writing and formed a close friendship with the young woman writer. In 1936, Xiao Hong traveled to Japan in order to break off her strained relationship with Xiao Jun, but she returned to Shanghai soon after learning of Lu Xun's death later that year.

The outbreak of full-scale war with Japan in 1937 sent Xiao Hong running again, this time to western China. "A Sleepless Night" is a short essay first published in the leftist journal *July* in 1937, just before she fled Shanghai. In it she evaluates her deteriorating relationship with Xiao Jun in terms of her ambivalence toward their native "homeland" in Manchuria.

After leaving Xiao Jun, Xiao Hong journeyed westward with another successful young writer from the northeast, Duanmu Hongliang. The two had an affair and were possibly married in the city of Xian, but by 1938 Xiao Hong again found herself pregnant, unwell, and alone. She made her way to Hong Kong not long after the child's birth. There she completed work on her masterpiece, *Tales of Hulan River* (1940), a novel based on her experiences growing up in the northeast, and began writing a comic novel entitled *Ma Bole*. She died suddenly of a respiratory infection in early 1942, despite efforts by American journalist and writer Agnes Smedley to get her proper treatment. One of the best and most widely translated writers of the 1930s, Xiao Hong was overshadowed for years by male leftist writers from her native region until efforts by scholars abroad, in particular Howard Goldblatt, revived interest in her work.

ABANDONED CHILD
(1933)

I

The water, like the horizon, flowed on endlessly as patches of sunlight sparkled on its surface. Adults, children, packages, all blurs of dark green. Silently, unhurriedly, small boats passed by on the current, one after another....

A woman, her belly protruding like a steamed bun, sat alone looking out the window. Her eyes were as dull and dark as lumps of coal, and her mouth hung open as she leaned on the windowsill and stared out vacantly.

There was a knock at the door. Who could it possibly be? A face, pale and sagging like a bag of flour, poked its way in. It began to speak. "What are you going to do? The water has already come up this high and in just a few more hours, don't you see what will happen? You must do something. Worthless creature, you've been staying on here for seven months already and owe 400 *yuan*. Your Mr. Wang won't be back. And when the man takes off, I've got no choice but to settle up with the woman. This simply can't go on any longer." The man straightened his hat and shook out his sleeves, his clothes hanging on him like an empty cloth sack. Only his eyebrows seemed alert.

The woman, her belly and expressionless face unchanged, moved to speak. "It will be taken care of tomorrow." She watched the innkeeper's feet below his gown as he waddled out the door like a duck.

Her belly wasn't so much like a steamed bun as a small basin pressed up against her; it showed no matter how loose a blouse she wore.

Her belly followed her even when she threw herself on the bed. She looked out at the shed roof, noticing how its reflection quivered slightly on the surface of the stream now flowing down the middle of the street. Loud noises continually poured in through the window. Someone's package has dropped in the water! A child has fallen into the gully! Over and over, these sounds continued endlessly as they echoed off the two facing walls.

"What will I do? I have no home, no friends. Where can I go? There's only that man I've just met and he's homeless too! The floodwaters outside have risen so high and that dog will soon be coming back for his money, I don't . . ." She could no longer check the flow of her thoughts; like the flood outside, she couldn't restrain herself. "When I first came here the snow was still falling and now it's the rainy season. When I got here my stomach was flat, now it has grown into this. . . ." She rubbed her hands over her belly and stared at the water ripples reflected on the ceiling. The bedclothes stank of sweat and oil.

II

At dusk, the owner and the guests of the inn left in a great commotion, carrying suitcases and dragging along children. Even those who had moved upstairs the day before to avoid the flood were now gone. The clamor departed with them. It was an empty building now; doors closed, long curtains, still and silent, showing through cracks in the windows. Only a family of peddlers, an inn servant, and a sick woman and her male companion stayed behind. Some windows of the building had been shut, others left open; dust carpeted the floor. The place was as desolate as a soldiers' barracks after a mobilization; everything was in a pitiful state of disorder.

The faint smell of water wafted in and the calmness of dusk hung in the air; someone's lost pig flailed about in the water, squealing desperately. The water rippled about the pig in rings, encircling it like a fly or a mosquito caught in a spider's web. The more it struggled, the more the web expanded. Then the pig rested on a plank of wood; it grew quiet as if it had been saved and a glimmer of hope showed in its eyes. But this glimmer mingled with the hungry look in the eyes of those watching, binding them together as if by an invisible rope.

The pig was carried off to a home across the way.

The dusk faded into night as if descending into a deep valley. The buildings on both sides of the road towered high, precipitous, and barren, like mountain cliffs; the water flowed between them like a mountain stream.

The countless everyday worries that once occupied the woman leaning on the windowsill had vanished, scared off by the endless mountains now looming before her. The pig that she had just seen carried away had now left her mind, and she sensed only a cool shiver running down her spine. When she dragged her feet across the dusty floor back to her room, her legs felt clumsy and numb like two wooden posts, or as though they belonged to someone else and had simply been attached to her body.

All night long she listened to the water as it flowed triumphantly through the streets.

III

The people who used to go down the road by rickshaw every day now boarded boats. The roads had all been transformed into small rivers and the sky had turned blue; the frail rickshaw pullers were now pulling boats. But is the sweat that pours from their brows any different from days gone by? It's still heavy with that salty, sour smell.

The Songhua River had breached its dikes for three days running and the streets were crowded with boats of all sizes. There were trunks being used as boats and wooden planks fashioned into makeshift rafts, and scores of rescue boats clamored about, yellow flags waving from their captains' hands.

The woman who had been living on the second floor was carried away in a boat, between the brick buildings that were now the banks of a narrow stream and on toward the vast ocean where yellow lights reflected off distant waves. She breathed in the open air, her first contact with the sunshine outside her window. The riverbanks were submerged under water, and the small homes that once bordered them were now resting on the riverbed. People squatted on the rooftops. Little boats flew back and forth like river hawks, sending waves rolling like slithering snakes. They crashed against the sides of the boat carrying the woman. As the boat tossed about on the waves, the color drained from the faces of the frightened passengers on board. The woman cried out and jumped up as if she wanted to get off the drifting boat and step on dry land. But where was there any dry land?

The boat was full of people, all of them strangers. But what wasn't strange? She spread her trembling, anxious hands over her protruding belly. The sky was strange, the sun was strange, and even the odor that drifted over the water's surface was strange. Only her own belly felt real and close, but what use was it to her?

The waves had passed, but her fingers still groped about, unable to find anything to hold on to—would she sleep at home tonight? Why hadn't Peili come to fetch her? Could he have taken a different route? What if they had overturned just now, wouldn't that have been the end? Then there would be no need to think of all this.

She hadn't been out on the street for six or seven months; she was bewildered by the sights and unaccustomed to the sounds and couldn't make out anything clearly. Her heart was in a state of turmoil. Yet despite her bewilderment at the myriad sights and sounds, she still carefully scrutinized every boat that passed to see if it contained Peili on his way to fetch her.

Her mouth hung open, her eyes stared off, and the remote sky and the sun shone in the distance.

IV

An old woman stood in the stairway of a building. Inside, a woman holding a baby ventured, "Are you Qin?"

Qin began talking with the woman of the house. As she sat in an armchair, her woolen winter shoes were conspicuously obvious to the lady. The woman said, "Didn't you see Peili on his way to meet you? He must have gone a different way." Her gaze bore into Qin and traveled up and down her entire body; every pore in Qin's body sweated nervously, anxiously, as she silently cursed herself for having left so early and missed Peili, making him take a trip for nothing.

Qin went to the window to take a breath of cool air, the hem of her worn old gown playing about her knees.

Later, when Peili and Qin walked along the lake shore circling the fractured reflection of the moon, it was already evening and only mosquitos were buzzing in the park. They leaned closely against each other and though the road before them appeared blocked by mosquitos, they pressed on through the swarms, through the forest, over two bridges, and sat down in a pavilion, their shadows mingling closely along the railing.

Way up in the tall trees, the tips of branches intertwined to block out the moon like a great gauze umbrella. The wind shook the umbrella and broken bits of moonlight spilled through like frenzied young girls frolicking on a spring day! Peili and Qin were both secretly excited.

V

Who knows what made the loneliness Qin felt at the inn disappear, and the agony Peili felt as he lay awake the previous night somehow vanish as well?

Peili had suffered the whole night for his new lover Qin, aching to go fetch her and bring her back to the Fei residence the second day of the flood. But he was as useless as a basket with a hole in it; he didn't have a penny to his name. Should he pawn his own worn-out quilt? Would anyone want it? He started to pull his best suit out from under the bed, brushing off the dust. Certainly he could pawn it for one *yuan*, he thought, and then use half the money to buy some things for her to eat and save the rest for the boat fare when he went to fetch her. He himself wouldn't need to take the boat. After all, hadn't he learned a few swim strokes at Sun Island? They would really come in handy now. His face brimming with excitement, he put the old suit, a gift from a friend, under his arm as if he were holding a precious pearl. Amid a forest of signs—store placards and restaurant ads—he spotted the gold sign of a pawnshop and broke out in a wide smile. But the pawnshop was closed; someone inside called out that the Zhengyang River had burst its dikes. He went home and collapsed on the bed, the frame as hard as a slab of stone. He hated himself; how could he have lost his belt when he went to see Qin yesterday? He had swum over there, but there had been no need for him to pull off his belt and leave it by the shore. Why had he been so excited? As Peili thought about this, he rubbed his hand over his newly purchased belt. Then suddenly he pulled it off and began whipping himself with it. Why had he wasted half a *yuan* on it? If only he had that money now, he could hold up his pants himself and fetch his lover. Feelings of regret plagued him all night as he lay on this slab of stone.

VI

He lived in a room at the back of a restaurant. He looked up at the swarms of flies on the ceiling and the waterbugs crawling between the cracks in the walls; he listened to the clang of spoons against metal woks, the clinking of wine cups in the dining room, the swishing of the dancing girls' costumes, the cries of beggars outside the door. These sounds, like arrows, like stars in the sky, shot through the cracked window and pierced Peili's heart. His eyes were bloodshot and unmoving. Calmly and silently, Peili took it all in. Was he a coward? Was he immune to pain? The stars twinkling in the sky understood him.

Like two soldiers retreating from the front line, bombs exploding behind them, Peili and Qin sat under the great umbrella listening to the wind rustle through the leaves.

Peili could scarcely keep his eyes open. In order to avoid Qin's notice he had tried to cover it up several times by saying that he had gotten up early and his eyes were tired. Qin understood Peili and she made an excuse for his pretense. "Well, then, let's go home and sleep."

A little gutter ran in front of the park gate and Fei's home stood diagonally across from it. They crossed the gutter and headed for the Fei residence.

VII

The two long shadows moving across the ground gradually faded. Like two wild dogs just taken in by someone, they sat out on the street, returning to the landlady's place only to eat and sleep.

Peili and his new love Qin had been staying at a friend's home for more than a week now. The time had flown by without notice. All day long, they sat on the overturned boat in the street. Even the park was submerged now and there was really nowhere else to go; all the nearby streets and alleyways were flooded as well; the water seemed to be chasing their love-filled hearts. They felt closer with each passing day, their hearts swollen like the Songhua River looking for an embankment to break through. It was no longer a matter of desire, but of necessity.

They searched on and on for that outlet, but the embankments about them grew higher and thicker with each passing day; they could feel their two hearts pulsating wildly as they clasped hands.

Peili had given up his room at the rear of the restaurant and moved into Fei's house too, although he and Qin slept separately as before. They rose early every morning, and if Peili didn't go into the inner room to nudge Qin to wake up, then Qin would get up early and stealthily pinch Peili's toes. He always rested his feet on the arms of the rattan chair, where they stuck out at an angle. Did he fix himself this way in preparation for Qin's touch? Or was the rattan chair too small to hold his legs? The pinching awoke Peili and he squirmed about like a big shrimp before finding his way out of the chair, as if it were a great shrimp cage that he had fallen into. He rubbed his eyes. Everything was a blur to him and his two outspread feet resting on the floor made him look like a frightened lost duck. The sky, as white as the underside of a fish, shone through the window and cast its sleepy eyes on the curtains.

Qin's belly grew larger and larger. The small basin had turned into a big one; a still thing into a moving one. She lay on the bed unable to sleep, mosquitos crawling playfully over her legs and the thing in her belly playing inside; she'd become a circus tent and everything played about her, inside and out.

She got out of bed and put on a pair of ragged slippers that looked like scrawny cats and shuffled into the outer room. As usual, Peili was curled up like a shrimp in a trap. Qin woke him up and showed him her legs, the little bumps on them now forming a neat row. If you didn't know they were mosquito bites, you would have mistaken them for lichen growing on a stone. Peili rubbed them with his hand, knit his brow and smiled at her again—how pained he felt! Having no idea of his feelings, Qin assumed that he was trying to make her laugh. She stretched out her hand, forgetting about the thing living in her belly, and threatened to pinch Peili's toes, trying her best to seem lighthearted.

Just then, as Mrs. Ying was pulling little Rong through the inner room into the kitchen, the little girl caught a glimpse of these two shrimps and noisily nudged her mother to look. Mrs. Ying, with a curious glare in her eyes, pointedly said: "When you two pinch each other's toes, is that an Oriental custom or a Western one?"

Four-year-old little Rong, mimicking her mother's intonations, sang out to them, half-mockingly, "Is that an Oriental or a Western custom?"

Both Qin and Peili narrowed their eyes like tigers.

For some reason, Peili's eyes had begun to gleam like diamonds, hard and cold. Over the last ten days Qin had watched them as they darted about constantly! Sometimes when their eyes met, a brief shadow of recognition fell over his eyes before disappearing again.

VIII

One evening as Qin sat with her, an uncomfortable smile appeared on Mrs. Ying's face and she shook her head. She tried to maintain a tactful tone as she said something to Qin, probably alluding to Fei having seen Qin and Peili on Central Avenue in broad daylight earlier that day.

As usual, Qin and Peili had taken a turn on the avenue. Peili still pressed Qin to go for a walk every day, although her legs didn't seem to want to cooperate and she felt irritable. The feeling she had while living at the inn two weeks earlier had returned; the mist that had once covered her heart threatened to enshroud it again. She toyed with the buttons on Peili's shirt, her eyes heavy with sleep, her head down. "I really don't know what she meant. Just because our clothes are ragged doesn't mean we're not good enough to walk out on the street!"

Peili wasn't sure who these words were directed at. He hesitated a moment before blurting out, "What?"

"Ying said," Qin tried to imitate the woman, "'You shouldn't go out on the street. You can do whatever you like at home, but there are too many people outside, it doesn't look good! It won't be good if people notice. Don't you realize? We have many friends on this street, and everyone knows you're living at our home. If you weren't staying here, then I wouldn't care how you looked.'" Qin continued to play with Peili's buttons.

Peili's eyes gleamed like diamonds and his heart burned as if it were the button she was playing with. He made a tight fist and hit himself on the head. When Qin rubbed the spot, Peili blushed and felt bad.

"What does it matter, rich or poor? Aren't poor people allowed to fall in love?"

The burning in their hearts faded and they sat on a wooden bench by the road. If she felt cold, there was only one thing to do—bury her head in the lapels of Peili's jacket.

After the park disappeared under the water, a single red electric light continued to burn in that desolate place. Finding the red light hanging low beneath the tree branches on an autumn night was like discovering a firefly in the middle of the ocean. They laughed and clapped their hands and returned every night to cheer the light on.

Suddenly she stopped clapping her hands and rubbed her belly. Peili helped her home. As they climbed the stairs, her tears flowed in the darkness.

IX

Fei's attitude toward Qin and Peili had changed and it was obvious that Mrs. Ying's words had really come from him.

He moved out, taking all the bedding with him and leaving the room to his mother-in-law. Qin slept on an earthen *kang*,[1] her head on a bundle of clothing. After sleeping like this for only two nights, her belly began to hurt terribly. She could do nothing but lie there and Peili stayed in as well. He squatted on the floor by the bed, his forehead leaning against the *kang* as he watched over her—two baby pigeons, fledglings who'd been turned out of their nests. Only they could understand each other, really help each other, because hunger and coldness weighed equally on both of them.

Qin's belly hurt even more terribly and she tossed about wildly on the *kang*, covering herself with dust like a clay figurine. Forgetting even to put on his hat, Peili raced downstairs and into the cold autumn rain falling outside. Two o'clock passed and Peili had still not returned; Qin continued to roll about on the *kang*. The rain outside fell harder. Three o'clock passed and Peili had still not come back. Qin could think only about ripping open her belly; she no longer even heard the sound of the rain.

X

Peili raced beneath the trees as the rain poured from the sky. Streams of rain pounded the stone-paved avenue as if trying to shatter the stones that staunchly resisted. As he ran down one street after another, through one sheet of rain after another, Peili's pockets were still empty and he was drenched like a waterfowl. As he burst through the door, his heart flew up the stairs and wrapped invisibly around Qin. She cried out like a wild animal; the sound shot through the window, past the driving

---

1. A heated brick bed common in northern China.

rain, smothering the sound of the rain, and firmly piercing Peili's heart like an arrow.

The arrow still in his heart, Peili bounded up the stairs. He thought Qin was finished, that she had called out her last. As she fainted from the pain in her belly, she unconsciously gripped Peili's hand, the dirt that she had clawed up from the earthen *kang* mixing with the rainwater dripping off him.

Peili's face was deathly pale as he recalled again how he had tried to borrow one *yuan* from Fei for the fare to take Qin to the hospital. But Fei had only said, "Be patient, things will be better in a few days, there's no hurry." He thought again: "Would a friend say that? But I see now that I am not Fei's economic equal, so we can't be friends."

In spite of Qin's cries, Peili was forced to go out again as the rain continued to fall in buckets.

XI

The pain in Qin's belly made her oblivious to the rest of the world and she barely looked human as she writhed about on the *kang*. Her face was white as a sheet of paper as she crawled across the floor in search of some water to drink. When she finally found a teacup, another unbearable spasm of pain gripped her, and the cup fell to the floor, shattering. Hearing the sound, Fei's jaundiced, wide-eyed mother-in-law came in, words pouring out of her mouth: "This has gone too far. We aren't running an inn here where just anybody can come along and stay."

Qin couldn't make out who was speaking; she pressed her belly against the *kang*, hoping to squeeze the little thing out of her. Her intestines felt like they had been knotted up or pulled out and cut apart. Sweat and tears poured from her.

XII

Sitting in the cart, Qin resembled a ghost as they streaked past the park and the circus grounds there, and down a dark alley. Peili held her tightly, but he only annoyed her now; every person walking on the road annoyed her. She tore at her hair and struggled in Peili's arms. She hated that she couldn't leap to the hospital in one bound, but the horse didn't seem to want to move. Instead it reeled about in the water. Peili began to panic and spoke in an unusual tone. "The water here is very deep, it will be dangerous if we fall into the gully." He jumped into the water and pulled on the horse's reins, leading it through the water.

Qin lay sprawled across the cart like a discarded sack or a bundle of trash.

The glow of the autumn moonlight only emphasized the tragedy of this image of oppressed humanity.

The iron gates were half closed and there was no light in the doorway; all was dark and the hospital looked closed. Peili went to knock at the door and Qin's heart surged with hope, but it was quickly followed by disappointment.

XIII

The horse cart carried her back, and again they passed the park and the circus. The ache in Qin's belly seemed to subside a bit, and she suddenly noticed a huge elephant at the circus, clumsily playing with its own trunk. Now that she could see it clearly, she had the energy to say to Peili, "Look at how cute that clumsy elephant is."

Peili hadn't eaten a thing all day and Qin's childishness amused and angered him all at once.

When the cart arrived back where it had started, Peili handed the entire half *yuan* he had managed to borrow over to the driver. Peili looked like a cabbage wilted after a terrible thunderstorm. The rain and wind had now let up, and he helped Qin back upstairs. He thought to himself, will it really be another month before the day comes? By that time I will certainly have found a way to borrow the fifteen-*yuan* hospital fee. Then Peili remembered to spread the tattered blanket over the *kang*. Qin lay stretched out on it, combing her disheveled hair with her fingers. Peili wanted to take off his wet shoes, so he kissed her and went to the outer room.

Again Peili heard moaning sounds and dashed back into the room, his eyes falling immediately on Qin's body. Her face was as ashen as a lead pot and he realized that it was not the pain but her heart that saddened her. He did his best to make himself believe what the doctor had just told them: another month at least.

XIV

He didn't question or plan—he now realized that the only way to get anything done was to be assertive. So the second time he took Qin to the hospital, he got her admitted even though he didn't have the fifteen-*yuan* fee.

Qin slept soundly in the third-class maternity ward for two days, dreaming about the horse reeling in the water. Later, she lay half awake, growing so anxious that sweat soaked her quilt and pillow. She felt that both her body and her spirit were equally exhausted. She showed little interest in anything, not in Peili or anything else in the world; it was all the same. When Peili came, he sat on a small stool and said a few words of little importance. The moment he left, Qin closed her eyes tightly again.

After three days, Qin could no longer sleep at night and her breasts had swollen up hard and full. She could only be heard complaining that her breasts hurt but asked nothing about the child.

There were five large beds in the maternity ward, with pregnant women sleeping on three of them; five cribs, all empty, stood nearby. A nurse pushed one of them over to the woman near the window, and another next to the other woman. When they heard the sound of the cribs being wheeled over, they lifted their heads from their covers, unable to restrain themselves. Strange smiles appeared on their faces as if they were already seeing their own little babies sleeping in the cribs. They didn't ask the nurse a single question, afraid that they might blush, but remained silent, saving their enthusiasm for the first moment they would meet the little creatures they had created.

When the nurse pushed a third crib in Qin's direction, her heart started to jump as if she were about to hear bad news. She waved her hand, "No, I don't want it . . . I don't want it . . . I don't!" Any motherly sentiment left in her voice snapped like an iron cable, and her entire body began to tremble.

XV

The autumn moonlight poured over the wall; the night was quiet and the people were silent, except for the baby crying in the next room.

The baby cried for five days after its birth as it lay on the cold planks of the crib. Mosquitos, newly hatched after the flood, swarmed through the window vent and crawled over the baby's face and body. It shivered and cried continuously. Was it cold? Hungry? Who would take care of this motherless newborn?

A quivering shadow moved across the moonlit wall as Qin made her way along the edge of the bed and pressed her face up against the wall. Little baby, don't cry, isn't Mama coming to hold you? So freezing cold, my poor baby!

At the sound of the child's coughing Qin's head shifted as she leaned against the wall. She jumped back onto the bed, tearing at her hair and beating her head with her fists. Selfish thing, thousands of little babies are crying, don't you hear them? Thousands of babies are starving to death, don't you see them? Even adults far more capable than little babies are starving to death, even I myself am nearly starving, but you don't realize it, what a truly selfish creature!

Sound asleep, Qin began to dream again. In her dream, Peili came to her bedside, lifted her in his arms, and began running, leaping over the wall, not paying the hospital fee, not taking the baby. Later in the same dream, she discovered that the child had been given as a maid to the hospital chief and beaten to death.

The baby continued to cry in the next room; it cried so long it began heaving. Qin woke up in a panic; confused and flustered, she quickly got out of bed. She thought that the hospital chief was killing her child; her shadow flashed across the wall and she fainted.

The autumn night flowed on in silence; the snow-white moonlight filled every room. On one side of the wall a mother's body slumped on the floor, on the other, a baby crying for its mother—only a wall separated the two, yet the love between mother and child was severed forever.

XVI

A woman, a little over thirty and wearing a long white gown, her sickly complexion masked with white powder, yellow and black blotches showing through, sat on the edge of Qin's bed. The woman nervously chattered on to Qin as the other women in the room sadly listened.

When Qin noticed the expressions on their faces, they pricked at her heart like needles. She covered her head with the blanket, unable to control herself. "Bundle it up and take it away. Say no more." What were these tears for? They flowed on under the covers.

The other two mothers rubbed their eyes as if moved to tears as well and the woman sitting on the edge of the bed said, "Who could bear to part with one's own child? I can't separate a mother and child." The woman turned away.

As if suddenly pressed by some force, Qin pushed aside the blanket covering her head and smiled, the tears and smile frozen together: "I can bear it. I have no use for a baby, you can take her away."

The baby in the next room slept on, completely unaware that her own mother had given her up.

The woman stood and went to the next room and tears poured from the nurse's eyes as she spoke to her. "The little baby was born six days ago and has never even seen her mother's face. She cries night and day and refuses to drink cows' milk, while her mother's breasts are so painfully swollen that her milk has to be squeezed out and thrown away. Oh, I don't understand it. I hear the baby's father is very rich too! What a strange woman; she doesn't even want to marry a rich husband."

The woman said to the nurse sympathetically, "Her little face is so cold and lonely. Truly a child to be pitied from birth." The woman's touch woke the baby and she pressed her face against the woman's hand. Thinking it was her mother, she began crying for attention.

Half an hour later, the overjoyed woman, now the baby's mother, walked down the stone steps of the hospital with a red bundle in her arms. Wrapped securely in a quilt, the baby had been carried by the stranger through the hallway, past the door of the maternity ward, past the mother in the ward, and down the stone steps.

The mother in the maternity ward didn't see a thing; she heard only a wave of commotion.

XVII

When Qin told Peili that she had given up the child, she stared straight into his eyes; he could only listen in silence. "We didn't get caught up in it this time," she said. "One child is sacrificed so that many others can be saved. Our problem now is the hospital fee."

Peili held onto Qin's hand tightly and thought—Qin is a woman of the time . . . she sees the positive side of things . . . she is the brave partner of my future! His blood boiled with excitement.

When Peili left the hospital each day, the clerk would ask him for the hospital fee, but Peili had long since given up trying to find the money. The next time he went to the pawnshop with his suit under his arm he was planning only to get enough money to pay a driver to take Qin home. But his suit had long since been gnawed apart by mice under the bed, and now even his last hope was dashed.

Peili began to run around in a desperate search for a half *yuan*.

XVIII

Qin had been in the hospital for nearly three weeks. The other women in the ward came and went home with their babies after a single week, and now she was the only one left in the room. The hospital chief no longer bothered asking her for the hospital fee; he just hoped that she would leave. But she had neither the cart fare nor any clothing to wear when she left the hospital, let alone the money to rent a room.

Alone in the ward at night, she enjoyed watching the moonlight cast shadows of the thin tree branches through the window, shadows that crawled over the walls and onto the floor. She remembered how, after her own mother had died when she was still just a child, she had slept beside her grandfather, watching the shadows the trees cast through the window. Now grandfather had gone to his grave and she had left home three years ago. Everything fades with time.

Outside the window the breeze blew a mournful tune through the trees; Qin heard a rooster crowing in the courtyard nearby.

XIX

The other new mothers, babies cradled in their arms, left the hospital by car or horse cart. Now Qin too was leaving the hospital. She didn't have a baby, or a car, just the road that stretched before her like barren land waiting to be cultivated.

Peili walked ahead, leading the way like a faithful partner.

Their two shadows—two determined shadows—stepped once again into the sea of humanity.

A SLEEPLESS NIGHT
(1937)

Why can't I sleep? I feel irritated, agitated, nauseated, and scared; my heart is pounding and I want to cry.

I wonder, do I feel this way because I've been thinking about my old home?

Outside the window, the sky seems far away; white clouds hang low and close like soft puffs of cotton. The slight scent of the grasslands seems to float in on the breeze announcing the arrival of autumn.

Back home, autumn is the most lovely season, with skies so blue they're nearly black and silver-tinted clouds that adorn the sky like heavy white blossoms about to drop; and, yes, the sky is extremely high—higher than seems possible.

Yesterday I visited several friends and listened to them as they discussed their many desires. All said and done, they all crave the same things. Some of them, for instance, said that if they could really go back to Manchuria right now, the first thing they'd do is boil up a pot of sorghum porridge. Still others talked of how huge the beans were on their land, using their hands as they spoke to show just how big—as big as bowls; and then there is the corn, they said, which has ears over a foot long that will pop open like flowers if you place them on the stove when they're dried. One after another they spoke of sorghum porridge and salted beans. As one of them put it: "If I could really go back to Manchuria, I'd fast for three days and nights and race straight back home waving a big flag, and the first thing I would do when I arrived would be to eat some sorghum porridge and salted beans."

The truth is, I'm not very fond of sorghum; it's too hard and difficult to digest (although this may have more to do with my own stomach problems than anything else). But after hearing so much talk about it, even I began to feel that I just had to have some.

When that will be, I don't know. Besides, since I'm not all that keen on sorghum anyway, it's not really something that I think about very often.

What I think about instead is the tall grass outside our door and the little purple flowers blossoming on the eggplants; I think of the cucumber vines creeping up the trellis in our backyard and the dewdrops that form at dawn with the rising sun!

Whenever I speak of the tall grass or cucumbers, San Lang waves his hand and shakes his head at me: "No, no, at our house there are two willow trees standing outside the front door and their shadows meet together to form a gate. Out front is a vegetable garden and beyond that— the mountains. A pyramid-shaped mountain peak faces the door of our house and the two sides of its base spread out to the east and west of the village like a bat's wings. There are cucumbers and eggplants growing in the backyard, but even more beautiful are the morning glories climbing up the cracks in the stone wall... they bloom at dawn, wet with dew..."

"But my home isn't like that, there aren't any mountains or willow trees... only..." I often cut him off in this manner.

Sometimes he doesn't even wait for me to finish speaking before continuing on. We always seem to be telling our stories to ourselves, not to each other.

There was only that one day. We had bought a map of "Natural Resources of the Northeast" and pinned it on the wall. Tiny horses, sheep, and a camel stood on the yellow-colored plains, and there was even a little person leading the camel. In the ocean were small fish, big fish, yellow fish, chubby red fish that looked like miniature bottles, and a huge black whale. Rows of mountains were drawn across the Xing'an and Liaoning regions like green waves.

His home was in these mountains not far from the Bohai Sea. He traced the mountain range with his fingernail. "This is Big Ling River . . . and here is Little Ling River . . . but, hey . . . it's not here, this map isn't complete, it's just a sketch. . . ."

"Ha! Day in and day out you talk about the Ling River, but where is it?" I don't know why, but anytime he began speaking of his home, I was always ready to knock him down a few notches.

"You don't believe me? I'll show you." And he went rummaging through his bookcase. "Here it is, Big Ling River . . . and Little Ling River . . . when I was a child I would catch small fish from the banks of the Ling River and then take them up to the mountains and roast them on slabs of stone. . . . And over here is Shen Family Terrace, it's two miles down the road from my house . . ." He was looking at another map spread out on the floor. As he spoke, he used his hands to sweep back the strands of hair that had fallen across his forehead.

The map of "Natural Resources of the Northwest" hung above our bed, and the next morning he grasped my hands the moment I opened my eyes. "I think that when I finally do go home, I'll buy two donkeys, one for you to ride and one for me . . . first we'll go to my aunt's home, and then to my sister's . . . on the way, maybe we'll visit my uncle. . . . My sister really adores me . . . whenever she came home for a visit after she got married, she'd start crying when she prepared to leave, and then I would cry, and then we'd both be crying . . . and now it's been seven or eight years since I last saw her! We've all grown older."

I could clearly make out the little red and black fish on the map as I looked up at it and listened to him. This time I didn't interrupt him or try to dampen his spirits.

"I'll buy black donkeys and hang bells around their necks so when they walk . . . ding-ling-ling, ding-ling-ling . . ." The noise he made sounded just like a real bell. "I'll take you to the market at Shen Family Terrace. Market day there is really lively! We'll hang a bottle of sorghum wine on the donkey, and . . . mutton is so cheap where we live . . . and the mutton stew . . . it's so delicious! Aiya! It's been years since I've eaten mutton!" Lines appeared on his forehead as he furrowed his brow.

I watched his reflection in the big mirror. He drew his hands away from mine and placed them on his chest. Then, after putting them back behind his pillow, he pulled them out again just as quickly and ran them through his hair before placing them back on the pillow.

"And what about me?" I was thinking to myself. "How would your family treat a 'daughter-in-law' brought home from somewhere else?" I then spoke my thoughts to him aloud.

Yet this probably isn't the reason why I can't sleep either. Those who buy donkeys will go on buying donkeys, and those who eat salted beans will continue eating salted beans, but what about me? No matter where we ride our donkeys, every place will always be unfamiliar to me, and wherever we end up stopping, the homes will always belong to strangers.

I have never really had strong feelings about the idea of "home," but when I hear other people reminisce about their homes, I grow anxious too! Even before that piece of land became Japanese, I never did have a "home."

My sleeplessness lasted right up until dawn. Just before daybreak, amid the sounds of artillery fire, I could hear the crowing of a rooster echoing over the open country—just like back "home."

GLOSSARY

"Abandoned Child"	《棄兒》
"After the Wedding Banquet"	《喜筵之后》
"After Victory"	《勝利以后》
All-China Writers' Resistance Association	中華全國文藝界抗敵協會
An E	安娥
"Another Man's Wife"	《生人妻》
"Aunty Liu"	《劉嫂》
Autobiography of a Girl Soldier	《女兵自傳》
Ba Jin	巴金
Bai Lang	白朗
Bai Wei	白薇

baihua	白話
Ban Zhao	班昭
Bao Huang Society	保皇會
Bao Kuang Party	飽狂黨
Beijing Post	京報
Beijing Women's Normal College	北京女子高等師範大學
Beijing Women's Post	北京女報
Big Dipper	北斗雜誌
Bing Xin (Xie Wanying)	冰心（謝婉瑩）
Bitter Heart	《棘心》
Bowei	波微
cainü	才女
Cao Dagu	曹大姑
Cao Ming	草明
Central Daily Newspaper	中央日報
Chen Baibing	陳白冰
Chen Duxiu	陳獨秀
Chen Fan	陳範
Chen Hengzhe	陳衡哲
Chen Xiefen	陳擷芬
Chen Xuezhao	陳學昭
Chen Ying	沉櫻
Chen Yuan	陳源
China Daily	中國日報
Chinese Students' Quarterly	留美學生季報
Chinese Women's News	中國女報
ci	詞
Contemporary Review	現代評論
Creation Quarterly	創造季刊
Creation Society	創造社
Crescent Monthly	新月月刊
Crescent Society	新月社
"Crisis in the Women's World"	《女界之可危》
Dagongbao	大公報
Dai Wangshu	戴望舒

"Day"	《日》
"Diary of a Madman"	《狂人日記》
Ding Ling	丁玲
Dream of the Red Chamber	《紅樓夢》
Dreams of Southern Winds	《南風的夢》
Duanmu Hongliang	端木蕻良
duli	獨立
Encompassing Love Society	共愛會
Feng Keng	馮鏗
Feng Youlan	馮友蘭
Feng Yuanjun (Gan Nüshi)	馮沅君（淦女士）
Fengzi	鳳子
The Field of Life and Death	《生死場》
"Flood"	《水》
Flowers in the Female Inferno	《女獄花》
funü wenti	婦女問題
funü wenxue	婦女文學
Gao Junyu	高君宇
Green Skies	《綠天》
Guan Lu	關露
guixiu	閨秀
Guo Mengliang	郭夢良
Guo Zhenyi	郭箴一
Guomindang	國民黨
Han Dan	邯鄲
"Harvest"	《收獲》
He Xiangning	何香凝
He Zhen	何震
History of the West	《西洋史》
Hongyu	紅玉
Hu Shi	胡適
Hu Yepin	胡也頻
huaju	話劇
Huang Chonggu	黃崇嘏
Huang Xinmian	黃心勉
Independent Critic	獨立評論
"Intoxicated"	《酒后》

Ivory Rings	《象牙戒指》
Jiang Bingzhi	蔣冰之
"The Journey"	《旅行》
July	七月
Kang Youwei	康有為
The Ladies' Journal	婦女雜志
The Ladies' Monthly	女子月刊
League of Left-Wing Writers	左翼作家聯盟
"Letters to Young Readers"	《寄小讀者》
Li Dazhao	李大釗
Li Tiwei	李緹維
Li Weijian	李唯建
Liang Qichao	梁啟超
Liang Sicheng	梁思成
Liang Zongdai	梁宗岱
Liberation Daily	解放日報
Lin Changmin	林長民
Lin Huiyin	林徽因
"Lin Nan's Diary"	《林楠的日記》
Lin Yutang	林語堂
Lin Zongsu	林宗素
Ling Shuhua	凌叔華
Linli	《琳麗》
Liu Hezhen	劉和珍
Lu Jingqing	陸晶清
Lu Kanru	陸侃如
Lu Ping	綠萍
Lu Xun	魯迅
Lu Yin (Huang Luyin)	廬隱（黃廬隱）
Luo Shi'an	羅世安
Luo Shu (Luo Shimi)	羅淑（羅世彌）
Luo Yanbin	羅燕斌
"Lusha"	《露莎》
Ma Yanxiang	馬彥祥
Ma Zongrong	馬宗融
Midstream	中流
Market Street	《商市街》

May Fourth Movement	五四運動
"Mengke"	《夢珂》
"Miss Sophia's Diary"	《莎菲女士的日記》
The Morning Post	晨報
Mother	《母親》
Mulan	木蘭
My Tragic Life	《悲劇生涯》
Myriad Stars	《繁星》
nannü pingdeng	男女平等
National Dispatch	國訊
national resistance literature	國防文學
"native soil" literature	鄉土文學
New China	新中國
New Chinese Women	中國新女界
New Culture Movement	新文化運動
New Fiction	新小說
New War Diary	《新從軍日記》
The New Woman	新女性
"The New Woman I Want to Be"	《我所希望的新婦女》
New Woman Magazine	新女性
new woman (xin nüxing)	新女性
New Youth	新青年
"News from the Seashore"	《海濱消息》
"Ninety-Nine Degrees"	《九十九度中》
nübao	女報
nüguomin	女國民
nüjie	女界
nüquan	女權
nüshi	女士
nüzuojia	女作家
Nu'er jing	《女兒經》
"On the Gate Tower"	《城樓上》
"Once Upon a Time"	《說有這麼一回事》
"One Day"	《一日》
"Our Mistress' Parlor"	《我們太太的客廳》
Peace Daily	和平日報

"Peach Blossom Spring"	《桃花源記》
Precepts for Women	《女誡》
Protect the Emperor Society	保皇會
Qian Xingcun (A Ying)	錢杏村（阿英）
Qin Liangyu	秦良玉
Qiu Jin	秋瑾
"Random Notes: Number Nine"	《素箋。箋九》
Red and Black Magazine	紅黑半月刊
"Remembering Paris"	《憶巴黎》
Revolutionary Alliance	同盟會
Ruan Lingyu	阮玲玉
Sancong side	三從四德
Seaside Friends	《海濱故人》
"Separation"	《隔絕》
Shen Congwen	沈從文
Shen Yunying	沈雲英
shi	詩
Shi Pingmei (Shi Rubi)	石評梅（石汝璧）
Shi Zhicun	施蟄存
Shibao (Times)	時報
Shimoda Utako	下田歌子
Short Story Monthly	小說月報
"Sitting Quietly"	《靜坐》
"A Sleepless Night"	《失眠之夜》
Song Qingling	宋慶齡
Southeast Flies the Peacock	《孔雀東南飛》
Spring Water	《春水》
"Still"	《仍然》
Stones of the Jingwei Bird	《精微石》
Su Qing	蘇青
Su Xuelin (Lu Yi)	蘇雪林（綠猗）
Subao	蘇報
suhua	俗話
The Sun Shines on the Sanggan River	《太陽照在桑干河上》
Tales of Hulan River	《呼蘭河傳》

Tan Sheying	談社英
tanci	彈詞
Tao Yuanming	陶淵明
Temple of Flowers	《花之寺》
Tianyi	天義報
The Times	時報
Torrents	奔流
Two Little Brothers	《小哥兒倆》
Untitled	《無題集》
Vernacular News	白話報
Village in August	《八月的鄉村》
Wanderings	《流浪集》
Wang Huiwu	王會悟
Wang Liming	王立明
Wang Lixi	王禮錫
Wang Miaoru	王妙如
Wang Xifeng	王熙鳳
Wanqing	浣青
War Diary	《從軍日記》
Wei Yuelu	韋月侶
wenti xiaoshuo	問題小說
wenxue geming	文學革命
wenyan	文言
"Wife"	《妻》
Wild Rose Association	薔薇社
The Wild Rose Weekly	薔薇周刊
"The Woes of the Modern Woman"	《現代女子的苦悶問題》
"Woman"	《女性》
A Woman Writer	《一個女作家》
Woman Writer Magazine	女作家雜志
Women's Bookstore	女子書店
Women	《女人》
Women Poets of the Tang Dynasty	《唐代女詩人》
Women Writers Special lssue	《女作家號》
Women's Life	婦女生活

Women's Paper	女報
Women's Review	婦女評論
Women's Studies	女學報
Women's Weekly	婦女周刊
Working Is Beautiful	《工作著是美麗的》
The World Daily	世界日報
Wu Shutian	吳曙天
Wu Wenzao	吳文澡
Xiang Jingyu	向警予
Xiao Hong (Zhang Naiying)	蕭紅（張乃瑩）
Xiao Jun	蕭軍
xiaopin	小品
xiaoshi	小詩
Xie Bingying	謝冰瑩
Xie Daoyun	謝道韞
xin ganjuepai	新感覺派
xin nüxing	新女性
xin xiaoshuo	新小說
Xu Zhimo	徐志摩
Xue Jinqin	薛錦琴
Xun Guan	荀灌
Yan'an Interviews	《延安訪問記》
Yang Duanliu	楊端六
Yang Gang	楊剛
Yang Guifei	楊貴妃
Yang Jiang	楊絳
Yang Mo	楊沫
Yang Sao	楊騷
Yanjing University	燕京大學
Yan'an	延安
Yosano Akiko	與謝野晶子
Yu Dafu	郁達夫
Yuan Changying	袁昌英
Yuan Mei	袁枚
Yuan Shikai	袁世凱
yuefu	樂府
zaju	雜劇

H. C. Zen	任鴻雋
Zhadan yu zhengniao	《炸彈與征鳥》
Zhang Ailing	張愛玲
Zhao Qingge	趙清閣
Zheng Zhenduo	鄭振鐸
Zhenmeishan	真美善
Zhou Zuoren	周作人
Zong Pu	宗璞
Zuofen	左芬

SUPPLEMENTAL READINGS

The following bibliographic list is divided into two parts: 1) critical and historical works pertaining to Chinese women's writing, and 2) additional translations and primary sources for individual writers represented in this anthology. We have included Chinese and English-language materials in both sections. The list is not exhaustive, but intended as a starting point for those wishing to pursue future reading and research on women's writing of early twentieth-century China.

I. Critical and Historical Research

Bai, Shurong. *Shiwei nüzuojia* (Ten women writers). Tianjin: Chunzhong chubanshe, 1986.
Barlow, Tani E. "Gender and Identity in Ding Ling's *Mother*." In Michael S. Duke, ed., *Modern Chinese Women Writers: Critical Appraisals*, 1–24. Armonk, NY: M.E. Sharpe, 1989.
———, ed. *Gender Politics in Modern China: Writing and Feminism*. Durham: Duke University Press, 1993.

——. "Theorizing Women: Funü, Guojia, Jiating (Chinese Women, State, and Family)." *Genders* 10 (Spring 1991): 132–60.
Beahan, Charlotte. "Feminism and Nationalism in the Chinese Women's Press 1902–1922." *Modern China* 1 (4): 379–416.
——. "In the Public Eye: Women in Early Twentieth-Century China." In Richard W. Guisso and Stanley Johannesen, eds., *Women in China: Current Directions in Historical Scholarship*, 215–28. Youngstown, NY: Philo Press, 1981.
Bien, Gloria. "Images of Women in Bing Xin's Fiction." In Angela Jung Palandri, ed., *Women Writers of Twentieth-Century China*, 19–33. Eugene: Asian Studies Program, University of Oregon, 1982.
Borthwick, Sally. "Changing Concepts of the Role of Women from the Late Qing to the May Fourth Period." In David Pong and Edmund S. K. Fung, eds., *Ideal and Reality: Social and Political Change in Modern China, 1860–1949*, 63–91. Lanham, MD: University Press of America, 1985.
Chen, Dongyuan. *Zhongguo funü shenghuo shi* (The history of Chinese women's lives). Shanghai: Shangwu yinshuguan, 1928; reprint, Taibei: Taiwan Commercial Press, 1994.
Chen, Jingshi. *Xiandai wenxue zaoqi de nüzuojia* (Early modern women writers). Taibei: Chengwen chubanshe, 1980.
Chow, Rey. "Virtuous Transactions: A Reading of Three Stories by Ling Shuhua." In Tani E. Barlow, ed., *Gender Politics in Modern China: Writing and Feminism*, 90–105. Durham: Duke University Press, 1993.
——. *Woman and Chinese Modernity: The Politics of Reading Between West and East*. Minneapolis: University of Minnesota Press, 1991.
Chow, Tse-tsung. *The May Fourth Movement: Intellectual Revolution in Modern China*. Cambridge: Harvard University Press, 1960.
Croll, Elisabeth. *Feminism and Socialism in China*. New York: Schocken Books, 1978.
——. *Changing Identities of Chinese Women: Rhetoric, Experience, and Self-Perception in Twentieth-Century China*. London: Zed Press, 1995.
Cuadrado, Clara Yu. "Portraits by a Lady: The Fictional World of Ling Shuhua." In Angela Jung Palandri, ed., *Women Writers of Twentieth-Century China*, 41–62. Eugene: University of Oregon Press, 1982.
Fairbank, Wilma. *Liang and Lin: Partners in Exploring China's Architectural Past*. Philadelphia: University of Pennsylvania Press, 1994.
Feuerwerker, Yi-tsi Mei. "Women as Writers in the 1920s and 1930s." In Margery Wolf and Roxanne Witke, eds., *Women in Chinese Society*, 143–68. Stanford: Stanford University Press, 1975.
——. *Ding Ling's Fiction: Ideology and Narrative in Modern Chinese Literature*. Cambridge: Harvard East Asian Series, 1982.
Gálik, Marián. "On the Literature Written by Chinese Women Prior to 1917." *Asian and African Studies* 15 (1979): 65–99.
Gerstlacher, Anna, ed. *Women and Literature in China*. Bochum, West Germany: Studienverlag Brockmeyer, 1985.
Gilmartin, Christina Kelley. *Engendering the Chinese Revolution: Radical Women, Communist Politics, and Mass Movements in the 1920s*. Berkeley: University of California Press, 1995.

Gilmartin, Christina K., Gail Hershatter, Lisa Rofel, and Tyrene White, eds. *Engendering China: Women, Culture, and the State*. Cambridge: Harvard University Press, 1994.
Gipoulon, Catherine. "The Emergence of Women in Politics in China, 1898–1927." *Chinese Studies in History* 32 (2): 46–67.
Goldblatt, Howard. *Hsiao Hung*. Boston: Twayne Publishers, 1976.
Guisso, Richard and Stanley Johanneson, eds. *Women in China: Current Directions in Historical Scholarship*. Youngstown, N.Y.: Philo Press, 1981.
He, Yubo. *Zhongguo xiandai nüzuojia* (Modern Chinese women writers). Shanghai: Xiandai shuju, 1932.
Huang Renying, ed. *Dangdai Zhongguo nüzuojia lun* (On contemporary Chinese women writers). Shanghai: Guanghua shuju, 1933; reprint, Shanghai: Shanghai shudian, 1985.
Ko, Dorothy. *Teachers of the Inner Chambers: Women and Culture in Seventeenth-Century China*. Stanford: Stanford University Press, 1994.
Larson, Wendy. "The End of 'Funü Wenxue': Women's Literature from 1925–1935." In Tani E. Barlow, ed., *Gender Politics in Modern China: Writing and Feminism*, 58–73. Durham: Duke University Press, 1993.
———. "Female Subjectivity and Gender Relations: The Early Stories of Lu Yin and Bing Xin." In Kang Liu and Xiaobing Tang, eds., *Politics, Ideology and Literary Discourse in Modern China*, 124–43. Durham: Duke University Press, 1993.
Li, Youning and Yufa Zhang, eds. *Jindai Zhongguo nüquan yundong shiliao, 1842–1911* (Documents on the feminist movement in modern China, 1842–1911). 2 vols. Taibei: Zhuanji wenxueshi, 1975.
———. *Zhongguo funüshi lunwenji* (Collected essays on Chinese women's history). Taibei: Taiwan Shangwu yinshuguan, 1981.
Liang, Yizhen. *Qingdai funü wenxue shi* (A history of women's literature in the Qing dynasty). Shanghai: Zhonghua shuju, 1926; reprint, Taibei: Zhonghua shuju, 1979.
Lieberman, Sally. *The Mother and Narrative Politics in Modern China*. Charlottesville: University Press of Virginia, 1998.
Liu, Huiying. *Zouchu nanquan chuantong de fanli: Wenxuezhong nanquan yishi de pipan* (Transcending the limits of the patriarchal tradition: a critique of patriarchal consciousness in literature). Beijing: Sanlian shudian, 1995.
Liu, Jucai. *Zhongguo jindai funü yundongshi* (The history of the modern Chinese women's movement). Liaoning: Zhongguo funü chubanshe, 1989.
Liu, Lydia H. "The Female Body and Nationalist Discourse: Manchuria in Xiao Hong's *Field of Life and Death*." In Angela Zito and Tani E. Barlow, eds., *Body, Subject, and Power*, 157–77. Chicago: University of Chicago Press, 1994.
———. "Invention and Intervention: The Making of a Female Tradition in Modern Chinese Literature." In Ellen Widmer and David Der-wei Wang, eds., *From May Fourth to June Fourth: Fiction and Film in Twentieth-Century China*, 194–220. Cambridge: Harvard University Press, 1993.
———. *Translingual Practice: Literature, National Culture, and Translated Modernity— China, 1900–1937*. Stanford: Stanford University Press, 1995.

Liu, Nienling. "The Vanguards of the Women's Liberation Movement—Lu Yin, Bingxin, and Ding Ling." *Chinese Studies in History* 23 (2): 22–45.

Lü, Meiyi, and Zheng Yongfu. *Zhongguo funü yundong: 1840–1921* (The Chinese women's movement: 1840–1921). Zhengzhou: Henan renmin chubanshe, 1990.

Lu, Tonglin, ed. *Gender and Sexuality in Twentieth-Century Chinese Literature and Society*. Albany: State University of New York Press, 1993.

Mann, Susan. *Precious Records: Women in China's Long Eighteenth Century*. Stanford: Stanford University Press, 1997.

Meng, Yue and Dai Jinhua. *Fuchu lishi dibiao: xiandai funü wenxue yanjiu* (Emerging from the horizon of history: a study of modern Chinese women's literature). Zhengzhou: Henan renmin chubanshe, 1989.

Nivard, Jacqueline. "Women and the Women's Press: The Case of the Ladies' Journal (Funü Zazhi) 1915–1931 (1)." *Republican China* 10 (16): 37–55.

Ono, Kazuko. *Chinese Women in a Century of Revolution, 1850–1950*. Joshua A. Fogel, ed. Stanford: Stanford University Press, 1989.

Rankin, Mary Backus. "The Emergence of Women at the End of the Ch'ing: The Case of Ch'iu Chin." In Margery Wolf and Roxane Witke, eds., *Women in Chinese Society*, 39–66. Stanford: Stanford University Press, 1975.

Schwarcz, Vera. *The Chinese Enlightenment: Intellectuals and the Legacy of the May Fourth Movement of 1919*. Berkeley: University of California Press, 1986.

Stacey, Judith. *Patriarchy and Socialist Revolution in China*. Berkeley: University of California Press, 1983.

Sung, Marina H. "T'an-Tz'u and T'an-Tz'u Narratives." *T'oung Pao: International Journal of Chinese Studies* 79 (1993): 1–22.

Tan, Zhengbi. *Zhongguo nüxing de wenxue shenghuo* (The literary life of Chinese women). Shanghai: Guangming shuju, 1930; reprint, Taibei: Zhuangyan chubanshe, 1982.

Wang, Jialun. *Zhongguo xiandai nüzuojia lunwang* (A discussion of modern Chinese women writers). Beijing: Zhongguo funü chubanshe, 1992.

Wei, Karen. *Women in China: A Selected and Annotated Bibliography*. Westport, Conn.: Greenwood Press, 1984.

Widmer, Ellen. "The Epistolary World of Female Talent in Seventeenth-Century China." *Late Imperial China* 10 (2): 1–43.

———. "Xiaoqing's Literary Legacy and the Place of the Woman Writer in Late Imperial China." *Late Imperial China* 13 (1): 111–55.

Widmer, Ellen and Kang-i Sun Chang, eds. *Writing Women in Late Imperial China*. Stanford: Stanford University Press, 1997.

Wolf, Margery and Roxane Witke, eds. *Women in Chinese Society*. Stanford: Stanford University Press, 1975.

Yin, Guoming and Zhihong Chen. *Zhongguo xiandangdai xiaoshuozhong de zhishi nüxing* (Female intellectuals in modern and contemporary Chinese fiction). Guangzhou: Guangdong gaodeng jiaoyu chubanshe, 1990.

Young, Marilyn B., ed. *Women in China: Studies in Social Change and Feminism*. Ann Arbor: Center for Chinese Studies, University of Michigan, 1973.

Zito, Angela and Tani Barlow, eds. *Body, Subject, and Power in China*. Chicago: University of Chicago Press, 1994.

II. Additional Translations of and Primary Sources for Individual Writers

BING XIN

Bing Xin. *Bing Xin xuanji* (The selected works of Bing Xin). 6 vols. Shijiazhuang: Hebei jiaoyu chubanshe, 1992.
——. "Chang Sao." Trans. Samuel Ling. In Vivian Ling Hsu, ed., *Born of the Same Roots: Stories of Modern Chinese Women*, 56–61. Bloomington: Indiana University Press, 1981.
——. "Loneliness." In R. A. Roberts and Angela Knox, eds., *One Half of the Sky: Selections from Contemporary Women Writers of China*, 1–14. London: Heinemann, 1987.
——. "Miss Winter." Jennifer Anderson and Theresa Munford, eds. and trans. In *Chinese Women Writers: A Collection of Short Stories by Chinese Women Writers of the 1920s and 1930s*, 32–40. San Francisco: China Books and Periodicals, 1985.
——. "On 'Literary Criticism.'" Trans. Wendy Larson. In Kirk A. Denton, ed., *Modern Chinese Literary Theory: Writings on Literature, 1893–1945*, 233–34. Stanford: Stanford University Press, 1996.
——. *The Photograph*. Beijing: Chinese Literature Press, 1992.
——. "Special Section on Bing Xin." *Renditions* 32 (Autumn 1989): 83–145.
——. "West Wind." Trans. Samuel Ling. In Vivian Ling Hsu, ed., *Born of the Same Roots: Stories of Modern Chinese Women*, 44–56. Bloomington: Indiana University Press, 1981.

CHEN HENGZHE

Chen Hengzhe. *Xiao yudian* (Little raindrop). 1928; reprint, Shanghai: Shanghai shudian, 1985.
——. *Chen Hengzhe sanwen xuanji* (Selected essays of Chen Hengzhe). Zhu Weizhi, ed. Tianjin: Baihua wenyi chubanshe, 1991.
——. "Influences of Foreign Cultures on the Chinese Woman." In Yu-ning Li, ed., *Chinese Women Through Chinese Eyes*, 59–71. Armonk, NY: M. E. Sharpe, 1992.
——. "My Childhood Pursuit of Education." Trans. Janet Ng. In Janet Ng and Janice Wickeri, eds., *May Fourth Women Writers: Memoirs*, 35–47. Hong Kong: Renditions, 1997.
——. "Remembrances of an Elderly Aunt." In Yu-ning Li, ed., *Chinese Women Through Chinese Eyes*, 129–32. Armonk, NY: M. E. Sharpe, 1992.

CHEN XUEZHAO

Chen Xuezhao. *Surviving the Storm: A Memoir*. Trans. Hua Ti and Caroline Green. Armonk: M. E. Sharpe, Inc., 1990.

CHEN YING

Chen Ying. "Careers." Jennifer Anderson and Theresa Munford, eds. and trans. In *Chinese Women Writers: A Collection of Short Stories by Chinese Women Writers of the 1920s and 1930s*, 137–67. San Francisco: China Books and Periodicals, 1985.
———. *Xiyan zhihou; Mou shaonü; Nüxing* (After the banquet; a girl; woman). Beijing: Renmin wenxue chubanshe, 1987.

DING LING

Ding Ling. *Ding Ling wenji* (The collected works of Ding Ling). Changsha: Hunan renmin chubanshe, 1983.
———. *Miss Sophie's Diary and Other Stories*. Trans. W. J. F. Jenner. Beijing: Chinese Literature Press, 1985.
———. "A House in Qingyun Lane." Jennifer Anderson and Theresa Munford, eds. and trans. In *Chinese Women Writers: A Collection of Short Stories by Chinese Women Writers of the 1920s and 1930s*, 4–12. San Francisco: China Books and Periodicals, 1985.
———. *I Myself Am a Woman: Selected Writings of Ding Ling*. Tani E. Barlow and Gary J. Bjorge, eds. Boston: Beacon Press, 1989.
———. "From Morning to Night." Trans. Ruth Nybakken. In Marian Arkin and Barbara Shollar, eds., *Longman Anthology of World Literature by Women*, 402–7. New York: Longman, 1989.
———. "New Year." Jennifer Anderson and Theresa Munford, eds. and trans. In *Chinese Women Writers: A Collection of Short Stories by Chinese Women Writers of the 1920s and 1930s*, 13–31. San Francisco: China Books and Periodicals, 1985.

FENG YUANJUN

Feng Yuanjun. *Feng Yuanjun chuangzuo yiwen ji* (The collected writings and translations of Feng Yuanjun). Jinan: Shandong renmin chubanshe, 1983.
———. "The Journey." Jennifer Anderson and Theresa Munford, eds. and trans. In *Chinese Women Writers: A Collection of Short Stories by Chinese Women Writers of the 1920s and 1930s*, 168–78. San Francisco: China Books and Periodicals, 1985.
———. *An Outline History of Classical Chinese Literature*. Trans. Yang Xianyi and Gladys Yang. Hong Kong: Joint Publishing Co., 1983.

LIN HUIYIN

Lin Huiyin. "Do Not Throw Away," "Meditation," and "Sitting in Quietude." Trans. Michelle Yeh. In Michelle Yeh, ed. and trans., *Anthology of Modern Chinese Poetry*, 29–31. New Haven: Yale University Press, 1992.
———. "Hsiu Hsiu." Trans. Janet Ng. In Janet Ng and Janice Wickeri, eds., *May Fourth Women Writers: Memoirs*, 19–34. Hong Kong: Renditions, 1997.

———. *Lin Huiyin shiji* (The collected poems of Lin Huiyin). Beijing: Renmin wenxue chubanshe, 1985.

LING SHUHUA

Ling Shuhua. *Ancient Melodies*. With an introduction by V. Sackville-West. 1953; reprint, New York: Universe Books, 1988.
———. "Embroidered Pillows." In Joseph S. M. Lau, C. T. Hsia, and Leo Ou-fan Lee, eds., *Modern Chinese Stories and Novellas: 1919–1949*, 197–200. New York: Columbia University Press, 1981.
———. *Ling Shuhua xiaoshuo ji* (The collected fiction of Ling Shuhua). 2 vols. Taibei: Hongfan shudian, 1986.
———. "Little Liu." Trans. Vivian Hsu with Julia Fitzgerald. In Vivian Ling Hsu, ed., *Born of the Same Roots: Stories of Modern Chinese Women*, 62–80. Bloomington: Indiana University Press, 1981.
———. "The Lucky One." Jennifer Anderson and Theresa Munford, eds. and trans. In *Chinese Women Writers: A Collection of Short Stories by Chinese Women Writers of the 1920s and 1930s*, 62–74. San Francisco: China Books and Periodicals, 1985.
———. "The Night of Midautumn Festival." Trans. Nathan K. Mao. In Joseph S. M. Lau and Howard Goldblatt, eds., *The Columbia Anthology of Modern Chinese Literature*, 110–19. New York: Columbia University Press, 1995.
———. "The Sendoff." Trans. Donald Holoch. In Marian Arkin and Barbara Shollar, eds., *Longman Anthology of World Literature by Women*, 413–19. New York: Longman, 1989.

LU JINGQING

Lu Jingqing. "Wanderings (Excerpts)." Trans. Amy D. Dooling. In Janet Ng and Janice Wickeri, eds., *May Fourth Women Writers: Memoirs*, 73–93. Hong Kong: Renditions, 1997.

LU YIN

Lu Yin. "Autobiography (Excerpts)." Trans. Kristina M. Torgeson. In Janet Ng and Janice Wickeri, eds. *May Fourth Women Writers: Memoirs*, 94–119. Hong Kong: Renditions, 1997.
———. "Factory Girl." Jennifer Anderson and Theresa Munford, eds. and trans. In *Chinese Women Writers: A Collection of Short Stories by Chinese Women Writers of the 1920s and 1930s*, 85–95. San Francisco: China Books and Periodicals, 1985.
———. *Lu Yin xuanji* (The selected works of Lu Yin). 2 vols. Hong Qian, ed. Fuzhou: Fujian renmin chubanshe, 1985.
———. "My Opinions on Creativity." Trans. Paul Foster and Sherry Mou. In Kirk A. Denton, *Modern Chinese Literary Theory: Writings on Literature, 1893–1945*, 235–36. Stanford: Stanford University Press, 1996.

LUO SHU

Luo Shu. *Luo Shu xuanji* (The selected works of Luo Shu). Chengdu: Sichuan renmin chubanshe, 1980.
———. "Wife of Another Man." Jennifer Anderson and Theresa Munford, eds. and trans. In *Chinese Women Writers: A Collection of Short Stories by Chinese Women Writers of the 1920s and 1930s*, 41–61. San Francisco: China Books and Periodicals, 1985.

SHI PINGMEI

Shi Pingmei. "Amid the Sound of Firecrackers on New Year's Eve." Trans. Janet Ng. In Janet Ng and Janice Wickeri, eds. *May Fourth Women Writers: Memoirs*, 63–72. Hong Kong: Renditions, 1997.
———. *Shi Pingmei zuopin ji* (The collected works of Shi Pingmei). 3 vols. Yang Yang, ed. Beijing: Shumu wenxian chubanshe, 1984–1985.

QIU JIN

Qiu Jin. "A Warning to My Sisters." Trans. Katherine Carlitz. In Marian Arkin and Barbara Shollar, eds., *Longman Anthology of World Literature by Women*, 178–80. New York: Longman, 1989.
———. "Poems." In Irving Yucheng Lo and William Schultz, eds., *Waiting for the Unicorn: Poems and Lyrics of China's Last Dynasty, 1644–1911*, 399–403. Bloomington: Indiana University Press, 1986.
———. *Qiu Jin ji* (The collected works of Qiu Jin). Shanghai: Shanghai guji chubanshe, 1979.

SU XUELIN

Su Xuelin. *Su Xuelin xuanji* (The selected works of Su Xuelin). Hefei: Anhui wenyi chubanshe, 1989.

XIAO HONG

Xiao Hong. *The Field of Life and Death and Tales of Hulan River*. Trans. Howard Goldblatt. Bloomington: Indiana University Press, 1979.
———. "Hands." Trans. Howard Goldblatt. In Joseph S. M. Lau and Howard Goldblatt, eds., *The Columbia Anthology of Modern Chinese Literature*, 174–87. New York: Columbia University Press, 1995.
———. *Market Street: A Chinese Woman in Harbin*. Trans. Howard Goldblatt. Seattle: University of Washington Press, 1986.
———. *Selected Stories of Xiao Hong*. Trans. Howard Goldblatt. Beijing: Chinese Literature Press, 1982.

———. *Xiao Hong quanji* (The complete works of Xiao Hong). 2 vols. Harbin: Ha'erbin chubanshe, 1991.

XIE BINGYING

Xie Bingying. *Autobiography of a Chinese Girl*. Trans. Tsui Chi. With an introduction by Elisabeth Croll. 1943; reprint, London and New York: Pandora, 1986.

———. *Girl Rebel: The Autobiography of Hsieh Pingying, with Extracts from Her New War Diaries*. Trans. Adet and Anor Lin. 1940; reprint, New York: De Capo Press, 1975.

———. "Letters of a Chinese Amazon." In Yutang Lin, ed. and trans., *Letters of a Chinese Amazon and War-Time Essays*, 3–47. Shanghai: The Commercial Press, 1930.

———. *Xie Bingying sanwen xuanji* (The selected essays of Xie Bingying). Demin Fu, ed. Tianjin: Baihua wenyi chubanshe, 1992.

———. *Xie Bingying zuopin xuan* (The selected works of Xie Bingying). Changsha: Hunan renmin chubanshe, 1985.

YUAN CHANGYING

Yuan Changying. *Kongque dongnan fei ji qita dumuju* (Southeast flies the peacock and other one-act plays). Su Xuelin, ed. 1930; reprint, Taibei: Shangwu yinshuguan, 1983.

———. *Yuan Changying xuanji* (The selected works of Yuan Changying). Su Xuelin, ed. Taibei: Hongfan shudian, 1986.

TRANSLATORS

Jennifer Carpenter is a doctoral candidate in Chinese history at Columbia University.

Amy D. Dooling is a doctoral candidate in modern Chinese literature in the East Asian Languages and Cultures Department at Columbia University. Her dissertation explores feminist narrative strategies in modern Chinese women's writing.

Janet Ng is assistant professor of Asian Literature at the City University of New York, College of Staten Island. She is editor, with Janice Wickeri, of *May Fourth Women Writers: Memoirs*.

Kristina M. Torgeson is a doctoral candidate in modern Chinese literature in the East Asian Languages and Cultures Department at Columbia University. She is editor and translator of *The Courage to Stand Alone: Letters from Prison and Other Writings* by Wei Jingsheng.

OTHER WORKS IN THE COLUMBIA ASIAN STUDIES SERIES

Modern Asian Literature Series

Modern Japanese Drama: An Anthology, ed. and tr. Ted. Takaya. Also in paperback ed. 1979

Mask and Sword: Two Plays for the Contemporary Japanese Theater, by Yamazaki Masakazu, tr. J. Thomas Rimer 1980

Yokomitsu Riichi, Modernist, Dennis Keene 1980

Nepali Visions, Nepali Dreams: The Poetry of Laxmiprasad Devkota, tr. David Rubin 1980

Literature of the Hundred Flowers, vol. 1: *Criticism and Polemics*, ed. Hualing Nieh 1981

Literature of the Hundred Flowers, vol. 2: *Poetry and Fiction*, ed. Hualing Nieh 1981

Modern Chinese Stories and Novellas, 1919 1949, ed. Joseph S. M. Lau, C. T. Hsia, and Leo Ou-fan Lee. Also in paperback ed. 1984

A View by the Sea, by Yasuoka Shōtarō, tr. Kären Wigen Lewis 1984

Other Worlds; Arishima Takeo and the Bounds of Modern Japanese Fiction, by Paul Anderer 1984

Selected Poems of Sō Chōngju, tr. with introduction by David R. McCann 1989

The Sting of Life: Four Contemporary Japanese Novelists, by Van C. Gessel   1989
Stories of Osaka Life, by Oda Sakunosuke, tr. Burton Watson   1990
The Bodhisattva, or Samantabhadra, by Ishikawa Jun, tr. with introduction by William Jefferson Tyler   1990
The Travels of Lao Ts'an, by Liu T'ieh-yün, tr. Harold Shadick. Morningside ed.   1990
Three Plays by Kōbō Abe, tr. with introduction by Donald Keene   1993
The Columbia Anthology of Modern Chinese Literature, ed. Joseph S. M. Lau and Howard Goldblatt   1995
Modern Japanese Tanka, ed. and tr. by Makoto Ueda   1996
Masaoka Shiki: Selected Poems, ed. and tr. by Burton Watson   1997

Translations from the Asian Classics

Major Plays of Chikamatsu, tr. Donald Keene   1961
Four Major Plays of Chikamatsu, tr. Donald Keene. Paperback ed. only.   1961
Records of the Grand Historian of China, translated from the Shih chi of Ssu-ma Ch'ien, tr. Burton Watson, 2 vols.   1961
Instructions for Practical Living and Other Neo-Confucian Writings by Wang Yang-ming, tr. Wing-tsit Chan   1963
Hsün Tzu: Basic Writings, tr. Burton Watson, paperback ed. only.   1963
Chuang Tzu: Basic Writings, tr. Burton Watson, paperback ed. only.   1964
The Mahābhārata, tr. Chakravarthi V. Narasimhan. Also in paperback ed.   1965
The Manyōshū, Nippon Gakujutsu Shinkōkai edition   1965
Su Tung-p'o: Selections from a Sung Dynasty Poet, tr. Burton Watson. Also in paperback ed.   1965
Bhartrihari: Poems, tr. Barbara Stoler Miller. Also in paperback ed.   1967
Basic Writings of Mo Tzu, Hsün Tzu, and Han Fei Tzu, tr. Burton Watson. Also in separate paperback eds.   1967
The Awakening of Faith, Attributed to Aśvaghosha, tr. Yoshito S. Hakeda. Also in paperback ed.   1967
Reflections on Things at Hand: The Neo-Confucian Anthology, comp. Chu Hsi and Lü Tsu-ch'ien, tr. Wing-tsit Chan   1967
The Platform Sutra of the Sixth Patriarch, tr. Philip B. Yampolsky. Also in paperback ed.   1967
Essays in Idleness: The Tsurezuregusa of Kenkō, tr. Donald Keene. Also in paperback ed.   1967
The Pillow Book of Sei Shōnagon, tr. Ivan Morris, 2 vols.   1967
Two Plays of Ancient India: The Little Clay Cart and the Minister's Seal, tr. J. A. B. van Buitenen   1968
The Complete Works of Chuang Tzu, tr. Burton Watson   1968
The Romance of the Western Chamber (Hsi Hsiang chi), tr. S. I. Hsiung. Also in paperback ed.   1968
The Manyōshū, Nippon Gakujutsu Shinkōkai edition. Paperback ed. only.   1969

Records of the Historian: Chapters from the Shih chi of Ssu-ma Ch'ien, tr. Burton Watson. Paperback ed. only.   1969
Cold Mountain: 100 Poems by the T'ang Poet Han-shan, tr. Burton Watson. Also in paperback ed.   1970
Twenty Plays of the Nō Theatre, ed. Donald Keene. Also in paperback ed.   1970
Chūshingura: The Treasury of Loyal Retainers, tr. Donald Keene. Also in paperback ed.   1971
The Zen Master Hakuin: Selected Writings, tr. Philip B. Yampolsky   1971
Chinese Rhyme-Prose: Poems in the Fu Form from the Han and Six Dynasties Periods, tr. Burton Watson. Also in paperback ed.   1971
Kūkai: Major Works, tr. Yoshito S. Hakeda. Also in paperback ed.   1972
The Old Man Who Does as He Pleases: Selections from the Poetry and Prose of Lu Yu, tr. Burton Watson   1973
The Lion's Roar of Queen Śrīmālā, tr. Alex and Hideko Wayman   1974
Courtier and Commoner in Ancient China: Selections from the History of the Former Han by Pan Ku, tr. Burton Watson. Also in paperback ed.   1974
Japanese Literature in Chinese, vol. 1: Poetry and Prose in Chinese by Japanese Writers of the Early Period, tr. Burton Watson   1975
Japanese Literature in Chinese, vol. 2: Poetry and Prose in Chinese by Japanese Writers of the Later Period, tr. Burton Watson   1976
Scripture of the Lotus Blossom of the Fine Dharma, tr. Leon Hurvitz. Also in paperback ed.   1976
Love Song of the Dark Lord: Jayadeva's Gītagovinda, tr. Barbara Stoler Miller. Also in paperback ed. Cloth ed. includes critical text of the Sanskrit.   1977
Ryōkan: Zen Monk-Poet of Japan, tr. Burton Watson   1977
Calming the Mind and Discerning the Real: From the Lam rim chen mo of Tsoṇ-kha-pa, tr. Alex Wayman   1978
The Hermit and the Love-Thief: Sanskrit Poems of Bhartrihari and Bilhaṇa, tr. Barbara Stoler Miller   1978
The Lute: Kao Ming's P'i-p'a chi, tr. Jean Mulligan. Also in paperback ed.   1980
A Chronicle of Gods and Sovereigns: Jinnō Shōtōki of Kitabatake Chikafusa, tr. H. Paul Varley.   1980
Among the Flowers: The Hua-chien chi, tr. Lois Fusek   1982
Grass Hill: Poems and Prose by the Japanese Monk Gensei, tr. Burton Watson   1983
Doctors, Diviners, and Magicians of Ancient China: Biographies of Fang-shih, tr. Kenneth J. DeWoskin. Also in paperback ed.   1983
Theater of Memory: The Plays of Kālidāsa, ed. Barbara Stoler Miller. Also in paperback ed.   1984
The Columbia Book of Chinese Poetry: From Early Times to the Thirteenth Century, ed. and tr. Burton Watson. Also in paperback ed.   1984
Poems of Love and War: From the Eight Anthologies and the Ten Long Poems of Classical Tamil, tr. A. K. Ramanujan. Also in paperback ed.   1985
The Bhagavad Gita: Krishna's Counsel in Time of War, tr. Barbara Stoler Miller   1986
The Columbia Book of Later Chinese Poetry, ed. and tr. Jonathan Chaves. Also in paperback ed.   1986

The Tso Chuan: Selections from China's Oldest Narrative History, tr. Burton Watson   1989
Waiting for the Wind: Thirty-six Poets of Japan's Late Medieval Age, tr. Steven Carter   1989
Selected Writings of Nichiren, ed. Philip B. Yampolsky   1990
Saigyō, Poems of a Mountain Home, tr. Burton Watson   1990
The Book of Lieh-Tzǔ: A Classic of the Tao, tr. A. C. Graham. Morningside ed.   1990
The Tale of an Anklet: An Epic of South India—The Cilappatikāram of Iḷaṅkō Aṭikaḷ, tr. R. Parthasarathy   1993
Waiting for the Dawn: A Plan for the Prince, tr. and introduction by Wm. Theodore de Bary   1993
Yoshitsune and the Thousand Cherry Trees: A Masterpiece of the Eighteenth-Century Japanese Puppet Theater, tr., annotated, and with introduction by Stanleigh H. Jones, Jr.   1993
The Lotus Sutra, tr. Burton Watson. Also in paperback ed.   1993
The Classic of Changes: A New Translation of the I Ching as Interpreted by Wang Bi, tr. Richard John Lynn   1994
Beyond Spring: T'zu Poems of the Sung Dynasty, tr. Julie Landau   1994
The Columbia Anthology of Traditional Chinese Literature, ed. Victor H. Mair   1994
Scenes for Mandarins: The Elite Theater of the Ming, tr. Cyril Birch   1995
Letters of Nichiren, ed. Philip B. Yampolsky; tr. Burton Watson et al.   1996
Unforgotten Dreams: Poems by the Zen Monk Shōtetsu, tr. Steven D. Carter   1997
Sutra on the Expositions of Vimalakirti, tr. by Burton Watson   1997

Studies in Asian Culture

The Ōnin War: History of Its Origins and Background, with a Selective Translation of the Chronicle of Ōnin, by H. Paul Varley   1967
Chinese Government in Ming Times: Seven Studies, ed. Charles O. Hucker   1969
The Actors' Analects (Yakusha Rongo), ed. and tr. by Charles J. Dunn and Bungō Torigoe   1969
Self and Society in Ming Thought, by Wm. Theodore de Bary and the Conference on Ming Thought. Also in paperback ed.   1970
A History of Islamic Philosophy, by Majid Fakhry, 2d ed.   1983
Phantasies of a Love Thief: The Caurapañcāśikā Attributed to Bilhaṇa, by Barbara Stoler Miller   1971
Iqbal: Poet-Philosopher of Pakistan, ed. Hafeez Malik   1971
The Golden Tradition: An Anthology of Urdu Poetry, ed. and tr. Ahmed Ali. Also in paperback ed.   1973
Conquerors and Confucians: Aspects of Political Change in Late Yüan China, by John W. Dardess   1973
The Unfolding of Neo-Confucianism, by Wm. Theodore de Bary and the Conference on Seventeenth-Century Chinese Thought. Also in paperback ed.   1975

To Acquire Wisdom: The Way of Wang Yang-ming, by Julia Ching   1976
Gods, Priests, and Warriors: The Bhṛgus of the Mahābhārata, by Robert P. Goldman   1977
Mei Yao-ch'en and the Development of Early Sung Poetry, by Jonathan Chaves   1976
The Legend of Semimaru, Blind Musician of Japan, by Susan Matisoff   1977
Sir Sayyid Ahmad Khan and Muslim Modernization in India and Pakistan, by Hafeez Malik   1980
The Khilafat Movement: Religious Symbolism and Political Mobilization in India, by Gail Minault   1982
The World of K'ung Shang-jen: A Man of Letters in Early Ch'ing China, by Richard Strassberg   1983
The Lotus Boat: The Origins of Chinese Tz'u Poetry in T'ang Popular Culture, by Marsha L. Wagner   1984
Expressions of Self in Chinese Literature, ed. Robert E. Hegel and Richard C. Hessney   1985
Songs for the Bride: Women's Voices and Wedding Rites of Rural India, by W. G. Archer; eds. Barbara Stoler Miller and Mildred Archer   1986
A Heritage of Kings: One Man's Monarchy in the Confucian World, by JaHyun Kim Haboush   1988

Companions to Asian Studies

Approaches to the Oriental Classics, ed. Wm. Theodore de Bary   1959
Early Chinese Literature, by Burton Watson. Also in paperback ed.   1962
Approaches to Asian Civilizations, eds. Wm. Theodore de Bary and Ainslie T. Embree   1964
The Classic Chinese Novel: A Critical Introduction, by C. T. Hsia. Also in paperback ed.   1968
Chinese Lyricism: Shih Poetry from the Second to the Twelfth Century, tr. Burton Watson. Also in paperback ed.   1971
A Syllabus of Indian Civilization, by Leonard A. Gordon and Barbara Stoler Miller   1971
Twentieth-Century Chinese Stories, ed. C. T. Hsia and Joseph S. M. Lau. Also in paperback ed.   1971
A Syllabus of Chinese Civilization, by J. Mason Gentzler, 2d ed.   1972
A Syllabus of Japanese Civilization, by H. Paul Varley, 2d ed.   1972
An Introduction to Chinese Civilization, ed. John Meskill, with the assistance of J. Mason Gentzler   1973
An Introduction to Japanese Civilization, ed. Arthur E. Tiedemann   1974
Ukifune: Love in the Tale of Genji, ed. Andrew Pekarik   1982
The Pleasures of Japanese Literature, by Donald Keene   1988
A Guide to Oriental Classics, eds. Wm. Theodore de Bary and Ainslie T. Embree; 3d edition ed. Amy Vladeck Heinrich, 2 vols.   1989

Introduction to Asian Civilizations
Wm. Theodore de Bary, General Editor

Sources of Japanese Tradition, 1958; paperback ed., 2 vols., 1964
Sources of Indian Tradition, 1958; paperback ed., 2 vols., 1964; 2d ed., 2 vols., 1988
Sources of Chinese Tradition, 1960; paperback ed., 2 vols., 1964
Sources of Korean Tradition, paperback ed., vol. 1, 1997

Neo-Confucian Studies

Instructions for Practical Living and Other Neo-Confucian Writings by Wang Yang-ming, tr. Wing-tsit Chan   1963
Reflections on Things at Hand: The Neo-Confucian Anthology, comp. Chu Hsi and Lü Tsu-ch'ien, tr. Wing-tsit Chan   1967
Self and Society in Ming Thought, by Wm. Theodore de Bary and the Conference on Ming Thought. Also in paperback ed.   1970
The Unfolding of Neo-Confucianism, by Wm. Theodore de Bary and the Conference on Seventeenth-Century Chinese Thought. Also in paperback ed.   1975
Principle and Practicality: Essays in Neo-Confucianism and Practical Learning, eds. Wm. Theodore de Bary and Irene Bloom. Also in paperback ed.   1979
The Syncretic Religion of Lin Chao-en, by Judith A. Berling   1980
The Renewal of Buddhism in China: Chu-hung and the Late Ming Synthesis, by Chün-fang Yü   1981
Neo-Confucian Orthodoxy and the Learning of the Mind-and-Heart, by Wm. Theodore de Bary   1981
Yüan Thought: Chinese Thought and Religion Under the Mongols, eds. Hok-lam Chan and Wm. Theodore de Bary   1982
The Liberal Tradition in China, by Wm. Theodore de Bary   1983
The Development and Decline of Chinese Cosmology, by John B. Henderson   1984
The Rise of Neo-Confucianism in Korea, by Wm. Theodore de Bary and JaHyun Kim Haboush   1985
Chiao Hung and the Restructuring of Neo-Confucianism in Late Ming, by Edward T. Ch'ien   1985
Neo-Confucian Terms Explained: Pei-hsi tzu-i, by Ch'en Ch'un, ed. and trans. Wing-tsit Chan   1986
Knowledge Painfully Acquired: K'un-chih chi, by Lo Ch'in-shun, ed. and trans. Irene Bloom   1987
To Become a Sage: The Ten Diagrams on Sage Learning, by Yi T'oegye, ed. and trans. Michael C. Kalton   1988
The Message of the Mind in Neo-Confucian Thought, by Wm. Theodore de Bary   1989

10/2000 4